Praise for Boris Akunin

'Boris Akunin shows how it should be done ... an absurdly imaginative story, surreal and comic – irresistible' *The Times*

'Extraordinarily readable, full of incident and excitement, swift-moving and told with a sparkling light-heartedness which is impossible to resist' *Evening Standard*

'Self-indulgently enjoyable ... [Akunin's] artfully constructed novel also nods in the direction of Arthur Conan Doyle
Financial Times

'A special treat for Akunin's fans' *Literary Review*

'Hugely entertaining, cunningly plotted detective novels ... clever, witty, wry page-turners to be commended to anyone with a taste for crime fiction' *Daily Telegraph*

'Akunin's work is gloriously tongue-in-cheek but seriously edge-of-your seat at the same time' *Daily Express*

'A witty, rip-roaring thrill-fest' *Time Out*

'Pastiche of the highest order, absurd and completely gripping at the same time' *Sunday Times*

Boris Akunin is the pseudonym of Grigory Chkhartishvili. He has been compared to Gogol, Tolstoy and Arthur Conan Doyle, and his Erast Fandorin books have sold more than twenty-five million copies in Russia alone. *The Coronation* was longlisted for the Independent Foreign Fiction Prize 2010. He lives in Moscow.

By Boris Akunin

FEATURING ERAST FANDORIN

The Winter Queen
Murder on the Leviathan
Turkish Gambit
The Death of Achilles
Special Assignments
The State Counsellor
The Coronation
She Lover of Death
He Lover of Death
The Diamond Chariot

FEATURING SISTER PELAGIA

Pelagia and the White Bulldog
Pelagia and the Black Monk
Pelagia and the Red Rooster

HE LOVER
OF DEATH

BORIS AKUNIN

Translated by
Andrew Bromfield

PHOENIX

A PHOENIX PAPERBACK

First published in Great Britain in 2010
by Weidenfeld & Nicolson.
This paperback edition published in 2011
by Phoenix,
an imprint of Orion Books Ltd,
Orion House, 5 Upper St Martin's Lane,
London WC2H 9EA

An Hachette UK Company

First published in Russian by Zakharov Publications,
Moscow, Russia and Edizioni Frassinelli, Milan, Italy.

Published by arrangement with Linda Michaels Limited,
International Literary Agents

5 7 9 10 8 6 4

A CIP catalogue record for this book
is available from the British Library

ISBN 978-0-7538-2806-9

Typeset by Input Data Services Ltd, Bridgwater, Somerset

Printed in Great Britain by Clays Ltd, St Ives Plc

The Orion Publishing Group's policy is to use papers that
are natural, renewable and recyclable products and made
from wood grown in sustainable forests. The logging and
manufacturing processes are expected to conform to
the environmental regulations of the country of origin.

www.orionbooks.co.uk

HE LOVER OF DEATH

How Senka First Saw Death

Of course, that wasn't what she was called to begin with. It was something ordinary, a proper Russian name. Malaniya, maybe, or Agrippina. And she had a family name to go with it, too. Well everyone's got one of them, don't they? Your lop-eared mongrel Vanka doesn't have a family name, but a person's got to have one, because that's what makes them a person.

Only when Speedy Senka saw her that first time, she already had her final moniker. Nobody ever spoke about her any other way – they'd all forgotten her first name *and* her family name.

And this was how he happened to see her.

He was sitting with the lads on the bench in front of Deriugin's corner shop. Smoking baccy and chewing the fat.

Suddenly, up drives this jaunty little gig. Tyres pumped fat and tight, spokes painted all golden, yellow leather top. And then out steps a bint, the like of which Senka has never seen before, not on the swanky Kuznetsky Most, not even in Red Square on a church holiday. But no, she *wasn't* a bint – a lady, *that's* what she was, or, better still, a *damsel*. Black plaits in a crown on top of her head, a fancy coloured silk shawl on her shoulders, and her dress was silk too, it shimmered. But the shawl or the dress didn't matter, it was her face, it was so . . . so . . . well, there's just no words for it. One look, and you melted inside. And that was what Senka did, melted inside.

'Who's that fancy broad?' he asked, and then, so as not to give himself away, he spat through closed teeth (he could gob farther than anyone else like that, at least six feet – that gap at the front was very handy). 'It's plain to see, Speedy,' Prokha said, 'that you're new round here.' And right enough, Senka was still settling into Khitrovka back then, it was only a couple of weeks since he'd taken off from Sukharevka. 'That ain't a broad,' says Prokha. 'That's Death!' Senka didn't twig straight off what death had to do with anything. He thought it was just Prokha's fancy way of talking – like, she's dead beautiful.

And she really was beautiful, no getting away from that. High clear forehead, arched eyebrows, white skin, scarlet lips and o-o-oh – those eyes! Senka had seen eyes like that on Cavalry Square, on the Turkestan horses: big and moist, but glinting with sparks of fire at the same time. Only the eyes of the damsel who got out of that fancy carriage were lovelier even than the eyes on those horses.

Senka's own eyes popped out of his head as he gaped at the miraculously beautiful damsel, and Mikheika the Night-Owl brushed the baccy crumbs off his lip then elbowed him in the side: 'Ogle away, Speedy,' he says, 'but don't overdo it. Or the Prince will lop your ear off and make you eat it, like he did that time with that huckster from Volokolamsk. He took a shine to Death too, that huckster did. But he ogled too hard.'

And Senka didn't catch on about Death this time either – he was too taken by the idea of eating ears.

'What, and did the huckster eat it, then?' he asked in amazement. 'I wouldn't do that, no way.'

Prokha took a swig from his beer. 'Yes you would,' he said. 'If the Prince asked you nice and polite, like, you'd be only too happy to do it and you'd say thank you, that was very tasty. That huckster chewed and chewed on his ear, but he couldn't swallow it, and then the Prince lopped off the other one and stuck it in his mouth. And to make him get a move on, he kept pricking him in the belly with his pen – his knife, I mean. That huckster's head swelled up afterwards and went all rotten. He howled for a couple of days, and then croaked, never did get back to that

Volokolamsk of his. That's the way things are done in Khitrovka. So just you take note, Speedy.'

It goes without saying that Speedy had heard about the Prince, even though he hadn't been doing the rounds in Khitrovka for long. Who hadn't heard about the Prince? The biggest hotshot bandit in the whole of Moscow. They talked about him at the markets, they wrote about him in the papers. The coppers were hunting him, but they couldn't even get close. Khitrovka didn't give up her own – everyone there knew what happened to squealers.

But I still wouldn't eat my ear, thought Senka. *I'd rather take the knife.*

'So, is she the Prince's moll, then?' he asked about the amazing damsel, out of simple curiosity, like. He'd decided he wasn't going to gape at her any more, wasn't really that interested, was he? And anyway, there was no one to gape at, she'd already gone into the shop.

'Ith she?' Prokha teased him (not all of Senka's words came out right since one of his teeth was smashed out). 'You're the one who's a moll.'

In Sukharevka, if you called one of the lads a moll, you earned yourself a right battering, and Senka took aim, ready to smash Prokha in his bony kisser, but then he changed his mind. Well, for starters, maybe the customs were different round here, and it wasn't meant to be an insult. And then again, Prokha was a big strapping lad, so who could tell which of them would get the battering? And last but not least, he was really dying to hear about that girl.

Well, Prokha kept putting him off for a while, but then the story came out.

She used to live all right and proper, with Mum and Dad, out in the Dobraya Sloboda district, or maybe Razgulyai – anyway, somewhere over on that side of town. She grew up a real good-looker, as sweet as they come, and she had no end of admirers. So, just as soon as she came of age, she was engaged. They were on their way to the church to get married, she and her bridegroom, when suddenly these two black stallions, great huge brutes, darted right in front of their sleigh. If only they'd guessed they ought to say a prayer right then, things would have gone different. Or at least crossed themselves. Only no one guessed, or maybe there wasn't enough time. The horses were startled something wicked by the black stallions and they went flying off the bank into the Yauza river on a bend. The bridegroom was crushed to death and the driver drowned, but the girl was fine. Not a scratch on her.

Well, all right, all sorts happen, after all. They took the lad off to bury him. And the bride walked beside the coffin. Grieving something awful, she was – they said she really did love him. And when they start crossing the bridge, right by the spot where it all happened, she suddenly shouts out: 'Goodbye, good Christian people,' and leaps head-first over the railings, down off the bridge. There had been a hard frost the day before, and the ice on the river was real thick, so by rights she should have smashed her head open or broken her neck. Ah, but that wasn't what happened. She fell straight into this gap with just a thin crust of ice, dusted over with snow, plopped under the water – and was gone.

Well, everybody thinks, she's drowned, and they're running around, waving their arms in the air. Only she wasn't drowned, she was dragged about fifty fathoms under the ice and cast up through a hole where some women were doing their laundry.

They snagged her with a boathook or some such thing and dragged her out. She looked dead, all white she was, but after she lay down for a while and warmed up again, she was as good as new. Alive and kicking.

Because she was harder to kill than a cat, they called her Lively, and some even called her the Immortal, but that wasn't her final moniker. That changed later.

A year went by, or maybe a year and a half, and then didn't her parents try to marry her off again. And by now the girl was

4

a more beautiful blossom than ever. Her bridegroom was this merchant, not young, but filthy rich. It was all the same to her – Lively, I mean – a merchant would do as well as anyone. Those that knew her then say she was pining badly for her bridegroom, the one who was killed.

So then what happens? The day before the wedding, at the morning service in church, the new bridegroom suddenly starts wheezing and flinging his arms about and then flops over on his side. He twitched a leg and flapped his lips for a bit, and went to his eternal rest. Carried off by a stroke.

After that, she didn't try to get married any more, and before long she ran away from her parents' house with this gent, a military man, and started living in his house, on Arbat Street. And she turned into a real swanky dame: dressed up like a lady and came to visit her mama and papa in a shiny varnished carriage, with a lacy parasol. The officer couldn't marry her, he didn't have his father's blessing, but he adored her madly, absolutely doted on her.

Only number three was done for as well. He was a strong young gent, with bright rosy cheeks, but after he lived with her for a while, all of a sudden he started wasting away. He turned all pale and feeble, his legs wouldn't hold him up. The doctors tried everything they could think of, sent him away to take the waters, and off to foreign parts, but it was all a waste of time. They said there was some kind of canker growing inside him, and it had nibbled all his insides away.

Well then, after she buried her officer, even the slow-witted could see there was something wrong with the girl. And that was when they changed what they called her.

There was no way she could go back to Dobraya Sloboda, and she didn't want to anyway. Her life was all different now. Ordinary folks steered clear of her. When she walked by, they crossed themselves and spat over their shoulders. But everyone knows the kind that did cosy up – rakish, dashing types who couldn't give a damn for death. And after she sucked all the juice out of that last gent – well, you've seen for yourself what she turned into then. Far and away the best-looker in the whole of Moscow.

And it carried on. Kolsha the Spike (he was a big-time bandit, used to work the Meshchani patch) stepped out in style with her for a couple of months – then his own lads took their knives to him, because he wouldn't divvy up the loot.

Then there was Yashka from Kostroma, the horse thief. Used to walk pure-blood trotters straight out of the stable, sold them to the gypsies for huge money. Carried thousands of roubles around in his pockets sometimes. He begrudged her nothing, she was swimming in gold. But the police narks shot Yashka down six months past.

And now there's the Prince. Three months and counting. Sometimes he puts on a brave face, but sometimes he rants and raves. He used to be a respectable thief, but now doing someone in means no more to him than squashing a fly. And all because now he's taken up with Death, he knows he isn't long for this world. It's like that saying: invite death to come visiting, and you end up in the graveyard. People don't get their monikers for nothing, especially one like that.

'What moniker d'you mean?' Senka asked eagerly after he'd listened to the story with his mouth hanging open. 'You still haven't told me, Prokha.'

Prokha stared at him, then tapped his knuckles on his own forehead. 'Why, you half-baked simpleton,' he said. 'So what do they call you Speedy for? I've just spent the best part of an hour explaining that to you. Death – that's her moniker. That's what everyone calls her. She don't mind, she answers to it, she's well used to it.'

How Senka Became a Khitrovkan

Prokha thought Senka was called Speedy, him being a smart lad, with lots of gumption, eyes darting about left and right, always quick with an answer, never stuck for a word. But actually Senka's nickname came from his surname. His father's name used to be Trifon Stepanovich Spidorov. What his name was now, only God knew. Maybe he wasn't Trifon Stepanovich any longer, but the Angel Trifaniil instead. Except that his old dad wasn't likely to have been made an angel – he drank too much, although he was a good man. But as for his mum, she was definitely somewhere not too far from the Throne of Light.

Senka often thought about that – which of his parents had ended up where. He wasn't sure about his father, but he had no doubts about his mother and brothers and sisters, the ones who'd died from cholera with their parents. He didn't even pray for them to get into the Kingdom of Heaven – he knew they were already there.

When the cholera hit their suburb three years before, it had carried off a lot of folk. Senka and his little brother Vanya were the only Spidorovs who kept a tight grip on this world. And whether that was good or bad depended on which way you looked at it.

For Senka it was probably bad, because his life was altogether different after that. His dad worked behind the counter in a big tobacco shop. He got a good wage and free baccy. When he was little, Senka always had clothes to wear and shoes on his feet. A full belly and a clean face, as they say. He was taught reading, writing and arithmetic at the usual age, he even went to commercial college for half a year, only when he was orphaned, that put an end to his studies. But then never mind his studies, that wasn't the reason he was so miserable.

His brother Vanka was lucky. He was taken in by Justice of the Peace Kuvshinnikov – the one who always used to buy English baccy from their dad. The magistrate had a wife, but no children, and he took Vanka, because he was small and chubby. But Senka was already big and bony, the magistrate wasn't interested in someone like that. So Senka was taken in by his second uncle, Zot Larionovich, in Sukharevka. And that was where Senka ran wild.

Well, what else could he do *but* run wild?

His uncle, the fat-bellied bastard, starved him. Didn't even give Senka a seat at the table, even though he was flesh and blood. On Saturdays he used to beat him, sometimes for a reason, but mostly just for the hell of it. He didn't pay him a kopeck, although Senka slaved away in the shop just as hard as the other boys, and they were paid eight roubles each. And the most hurtful thing of all was that every morning he had to carry his second cousin Grishka's satchel to the grammar school for him. Grishka walked on ahead, full of himself, sucking on a fancy boiled sweet, and Senka trudged along behind, like a serf from the olden days, lugging that unbelievably heavy satchel (sometimes Grishka put a brick in it out of sheer mischief). He'd have loved to squeeze all the pus out of that Grishka like a fat, ripe boil, so he'd stop putting on airs and share his sugar candy. Or smash him across the head with that brick – but he couldn't, he just had to lump it.

Well, Senka lumped it for as long as he could. For three whole years, near enough.

Of course, he used to get his own back too, whenever he could. You have to find some way of letting off steam.

Once he put a mouse inside Grishka's pillow. During the night it gnawed its way to freedom and got tangled in his second cousin's hair. That was a fine ruckus in the middle of the night. But it went off all right, no one suspected Senka at all.

Or that last Shrovetide, when they baked and boiled and roasted all that food, and gave the orphan only two little pancakes with holes in them and a tiny scraping of vegetable oil. Senka flew into a fury and he splashed some of that oat 'decoction' they took for constipation into the big pot with the thick cabbage soup. That'll make you run, you greaseballs, let's see you twitch and heave! And he got away with that too – they blamed the sour cream for going off.

When he got the chance, he used to steal all sorts of small things from the shop: thread maybe, or a pair of scissors, or some buttons. He sold what he could at the Sukharevka flea-market and threw away the things that were no use. He got beaten for it sometimes, but only on suspicion – he was never caught in the act.

But when he finally did get his fingers burned, it was really bad, the smoke was thick and the fiery sparks flew. And it was Senka's compassionate heart to blame for the whole thing, for making him forget his usual caution.

After he hadn't heard anything about his brother for three whole years, he finally got word from him. He often used to comfort himself by thinking how lucky Vanka was, and how happy he must be, living with Justice of the Peace Kuvshinnikov, not like Senka. And then this letter came.

It was amazing it ever got there at all. On the envelope it said: '*My brother Senka hoo lives with Uncle Zot in Sukharevka in Moscow*'. It was lucky Uncle Zot knew one of the postmen who worked at the Sukharevka post office, and he guessed where to bring it, may God grant him good health.

This was what the letter said:

Deer bruther Senka, how are you geting on. Im very unhapy living heer. They teech me letters and scowld me and misstreet me, even thow its my naym day soon. I askd them for a horsy,

9

but they tayk no notiss. Come and tayk me away from these
unkind peeple.
Yor little bruther Vanka.

When Senka read it, his hands started trembling and the tears came pouring out of his eyes. So this was his lucky brother! That magistrate was a fine one. Tormenting a little child, refusing to buy him a toy. Then why did he want to raise the orphan in the first place?

Anyway, he took serious offence for Vanka, and decided it would be cruel and heartless to abandon his brother so.

There wasn't any return address on the envelope, but the postman told him the postmark was from Tyoply Stan, and that was about eight miles outside Moscow if you took the Kaluga Gate. And he could ask where the magistrate lived when he got there.

Senka didn't take long to make up his mind. After all, the next day was St Ioann's day – little Vanka's name day.

Senka got ready to set out and rescue his brother. If Vanka was so unhappy, he was going to take him away. Better to suffer their grief together than apart.

He spotted a little lacquered horse in the toy shop on Sretenka Street, with a fluffy tail and white mane. It was absolutely beautiful, but really pricey – seven and a half roubles. So at midday, when there was only deaf old Nikifor left in his uncle's shop, Senka picked the lock on the cash box, took out eight roubles and did a runner, trusting to God. He didn't think about being punished. He wasn't planning on ever coming back to his uncle, he was going away with his brother to live a free life. Join a gypsy camp, or whatever came along.

It took him an awful long time to walk to that Tyoply Stan, his feet were all battered and bruised, and the farther he went, the heavier the wooden horse got.

But then it was very easy to find Justice of the Peace Kuvshinnikov's house, the first person he asked there pointed it out. It was a good house, with a cast-iron canopy on pillars, and a garden.

He didn't go up to the front door – he felt too ashamed. And they probably wouldn't have let him in anyway, because after the long journey Senka was covered in dust, and he had a cut right across his face that was oozing blood. That was from outside the Kaluga Gate, when he was so knackered, he hung on to the back of an old cart, and the driver, the rotten louse, lashed him with his whip – it was lucky he didn't put his eye out!

Senka squatted down on his haunches, facing the house, and started thinking about what to do next. There was a sweet tinkling sound coming from the open windows – someone was slowly trying to bash out a song that Senka didn't know. And sometimes he could hear a thin little voice he thought must be his Vanka's.

Senka finally plucked up his courage, walked closer, and stood on the step to glance in the window.

He saw a big, beautiful room. And sitting at a great big polished wooden box (it was called a 'piano', they had one like it in the college too) was a curly-haired little boy in a sailor suit, stabbing at the keys with his little pink fingers. He looked like Vanka, and not like him at the same time. So peachy and fresh, you could just gobble him up like a spice cake. Standing beside him was a young lady in glasses, using one hand to turn the pages of a copy book on a little stand, and stroking the little lad's golden hair with the other. And in the corner there was a great big heap of toys. With toy horses, too, much fancier than Senka's – three of them.

Before Senka could make any sense of this amazing sight, a carriage drawn by two horses suddenly came out from round the corner. He only just managed to jump down in time and squeeze up against the fence.

Justice of the Peace Kuvshinnikov himself was sitting in the carriage. Senka recognised him straight off.

Vanka stuck his head out of the window and shouted as loud as he could:

'Did you bring it? Did you bring it?'

The magistrate laughed and climbed down on to the ground. 'I did,' he said. 'Can't you see for yourself? What are we going to call her?'

That was when Senka spotted the horse tethered to the back of the carriage, a sorrel foal with plump round sides. It looked like a grown-up horse, only it was really small, not much bigger than a goat.

Vanka started chirruping away: 'A pony! I'm going to have a real pony!' And so, Senka turned back and trudged all the way to the Kaluga Gate. He left the wooden horse in the grass at the side of the road. Let it graze there. Vanka didn't need it – maybe some other kid would get good use out of it.

As Senka walked along, he dreamed about how time would pass and his life would change miraculously, and he would come back here in a big shiny carriage. The servant would carry in a little card with gold letters, with everything about Senka written in the finest fancy style, and that young lady with the glasses would say to Vanka: 'Ivan Trofimovich, your brother has come to visit'. And Senka would be wearing a cheviot wool suit and button-down spats, and carrying a cane with an ivory knob on it.

It was already dark when he finally staggered home. It would have been better if he hadn't come back at all, just run off straight away.

Right there in the doorway Uncle Zot thumped him so hard he saw stars, and knocked out the front tooth that left such a handy gap for spitting. Then, when Senka fell down, his uncle gave his ribs a good kicking: 'That's just for starters, you'll get what you deserve later. I went to the police about you,' he yelled, 'I wrote out a complaint for the local sergeant. You'll go to jail for stealing, you little bastard, they'll soon straighten you out in there.' And he just kept on and on barking out his threats.

So Senka did run away. When his uncle got tired kicking and punching and went to take the yoke down off the wall – the one the women used to carry water – Senka darted out of the porch, spitting blood and smearing the tears across his face.

He shuddered through the night at the Sukharevka market, under a load of hay. He was feeling miserable and sorry for himself, his ribs ached, his battered face hurt, and he was really hungry too. He'd spent the half-rouble left over from the horse on food the day before, and now he had nothing but holes in his pockets.

Senka left Sukharevka at dawn, to get well out of harm's way. If Uncle Zot had snitched on him to the coppers, the first constable who came along would grab him and stick him in the jug, and once you were in there, you didn't get out in a hurry. He had to make for somewhere where no one knew his face.

He walked to another market, the one on Old Square and New Square, under the Kitaigorod wall, and hung about beside the row of food stalls, breathing in the smell of the pies and the baked goods, shooting quick glances this way and that in case any of the tradeswomen got careless. But he didn't have the nerve to snitch anything – after all, he'd never stolen openly like that before. And what if he got caught? They'd kick him so hard, it would make Uncle Zot seem like a doting mother.

He wandered round the market, keeping well away from Solyanka Street. He knew that over there, behind that street, was Khitrovka, the most terrible place in all Moscow. Of course, there were plenty of con merchants and pickpockets in Sukharevka too, but they were no match for the thieves of Khitrovka. From what he'd heard, it was a terrifying place. Stick your nose in there, and they'd have you stripped naked before you could say knife, and you could be grateful if you managed to escape with your life. The flophouses there were really frightening, with lots of cellars and underground vaults. And there were runaway convicts there, and murderers, and all sorts of drunken riff-raff. And they said that if any youngsters happened to wander in there, they disappeared without a trace. They had some special kind of crooks there, grabbers, they were called, or so people said. And these grabbers caught young boys who had no one to look out for them and sold them for five roubles apiece to the Yids and the Tartars for depraved lechery in their secret houses.

But as it turned out that was all horseshit. Well, everything about the flophouses and the drunken riff-raff was true, but there weren't any grabbers in Khitrovka. When Senka let slip about the grabbers to his new mates, they laughed him down something rotten. Prokha said that if someone wanted to grab a bit of easy money off kids, that was fine, but forcing youngsters into doing filthy things – that just wasn't on. The Council wouldn't stand for anything like that. Slitting a throat or two in the middle of the night wasn't a problem, if some gull showed up because he was drunk or just plain stupid. They'd found someone in Podkopaevsky Lane just recently, head smashed in like a soft-boiled egg, fingers cut off to get the rings, and his eyes gouged out. It was his own fault. You shouldn't go sticking your nose in where you aren't invited. The mice shouldn't play where the cats are waiting.

'Only why put his eyes out?' Senka asked in fright.

But Mikheika the Night-Owl just laughed and said: 'Go and ask them as put them out.'

But that conversation came later, when Senka was already a Khitrovkan.

It all happened very quickly and simply – before he even had time to sneeze, you might say.

There was Senka walking along the row of spiced tea stalls, sizing up what there was to filch and plucking up his courage, and suddenly this almighty ruckus started up, with people shouting on all sides, and this woman was yelling. 'Help! I've been robbed, they've took me purse, stop thief!' And two young lads, about the same age as Senka, came dashing along the line of stalls, kicking up the bowls and mugs as they ran. A woman selling spiced tea grabbed one of them by the belt with a great ham of a hand and pulled him down on to the ground. 'Gotcha,' she shouted, 'you vicious little brute! Now you're for it!' But the other young thief, with a sharp pointy nose, leapt off a hawker's stand and thumped the woman on the ear. She went all limp and slipped over on her side (Prokha always carried a lead bar with him, Senka learnt that later). The lad with the pointy nose jerked the other one up by the arm to get him to keep on running, but people had already closed in from all sides. They'd probably have beaten the two of them to death for hurting the woman, if it wasn't for Senka.

He roared at the top of his voice:

'Good Orthodox people! Who dropped a silver rouble?'

Well, they all went dashing over to him: 'I did, I did!' But he squeezed through between their outstretched hands and shouted to the young thieves:

'Don't stand there gawping! Leg it!'

They sprinted after him, and when Senka hesitated at a gateway, they overtook him and waved for him to follow.

After they stopped at a quiet spot to get their breath back and shook hands. Mikheika the Night-Owl (the one who was shorter, with fat cheeks) asked him: 'Who are you? Where are you from?'

And Senka answered: 'Sukharevka.'

The other one, who was called Prokha, bared his teeth and grinned, as if he'd heard something funny. 'So what made you leave Sukharevka in such a hurry?'

Senka spat through the gap in his teeth – he hadn't had time to get used to the novelty of it yet, but he still spat a good six feet.

And all he said was: 'Can't stay there. They'll put me in jail.'

The two lads gave Senka a respectful kind of look. Prokha slapped him on the shoulder. 'Come and live with us, then. No need to be shy. No one gets turned in from Khitrovka.'

How Senka Settled in at the New Place

So this was the way he and the lads lived.

During the day they went 'snitching', and at night they went 'bombing'.

They did most of their thieving round that same Old Square where the market was, or on Maroseika Street, where all the shops were, or on Varvarka Street, from the people walking by, and sometimes on Ilinka Street, where the rich merchants and stockbrokers were, but definitely no farther than that, oh no. Prokha – he was their leader – called it 'a dash from Khitrovka'. Meaning that if anything went wrong, you could hightail it to the Khitrovka gateways and side alleys, where there was no way anyone could catch a thief.

Senka learned how to go snitching quickly enough. It was easy work, good fun.

Mikheika the Night-Owl picked out a 'gull' – some clueless passer-by – and checked to make sure he had money on him. That was his job. He moved in close, rubbed up against the gull and then gave them the nod: *yeah he's got a wallet on him, over to you*. He never pinched anything himself – his fingers weren't quick enough for that.

Then it was Senka's turn. His job was to surprise the gull so his jaw dropped open and he forgot all about his pockets. There were several ways of going about it. He could start a fight with Night-Owl – people loved to gawp at that. He could suddenly start walking down the middle of the road on his hands, jerking his legs about comically (Senka had been able to do that ever

16

since he was a little kid). But the simplest thing of all was just to collapse at the gull's feet, as if he was having a fit, and start yelling: 'I feel real bad, mister (or missus, depending on the circumstances). I'm dying!' If it was someone soft-hearted, they were bound to stop and watch the young lad writhing about; and even if you'd picked a real cold fish, he'd still look round, out of sheer curiosity, like. And that was all Prokha needed. In and out like a knife, and the job was done. It used to be your money, but now it's ours.

Senka didn't like bombing so much. In fact, you could say he didn't like it at all. In the evening, somewhere not far from Khitrovka, they picked out a 'beaver' who was all on his own (a beaver was like a gull, only drunk). Prokha did the important work here too. He ran up from behind and smashed his fist against the side of the beaver's head – only he was holding a lead bar in that fist. When the beaver collapsed, Speedy and Night-Owl came dashing in from both sides: they took the money, the watch and a few other things, and tugged off the jacket and the low boots, if they looked pricey. If the beaver was some kind of strongman who wasn't felled by the lead bar, they didn't mess with him: Prokha legged it straight away, and Skorik and Filin never stuck their noses out of the gateway.

So bombing wasn't exactly complicated, either. But it was disgusting. At first, Senka was terrified Prokha would hit someone so hard he'd kill them, but then he got used to that. For starters, it was only a lead bar, not knuckledusters or a blackjack. And anyway, everyone knew that God himself looked after drunks. And they had thick heads.

The lads sold their loot out of Bunin's flophouse. Sometimes they only made a rouble between them, but on a good day it could be as much as fifty. If it was just a rouble, they ate 'dog's delight' – cheap sausage – with black rye bread. But if the takings were good, they went to drink wine at the Hard Labour or the Siberia. And after that the thing to do was visit the tarts ('mamselles' they were called in Khitrovka), and horse around.

17

Prokha and Filin had their own regular mamselles. Not molls, of course, like proper thieves had – they didn't earn enough to keep a moll just for themselves – but at least not streetwalkers. Sometimes the mamselles might even feed them, or lend them some money.

Senka soon acquired a little lady-friend of his own too. Tashka, her name was.

That morning Senka woke up late. He couldn't remember anything that had happened the day before, he had been too drunk. But when he looked, he saw he was in a small room, with just one window, curtained over. There were plants in pots on the windowsill, with flowers – yellow, red and blue. In the corner, lying on the floor, was a withered old woman, a bag of bones, tearing herself apart with this rasping cough and spitting blood into a rag – she had consumption, for sure. Senka was lying on an iron bedstead, naked, and there was a girl about thirteen years old, sitting at the far end of the bed with her legs crossed under her, looking at some book and laying out flowers and muttering something under her breath.

'What's that you're doing?' Senka asked in a hoarse voice.

She smiled at him. 'Look,' she said, 'that's white acacia – pure love. Red celandine – impatience. Barberry – rejection.'

Queer in the head, he thought. He didn't know then that Tashka was studying the language of flowers. Somewhere or other she'd picked up this book called *How to Speak with Flowers*, and she'd really taken to the idea of talking with flowers instead of words. She'd spent almost all the three roubles she got from Senka the night before on flowers – run to the market first thing and bought a whole bundle of leafy stuff, then started sorting it all out. That was what Tashka was like.

Senka spent almost the whole day with her that time. First he drank brine to cure his sore head. Then he drank tea with some bread. And after that they sat there doing nothing. Just talking.

Tashka turned out to be a nice girl, only slightly touched.

Take the flowers, for instance, or that mum of hers, the miserable drunk with consumption, no good for anything. Why did she bother with her, why waste her money like that? She was going to die anyway.

And in the evening, before she went out on the street, Tashka suddenly said: 'Senka, let's you and me be mates, shall we?'

'All right,' he said.

They hooked their little fingers together and shook them, then kissed each other on the lips. Tashka said that was what mates were supposed to do. And when Senka tried to paw her after the kiss, she said to him: 'Now what do you think you're doing? We're mates. And mates don't go horsing around. And you shouldn't do it with me, anyway, I've got the frenchies, picked it up off this shop clerk. You do the jig-a-jig with me and that snotty nose of yours will fall right off.'

Senka was upset.

'What do you mean, the frenchies? Why didn't you say anything yesterday?'

'Yesterday,' she says, 'you was no one, just a customer, but now we're mates. Never mind, Senka, don't be scared, it ain't a sickness that takes to everyone, especially not from just one time.'

He calmed down a bit then and started feeling sorry for her.

'What about you?'

'Phooey,' she said. 'There's plenty round here have got that. They keep going somehow. Some mamselles with the frenchies lives to be thirty, even longer, sometimes. Thirty's more than enough, if you ask me. Mum over there's twenty-eight, and she's an old woman – her teeth have all fallen out, and she's covered in wrinkles.'

Senka still called Tashka his mamselle in front of the lads. He was ashamed to tell them the truth – they'd just laugh him down. But it was okay, what did that matter anyway? You could horse around with anyone you wanted if you had three roubles, but where could he find another good mate like her?

Anyway, it turned out it was possible to live in Khitrovka, and even better than in some other places. Of course, the place had its own laws and customs, like anywhere else, you had to have those, to make it easier for people to live together and understand what they could and couldn't do. There were lots of laws, and you needed to live in Khitrovka a long time to remember them all. Mostly the way of things was clear and simple, you could figure it out for yourself: treat outsiders any way you like, but don't touch your own; live your own life, cause your neighbour no strife. But there were some laws you couldn't make any sense of, no matter how hard you racked your brains.

For instance, if someone crowed like a cock any earlier than two in the morning – out of mischief, or drunkenness, or just playing the fool – you were supposed to thrash him within an inch of his life. But no one in Khitrovka could explain to Senka why. There must have been some point to it at some time, only now even the oldest old men couldn't remember what that was. But even so, you still couldn't crow like a cock in the middle of the night.

Or take this, for instance. If any of the mamselles started putting on airs and cleaning her teeth with shop powder, and her client caught her out, then he had the right to knock all her teeth out, and the mamselle's pimp had to accept the loss. Clean them with crushed chalk if you want to be posh, but stay clear of that powder, that was invented by the Germans.

There were two kinds of laws in Khitrovka: those from times gone by, the way things used to be in the olden days, and new ones – those were announced by the Council when they were needed. Say, for instance, a horse-tram sets off down the street. Who ought to work it – the 'twitchers', who dip their fingers in all the pockets, or the 'slicers', who cut them open with a sharpened coin? The Council deliberated, and decided it wasn't a job for the slicers, because the same crowd rode the horse-tram all the time, and soon they wouldn't have any pockets left.

The Council was made up of 'grandfathers', the most

respected thieves and tricksters, those who had come back from doing hard labour, or were so old and feeble they didn't work any more. The grandfathers could untangle any kind of tricky knot, and if anyone offended against the Council's rules, they meted out the punishment.

If someone made everybody else's life a misery, they threw him out of Khitrovka. If he really fouled things up, they could even take his life. Sometimes they might give someone up to the law, but not for what the Council really thought he was guilty of – they ordered him to take the rap for someone else's crimes, one of the 'businessmen's'. That way things worked out fairer all round. If you tried to cheat Khitrovka, you had to answer for it: purge your crime, bleach yourself white and help the good people, and they'd put in a good word for you in the jailhouse or in Siberia.

And they didn't hand over a rogue they'd convicted to just anyone in the police, only to their own man, Boxman, the senior constable in the Khitrovka precinct.

This Boxman had served more than twenty years around here; Khitrovka wouldn't be Khitrovka without him. If Khitrovka was a world, then he was like the whale it rested on, because Boxman was authority, and people can't live without any authority at all, otherwise they start forgetting who they are. There has to be a little bit of authority, a tiny little bit, and not according to some rules on a piece of paper, thought up by some outsider in some place no one had ever seen, but according to justice – so that every man could understood why his face was getting blacked.

Tough but fair, that was what everybody said about Boxman, and Boxman really was his surname. He wouldn't deliberately do you wrong. Everyone called him 'Ivan Fedotovich' to his face, as a mark of respect. Only Senka couldn't tell if it was just a nickname that he'd got from his surname, or if it was because in olden times, so they said, all the constables in Moscow were called 'boxmen', because of the kiosks they used to stand in. Or maybe it was because he lived in the official police box on the edge of the Khitrovka market. Any time when he wasn't pounding his beat, he sat at home in front of an open window, keeping a watch on the square, reading books and newspapers and drinking tea from his famous silver samovar with medallions that were worth a thousand roubles. And there weren't any locks on the box. What would Boxman want locks for? In the first place, what good were they, when the place was surrounded by top-class lock-pickers and window-men? They could open any lock, easy as falling off a log. And in the second place, no one would go trying to filch anything from Boxman – not unless he was tired of living, that is.

From his window the constable could hear everything and see everything, and what he couldn't see or hear was whispered to him by his loyal informers. That was above board, it wasn't forbidden by the Council, because Boxman was part of Khitrovka. If he'd lived by the written laws and not the laws of Khitrovka, they'd have knifed him ages back. No, when he took someone into the station, it was all done with the proper understanding: he had to do it, to show his bosses he was doing *something*. Only Boxman didn't put anyone away very often – not unless he absolutely had to – mostly he taught people their lesson with his own hands, and they kowtowed to him and said thank you very much. In all the years he'd been there, only one pair of shysters had ever gone for him with a knife – escaped convicts, they were, not from Khitrovka. He beat the two of them to death with his massive great fists, and the police superintendent gave him a medal. Everyone respected him for it, and the Council gave him a gold watch for the inconvenience.

So once Senka had settled in a bit, it was clear enough that Khitrovka wasn't such a terrible place. It was more cheerful there, and freer, and it goes without saying that he ate better. In winter, when it got cold, it would probably be tough, but then winter was still a long way off.

How Senka Got to Know Death

It happened about ten days after Senka saw Death that first time.

He was hanging about on the Yauza Boulevard, in front of her house, spitting at the bollard they tied the horses to and staring at the half-open windows.

He already knew where she lived, the lads had shown him and, to tell the truth, this wasn't the first day he'd spent cooling his heels here. Twice he'd been lucky and caught glimpses of her from a distance. One time, four days before, Death had come out of the house wearing a black shawl on her head and a black dress, got into the fancy gig that was waiting for her and driven off to church for Mass. And just yesterday he'd seen her arm in arm with the Prince: dressed up like a lady, wearing a hat with a feather in it. Her beau was taking her somewhere – to a restaurant, maybe, or the theatre.

He took a gander at the Prince at the same time. Well, what was there to say, a superb figure of a man. After all, he was the most important hold-up artist in all of Moscow, and that's no small potatoes. The governor-general, Simeon Alexandrovich, had it easy, he was born the tsar's uncle, no wonder he was a governor and a general, but just you try climbing up to the top of the heap and making yourself mister big, number one, out of all the crooks in Moscow. It was a real rags-to-riches story. And his sidekicks were all really grand lads, everyone said so. They said some of them were really young too, not much older than Senka. Would you believe some people's luck, ending up in the Prince's gang straight off like that, when you were still green and sappy! They had respect, any girls they wanted, more money than they could ever count, and they dressed up like real fancy dandies.

When Senka saw him, the famous bandit was wearing a red silk shirt, a lemon satin waistcoat, and a crimson velvet frock coat. He had a boater perched on the back of his head, gold rings with precious stones on his fingers and calf boots that shone like mirrors. A real sight for sore eyes! A dashing light-brown forelock, blue eyes with a bold stare to them, a gold crown glinting in his red teeth, and a chin like chiselled stone, with a dimple right in the middle of it. *They're not just a couple – a real picture, that's what they are*, Senka thought, and sighed.

Not that he had any stupid dreams in his head that should give him reason to sigh, God forbid. He wasn't trying to get Death to notice him either. He just wanted to get another look at her, so he could properly make out what was so unusual about her and why his insides clenched up tight, like a fist, the moment he laid eyes on her. So he'd been wearing down his soles here on the boulevard for days now. As soon as he finished thieving with the lads, he went straight to the Yauza.

He'd examined the house thoroughly from the outside. And he knew what it was like on the inside too. The plumber Parkhom, who fixed Death's washbasin, told him the Prince had set up his lady love in real classy style, even laid in water pipes. If Parkhom wasn't lying, then Death had a special room with a big china tub that was called a bath, and the hot water flowed into it straight out of a pipe, from this boiler up on the wall – gas-heated, it was. Death got washed in that tub almost every day that God sent. Senka imagined her sitting there all pink and steamy, scrubbing her shoulders with the sponge, and the fantasy made him feel all hot and steamy too.

The house was pretty impressive from the outside too. There used to be some general's manor house here, but it burned down, and just this wing was left. It was pretty small, with only four windows along the boulevard. But this was a special spot, right smack on the boundary line between the Khitrovka slums and the well-heeled Serebryaniki district. On the other side of the Yauza, the houses were taller and cleaner, with fancier plastering, but here on the Khitrovka side, they weren't so smart. Like the horses they sold at the horse market: look at it from the rump, and it seems like a horse all right, but from any other angle it's definitely an ass.

And so the front of Death's house that overlooked the boulevard was neat and dignified, like, but the back led out into a really rotten passage, and a gateway only spitting distance from Rumyantsev's flophouse. You could see what a handy home the Prince had found for his girl – if anything happened, if he was ambushed at her place, he could dash out the back way, or even jump out of a window and make a beeline for the flophouse, and there was no way anyone could ever find him in all the underground collidors and passages there.

But from the boulevard, where the well-bred people strolled about between the trees, you couldn't see the back passage, let alone Rumyantsev's place. Khitrovkans couldn't go out past the fancy railings – the coppers would sweep them up with their broom in a flash and stick them in their rubbish cart. Even here, on the Khitrovka waterside, Senka tried not to make himself too obvious, he stuck close to the wall of the house. He was behaving himself proper too, not like some kind of riff-raff, but even so, Boxman spotted him with his eagle eye as he was walking past and stopped.

'What are you doing skulking over there?' he asked. 'You better watch yourself, Speedy, I'm warning you.'

Now that was him all over! He already knew who Senka was and what his moniker was, even though Senka was still new in Khitrovka. That was Boxman for you.

'Don't you dare nick a thing,' he said, 'you're out of your jurisdiction, because this ain't Khitrovka, it's a civil promenade. You look out, young Speedy, you sly little monkey, I've got you under special observation until the first contravention of legality, and if I catch you, or even suspect you, I'll issue you a reprimand across that ugly mug of yours, fine you a clout round the ear and sanction you round the ribs with my belt.'

'I'm not up to nothing, Uncle Boxman,' Senka whined, pulling a face. 'I just, you know, wanted to take the air.'

And for that he got a cast-iron mitt across the back of his head, smack crunch between the ears.

'I'll teach you what for, snarling "Boxman" like that. What a damned liberty! I'm Ivan Fedotovich to you, all right?'

And Senka said meekly:

'All right, Uncle Ivan Fedotovich.'

Boxman stopped scowling then. 'That's right, you snot-nosed little monkey.' And he walked on – big, solemn and slow, like a barge floating off down the Moscow river.

So Boxman went and Senka stayed right where he was, looking. But now he wanted more so he tried to figure out how to get Death to come to the window.

He had nothing better to do, so he took the green beads out of his pocket, the ones he'd snaffled just that morning, and started studying them.

What happened with the beads was this.

As Senka was walking away from Sukharevka through the little lanes around Sretenka Street . . .

No, first you need to be told why he went to Sukharevka. Now that was really something to be proud of . . .

Senka didn't just go off to Sukharevka for no reason, he went on good honest business – to get even with his Uncle Zot. He lived according to the laws of Khitrovka now, and those laws said you should never let a bad man get away with anything. You had to settle every score, and it was best to pay it back with interest, otherwise you weren't really one of the lads – just some wet-tailed little minnow.

So Senka set out, and Mikheika the Night-Owl tagged along as well, to keep him company. If not for Mikheika, he probably wouldn't have dared try anything like that in broad daylight, he would have done the job at night, but now he had no choice, he had to play the hard man.

And it all turned out fine, really grand in fact.

They hid in the attic of the Möbius pawnshop, opposite his uncle's shop. Mikheika just sat and gawped, it was Senka that did everything, with his own two hands.

He took out a lead pellet, aimed his catapult and shot it right into the middle of the shop window – crash! Uncle Zot had three of those huge glass windowpanes with 'Haberdashery' written across them in silver letters. And he was very proud of them. Sometimes he would send Senka to scrub those rotten panes as many as four times a day, so Senka had a score to settle with the windows as well.

The jangling and the spray of broken glass brought Uncle Zot running out of the shop in his apron, holding a tray of Swedish ivory buttons in one hand and a spool of thread in the other – he'd been serving a customer all right. He turned his head this way and that, and his jaw dropped open – he just couldn't figure out how this awful thing could have happened to his window.

Then Senka fired again – and the second window shattered into jagged splinters. His uncle dropped his wares, flopped down on his knees and started collecting up the splinters of glass, like a total fool. It was just hilarious!

But Senka already had the third window in his sights. And the way it smashed was a real delight. There you go, dear Uncle Zot, take that, for all the care and affection you gave a poor orphan.

Feeling all giddy, Senka fired the last pellet, the biggest and heaviest, right at the top of his uncle's head. The bloodsucker collapsed off his knees onto his side and just lay there, with his eyes popping out of his head. He stopped yelling completely – he was so astonished by it all.

Mikheika was cock-a-hoop at Senka's daring: he whistled through four fingers and hooted like an owl – he was great at that, that was how he got the moniker Night-Owl.

And on the way back, as they were walking along Asheulov Lane, up behind Sretenka Street (Senka all calm and composed, Mikheika rattling away twenty to the dozen in admiration), they saw two carriages in front of some house there. They were carrying in suitcases with foreign labels on them, and some kind of boxes and crates. It seemed like someone had just arrived and was moving in there.

Senka was on a roll. 'Shall we lift something?' he said, nodding at the luggage. Everybody knew the best time for thieving was during a fire or when someone was moving house.

Mikheika was keen to show what he was made of too. 'Yeah, why not?' he said.

The first to walk in through the doorway was the gent. Senka didn't really get a proper look at him – all he saw were the broad shoulders and straight back, and a grey-haired temple under a top hat. But from the sound of his voice the gent wasn't old, even if he did have grey hair. He shouted from inside the hallway, with a slight stammer.

'Masa, t-take care they don't break the headlamp!'

The servant was left in charge. A Chinee, or some kind of Turkestani, he was – squat and bandy-legged with narrow eyes. And he was wearing a weird outfit – a bowler hat and a shantung silk three-piece, and instead of shoes on his feet he had white stockings and funny wooden sandals like little benches. An Oriental all right.

The porters with their leather aprons and their badges (that meant they were from the station, so the gent must have arrived by railway) carried all sorts of stuff into the building: bundles of books, some wheels with rubber tyres and shiny spokes, a shiny copper lamp, pipes with hoses.

Standing beside the Chinee, or whoever he was, was a man with a beard, obviously the landlord of the apartment, watching politely. He asked about the wheels: what did Mr Nameless need them for, and was he a wheel-maker by any chance?

The Oriental didn't answer, just shook his fat face.

One of the drivers, clearly fishing for a tip, barked at Senka and Mikheika: 'Hey, keep out of it, you little cretins!'

Let him yell, he'd never be bothered to get down off the box.

Mikheika asked in a whisper: 'Speedy, what shall we nick? A suitcase?'

'A suitcase? Don't be daft,' Senka hissed, curling up his lip. 'Take a gander at the tight hold he's keeping on that stuff.'

The Chinee was holding a travelling bag and a little bundle – chances were they were the most valuable things, which couldn't be trusted to anyone else.

Mikheika hissed back: 'But how do we get it? Why would he let go, if he's holding on so tight?'

Senka thought about that for a bit and had an idea.

'Just don't you start snickering, Night-Owl, keep a straight face.'

He picked a small stone up off the ground, flung it and knocked the Oriental's hat straight off his head – smack! Then he stuck his hands in his pockets and opened his mouth – a real angel, he was.

When Slanty-Eyes looked round, Senka said to him, very respectful, like:

'Uncle Chinaman, your hat's fallen off.'

And good for Mikheika – he didn't even twitch, just stood there, batting his eyelids.

Righto, now let's see what this pagan puts down on the step so he can pick up his hat – the travelling bag or the bundle.

The bundle. The travelling bag stayed in the servant's left hand.

Senka was at the ready. He leapt forward like a cat pouncing on a sparrow, grabbed the bundle and shot off down the lane as fast as his legs could carry him.

Mikheika set off too, hooting like an eagle owl and chortling so much he dropped his cap. But it was a rubbishy old cap anyway, with a cracked peak, he wouldn't miss it.

The Chinee stuck with them, though, he didn't fall behind for a long while. Mikheika soon darted off into a gateway, so the Oriental had only Senka to chase after. He obviously wasn't going to give up. Those little wooden benches kept clacking along the roadway, getting closer all the time.

By the corner of Sretenka Street, Senka felt like flinging that damn bundle away (he wasn't feeling quite so bold without Mikheika), but then there was a crash behind him – the Chinee had caught one of his stupid sandals on a bottle and gone sprawling flat out.

Oho!

Senka carried on, dodging and twisting through the alleys for a while, before he stopped and untied the bundle to see what precious treasures were hidden inside. He found a set of round green stones on a string. They didn't look like much, but who could tell, maybe they were worth a thousand.

He took them to a dealer he knew. The dealer fingered them and tried gnawing on them. 'Cheap stuff,' he said. 'Chinese marble, jade stone it's called. I can give you seventy kopecks.'

Senka didn't take the seventy kopecks, he kept them for himself instead. The way those little stones clicked together was much too dainty altogether.

But never mind the blasted stones, we were talking about Death.

So, Senka was mooning around in front of the house, still trying to think of a way to lure Death to the window.

He took out the string of green beads and clicked them together – clack, clack, clack, they went. *Like little china hammers*, he thought, *but what kind of hammers could you make out of china?*

Then suddenly something clicked inside his head – clear and crisp just like those beads. Right, that'll catch her eye! Dead simple.

He looked round and picked up a piece of glass. Then he caught a ray of late summer sunlight and shot a bright beam in through the gap in the curtains.

And who'd have thought it? Less than a minute later the curtains parted and Death herself glanced out.

Senka was so dazzled by the suddenness of it all, he forgot to hide the hand that was holding the piece of glass and the patch of sunlight started dancing about on Death's face. She put her hand over her eyes, peered out and said:

'Hey, boy!'

Senka took offence: *I ain't a boy*, he thought. *I ain't even dressed like one: with my shirt and my belt, corduroy pants, these fancy new boots and a decent cap too, I took it off a drunk just two days back.*

'You can stick your boy up your . . . joy,' Senka hissed back, although he didn't like rude words, and almost never used them – they used to laugh at him for that. But this time the phrase just slipped out by itself – he was so blinded by the sight of Death, as if she was the one taunting him with the patch of sunlight.

She didn't get embarrassed or angry – no, she just laughed.

'Well, we've got a real Pushkin here. Do you live in Khitrovka? Come in, I've got a job for you. Come in, don't be afraid, it's not locked.'

'What's to be afraid of?' Senka muttered, and set off towards the porch. He couldn't rightly tell whether he was dreaming or awake. But his heart was hammering away.

He didn't get a proper look at what Death had in her porch. She was standing in the doorway of the sitting room, leaning against the doorpost. Her face was in shadow, but her eyes still sparkled, like the light glinting on a river at night.

'Well, what d'you want?' Senka asked even more rudely, he was feeling so nervous.

He didn't even look at the lady of the house, just stared down at his feet or glanced around.

It was a fine room. Big and bright. With three white doors, one across from the entrance and two more, one on each side. A Dutch stove with tiles, embroidered doilies all over the place, and the tablecloth was covered in fancy needlework too, so bright it was almost dazzling. The pattern was amazing:

31

butterflies, birds of paradise, flowers too. Then he took another look and saw that all the butterflies and birds, and even the flowers, had human faces – some were crying, some were laughing, and some were snarling viciously with their sharp teeth.

Death asked him: 'Do you like it? That's my embroidery work. I have to do something with my time.'

He could feel her looking him up and down, and he desperately wanted to take a look at her from close up, but he was afraid – even without looking at her he was feeling hot one minute and cold the next.

Eventually he got up the courage to raise his head. Death was the same height as him. And he was surprised to see her eyes were black all over, like a gypsy girl's.

'What are you staring at, freckle-face? Why did you shine sunbeam light in through my window? I spotted you ages ago, hanging around outside. Fallen in love, have you?'

Then Senka saw her eyes weren't completely black, they had thin rims of blue round them, and he guessed her pupils were open wide, the way his uncle's favourite cat's eyes went when they gave him valerian to drink for a laugh. And that eerie black stare was really frightening.

'Yeah, right,' he said. 'I don't want you.'

And he twisted his bottom lip up into a sneer. She laughed again.

'Ah, you're not just freckly, you're gap-toothed too. You don't want me, but maybe you wouldn't mind some of my money. Just run an errand for me, I'll tell you where to go. It's not far, just the other side of Pokrovka Street. And when you get back, I'll give you a rouble.'

Senka was so shaken, he blurted out:

'I don't want your rouble either.'

He was petrified, or he'd have come up with some smarter answer.

'Then what do you want? Why are you skulking around

outside? I swear to God, you're in love. Come on, look at me.'
And she took hold of his chin with her fingers.

He slapped her hand away – *don't you paw me!*

'I ain't in love with you, no way. What I want from you is . . .
different.' He had no idea what to come out with, and then
suddenly, like an inspiration from God, it just slipped out. 'I want
to join the Prince's gang. Put in a word for me. Then I'll do
anything for you.'

He was really pleased with himself for saying something so
smart. For starters, it wasn't anything shameful – and she'd been
going on and on: 'You're in love, you're in love'. And what's
more, he'd shown he was someone to be taken seriously, not
just some young scruff. And then – what if she really did set him
up with the Prince? Wouldn't Prokha be green with envy!

Her face went dead and she turned away.

'That's no place for you. So that's all the little beast wants!'

She grasped her shoulders in her hands, as if she was feeling
chilly, although it was warm in the room. She stood like that for
about half a minute, then turned back to Senka and pleaded
with him, even took hold of his hand.

'Go for me, will you? I'll give you three roubles, not one. Do
you want five?'

But by now Senka had realised he was the one in charge here,
he had the power, although he didn't have a clue why. He could
see Death wanted something from Pokrovka Street very, very
badly.

He snapped back:

'No, you can give me a twenty-five note, and I still won't go.
But if you whisper in the Prince's ear, I'll be there and back in a
flash.'

She pressed her hands to her temples and twisted up her face.
It was the first time Senka had ever seen a dame wrinkle herself
up like that and still look beautiful.

'Damn you. Do what I tell you then we'll see.'

And she told him what she wanted.

'Go to Lobkovsky Lane, the Kazan boarding house. There's a cripple with no legs at the gate. Whisper this special word to him, "*sufoeno*". And don't you forget it, or you'll be in big trouble. Go into the boarding house and let them take you to a man, his name's Deadeye. Tell him quietly, so no one else hears: "Death's waiting, she's desperate". Take what he gives you and get back here quick. Do you remember all that? Repeat it.'

'I'm no parrot.'

Senka stuck his cap on his head and dashed out into the street.

And he set off down the boulevard so fast, he even overtook two cabs.

How Senka Caught Destiny by the Tail

It was a good thing Senka knew where that Kazan lodging house was, or there was no way in hell he could have found it. There was no sign, nothing. The gates were locked tight shut, with only the little wicket gate slightly open, but you couldn't walk straight in, just like that. Right in front of the iron bars there was a crippled beggar perched on his dolly, with empty trousers folded up where his legs ought to be. He had big broad shoulders, though, and a red face like tanned leather, and the arms sticking out of the sleeves of his sailor's vest were covered in coarse red hairs. He might be a cripple, but a smack from that mallet he used to push his dolly about would knock the life clean out of you.

Senka didn't go up to the man with no legs straight off, he took a good look at him first.

The man wasn't just sitting there doing nothing, he was selling bamboo whistles. Shouting his wares lazily in a hoarse bass voice: 'Roll up now, if you've any brains in your heads, bambood whistels, only three kopecks a time.' There were little kids jostling round the cripple, sampling his goods by blowing into the smooth yellow sticks. Some of them bought one.

One boy pointed to the little brass pipe hanging round the invalid's thick neck and said: 'Let me try that whistle, mister.' The cripple flicked the boy's forehead: 'That ain't no toy whistle, that's a bosun's pipe, it ain't meant for snot-nosed kids like you to blow.'

That told Senka everything he needed to know. This sailor

was only plying his trade for show, of course, he was really a lookout. It was a smart set-up: any sign of trouble, and he'd blow on that brass whistle of his – it must make a loud piercing sound – and that was the signal for the others to look sharp and clear out. And the magic word that Death had told him, '*sufoeno*', that was 'one of us', only back to front, like. Since olden times the bandits and thieves in Moscow had always mangled the language, so outsiders wouldn't understand: they added bits onto words or swapped them around, or thought up other tricks.

He walked up to the lookout, leaned right down to his ear and whispered the word he'd been told to say. The sailor gave him a sharp glance from under bushy eyebrows, twitched his big ginger moustache and didn't say a word, just shifted his dolly away from the gate a bit.

Senka went into the empty yard and stopped. Was this really the place where the Prince and his gang had their hideout?

He pulled his shirt down and brushed one sleeve across his boots to make them shiny. He took off his cap, then put it back on. At the door of the building he crossed himself and muttered a little prayer – a special one about granting wishes that a certain good person had taught him a long time ago: 'Look down, O Lord, in Thy mercy, heed the prayers of the humble and meek and reward me not according to my deserts, but according to my desires.'

He plucked up his courage and tugged at the door – it was locked. So then he knocked.

It was a few moments before it opened, and even then it was only by a crack. An eye glinted in the darkness.

Just to be on the safe side, Senka repeated: '*Sufoeno*.'

Someone behind the door asked: 'What do you want?'

'I'd like to see Deadeye . . .'

At that the door opened wide and Senka saw a young lad in a silk shirt with a fancy belt and Moroccan leather boots. He had a silver chain dangling out of his waistcoat pocket with a little silver skull on it – you could see straight off he was a real top-notch businessman. And he had that special kind of glance, like all the businessmen did: quick and piercing, it didn't miss a thing. Senka felt really jealous: the lad was the same age as him, and not even as tall. Some people have all the luck!

'This way,' the lad said, and walked on in front, without looking at Senka any more.

The dark collidor led to a room where two men were playing cards, slapping them down hard on a bare table. Each of them had a heap of banknotes and gold imperials lying in front of him. Just as Senka and his guide walked in, one of the players flung his cards down and yelled:

'You're cheating, you whore's tripes! Where's the queen?' And he punched the other man smack on the forehead.

The other man got up from the table and fell backwards. Senka gasped – he was afraid the man would smash the back of his head open. But as he fell, he turned a backward somersault, just like an acrobat in the circus big top, then jumped up smartly on to the table and lashed the man who had hit him across the kisser with his foot! 'You're the cheat!' he shouted. 'The queen's been played!'

Well, of course, the one with the boot in his face tumbled over. Gold went rolling and jangling across the floor, and paper money went flying in all directions – what a sight!

Senka was scared, he thought someone was about to get killed. But the other lad just stood there grinning – he thought it was funny.

The man who had started the fight rubbed his cheekbone.

'The queen's been played, you say? Why, so it has. All right, let's get on with the game.'

And they sat down as if nothing had happened and gathered up the scattered cards.

Senka looked a bit closer and his jaw dropped in amazement and his eyes almost popped out of his head. Looking closer, he saw the two players had the same face, you couldn't tell them apart. They both had snub noses, yellow hair and thick lips, and they were dressed exactly the same. It was incredible!

'What's your problem?' his guide asked, tugging on Senka's sleeve. 'Let's go.'

They walked on. Another collidor, and another room. This one was quiet, with someone sleeping on a bed. He had his kisser turned to the wall, all you could see was a fat cheek and a jug-ear. The great hefty hulk was stretched out, snoring away with his boots still on.

Senka's guide took small steps, walking quietly on the tips of his toes. Senka did the same, only quieter.

But, as the hulk went on snoring, one hand stuck out from under the blanket, and a black gun barrel glinted in it.

'It's me, Lardy, it's me,' the young businessman said quickly.

The hand went back down, but the sleeper still didn't turn towards them.

Senka took off his cap and crossed himself – the wall was covered with icons, just like the icon screen in a church. There were holy saints, and the Virgin, and the Most Holy Cross.

A man was sitting by the opposite wall with his long legs stretched out, and his feet propped up on a table in shiny bright half-boots. He had specs and long straight flaxen hair and he was twirling a sharp little knife, no bigger than a teaspoon in his fingers. He was dressed neatly too, like a gent, even had a string tie. Senka had never laid eyes on a bandit dressed like that before.

Senka's guide let him go ahead and said:

'Deadeye, the ragamuffin's to see you.'

Senka gave him an angry sideways glance. He could have thumped him for that word, 'ragamuffin'. But then the man called Deadeye did something that made Senka gasp: he flicked his hand, and the little knife flashed across the room in a silver streak and stuck dead in the eye of the Most Blessed Virgin.

And that was when Senka spotted that the eyes had been gouged out of all the saints on the icons, and the Saviour on the Cross had little knives sticking out where there ought to be nails.

Deadeye took another knife out of his sleeve and flung it into the eye of the Infant Jesus, as he lay in Mary's arms. And after that he turned to look at Senka, who was stupefied.

'Well, what do you want, kid?'

Senka walked up to him, glanced round at the other lad, who was hanging about by the door, and said quietly, just like he'd been told to:

'Death's waiting, she's desperate.'

Once he'd said it, he felt scared. What if Deadeye didn't understand? What if he asked: 'What's she waiting for?' Senka didn't have a clue.

But Deadeye didn't ask anything of the kind; instead he said to the other lad in a low, polite voice: 'Mr Sprat, would you please be so good as to conceal your face behind the door.'

Senka realised that he'd told the other lad to push off, but Sprat didn't seem to twig, and just stood there.

So Deadeye launched another falcon – a knife, that is – out of his right sleeve and it stuck in the doorpost, thwack, just an inch from Sprat's ear. Then, the lad disappeared in a flash.

Deadeye examined Senka through his specs. The eyes behind the lenses were as pale and cold as two little lumps of ice. He took a square of folded paper out of his pocket and held it out. Then he said in a polite voice: 'There you are, kid. Say I'll call round tonight at about eight o'clock . . . No, wait.'

He turned towards the door and called: 'Hey, Mr Sixer, are you still here?'

Sprat stuck his head back in through the door. So he had two nicknames, then, not just the one?

He sniffed and asked warily: 'You won't do that again with the knife, will you?'

Deadeye's reply was impossible to understand: 'I know the pen of gentle Parni is not in fashion in our day.[1] When is our rendezvous, by which I mean the meet with the Ghoul?'

Sprat-Sixer understood, though. 'At seven,' he said.

---

[1] Pushkin, *Yevgeny Onegin*.

'Thank you,' the odd man said with a nod. Then he turned to Senka. 'No, I can't make it at eight. Say I'll be there at nine, or maybe not till ten.'

Then he turned away and started gazing at the icons again. Senka realised the conversation was over.

On his way back, cutting through the yards and alleys of Khitrovka to shorten the way, he thought: *They're the real thing, all right!* It was no wonder the Prince was Moscow's number-one bandit with eagles like that in his gang. He thought there was nothing he wouldn't give for the chance to hang out in the den with them, like one of the boys.

Once he was past Khitrovka Lane, where the labourers were kipping in lines, Senka stopped under a withered poplar tree and unfolded the little package. He was curious to see what was so precious that Death was willing to hand over a fiver to get it.

White powder, it looked like saccharine. He licked it – sweetish, but it wasn't saccharine, that was a lot sweeter.

He was so distracted, he didn't see Tashka come walking up.

'What's this, Senka,' she said, 'are you doing candy cane now?'

That was when Senka finally twigged. Of course, it was cocaine, why hadn't he guessed? That was why Death's pupils were blacker than night. That was it, and that meant . . .

'You don't lick it, you sniff it up your nose,' Tashka explained.

It was still early, so she wasn't dolled up or wearing make-up, and she had her purse in her hand – she must be going to the shop.

'Don't do it, Senka,' she said. 'You'll rot your brains away.'

But he still took a pinch anyway, stuck it in his nostril and breathed in as hard as he could. Why, it was disgusting! The tears streamed out of his eyes, and he sneezed and sneezed until his nose started running.

'Well, you ninny, happy now?' asked Tashka, wrinkling up her nose. 'Chuck it, if you know what's good for you. Why don't you tell me what I've got here?'

And she pointed to her head. She had a daisy and two flowers that Senka didn't recognise in her hair.

'A meadow for cows, that's what.'

'It ain't a meadow, it's three messages. The marjoram signifies "I hate men", the daisy signifies indifference and the silver-leaf signifies "cordially inclined". Say I'm going with a customer who makes me feel sick. I stick the marjoram in my hair to show I despise him, and the thickhead's none the wiser. Or I'm standing here with you, and I have the silver-leaf in my hair, because we're mates.'

She took the other two out and left just the silver-leaf to make Senka feel happy.

'And what do you use the indifference for?'

Tashka's eyes glinted and she ran her tongue over her cracked lips. 'That's for when someone falls in love with me and starts giving me sweets and beads and stuff. I won't send him packing, because maybe I like him, but I still have to keep my pride. So I stick on the daisy, let him suffer . . .'

'Who's the admirer?' Senka snorted, wrapping up the cocaine the way it was before. He stuck it in his pocket, and something in there clicked – the green beads he'd lifted off the Chinee. So, since they were on the subject anyway, he said: 'How would you like me to give you some beads without any courting?'

He took them out and waved them under Tashka's nose. She lit up.

'Oh,' she said, 'they're really lovely. And my favourite colour, "esmerald", it's called! Will you really give them to me?'

'Yes, take them, I don't mind.'

So he gave them to her – seventy kopecks was no great loss.

Tashka put the beads round her neck straight away. She gave Senka a quick peck on the cheek and legged it off home, as quick as she could – to get a look in the mirror. And Senka ran off too, to the Yauza Boulevard. Death was probably tired of waiting by now.

He showed her the little packet, keeping her at arm's length, then put it back in his pocket.

She said: 'What are you doing? Give it here, quick!'

Her eyes were all wet and watery, and her voice was shaking.

Senka said: 'Ah, but what did you promise me? You write the Prince a note, so he'd take me into his gang.'

Death dashed at him and tried to take it by force, but she was wasting her time – Senka ran round the table to get away from her. After they'd played catch for a while, she begged him: 'Give me it, you fiend, don't torture me.'

Senka suddenly felt sorry for her: she was so beautiful, but so unhappy. That rotten powder was no good for her. And then it occurred to him: maybe the Prince wouldn't listen to what a mamselle thought about important business, not even the lover he truly adored. Ah, but no, the lads had told him the Prince could never refuse her a thing.

While he was wondering whether to give her the cocaine or not, Death suddenly went limp and dropped her head. She sat down at the table and propped her forehead on her hands, like she was really, really tired, and said:

'Oh, to hell with you, you little beast. You'll grow up into a big bad wolf anyway.'

She gave a quiet moan, as if she was in pain. Then she took a scrap of paper, wrote something on it in pencil and tossed it to Senka.

'Here, may you choke on it.'

When he read the note, he could hardly believe his luck. The sprawling handwriting said:

'Prince, take this youngster on. He's just the kind you need. Death.'

How Senka Showed What He Was Made Of

'I need you, do I? What good are you to me?'

The Prince rubbed the dimple in his chin furiously and gave Senka a scorching glance from his black eyes. Senka cringed, but this was no time to be shy.

'She told me, "Go to him, Speedy, don't you have no doubts, you'll definitely be useful to the Prince, I ought to know,"' that's what she said.'

Senka tried to look at the big man with fearless devotion, but his knees were trembling. The whole gang was standing behind him: Deadeye, Sprat-Sixer, the pair with the same face and another one with fat cheeks (it must have been him who was dozing with his devolvert in his hand). Only the cripple with no legs was missing.

The Prince's lodgings in the Kazan were right at the end of the collidor that Senka had been led along the day before. From the room with the desecrated icons, where Deadeye flung his knives about, you just had to go a little bit farther and turn a corner, and there was a big room, with a separate bedroom. Senka saw the bedroom only through the half-open door (well, it was just an ordinary bedroom: a bed covered with a coloured counterpane, a flail – a spiked steel ball on a chain – lying on the floor, and that was all he could make out), but the Prince's sitting room was really grand. The Persian carpet covering the whole floor, so incredibly fluffy it was like walking on moss in a forest; carved wooden chests along the walls (oh, there must be some fine stuff in there!); bottles of vodka and cognac in a row on the huge table, with silver goblets, a well-hacked ham and a jar of pickled cucumbers. Every now and then the Prince stuck his hand into this jar, fished out the cucumbers with the most pimples and crunched on them with relish, making Senka's mouth water. The big boss's face was handsome all right, but it looked a bit puffy and creased. He'd obviously done some hard drinking, and a fair bit of sleeping too.

The Prince wiped his mouth with the hem of his silk shirt. He picked up the note again.

'Has she gone crazy, or what? As if she didn't know I've got a full deck. I'm the King, right?'

He bent down one finger, and Deadeye said:

'Soon you'll have as many titles as His Majesty the Emperor. Prince by name and king by nature, and soon you'll be an ace too. By the grace of God, Ace of all Moscow, King of Khitrovka and Prince of Piss-ups.'

Senka thought the bit about 'piss-ups' was too brazen by half, but the Prince liked the joke and roared with laughter. All the others chuckled along. Senka didn't really get what was so amusing, but just to be on the safe side, he smiled too.

'When I'm Ace, there'll be no more banter like that,' said the Prince, putting down the note and bending his fingers down as he carried on counting. 'Death's my Queen, right? You, Deadeye, are the Jack. Lardy's the tenner, Bosun's the niner. Maybe's the eighter, Surely's the sevener. This ragamuffin's a sixer at best, and I've already got one of those. Right, Sprat?'

'Yes,' said the lad from the day before.

Now Senka realised what the Prince was on about. The lads had told him that real businessmen, the ones who lived by bandit laws, had gangs called 'decks', and every deck had its own set. A set was made up of eight bandits, and they all had their own position. The top brass was the 'King', who had a moll or 'Queen'; then there was the 'Jack', a kind of deputy; and then came the gang members from tenner to sixer. And no one had more than eight in their gang, it had been that way ever since

44

the old days. That must be where the name 'Jack' came from, because he often used a black jack.

Senka gave Deadeye a look of special respect: *so you're the Jack*. On top of being the King's right-hand man, the Jack was usually responsible for 'wet jobs' – killings, that is.

'There are no vacancies available presently,' said Deadeye, using fancy words as usual, but Senka understood what he meant, that there were no free places in the gang.

But strangely enough, the Prince didn't throw the little squirt out. He just stood there, scratching his head.

'Two sixers – what kind of deck's that? Whatever will the Council say to that?' The Prince sighed. 'Oh, Death, my little darling, the things you do to me ...'

And from the way he sighed, Senka twigged that though the Prince might grouse and grumble, he didn't have the nerve not to do Death's bidding, even though he was such a big hero. Senka cheered up, stopped feeling wary, straightened his shoulders and looked round at the bandits. He stood proud, as though to say: *You can sort this little snag out yourselves, I've done my bit. It's Death's fault, anyway.*

'All right,' said the Prince. 'What's your name? Speedy? You stay put for the time being, Speedy, without any number. We'll work out where to put you later.'

Senka squeezed his eyes shut, he was so happy.

Maybe he didn't have a number, but now he was a real bandit, and more than that, he was in the number-one top gang in all of Moscow! Now then, Prokha, now then, Mikheika, let's see you choke on that! And as soon as he started getting his share of the swag, he could take Tashka as his moll, so she wouldn't go lying with anyone and everyone. She could sit at home and lay out her flowers.

The Prince waved his hand towards the table, and everyone but Deadeye poured himself a glass of vodka or cognac and started drinking. Senka took a nip of the brown booze too, just to try it (it was horrible, far worse than any homebrew). Even though he was hungry, he didn't take a single piece of the ham – he had to fit in right: play a lad who knew the rules, not a starving kid they picked up off the rubbish heap. He kept out of the way tactfully, watched and listened, didn't butt into conversations – oh God forbid. And the businessmen didn't even look at him – what would they want with a youngster like him? Only Sprat glanced at him a couple of times. Once he just looked, but the second time he winked. That was something to be grateful for, at least.

The Prince started telling the twins, the sevener and the eighter, about Death. 'You haven't been here long, Maybe and Surely, you still don't know what the mamselle's like. Sure, you've seen her, all right, but there's more to her than that. When I tell you what I did to get her, you'll understand. When her old fancy man, Yashka from Kostroma, took a dose of lead poisoning and she was free, I started to make a move. I'd had my eye set on her for a long time, but while Yashka was still alive, I didn't dare do anything about it. Had great respect from the Council, he did, and back then I was just a simple robber. No deck, no decent den, I didn't deal in wet jobs, or do any big-time stuff. Sure, I wasn't exactly the lowest of the low in Khitrovka, but how could I compare with Yashka from Kostroma? But I still thought, come hell or high water, that doll's got to be mine. That was the first time I did a pawnshop and clouted the watchman with my flail. People started talking about me, and the big loot started rolling in. I start sending her presents: gold, and all sorts of fancy china, and Japanese silk. She sends it all back. If I show up, she throws me out, doesn't even want to talk to me.

'But I'm patient, I understand I'm not big enough for Death yet.

'Okay, so then I held up this post wagon, beat two men to death. Took forty thousand.

'I showed up at her place with a gypsy choir, at night. Forked out five hundred roubles to the coppers at the Myasnitsky station

46

so they wouldn't interfere. I left a satin box outside her door, and there was a diamond brooch in the box, this big it was.

'And what came of it? The gypsies and their women sang themselves hoarse, and she didn't open the door, didn't even look out the window.

'Well, I think, what the hell else do you want? It's not money, it's not presents, that much is clear. But what, then?

'So I got the idea of trying a different approach. I knew Death was soft on kids. She sent money and clothes and all sorts of sweets to the Mariinsky Home, where the Khitrovka orphans go. Yashka the horse thief once gave her a hundred gold imperials in a basket of violets, and the crazy bint kept the flowers and gave the money to the nuns at the orphanage, so they could build a bathhouse.

'Aha, I think to myself. If I can't get you by hook, then I'll get you by crook.

'I bought thirty pounds of the very finest Swiss chocolate and three bolts of Holland cloth, and some calico for underclothes. I took it there in person and gave it to the Reverend Mother Manefa. Take it, I said, a present from the Prince to the orphans.'

Here the fat-faced man, the tenner, cleared his throat and interrupted the Prince's story:

'Uhu, a right royal present it was, we remember.'

The Prince hissed at him. 'Lardy,' he said, 'don't you go barging in and spoiling the story. Well, what happens? I go breezing round to Death's place to see if she'll treat me any different. She opens the door, only it would have been better if she hadn't. She comes out, eyes blazing. Clear out and don't come back, she shouts. Don't you dare come anywhere near me, and all sorts of other stuff like that. She prods and pokes me out the door, after everything I'd done ... I took offence real bad, that time. Started drinking – I was wandering round in a haze for a week. And while I was drunk the memory that really stung was the way I'd bought that lousy chocolate with my hard-earned money and even felt the cloth in the shop – to check the quality.'

'Well, I still say they gave you that cloth for nothing,' Lardy put in again.

But the Prince said: 'That's not the point. I'd tried so hard, my feelings were hurt. Right, I think, you're too flighty altogether. This isn't going right. Damn you for that cloth and chocolate. That night I climbed over the orphanage wall, took the window out, broke down the door of their storeroom and started hacking away. I tipped the chocolate out on the floor and stamped on it. I slashed the cloth to shreds – now let's see you wear that! I cut all the calico to pieces. And I smashed up everything else they had in there. The watchman came to see what all the noise was about. "What are you doing, you bastard," he yells, "you're depriving the poor orphans!" Well, I stuck my blade straight in his heart, the blood splashed out all over my arm. I came out of the storeroom all covered in blood, threads hanging off me and my face as black as an Arab's with chocolate. And there's Mother Manefa coming straight at me, with a candle. Well, I did her in too. It's all the same to me, I think, I've damned my soul anyway. So screw my soul and the life eternal. I didn't want any kind of life at all without Death . . .'

'Yes,' said Lardy with a nod. 'That set Moscow on its ear. You might have been drunk, but you didn't leave any tracks or witnesses. In the end they realised it was you running wild, of course, but there was no way to prove it.'

The Prince laughed. 'The important thing was that our lot found out about it straight away, and they told Death. When I got back from the orphanage I slept for two days straight, didn't wake up once. And when I came round, they gave me a note from her, from Death. "Come to me, you'll be mine" – that was what it said. So that's what she's like, Death. Just try to understand her.'

Senka listened eagerly to the story, and afterwards he racked his brains trying to make sense of it, but he just couldn't.

But that day, he didn't have time to rack his brains, so many different things happened.

After the Prince announced his decision and treated his deck to vodka and cognac, Sprat took the new boy back to his place (he had a little room behind a chintz curtain near the way in).

He turned out to be a mighty fine lad, with no side to him at all, even though he had a number in the gang, and Senka had just turned up out of nowhere. He didn't put on airs, he spoke simply and told Senka lots of useful things, as if he was one of them, almost a card in the deck.

'It's OK, Speedy,' he said, 'if Death herself asked for you, you'll be in the deck, there's no way round it. Maybe one of us will get put away or done in, and then they'll take you as sixer and I'll move up to sevener. You stick with me, and you'll be all right. And you can live right here. It's more fun snoring together.'

(They never did get to snore together, but we'll come to that later.)

Because everyone knew about the Prince, and Senka knew as much about Death as Sprat did, he started asking about the others.

'Everyone's afraid of our Jack,' said Sprat, 'even the Prince is wary of him, because Deadeye has these fits. Most of the time, he's calm and quiet, though he's always using strange words and talking in poetry, but sometimes he just goes berserk, and then he gets really scary, like a devil, he is. He's a gent from a good family, used to be a student, but he stabbed someone to death over some candy cane and got hard labour for life. You keep clear of him,' Sprat advised. 'The Prince can smack you in the kisser, even beat you to death, but at least you'll know why and what for, but that Deadeye's a crazy man.'

The next one in the deck, Lardy, was Ukrainian, that was how he got his moniker, because they eat lard there. He was a key man, with big connections among the fences in other cities – all the swag passed through his hands and came back as 'crunch', that is, money.

Sprat told Senka that the legless Bosun had really been a bosun in the fleet, a hero proper, known all over the Black Sea. When he started to tell you about the Turks or the high seas, he was absolutely fascinating. His legs were crushed by a steam boiler on board ship. He had crosses and medals and a hero's pension, but he wasn't the sort to spend his old age in peace and quiet. What he wanted was something to test his luck, a bit of gusto and excitement. He almost never took his share of the swag, either, and a niner's share was a fair size, not like Sprat's.

The sevener and eighter were twin brothers from the Yakimanka District. A smart, dashing pair of lads. The Prince had been advised to take them on by a constable he knew at the First Yakimanka Station. He said the lads were real desperadoes, it would be a shame if they didn't make the big time, a real waste. And they were nicknamed Maybe and Surely because they had more daring than brains. Maybe wasn't that bad, that was why he had a higher number, but Surely was a total loon. If the Prince told him to steal the double-headed eagle off the Saviour's Tower at the Kremlin, he'd start climbing without a second thought.

Then at the end Sprat sighed, rubbed his hands together and said: 'Anyway, you'll see us all in action on the job tonight.'

'What's the job?' Senka's heart stood still – how about that, straight into a job on the very first day! 'Are we going bombing?'

'Nah, bombing's nothing. This is a really wild job. The Prince and the Ghoul have a meet today.'

Senka remembered that Deadeye had asked about the meet too.

'Is that the one at seven o'clock? What's it about? This Ghoul, that's Kotelnichesky, right?'

'That's the one. The Prince and him are going up for Ace of Moscow, if you get my drift.'

Senka whistled. So that was it.

The ace was like the tsar of bandits, there was just one for all of Moscow. The ace used to be Kondrat Semyonich, a really big man, everyone in Moscow was afraid of him. They used to say all sorts of things about Kondrat Semyonich, though. That he'd got old and rusty, he didn't give the young men a chance. Some condemned him for living a life of luxury, not in Khitrovka, like the ace was supposed to do, but in a house on the Yauza. And he didn't die like a bandit, from a knife or a bullet, or in jail. He drew his last breath on a soft feather bed, like some merchant.

Anyway, the Council had decreed that the ace should be one of the two: the Prince or the Ghoul.

The case for the Prince was clear enough – he was a man on the make. He'd appeared from nowhere, and the jobs he did were breathtaking. But the problem was he was in too much of a hurry and he was obstinate, those were his only flaws. The grandfathers were afraid that power like that might go to his head.

The Ghoul was a different matter altogether. He was from the old guard – the less showy bandits who'd plodded their way to the top. The Ghoul didn't have any famous jobs to his name, his deck didn't fire any broadsides, but people were just as much afraid of him as they were of the Prince.

The Ghoul's deck didn't make a living from hold-ups, though, they had a new business, one that was kept very quiet: they skimmed from the grain merchants and shopkeepers. Their kind of businessmen were called 'milkers'. If you wanted your shop to stay safe, and you didn't want the sanitary inspector picking on you, or the coppers bothering you – then you gave the milker his dough and carried on trading in peace. But as for those who didn't pay – who thought they could manage or were just plain mean – all sorts happened to them.

One stubborn grocer was hit over the head from behind in a dark alleyway, he didn't see who did it. He fell down and tried to get up, but he couldn't – the ground was spinning in front of his eyes. Suddenly he saw a horse and cart coming straight at him, and the cart held a great heap of paving stones. He yelled and waved his arms, but the driver didn't seem to hear him. The horse stepped over the grocer, so its hooves missed him, but the wheels of the cart ran right over his legs and smashed them to bits. Now they pushed that grocer around in a chair on wheels, and he paid the Ghoul promptly. And there was an ice-cream seller too, they ambushed his daughter, who was engaged, put a sack over her head and violated her, and not just one of them, no, half a dozen thugs. Now she sat at home and never showed her face outside, and she'd been taken down from a noose twice. If only the ice-cream seller had paid, none of that would ever have happened.

But even the Ghoul wasn't to the liking of all the grandfathers, Sprat explained. Those who were older and remembered times past didn't approve of the Ghoul's trade. Back then it wasn't done to suck people's blood like that.

Anyway, today was the day of the meet.

'They'll do each other in!' Senka gasped. 'They'll stab each other, or shoot each other.'

'They can't, that's against the law. They can break a few ribs or crack someone's head open, but that's all. You can't take weapons to a meet, the Council doesn't allow it.'

At five o'clock the mediators came from the Council, two calm, slow-moving 'grandfathers' who used to be respected thieves. They named the spot for the meet – the Cows' Meadow in the Luzhniki District – and the time: seven o'clock on the dot. They said the Ghoul wanted to know whether his whole deck should come or what.

They sat the grandfathers down to drink tea in the front room, and all crowded round the Prince at the table. Even the Bosun trundled in from the street, afraid they'd settle things without him.

Maybe shouted out first: 'Let's all go! We'll give the ghoulies a beating to remember.'

The Prince hissed at him:

'Think before you speak, smartarse. Do we have a Queen

52

with us? No. Death won't traipse across to Cows' Meadow, will she now?'

Everyone smiled at the joke, and waited to see what the Prince would say next.

'But the Ghoul's Queen is Pockface Manka. Last year she smacked two narks' heads together so hard, they never got up again,' the Prince went on, polishing his fingernails with a little brush. He was sitting with his legs crossed and easing his words out slowly – no doubt already seeing himself as the ace.

'We know Manka, she's a woman to be reckoned with,' the Bosun agreed.

'Right, then. So think on a bit. You're a cripple, Bosun – no offence meant – what good are you at a meet?'

The Bosun bounced on his stumps and started getting excited.

'Why I ... I'll smack 'em so hard with this mallet – that's enough to double anyone over. You know me, Prince!'

'A mallet!' the Prince mocked him, biting off a hangnail. 'And the Ghoul's niner is Vasya Ugreshsky. What good will it do to swing your mallet at him? You see?'

The Bosun went all sad and started sniffing.

'Now let's take Sixer,' said the boss, nodding at Sprat.

'What about me?' said Sprat, jerking his head up.

'I tell you what. Their sixer is Cudgel. He can hammer a six-inch nail into a log of wood with that great big fist of his, and anyone can knock you down with a feather, Sprat. So where does that leave us, my brave gents? With this – at a meet, their deck will leave us for dead, as sure as God's holy. And then they'll say the Prince had his whole deck with him, they won't bother working out who's too small, who's crippled and who wasn't even there. That's what they'll say, oh yes they will,' the Prince declared in response to their dull muttering.

The room was suddenly quiet and downbeat.

Senka was sitting in the corner farthest away, afraid they might throw him out. He wasn't too upset about them not taking him to the meet, he didn't much fancy fisticuffs, especially not against real fighters. They'd batter a youngster like him down and trample him into the ground.

The Prince admired his nails, then bit off another hangnail and spat it out.

'Call the grandfathers. I decide. And not a word! Keep your traps shut.'

Sprat ran off to get the mediators. They came and stood just inside the door. The Prince stood up too.

'Two of us should go to the meet, that's my opinion.' He looked at them merrily and shook his forelock. 'The King and one other chosen by the King. Tell the Ghoul that.'

Deadeye sighed and the others frowned but not a word was spoken. It clearly wasn't on to haggle in front of outsiders, Senka thought.

But even when the grandfathers left, there was no yapping. Once the Prince had decided, that was that.

Sprat winked at Senka: *come on outside*. In the collidor he sniffed as he whispered: 'I know that spot very well. There's a little barn there, a good place to hide. We'll wait and watch them from there.'

'But what if they see us?'

'Then we're for it, no question,' Sprat said with a careless wave of his hand. 'They're real strict about stuff like that. But don't you get the wind up, they won't see us. That barn's a great spot, I tell you. We'll burrow into the hay. No one will twig, and we'll be able to see everything.'

Senka suddenly felt afraid and he hesitated. But Sprat spat on the floor and said: 'You can please yourself, Speedy. I'm running over there right now. While they're dragging things out, I'll get there ahead of them.'

Of course, Senka went with him – what else could he do? He couldn't act scared like some girl. And he really did want to watch: this was serious stuff, a proper bandit meet, to decide who would be Ace of Moscow. How many people had ever seen something like that?

Naturally, they didn't actually run there, that was just Sprat's way of talking. The young bandit had a wad of cash in his pocket. They walked to Pokrovka Street, hired a cab and drove out of town to Luzhniki. Sprat promised the driver an extra rouble to drive like the wind. It took them twenty-three minutes – Sprat timed it with his silver watch.

The Cows' Meadow was just that, a meadow – all yellow grass and burdock. On one side, across the river, were the Sparrow Hills, and on the other side was the Novodevichy Convent, with its vegetable gardens.

'This is where they'll have the meet, there's no other option,' said Sprat, pointing to a trampled bald patch where four paths came together. 'They won't go into the grass, there's cowpats all over the place, they'll get their shoes filthy. And that's the barn right there.'

The barn was rotten – sneeze and it would collapse. It had been built once upon a time to store straw, but it wouldn't stay standing much longer, that was clear. It was less than a stone's throw from the bald patch, ten paces or maybe fifteen.

They climbed up the ladder into the loft, full of last year's straw. Then they settled into the hideaway, pulling the ladder up after them, so no one would get inquisitive and come over.

Sprat glanced at his watch again and said: 'Three and a half minutes past five. Almost two hours to go. Why don't we play a hand or two, fifty kopecks a time?'

He pulled a deck of cards out of his pocket. Senka was so frightened his hands and feet were freezing, he had cold shivers running up and down his spine, and Sprat wanted to play cards!

'I ain't got any money.'

'We can play flicks. Only straight ones, mind, no twisting, my head's not that hard.'

As soon as they'd dealt the cards, they heard voices. Someone had come up from behind, from the direction of the railway.

Sprat put his eye to a crack and whispered: 'Hey, Speedy, take a gander!'

There were three men walking round the barn. They looked like bandits all right, but Senka didn't know them. One was huge, with big, broad shoulders and a small head, shaved clean; one was wearing a cap, but even from up there you could still see that his nose had caved in; the third was short, with long arms, and his jacket was buttoned right up.

'The bastard,' Sprat hissed right in Senka's ear. 'That's what he's up to! What a lousy cheat!'

The men came into the barn, but Senka and Sprat could still see them through the cracks in the ceiling. All three men lay down and covered themselves with straw.

'Who's a lousy cheat?' Senka whispered. 'Who are they?'

'The Ghoul's a lousy cheat, that's who. Those are his fighters, from his deck. The big one's Cudgel, the sixer. The one with no nose is Beak, he's the eighter. And the little one's Yoshka, the Jack. Ah, this is really bad. This'll be the death of us.'

'Why?' Senka asked, frightened.

'Yoshka's no good in a fight, but he never misses with that gun of his. He used to work in a circus, snuffing candles out with bullets. If they brought Yoshka it means there'll be shooting. But our two will have left their guns at home. And there's no way to warn them . . .'

This news set Senka's teeth chattering. 'What're we going to do?'

Sprat had turned all pale too. 'Hell only knows . . .'

They just sat there, shaking. Time dragged by, then seemed to stop completely.

Down below it was quiet. Just once they heard a match being struck and caught a whiff of tobacco smoke, then someone hissed: 'Cudgel, you ugly mug, d'you want to burn us alive? I'll shoot you!'

There was silence again. And then, just before the clock struck seven, there was a metal click. Sprat mimed for Senka: that was the hammer being cocked.

Oh, this was really bad!

Two light carriages drove up to the bald spot from different directions.

Sitting on the box of one carriage – a classy number in red lacquer – was Deadeye, wearing a hat and a sandy-coloured three-piece suit, and holding a cane. The Prince was sprawled on the leather seat, smoking a *papyrosa*. He was done up like a dandy too, in a sky-blue shirt and thin scarlet belt.

Sitting on the box of the other carriage, which wasn't as fancy as the first, but still pretty smart, was a woman with hands the size of ham hocks. Her fat red cheeks stuck out from the bright flowery shawl wrapped tight round her head. It looked as though two watermelons had been stuck down the front of her blouse – Senka had never seen breasts like that before. The Ghoul was riding behind, like the Prince. He looked pretty ordinary: stringy and balding, narrow snaky eyes, greasy hair hanging down like icicles. He was no eagle from the look of him, no way was he a match for the Prince.

They met in the middle of the bald patch, but didn't bother shaking hands. The Ghoul lit up, and glared at the prince. Deadeye and the huge woman stood a bit farther back – Senka supposed that must be the way it was done.

'Shall we kick up a racket, eh, Speedy?' Sprat asked in a whisper.

'But what if the Ghoul only put his men in the barn just in case? Because he was afraid the Prince might try something? Then it's the shiv for you and me.'

Senka was really afraid of making a racket. What if that Yoshka started firing bullets through the ceiling?

Sprat whispered: 'Who can tell . . . OK, let's watch for a bit.'

The men in the meadow finished their *papyroses* and threw them away.

The Prince was the first to speak. 'Why didn't you come with your Jack?'

'Yoshka's teeth have been bothering him, his cheek's swollen right up. And why do I need my Jack? I'm not afraid of you, Prince. You're the one who's scared of me. You brought Deadeye along. A woman's a match for you.'

Manka chuckled in a loud, deep voice.

The Prince and Deadeye locked eyes once more. Senka saw Deadeye drum his fingers on his cane. Maybe they'd guessed there was something shady going on.

'If you want to bring a woman, that's your business.' The Prince put his hands on his hips. 'Lording it over women is all you're good for. When I'm the ace, I'll let you run the mamselles of Khitrovka. It'll be just the job for you.'

The Ghoul didn't rise to the bait, he just smiled and cracked his long fingers: 'Of course, you, Prince, are an outstanding hold-up artist, a man on the make, but you're still wet behind the ears. What kind of ace would you make? It's barely five minutes since you got your deck together. And you're far too reckless. Every last nark in Moscow's after you, but I'm a safe pair of hands. Do the decent thing and stand down.'

The words were peaceable, but the voice was jeering – you could see he was riling the Prince, trying to wind him up.

The Prince said: 'I soar like an eagle, but you scrounge like a jackal, you feed on carrion! You're a fine talker but Moscow isn't big enough for the two of us! You've got to be under me, or . . .' And he slashed a finger across his throat.

The Ghoul licked his lips, cocked his head and said slowly, almost gently: 'Or what, my little Prince? Be under you . . . or death, is that it? And what if that Death of yours has already been under me? She's a handsome girl. Soft to lie on, springy, like a duck-down bed . . .'

Manka laughed again, and the Prince turned crimson – he knew what the Ghoul meant. And the Ghoul got what he wanted – he'd driven his enemy wild with fury.

The Prince lowered his head, howled like a wolf and went for the man who had insulted him.

But Manka and the Ghoul obviously had everything arranged. He jumped to the left and she jumped to the right, stuck two fingers in her mouth and whistled.

Down below the hay rustled, a door banged and Yoshka flew from the barn, though the other two stayed put. He had a shooter in his hand – black, with a long barrel.

'Stop right there!' he cried. 'Look this way. You know me, old friend, I never miss.'

The Prince froze on the spot.

'So that's how you operate, is it, Ghoul?' he asked. 'No respect for the rules?'

'Quite correct, my little Princeling, quite correct. I've got brains, and the rules aren't made for people like me. Now both of you get down on the ground. Get down, or Yoshka will shoot you.'

The Prince grinned, as if he thought that was funny. 'You don't have brains, Ghoul, you're a fool. You're no match for the Council. You're done for now. I don't have to do a thing, the grandfathers will do it all for me. Let's lie down, Deadeye, and take a rest. The Ghoul's condemned himself.'

And he lay down on his back, crossed one leg over the other and took out a *papyrosa*.

Deadeye looked at him, and trailed the toe of his low boot across the ground – he must have been feeling bad about his suit – and lay down too, on his side, his head propped on his hand and his cane by his side.

'Well, now what?' the Prince asked. Then, turning to Yoshka: 'Fire away, my little sharpshooter. Do you know what our traditionalists do with rule-breakers like you? For a trick like this they'll dig you out from wherever you hide, then stick you straight back in the ground again.'

The way this meet was turning out was weird. What with

two men lying on the ground smiling, and three people standing there, just watching them.

Sprat whispered: 'They don't dare fire. They bury you alive for that, it's the law.'

The Ghoul's moll whistled again. Then Cudgel and Beak came dashing from the barn and pounced on the men on the ground: Cudgel dropped the entire weight of his carcass on the Prince, Beak turned Deadeye face down and neatly twisted his arms behind his back.

'There you go, little Prince.' The Ghoul laughed. 'Now Cudgel's going to beat your brains out with his great big fist. And Beak's going to smash your Jack's ribs. And no one will ever know about the shooter. Simple as that. We'll tell the Council we beat you up. Shame you couldn't handle the Ghoul and his woman. Right, lads, smash 'em now!'

Suddenly there was this fierce yell – 'A-a-a-a-gh!' – right beside Senka's ear.

Sprat launched himself up with his elbows, got to his knees and leapt straight down on to Yoshka's shoulders, screeching as he went. He couldn't hold on and went flying to the ground. Yoshka swung the handle of his gun and smashed it into Sprat's temple – but that brief moment, when Cudgel and Beak turned towards the noise, was enough for the Prince and Deadeye. They pushed off their enemies and jumped to their feet.

'I'll let them have it, Ghoul!' Yoshka shouted. 'It didn't work out like you planned! We can dig the bullets out afterwards! Maybe that'll work.'

And then Senka surprised himself by screeching even louder than Sprat and jumping on to Yoshka's back. He clung on for grim death, sinking his teeth into Yoshka's ear. He felt a salty taste in his mouth.

Yoshka swung round, trying to shake the kid off, but he couldn't. Senka bellowed, and kept ripping Yoshka's ear with his teeth.

He couldn't have held on for long, of course. But then Deadeye snatched his cane up off the ground and shook it, the wooden stick went flying off, and something long and steely glittered in the Jack's hand.

Deadeye bounded towards Yoshka, bent one leg and stretched out the other, straightened out like a spring, and elongated himself, like a viper attacking. He snagged Yoshka with his blade – right in the heart – and Yoshka stopped waving his arms and tumbled over, with Senka underneath him. Senka escaped, and looked round to see what would happen next.

He was just in time to see the Prince tear himself out of Cudgel's great mitts, take a run at Manka and smash his forehead into her chin – the enormous woman went down on her backside, sat there for a moment then collapsed. But the Prince had already taken the Ghoul by the throat and they went tumbling over and over, off the well-trodden path and into the grass, setting the dry stalks swaying furiously.

Cudgel was about to go and lend his King a hand, but Deadeye came flying up from behind, his left hand tucked behind his back and his right hand holding that pen – it was more than two feet long – swish-swish, backwards and forwards through the air, and there were red drops dripping off the steel.

'Oh, do not leave me,' he recited, 'stay a while. I have loved you for so long. Let my fiery caresses scorch you . . .'

Senka knew those lines – they were from this song, a real tear-jerker it was.

Cudgel turned towards Deadeye, fluttered his eyelids and staggered backwards. Beak was quicker off the mark, he'd scarpered straight off. And then the Prince and the Ghoul came tumbling back on to the bald patch, only now you could see who was getting the best of it. The Prince twisted his enemy round, grabbed hold of his face and started hammering his head against the ground.

The Ghoul wheezed: 'Enough, enough. You win! I'm a punk.'

That was a special kind of word. When anyone said that at a

meet, you weren't supposed to hit him any more. That was the law.

The Prince thumped him another couple of times, just to round things off, or maybe it was more than a couple – Senka didn't watch the end. He was squatting down next to Sprat, watching crimson blood streaming out of the black hole in the side of his head. Sprat was as dead as a doornail – Yoshka had smashed his head in with his shooter.

After that the grandfathers spent four days trying to decide whether a meet like that could decide anything. They ruled that it couldn't. Of course the Ghoul had cheated, but the Prince had blotted his copybook too: his Jack had come with a blade, and there were the two lads hiding in the barn. The Prince wasn't fit to be ace yet, that was the verdict. Moscow would have to manage a bit longer without a thieves' tsar.

The Prince went about in a fury, drinking all the time and threatening to put the Ghoul in the ground. There was no sign of the Ghoul, he was holed up somewhere, recovering from the treatment the Prince had doled out.

All Khitrovka was buzzing with sensational talk about the meet in Luzhniki.

And as for Speedy Senka, you could say these were golden days.

He was the Prince's sixer now, all fully legit. For his heroism the deck gave him a handsome ration and total respect – you can imagine how the lads in Khitrovka treated him now.

Senka went round there about three times a day, as if he had important secret business, but really just to cut a dash. All of Sprat's clothes went to him: the English cloth trousers with a crease in them, and the box calf boots, and the boulanger pea-jacket, and the captain's cap with the lacquered peak, and the silver watch on a chain with the little silver skull. The lads came running from all over to shake hands with the hero or gape from a distance as he told his story.

Prokha, who used to teach Senka what was good sense and put on airs around him, looked into Senka's eyes now and asked him in a quiet voice, so the others wouldn't hear, to fix him up as a sixer somewhere, even with a really feeble deck. Senka listened condescendingly and promised to think about it.

Oh, but it felt good.

True enough, his pockets were as empty as before, but surely that would all change when the first job came along.

It came along soon, and a real hotshot job it was too.

How Senka Went on a Real Job

The Prince got this tip-off from a reliable man, a waiter at the Slavyanskaya hotel where merchants stayed, over in Berezhki. He said a rich Kalmyk horse-trader and his right-hand man had arrived from the town of Khvalynsk to buy stud horses for a herd. This Kalmyk had a fat wad of crunch on him, and it had to be lifted quick, because tomorrow, on Sunday, he was going to the horse auction, and he could spend the whole lot there.

Late in the evening the whole deck got into three two-seaters and set off. The Prince rode up front with Deadeye, then came Lardy and the twins, with the Bosun and Senka at the rear. Their job was to stand lookout and make sure the horses could be started at a gallop if they had to scram.

As they flew across Red Square, down Vozdvizhenka Street and along Arbat Street, Senka's belly kept rumbling so bad he could have gone running to the lav. But later, after they clattered across the bridge, the sickening fear suddenly turned to jauntiness, like when Senka was a kid and his father took him to the Shrovetide Carnival that first time, to ride down the icy wooden slides.

The Bosun was merry right from the off and kept cracking jokes. 'Ah,' he said, 'Sebastopol, I'll meet my moll.' And again: 'Ah, Poltava, what a palaver.' Or else: 'Ah, Samara, we'll be there tomorra.'

He knew lots of different towns, some of them Senka hadn't even heard of.

The hotel was a drab-looking place, like a workers' bunkhouse. The lights were all out before ten – trading folk went to bed early, and it was market day tomorrow.

They drove through to the railway depot and jumped out. They didn't talk, they didn't need words now – everything had been talked through in advance.

Senka took the reins and steered the three carriages side by side, wheel to wheel, with the Bosun's rig in the middle. Then he handed the Bosun all three reins. The horses wouldn't play up with him, they were smart. When they sensed strength, they stood still and didn't stir. And the Prince's horses were special, miraculous – nothing could catch horses like that.

So there was the Bosun, sitting on the box, puffing on his long pipe, and Senka didn't know what to do with himself; he paced down the street, then back up the other side. He wasn't scared any more, just limp and fed up. He felt pretty useless.

He ran to one corner, then another, to check whether there was any need to scram. Not a thing, it was all quiet.

'Uncle Bosun, what's taking them so long?'

The Bosun took pity on the sixer. 'All right,' he said, 'why should a healthy young lad like you be hanging about back here? Run and see how the job's going. Take a look, then come back and tell me how they finish off the Kalmyks.'

Senka was surprised. 'Can't they just take the money? Do they have to finish them off?'

'That depends how much there is,' the Bosun explained. 'If there's not a lot of crunch, only a few hundred, you don't need to finish them off, the coppers won't look too hard. But if there's thousands, it's best to do them in. A merchant will offer the coppers a big reward for his thousands, to make sure they sweat real hard. Off you run, Speedy, don't you worry none. I'll manage here on my own. Ah, I'd go myself, like a shot, if I had any legs.'

Senka didn't need to be told twice. He was so tired of just hanging around, he didn't even go in through the gate, just climbed straight over the wall.

When he walked into the big hallway he saw a man in a long

coat lying there on the counter, squealing in fear. He had his hands over his head, and his shoulders were shaking. Lardy was standing beside him, yawning, with his fiddle in his hand (that was what bandits called a devolvert: a fiddle, a bludgeon or a chanter).

The man on the counter said in this feeble voice: 'Don't kill me, gentlemen. I didn't look at you, I closed my eyes straight away. Go easy on me . . . please? Don't take my life – I'm a family man, a good Orthodox Christian, eh?'

Senka answered, playing the big man: 'Don't you worry. You won't twitch much – we'll take pity on you.'

Then the man said to Senka. 'Curious? Go on, then, have a gander. They're taking their time over it.'

There was a collidor. Long it was, with doors in a row on both sides. Maybe was standing at the near end, and Surely at the far end (or the other way round, Senka still found it hard to tell the brothers apart). They had fiddles too.

'I came to have a look,' Senka said. 'Just a quick peep.'

'Be my guest,' said Maybe (or it could have been Surely), flashing his white teeth in a smile.

Just then, one of the doors started to open. He slammed it shut with his foot and barked: 'Come out here and you're for it!'

Someone wailed behind the door: 'What are you doing, you fooligan? I have to get to the lav.'

Maybe hooted with laughter: 'Puddle in your pants. But you kick up a racket, and I'll shoot through the door.'

'Holy God,' gasped the voice behind the door. 'Is it a hold-up, then? I won't bother you, lads, I'll be quiet.'

And the bolt rasped shut.

Maybe started giggling again (it was probably Surely after all – he was always grinning from ear to ear). He pointed with his devolvert to a half-open door halfway down the collidor: *That's where it is.*

Senka walked over and glanced inside.

He saw two men tied to chairs – they had swarthy skin and

narrow eyes. One was really old, about fifty, with a little goatee beard, a pair of good plaid trousers, and a silk waistcoat with a gold chain dangling out of the pocket. He had to be the horse-trader. The other one was young, without any beard or moustache, with a calico shirt hanging over his trousers – he was definitely the right-hand man.

The Prince was striding to and fro between the two men, waving his flail through the air.

Senka opened the door a bit wider – so where was Deadeye, then?

He was doing something really strange: he'd taken that pen of his (a foil, it was called) out of the cane, and was shredding the feather mattress on the bed with it, scattering fluff and feathers in the air.

'Can't think where else,' said Deadeye. 'Where could our friends from the steppe have concealed their *porte-monnaie*?'

The Prince sneezed – the fluff must have got up his nose.

'All right, Deadeye, don't get in a sweat.' He stopped in front of the foreman and grabbed hold of his hair with one hand. 'They'll spill the beans. Right, Yellow-face, are you going to blab? Or would you like to chew on this iron apple here?'

And he swung the flail in front of the foreman's face (which wasn't yellow at all, it was as white as chalk, as if it had been dusted with the stuff).

Deadeye stopped lashing his blade about and sprinkled some powder on his fingernail (candy cane, Senka guessed). As he threw his head back, Senka winced – now he'd start sneezing even worse than the Prince! But Deadeye wasn't bothered, he just squeezed his eyes shut, and when he opened them again, they'd turned all wet and shiny.

The Kalmyk foreman licked his lips – they were as white as his mug – and said: 'I don't know . . . Badmai Kekteevich doesn't tell me.'

'Right, then,' said the Prince with a nod. He let go of the foreman's hair and turned to the horse-trader. 'Well, Goat-beard?

Shall I chop you into little pieces, or are you going to talk?'

The horse-trader seemed like a tough old nut to crack. He spoke calmly and his voice didn't shake: 'I'm not so stupid as to keep my money here. I went to the market office today and put it in the safe. Take what there is and leave. This watch is gold. And there's money in the wallet. Enough for you.'

The Prince looked round at Deadeye, who was standing there, smiling at something. He confirmed the story.

'That's right. There is a safe at the horse market and the traders put their money in it for safe-keeping, so it won't get stolen and they can't binge it all away.'

Senka saw the trader and his man glance at each other, and Badmai fixed his eyes on something on the floor. Ah-ha! One leg of the foreman's chair was pressing down on a floorboard, and its edge was sticking up. The foreman shifted a bit and the floorboard fell back into place.

The trader's wallet was lying open on the table. The Prince took out the banknotes and rustled them.

The Prince took a step towards the horse-trader and smashed a fist into his cheekbone. The Kalmyk's head bobbed about, but he didn't shout out or start crying – he was a tough one.

'I got the whole deck out for three hundred. It's a flaming disgrace. Why, you squint-eyed snake!'

'All right,' said the Prince, tugging the watch out of the horse-trader's pocket – it was gold, good stuff. 'You can thank your Kalmyk god for keeping your fat purse safe. Let's go, Deadeye.'

He was already on his way to the door when Senka stuck his head in and said, all modest like:

'Uncle Prince, can I say something, please?'

'What are you doing here?' the Prince said with a scowl. 'A scram?'

And Senka said: 'Nah, no scram, but wouldn't it be a good idea to check over there, under the floor, eh?'

And he pointed to the floorboard.

The horse-trader jerked on his chair and wheezed something

Senka couldn't understand – it must have been a curse in his own language. The Prince looked at Senka, then at the floor. He thumped the foreman in the ear – the blow hadn't looked very hard, but the foreman tumbled over, taking his chair with him, and started snivelling.

The Prince bent down, hooked one finger under the edge of the floorboard and lifted it out – there was a hole in the floor underneath it. He put his hand in.

'Ah-ha.'

He took out a big leather wallet, and it was stuffed chock-full with crunch.

The Prince counted the swag. 'Why, there's three thousand here!' he said. 'Good for you, Sixer.'

Senka was flattered, of course. He looked at Deadeye to see whether he was admiring him too.

But Deadeye wasn't admiring Senka, and he wasn't looking at the wallet. Something strange was happening to him. He'd stopped smiling, and his eyes weren't gleaming now, they looked drowsy.

'I believed them . . .' Deadeye said slowly, and his whole face quivered, as if waves were running across it. 'I believed the Judases. They looked me in the eye! And they lied! They lied – to me!'

'Enough, enough, don't go kicking up the dust,' the Prince said – he was rather pleased with the find. 'They have to mind their own interests . . .'

Deadeye started moving, muttering: 'Goodbye, my darling Kalmyk girl . . . Your eyes are very narrow, true, your nose is flat, your forehead broad, you do not lisp in fluent French . . .'[2] He chuckled: 'Narrow, very narrow . . .'

Then suddenly he leapt forward – exactly the same way he had when he spiked Yoshka – and stuck his foil straight down into the foreman's eye. Senka heard a crunch (that was the steel

---

[2] Pushkin, 1830.

running through the skull and sticking in the floor) and he gasped and closed his eyes. When he opened them, Deadeye had already pulled the foil out and was watching curiously as something white, like cream cheese, dripped off the blade.

The foreman hammered his heels on the floor and opened his mouth wide, but no shout came out. Senka was afraid to look him in the face.

'What the . . . Are you crazy?' the Prince snarled.

Deadeye answered back in a hoarse, strained voice: 'I'm not crazy. It just sickens me that there's no truth in this world.'

He gave a flick of his wrist, there was a whistling sound, and the sharp point of the foil slit the horse-trader's throat. A tuft of beard that was sliced off went flying through the air, then the blood came spurting out in a thick jet – like water out of a fire hose.

Senka gasped again, but this time he forgot to close his eyes. He saw the horse-trader jerk up off the chair so hard that the ropes holding his hands broke. He jumped up, but he couldn't walk, his legs were still tied to the chair.

The life was gushing out of the horse trader in spurts of cherry red, and he kept trying to hold it back with his hands, to stuff it back in, but it was no good – the blood flowed through his fingers, the Kalmyk's face went blank and it was so terrifying that Senka screamed and went dashing out of that hideous room.

How Senka Sat in the Privy Cupboard

He began to recover his wits only on Arbat Street, when he was completely winded from running. He didn't remember flying out of the Slavyanskaya Hotel, or running across the bridge, and then right across the empty Smolensky market.

And even on Arbat Street he still wasn't himself. He couldn't run any longer, but he didn't think to sit down and take a rest. He staggered along the dark street like an old man, croaking and gasping. And he kept looking round, all the time; he still thought he could see the Kalmyk behind him, with his torn-open throat.

The way things had turned out, he was the one who killed the horse-trader and his man. It was all his fault. If he hadn't wanted to impress the Prince, if he hadn't pointed out the hiding place, the Kalmyks would still be alive. But he had to go and blab, didn't he? He was Speedy the Bandit, was he not?

But by Theatre Square, Senka was asking himself another question: *what kind of damn bandit are you?* A lousy worm of a bandit, that's what you are. Oh, Semyon Spidorov, you haven't got the stomach for real man's work now, do you?

He felt so ashamed for running away, he couldn't bear it. As he walked along Maroseika Street, he called himself every name he could think of, abused himself something rotten, but as soon as he remembered the Kalmyks, it was clear as day: there was no way back into the deck now. The Prince and his gang might forgive him – he could lie and say his stomach was turned or make up something else, but he couldn't lie to himself. If Senka was a businessman, a cow was a thoroughbred.

Oh, the shame of it.

Senka's legs carried him to the Yauza Boulevard before he had any idea where he was heading.

He sat on a bench for a while and got frozen right through. Then he paced up and down for a while. It started to get light. And it wasn't until he realised he was walking past Death's house for the third time that he understood what pain was gnawing hardest at his heart. He stopped in front of the door and suddenly his hand reached out of its own accord, so it did, and knocked. Loudly.

He felt scared and wanted to turn and run. He decided he would just hear the sound of her footsteps, her voice. When she asked 'Who's there?' he would scarper.

The door opened without a sound and without any warning. There were no footsteps, no questions.

Death appeared in the doorway. The loose hair flowing down over her shoulders was black, but all the rest of her was white: the nightshirt, the lacy shawl on her shoulders. And her feet – Senka was looking down at them – they were white too, the tips were peeping out from under the hem of her nightshirt.

Well, well, she never even asked who was knocking at that time in the morning. She was fearless, all right. Or was it all the same to her?

She was surprised to see Senka. 'You? Did the Prince send you? Has something happened?'

He shook his hanging head.

Then she got angry: 'What are you doing here at this unearthly hour? Why are you hiding your eyes, you little beast?'

All right, so he looked up. And then he couldn't look down again – he was lost in wonder. Of course, the dawn played a little trick of its own, peeping out from behind the roofs with its pink glow, lighting up the top of the doorway and Death's face and shoulders.

'Well, aren't you going to say something?' she said, frowning. 'You look like a ghost. And your shirt's torn.'

That was when Senka noticed that his shirt really was torn from the collar to the sleeve and it was hanging all askew. He must have snagged it on something when he was running out from the hotel.

'What's this, are you hurt?' asked Death. 'You've got blood on you.'

She reached out a hand and rubbed the spot of dried blood on his cheek. Senka guessed some of the spray must have hit him when the horse-trader's blood came spurting out.

But Death's finger was hot, and her touch came as such a surprise that Senka suddenly burst into tears.

He stood there, blubbing away, the tears streaming down his face. He felt terribly ashamed, but he simply couldn't stop. He tried hard to force them back, but they kept breaking through – it was so pitiful, just like a little puppy whimpering! Then Senka started cursing like he'd never cursed before, with the most obscene words he knew. But the tears kept on flowing.

Death took his hand: 'What's wrong, what is it? Come with me . . .'

She bolted the door shut and dragged him into the house after her. He tried to dig his heels in, but Death was strong. She sat him down at the table and took hold of his shoulders. He wasn't crying now, just sobbing and rubbing his eyes furiously.

She put a glass of brown stuff down in front of him. 'Go on, get that down you. It's Jamaican rum.'

He drank it. It made his chest feel hot, but otherwise it was all right.

'Now lie down on the sofa.'

'I'm not lying down!' Senka snarled, and he looked away again.

But he did lie down, because his head was spinning. And the instant his head touched the cushions, everything went blank.

When Senka woke up it was day, and not early in the day either – the sun was shining from the other side, not from where the street was but from the yard. Lying under a blanket – which was light and fluffy with a blue-and-green check – he felt free and easy.

Death was sitting at the table, sideways on to Senka sewing something, or maybe doing her embroidery. She looked incredibly beautiful from the side, only she seemed sadder than when you saw her from the front. He didn't open his eyes wide, just peeked out at her for a long time. He had to figure out how to behave after what had just happened. Why, for instance, was he lying there naked? Not completely naked, that is, he had his pants on, but no shirt and no boots. That had to mean she undressed him while he was asleep, and he didn't remember a thing.

Just then Death turned her head and Senka shut his eyelids quickly, but even so she realised he wasn't sleeping any more.

'Are you awake?' she said. 'Are you hungry? Sit at the table. Here's a fresh roll. And here's some milk.'

'I don't want it,' Senka muttered, offended by the milk. Why couldn't she offer him a man's drink – tea or coffee? But then, of course, what respect could he hope for after snivelling like a little kid?

She stood up, took the cup and bread roll off the table and sat down beside him. Senka was afraid Death would start feeding him by hand, like a baby, and he sat up.

Suddenly he felt so desperately hungry he started trembling all over. And he started gobbling down the bread and washing it down with milk. Death watched and waited. She didn't have to wait for long, Senka guzzled it all in a minute.

'Now tell me what the matter is.'

There was nothing else for it. He hung his head, scowled, and told her – briefly, but honestly, without keeping anything back. And this is how he finished: 'So I'm sorry, I've let you down. You vouched for me to the Prince, and I turned out too weak, you see. What kind of bandit would I make? I thought I was a falcon, and I'm nothing but a mangy little sparrow.'

And as soon as he finished, he looked up at her. She seemed so angry that Senka felt really terrible.

They didn't say anything for a little while. Then she spoke: 'I'm the one who owes you an apology, Speedy, for letting you get anywhere near the Prince. I wasn't myself at the time.' Then she shook her head and said to herself, not to Senka: 'Oh, Prince, Prince . . .'

'It wasn't the Prince, it was Deadeye,' he said. 'Deadeye killed the Kalmyks. I told you . . .'

'What can you expect from Deadeye, he's not even human. But the Prince wasn't always that way, I remember. At first I even wanted . . .'

Senka never found out what it was she wanted, because at that very moment they heard a knock, a special one: tap-tap, tap-tap-tap, and then two more times, tap-tap.

Death started and jumped up: 'It's him! Talk of the devil. Come on, get up, quick. If he sees you, he'll kill you. He won't care that you're just a kid. He's so awfully jealous.'

Senka didn't have to be asked twice – he was up off that sofa in a flash, he wasn't even offended by that 'kid'.

He asked in a frightened voice: 'Which way? The window?'

'No, it takes too long to open.'

Senka made for one of the two white doors at the back of the room.

'You can't go in the bathroom. The Prince is fussy about keeping clean, the first thing he always does is go and wash his hands. Go in there.' And she nodded to the other door.

Senka didn't care – he'd have climbed into a hot oven to get away from the Prince. He was knocking again now – louder than before.

Senka flew into a little room that was like a closet, or even a cupboard, only inside it was all covered in white tiles. On the floor by the wall there was a big vase or bowl – it was white too.

'What's this?' Senka asked.

She laughed. 'A water closet. A privy with flushing water.'

'And what if he gets the urge?'

She laughed even louder: 'Why, he'd burst before he'd go to the privy in front of a lady. He's a prince, after all.'

The door to the closet slammed shut, and she went to open up. Senka heard her shout: 'All right, I'm coming, I'm coming, no need for that racket!'

Then he heard the Prince's voice: 'What did you lock yourself in for? You never lock yourself in!'

'Someone filched a shawl from the porch, crept in during the night.'

The Prince was already in the room. 'That must have been a vagrant, passing through. No one in Khitrovka would dare do that. Don't worry, I'll put the word out, they'll get your shawl back and find the thief – he'll be sorry.'

'Oh, never mind about the shawl. It was old anyway, I was going to throw it out.'

Then it went quiet for a while, something rustled and there was a slobbery sound.

She said: 'Well, hello.'

'They're necking,' Senka guessed.

The Prince said: 'I'll go and wash my hands and face. I'm all dusty.'

Water started running on the other side of the wall, and the sound went on for a long time.

Meanwhile Senka looked around in the privy cupboard.

There was a pipe sticking out over the bowl, and higher up there was a cast-iron tank with a chain dangling from it – he had no idea what it was for. But then Senka had no time for idle curiosity – he had to scarper while he was still in one piece.

And right up by the ceiling was a bright little window – not very big, but he could get through it. If he stood on the china bowl, grabbed hold of the chain, and then the tank, he could reach it all right.

He didn't waste any time on second thoughts. He climbed up

on the bowl (oh, don't let the damn thing crack!) and grabbed the chain.

The bowl stood the test all right, but that chain played him a shabby trick: when he tugged on it, the pipe started roaring and water came gushing out!

Senka almost fainted, he was so afraid.

Death stuck her head in: 'What are you doing? Have you lost your wits?'

And just then the next door slammed as the Prince came out of the bathroom. So Death swung round towards him, as if she'd just finished her business.

She closed the door behind her, firmly.

Senka stood there for a while with his hand on his heart while he gathered his wits. Once he'd recovered a bit, he squatted down on his haunches and started wondering how beautiful women did the necessary. It was nature, they had to, but it was impossible to imagine Death doing anything like that. And where could you do it in here? Not in this snow-white china bowl! It was beautiful, the sort of thing you could eat fruit jelly off.

So Senka still wasn't sure – he found it easy to imagine that specially beautiful women had everything arranged in some special kind of way.

Once he got comfortable in the closet, he wanted to know what was going on outside.

He pressed his ear against the door and tried to listen, but he couldn't make out the words. He tried sticking his ear here and there and finally crouched down on all fours, with his ear on the floor. There was a crack under the door, so he could hear better that way.

He heard her voice first: 'I told you – I'm not in the mood for fooling around today.'

'But I brought you a present, a sapphire ring.'

'Put it over there, by the mirror.'

Footsteps. Then the Prince again, angry (Senka cringed):

'Seems like you're not in the mood very often. Other women can't wait to get on their back, but you're as prickly as a hedge-hog.'

She said (real reckless!): 'If you don't like me, then clear off, I won't try to stop you.'

He said (even angrier): 'Get off your high horse! You owe me an apology. Where did you find that snot-nosed kid Speedy?'

Oh, Lord in Heaven, thought Senka!

'Why, don't you like him?' Death asked. 'They told me he saved your life.'

'He's a bright enough lad, only he's too wet. If you see him, tell him this: once you're in my deck, there's only two ways you leave the Prince – the coppers put you away or you go into the cold damp ground.'

'What's he done?'

'He's done a runner, that's what.'

She said: 'Let him go. It's my mistake. I thought he'd be useful to you. But clearly he's not made of the right stuff.'

'I won't let him go,' the Prince snapped. 'He's seen everyone, he knows everything. You tell him: if he doesn't show up, I'll hunt him down and bury him. Anyway, that's enough of that nonsense. Last night, Death, my little darling, I picked up a fine load of loot, more than three thousand, and today I'm going to take even more, I've got a really grand lead. You know Siniukhin, the pen-pusher, lives in Yeroshenko's basement?'

'I know him. A drunk, used to be a clerk in the civil service. Has he given you a lead, then?'

The Prince laughed. 'Ah – it's not from him, it's *about* him.'

'But how can you get anything out of a miserable wretch like him? He can hardly feed his wife and children.'

'I can, Death, my little darling, I most certainly can! A certain little person whispered to Lardy, and Lardy whispered to me. The pen-pusher found old treasure somewhere underground, heaps and heaps of gold and silver. He's been drinking vodka for three days now, with salted mushrooms and salmon. He's bought his old woman dresses, and boots for the kids – Siniukhin, who never had more than ten kopecks to his name! He sold Hasimka the Fence some old money, a whole handful of silver coins, then he got drunk in the "Labour" and boasted he was not much longer for Khitrovka, he was going to live in an apartment of his own, like before, dine off fancy food on a white tablecloth. I'm going to have a little chat with Siniukhin tonight. Let him spread his good luck around a bit.'

Suddenly the room went quiet, but it wasn't just quiet, it was creepy. Senka pressed his ear hard up against the crack – he could tell there was something wrong.

Then the Prince roared: 'So what's this, then? Boots? And the sofa's all creased up?'

There was a clatter as a chair fell over, or something of the sort.

'You whore! You slut! Who is he? Who? I'll kill him? Hiding, is he? Where?'

Well, Senka didn't hang around after that. He closed the latch on the door, leapt up on the bowl, grabbed the chain, hauled himself up (ignoring the roar of the water), pushed open the window and dived out head first.

Behind him he heard a crunch and a crash as the door swung open, and then a bellowing voice: 'Stop right now! I'm going to rip you to pieces!'

But Senka skidded down like a fish. With a hand from God, or somehow else, he managed not to break his neck. He tumbled awkwardly then darted off across the broken stone and brick towards the passage.

But he didn't run very far. He stopped and thought: *He's going to kill her now, the Prince is. Kill her for nothing.*

His feet carried him back, of their own accord. Then he stood under the windows and listened. It was quiet. Had he done her in already?

Senka rolled an old barrel to the window of the privy, stood it on end and began to climb back in. He didn't know why he was doing it. He didn't want to think about it. He had this stupid thought running round his head: *you can't kill Death*. It wasn't possible – or was it – to kill Death? And then he thought: *I did enough running last night. I'm no hare, especially on broken bricks without boots.*

When he got back in the closet, it was clear the Prince hadn't killed her yet, and it didn't look like he was about to.

Suddenly Senka didn't feel so brave any more. Especially when, through the door, which was broken off its top hinge, he heard this: 'Tell me, in God's name. Nothing will happen to you, just say who it is.'

There was no answer.

Senka peeped out warily. Oh Lord, the Prince had a flick-knife and he was pointing it straight at Death's chest. Maybe he would kill her after all?

He even said: 'Don't play games with me – I might just lose control. Killing someone's like swatting a fly for the Prince.'

'But I'm not just anyone, I'm Death. Go on, then, swat me. Well, what are you gawping at? Either kill me, or get out.'

The Prince flung the knife at the mirror and ran out. The front door slammed.

Senka craned his neck and saw that Death had turned away. She was looking at herself in the broken mirror, and the cracks in the mirror were like a cobweb stretched over her face. The way she was looking at herself was weird, as if there was something she couldn't understand. She caught sight of Senka, swung round and said:

'You came back? That was brave. And you said you were a sparrow. You're not a hawk, I know, but you're not a sparrow, more like a swift.'

And she smiled – the whole thing was water off a duck's back to her. Senka sat down on the sofa and pulled on the boots that had caused the disaster. He was breathing hard; after all, he'd had a bad scare.

She handed him his shirt. 'Look, I've put my mark on you. From now on you'll be mine.'

Then he saw that she hadn't just stitched up his torn shirt, she'd embroidered a flower on it while he was sleeping, a strange flower with an eye like hers, like Death's eye, in the middle. And the petals were coloured snakes with forked tongues.

He realised she was joking about the sign. He put the shirt on and said, 'Thanks.'

Her face was really close to his, and it had a special kind of smell, sweet and bitter at the same time. Senka gulped and his eyelids batted, his mind went blank and he forgot everything, even the Prince. She didn't want to mess around with the Prince. Which meant she didn't love him, right?

Senka took a small step closer, and felt himself swaying, like a blade of grass in the wind. But he didn't have the nerve to move his hands and hug her or anything.

She laughed and tousled Senka's hair. 'Keep away from the flames, little gnat,' she said. 'You'll singe your wings. I'll tell you what you should do. You heard what the Prince said about the treasure? You know Siniukhin, the pen-pusher? He lives under Yeroshenko's flophouse, in the Old Rags Basement. A miserable man with a red nose like a big plum. I went to Siniukhin's place once, when his son was sick with scarlet fever – I took the doctor. Go and warn him to take his family and get out of Khitrovka fast. Tell him the Prince is going to pay him a visit tonight.'

A swift was all right, no offence taken, but Senka drew the line at that 'gnat'. She understood, and started laughing even harder. 'Stop sulking. All right, then, I'll give you just one little kiss. But no nonsense.'

He couldn't believe it – he thought she was mocking a poor orphan. But even so, he pursed his lips up and pushed them out. But would she really kiss him?

She didn't cheat, she touched his lips with hers, but then she started pushing him away.

'Off you go to Siniukhin, run. You can see what a wild beast the Prince has turned into.'

As he walked away from her house, Senka touched his lips gingerly with his little finger – oh Lord, they were burning up! Death herself had kissed them!

How Senka Ran and Hid
and then Got the Hiccups

It wasn't Senka's fault he didn't get to the pen-pusher, there was good reason.

He made an honest effort, set straight out from Death's house for Podkolokolny Lane, where Yeroshenko's flophouse was. It had apartments with numbers upstairs – as many as a thousand people would snore away up there – and down below, under the ground, there were these massive deep cellars, and people lived there too: 'diver-ducks' who altered stolen clothes, paupers who had nothing, and the pen-pushers were the kind that settled there. Pen-pushers were a heavy-drinking crowd, but they tried not to overdo it, they needed to keep hold of a pen and set the words out right on paper. That was their trade, scribing letters for the unlearned: begging, weepy letters as often as not. They were paid by the page: one was five kopecks, two was nine and a half, and three was thirteen.

It wasn't a long way from the Yauza Boulevard to the Yerokha (that was what Yeroshenko's flophouse was usually called), but Senka never got to where he was heading.

When he turned the corner on to Podkolokolny Lane (he could already see the door of the Yerokha), Senka spotted something that stopped him dead in his tracks.

There was Mikheika the Night-Owl, and standing beside him, holding him tight by the shoulder was a short-arse in a check two-piece and bowler – the same Chinee Senka had nicked the green beads off the week before. Once you'd seen someone like that, you never forgot him. Big fat cheeks the colour of ripe turnips, narrow slits for eyes, a blunt little nose, but with a hook in it too.

Night-Owl was acting calm and grinning. What had he got to be afraid of? There were two Khitrovka lads standing behind the Chinaman (the pudding-head didn't have a clue). Mikheika spotted Senka and winked: *just you wait, the fun's about to start.*

Well, he couldn't not watch, could he?

Senka came a bit closer, so he could hear, and stopped. The Chinee asked (the way he spoke was funny, but you could still make it out): 'Night-Owr-kun, where your friend? The one who run so fast. Thin, yerrow hair, grey eyes, nose with freckurs?'

Well, well, so he'd remembered everything, the yellow pagan, even the freckles. But the question was, how had he managed to find Mikheika? He must have just wandered into Khitrovka and run into him by chance.

But then Senka spotted a battered old cap with a cracked peak in the Chinaman's hand. Now, that was crafty! He hadn't just barged in by accident, he'd come on purpose, to look for his beads. He'd twigged that the lads were from Khitrovka (or maybe the cabbies had given him the hint, they were an eagle-eyed bunch), come dashing over and nabbed Night-Owl. Mikheika didn't know his letters, and he drew an owl on all his things so they wouldn't get nicked. And now look where that had got him. The oriental titch must have walked around with the cap, which had been dropped on Sretenka Street, asking whose it was. And now he'd found out, he was in trouble. Old Slanty-eyes had made a big mistake, coming here and grabbing Night-Owl by the sleeve. That flat pancake face was in for a good battering.

Mikheika answered back: 'What friend's that? All those Chinese radishes must have gone to your head. I've never seen you before.'

Night-Owl was showing off in front of the lads, naturally.

The Chinaman waved the cap. 'And what this? What bird this?' And he jabbed his finger at the lining.

What was the point, though? The lads would fling a load of seventy-kopeck lead pellets in his face, and that was all he'd take home. Senka even felt sorry for the heathen. Pike, a smart lad from Podkopaevsky Lane, quick on his feet, had already gone down on all fours behind the gull's back. Now Night-Owl would give Yellow-cheeks a shove and the fun would start. He'd leave with no pants, and they'd rearrange his teeth, and his ribs too.

There were gawkers grinning at the sight from the square and the lane. Boxman set off along the edge of the market, with an open newspaper in his hands – he stopped, looked over the top of the grey page, yawned and tramped on. Nothing unusual, just another gull getting what he had coming.

'Oh, oh, don't frighten me, mister, or I'll wet me pants,' Night-Owl mocked. 'But thank you most kindly for the cap. Please accept my regards, and this too, out of the generosity of my heart.'

And he smashed his fist into the Chinaman's teeth!

Or, rather, he aimed for the teeth, only Slanty-eyes bobbed down, Night-Owl's fist flailed at empty air, and the swing of it spun him right round. Then the Chinaman lashed out with his right hand and left leg, at the same time: his hand caught Mikheika round the back of the head (only gently, but Mikheika dived nose first into the dust then didn't move), and his heel smacked into Pike's ear. Pike went flat out too, and the third lad, a bit older than Pike – Drillbit, his moniker was – tried to hit the nimble heathen with his brass knuckles, but all he caught was empty air, too. The Chinee leapt sideways and smacked Drillbit on the chin with the toe of his boot (how could he fling his legs up that high?), and Drillbit fell flat on his back.

So before the gawkers could even drop their jaws, the three lads who'd tried to fleece the pagan gull were stretched out on the ground, and not getting up in a hurry.

People shook their heads in wonder and went on their way. But the Chinee squatted down beside Mikheika and grabbed his ear.

'Ver' bad, Night-Owr-kun,' he said. 'Ver', ver' bad. Where beads?'

Mikheika started shaking all over. And for real – he wasn't putting it on. 'I don't know about no beads! On me mother's grave! In the name of Christ!'

The Chinaman twisted his ear a bit and explained what he wanted. 'Littuw green baws, on thread. They were in bunduw.'

Then didn't Night-Owl go and yell: 'That wasn't me, it was Speedy Senka! Ow, my ear! That hurts! There's Senka, over there!'

Why, the Judas! Couldn't even stand a simple ear-twist. He needed a bit of training from Uncle Zot!

The Chinaman swung round to where Night-Owl was pointing, and saw Senka. Then the heathen got up and walked towards him – moving softly, like a cat. 'Senka-kun,' he said, 'don' run. Today I have soos, not *geta* – I catch you.'

And he pointed to his half-boots. As if to say: *not sandals, like the last time*.

But of course Senka ran away. He'd sworn never to kick up his heels again, but it seemed like that was his destiny now, to keep scampering off like a hare. Crack the whip and give 'em the slip.

And Senka had to run a lot harder now than he had a week ago. First he dashed right along Podkolokolny Lane, then down Podkopai Lane, and then Tryokhsvyatskaya Street, along Khitrovka Lane, across the square, and turned back onto Podkolokolny again.

Senka galloped so fast it was a wonder the heels didn't fly off his boots, but the Chinaman kept up, and the fat-faced blubber-bag even tried to reason as he ran: 'Senka-kun, don' run, you faw and hurt yourserf.'

He wasn't even panting, but Senka was almost out of breath already.

It was a good thing Senka decided to turn on to Svininsky Lane, where the Kulakovka was – the biggest and rottenest dosshouse in Khitrovka. It was the Kulakovka's cellars that saved Senka from the heathen Chinee. They were an even trickier maze than the Yerokha, no one knew every last inch of them. They'd dug so many tunnels and passages down there, the devil himself would never find you, and a Chinaman had no chance.

Senka didn't go in very far – if you didn't know the place, you could easily get lost in the dark. He just sat there and smoked a *papyrosa*. When he stuck his head out, the Chinee was squatting on his haunches beside the entry, squinting in the sunlight.

What could he do? He went back into the cellars and walked to and fro, to and fro again, smoked a bit more, spat at the wall (that was boring – you couldn't see what you hit in the dark). Folks who lived in the Kulakovka flitted past like shadows. No one asked him why he was hanging about. They could see he was one of them, a Khitrovkan, and that was good enough for them.

He stuck his head out for another look, later, when the lantern by the entranceway was lit. The lousy Chinee was still sitting there, he hadn't budged. The yellow race were a really stubborn lot!

This was starting to get Senka down. Was he going to hang about in the Kulakovka cellars for the rest of his life? He had cramps in his belly, and he had serious business to attend to – he had to warn that pen-pusher.

He went back down and started scouring the collidor (if you could call it a collidor – it was more like a cave really). The walls were slimy stone in some places, bare earth in others. There had to be another way out, right?

When the next Kulakovkan loomed out of the darkness, he grabbed him by the arm.

'Is there another way out, mate?'

The man pulled his arm away and gave Senka a mouthful of abuse. At least he didn't take a knife to him – you could expect that sort of thing in the Kulakovka.

Senka leaned back against the wall, and started wondering how he could get out of this miserable dive.

Suddenly this black, damp hole opened up right in front of where he was standing, and a shaggy head emerged and smacked Senka's knee.

He yelled: 'Lord, save me,' and jumped out of the way.

But the head started barking: 'What do you mean, by spreading yourself right across the burrow like that? Clumsy oafs all over the place, blocking the way!'

That was when Senka realised this was a 'mole' who had climbed out of his den. Underground, Khitrovka had this special class of 'moles', who stayed underground in the daytime, and came out only at night, if at all. People said they minded the secret hiding places for stolen goods, and the fences and dealers paid them a small share for food and drink, and they didn't need proper clothes – what good were clothes underground?

'Uncle Mole!' Senka called, dashing after him. 'You know all the ways in and out of this place. Take me out, only not through the door, some other way.'

'You can't get out any other way,' said the mole, straightening up. 'The only way out of the Kulakovka is on to Svininsky. If you hire me, I can take you to a different basement. The Buninka's ten kopecks, the Rumyantsevka's seven, the Yerokha's fifteen . . .'

Senka was delighted. 'The Yerokha's the one I want! That's even better than getting back outside!'

Siniukhin lived in the Yerokha.

Senka rummaged in his pockets – there was a fifteen-kopeck coin, his last one.

The mole took the money and stuck it in his cheek. He waved his hand: *follow me now*. Senka wasn't worried he'd run off with the money and dump him in the dark. Everyone knew the moles were honest, or why would anyone ever trust them with their swag?

But he had to mind not to fall behind. It was all right for the mole, he was used to it, he could see everything in the dark, but for Senka it was hit or miss, feeling his way round the bends one step at a time.

At first they went straight and downhill a bit, or that was how it felt. Then his guide went down on all fours (Senka guessed only from the sound he made) and scrambled through a hole on the left. Senka followed him. They crawled along for maybe fifty feet, then the ceiling got higher. They left the passage and turned to the right. Then to the left again, and the stone floor changed to soft earth that was boggy in places and squelched under their feet. Then they turned left and left again into a place just like a cave, and he could feel a draught. From the cave they walked up some steps, not very far, but Senka still missed his footing and bruised his knee. At the top an iron door clanged open and behind it there was a collidor. After the passage they'd crawled though on all fours, it seemed quite light in here to Senka.

'There, that's the Yerokha,' said the mole – the first time he'd spoken since they had set out. 'From here you can get out either through the Tatar Inn or on to Podkolokolny. Where do you want to go?'

'I want to go to the Old Rags Basement, Uncle, where the pen-pushers live,' Senka said, and then, just to be safe, he added a lie: 'I want a letter written to my father and mother.'

The underground man led him to the right, through a big stone cellar with high, round ceilings and fat-bellied brick columns, then along another collidor and through another big cellar till they came out in a collidor a bit wider than the others.

'Ah-ha,' said the mole as they turned a corner.

When Senka followed, the mole had disappeared, as if the ground had swallowed him up. There was grey light round the corner – the way out on to the street wasn't far – but it wasn't likely the mole had dashed out that way, he must have ducked into a burrow.

'Are we here, then?' Senka shouted, although there was no one there to hear.

The echo bounced off the ceiling and the walls: 'eerthen-eerthen-eerthen'.

And the hollow answer seemed to come from under the earth: 'Ah-ha'.

So this was it, the Old Rags Basement. Senka looked hard, and saw rough wooden doors along both walls. He knocked on one and shouted:

'Where do the Siniukhins live round here?'

There was a pause, then a rattly voice asked: 'What is it, want something written? I can do that. I write a better hand.'

'No,' said Senka. 'The snake owes me half a rouble.'

'A-a-ah,' the voice drawled. 'Go right. It's the third door along.'

Senka stopped in front of the door and listened. What if the Prince was there already? Then he'd be in really hot water.

But no, it was quiet inside.

He knocked, gently at first, then with his fist.

Still no sound.

Maybe they'd gone out. But no – when he looked he could see light coming out from under the door, very faint.

He pushed the door, and it opened.

A rough table and on it a candle-end in a clay bowl, with splints of wood lying beside it. That was about all he could see at first.

'Hello?' Senka called, and took off his cap.

No one answered. But he had to keep the banter brief – he didn't want the Prince to catch him here.

Senka lit one of the splinters and held it above his head. What was up with these Siniukhins, then? Why were they so quiet?

There was a woman lying on a bench by the wall, sleeping. And on the floor under the bench there was a kid – still a baby, only three, or maybe even two.

The woman was lying on her back, and she'd covered her eyes with something black. Uncle Zot's wife used to put cotton wool soaked in sage tea on her eyes at night, so she wouldn't get wrinkles. Women were fools, everyone knew that. They looked horrifying like that, as if they had holes in their faces, not eyes.

'Hey, Auntie, get up! This is the no time for dozing,' Senka said, approaching her. 'Where's the man of the house? I've got something to—'

He gagged. It wasn't cotton wool on the woman's eyes, it was mush. It had clotted in the hollows of her sockets and some had overflowed down her temple towards her ear. And it wasn't black, no, it was red. And Mrs Siniukhin's neck was all wet and shiny too.

Senka fluttered his peepers for a bit before he caught on: someone had slit the woman's throat and gouged her eyes out – that was it.

He tried to scream, but all that came out was: 'Hic!'

Then he squatted down on his haunches to take a look at the kid. He was dead too, and where his eyes should be there were two dark holes, only little ones – he wasn't too big himself.

'Hic,' Senka went. 'Hic, hic, hic.'

And he kept on hiccuping, he just couldn't stop.

Senka backed away from that horrible bench, stumbled over something soft and almost fell.

When he held the light down, he saw a young lad, about twelve, lying there. He had no eyes either, they'd been gouged out too.

'Blimey!' Senka finally managed to say. 'That's awful!'

He was all set to dash back to the door, but suddenly he heard a voice coming from a dark corner.

'Mitya,' the voice called, all low and pitiful. 'Has he gone? Did he hurt your mother? Eh? I can't hear . . . Look what he did to me, the animal . . . Come here, come . . .'

There was a chintz curtain hanging across the corner. Should he run for it or should he go over there?

He went over. Pulled the curtain back.

He saw a wooden bed. There was a man on it, feeling his chest – it was soaked in blood. And he had no eyes, just like the others. This had to be the pen-pusher, Siniukhin.

Senka tried to explain that Mitya, and his mum, and the little kid, had all been slaughtered, but all he did was hiccup.

'Shut up and listen,' said Siniukhin, licking his lips. He looked like he was smiling, and Senka turned away, so as not to see that no-eyed smile. 'Listen now, my strength's almost gone. I'm on my way out, Mitya. But never mind, that's all right. I lived a bad life, a sinful life, but at least I can die like a man. Maybe that will earn me forgiveness . . . I didn't tell him, you know! He ripped my chest open with that knife of his, but I bore it all . . . I pretended to be dead, but I'm still alive!' The pen-pusher laughed, and something gurgled in his throat. 'Listen, son, remember . . . That secret place I told you about, this is how you get there: you know the underground hall with the vaulting and the brick pillars? You know it, of course you do . . . Well, in there, behind the last pillar on the right, right in the very corner, you can take the bottom stone out . . . I came across it when I was looking for a place to hide a bottle from your mother. You take the stone out, and then you can take some more out, from above the first one . . . Crawl in there, don't be afraid. It's a secret passage. After that, it's easy: you just keep going . . . And you come out into the chamber where the treasure is. The important thing is, don't be frightened . . .' His voice had gone really quiet now, and Senka had to lean over him – the hiccups made it hard for him to listen properly too. 'The treasure . . . There's so much of it . . . It will all be yours. Live a good life. Don't think too badly of your old dad . . .'

Siniukhin didn't say anything else. Senka looked at him: his lips were set in a wide smile, but he wasn't breathing any more. He'd passed over.

Senka crossed himself and reached out to the departed, like you were supposed to, to close his eyes, then jerked his hand away.

He wasn't hiccuping any more, but he was trembling silently. And not from fear – he'd forgotten all about that.

Treasure! So much treasure!

How Senka Hunted for Treasure

Now of course, he was shaken up, after something like that.

He kept thinking: *There's a monster on the loose, he didn't even spare the little baby, cut his eyes out too, the fiend! And what does that make the Prince! If he's supposed to be an honest bandit, why does he keep a villain who gouges people's eyes out when they're still alive?*

But his thoughts kept skipping from these terrible things to the treasure. He couldn't imagine it properly, though: it was like the Holy Gate in the icon screen in church. With everything sparkling and shimmering, so you couldn't make anything out. He imagined chests too, full of gold and silver, and all sorts of precious stones.

But then his thoughts turned to his brother Vanka, and how Senka would go to see him and give him a present – not a wooden horse with a string tail, and not some dwarf pony, like Judge Kuvshinnikov did, but a genuine thoroughbred Arab racer, and a carriage on springs to go with it.

And he thought about Death a bit too – well, of course he did. If Senka had all these huge riches, maybe she'd see him differently then. Not some gap-toothed, freckly kid, not a gnat or a swift, but Semyon Trifonovich Spidorov, a substantial squire. And then . . .

He didn't really know what came 'then'.

When he left that hideous room he ran back to the first cellar, with the fat-bellied pillars – that had to be the one Siniukhin was talking about.

Last pillar 'on the right' – was that this end or the other?

93

Probably the other, the one farthest from Siniukhin's place

Senka was feeling a bit squiffy after everything that had happened, but he'd still grabbed the matches and a supply of splints off the table.

In the far corner he squatted down on his haunches and struck a match. He saw the dressed stonework of an ancient wall, every stone the size of a crate. Just try shifting one of those!

When the flame went out, Senka felt for the joint, tried pushing this way and that – a dead loss. He tried moving the next stone too – the same thing.

Right. He went over to the next corner on the right. This time he lit a splint, not just a match, and moved the light this way and that. The stones here looked the same, but one, at the bottom, was surrounded by black cracks. Was he in business?

He grabbed hold and pulled. The stone yielded, and quite easily too.

He tugged it out with a grunt and pushed it aside. The hole gave out a smell of damp and decay.

Senka started to shake again. Siniukhin was telling the truth! There *was* something there!

The next stone was even easier to get out – and a bit broader than the one underneath. The third was broader still, and it wasn't held in by mortar either. He took out five stones altogether. The top one must have weighed seventy-five pounds, if not more.

Now Senka was peering into a narrow gap – a man could quite easily get through it if he turned sideways and bent crooked.

So he crossed himself and clambered in.

Once he'd squeezed through, there was much more room. He hesitated, wondering whether he ought to put the stones back. But he didn't – what would anyone else want in the corner of the cellar? You'd never see the gap without a light, and the tenants in the Yerokha didn't carry lights.

Senka was really desperate to get to that treasure, and as quick as possible.

The passage was about a yard wide, with something trailing down off the ceiling – cobwebs maybe, or dust. And there was squeaking from the floor – rats. They were all over the place in the basements – the motherland of rats, those places were. One of them jumped up on Senka's boot and sank its teeth into the folds. He shook it off and another jumped on. They had no fear at all!

He stamped his feet: *scram, damn you*.

He walked on through the passage and every now and then the pointy-nosed grey vermin scuttled from under his feet. Their bright eyes glinted in the darkness, like little drops of water.

The lads had told him that last winter the rats went crazy with hunger, and they ate the nose and ears off a drunk who fell asleep in a basement. They often gnawed at babies if they were left unwatched. *Never mind*, thought Senka, *I ain't no drunk or little baby. And they can't bite through these boots.*

When the splint burned out, he didn't light another. What for? There was only one way to go.

It's hard to say how long he walked in the dark for, but it wasn't really that long.

He held his hands out and ran them along the walls, afraid of missing a turning or a fork.

He should have been feeling for the ceiling instead. He hit his forehead on a stone – the smack set his ears ringing and he saw stars. He bent his head down, took three short steps, and the walls disappeared from under his hands.

He lit a splint.

The passage had led out into some kind of vault. Could this be the chamber Siniukhin was talking about?

The ceiling here was smooth and curved, and made of narrow bricks – not exactly high, but high enough so he couldn't reach it. The bricks had flaked away in places, and the chips were lying around on the floor. It wasn't a very big space, but it wasn't small either. Maybe twenty paces across from wall to wall.

Senka couldn't see any chests.

But there was a heap of sticks lying by the wall on the right. When he walked over he saw they weren't sticks, they were iron rods, all black with age.

It looked like there used to be a door opposite the passage Senka had come out of, but it was blocked off with broken bricks, stones and earth – there was no way through.

So where was the huge treasure that Siniukhin and his family had suffered such a horrible death for?

Maybe it was under the floor, and Siniukhin didn't have time to say.

Senka went down on all fours and crawled round the floor, knocking as he went. The floor was brick too, and made a hollow sound.

In the middle of the chamber he found a big purse of thick leather, which had turned stiff and hard. It was tattered and useless – but something jingled inside. Now then!

He turned the purse inside out and shook it. Scales or flakes of some kind clinked as they fell to the ground. A couple of handfuls, the pieces no bigger than the nail on his pinkie.

Were they leaves of gold?

It didn't look like it – they didn't glitter bright enough.

Senka had heard that you tested gold with your teeth. He gnawed on one of the flakes. It tasted dusty, but there was no way he could bite through it. So maybe it was gold. God only knew.

He tipped the flakes into his pocket and crawled on. He lit another three splints and scrubbed the whole floor with his knees, but still he didn't find anything more.

Then he sat down on his backside, put his head in his hands, and started feeling miserable.

Some treasure. Was Siniukhin just raving? Or maybe there was a hiding place in the wall.

He jumped to his feet, picked an iron rod out of the heap and started sounding the walls out.

And a fat lot of good that did him – all he got was earache from the noise.

Senka took one of the flakes out of his pocket and held it close to the flame. He could make out a stamp: a man on a horse, some initials. It looked like a coin, only kind of crooked, like someone had chewed it.

Feeling all frustrated, he stuck his hand back in the purse and felt under the lining. He found another flake and then a coin – a proper round coin, bigger than a rouble, with a bearded man stamped on it, and some letters too. It was silver money, Senka realised that straight off. There had quite likely been a whole bagful here, which Siniukhin had taken and hidden. No way he would ever find them now.

There was nothing else for it – Senka set off back along the underground passage, with almost nothing to show for his pains.

Well, a round piece of silver. And those flakes – maybe silver, maybe copper, who could tell? And even if they were silver, they wouldn't add up to real riches.

He took the iron rod he'd used to tap the walls, to keep the rats away. And he was sure it would come in handy – it had a good hefty feel to it.

How Senka Was Nabbed

Even though there wasn't any treasure in the vault, when Senka came out of the passage, into the cellar with the brick pillars, he pushed the stones back in place anyway. He'd have to come back with an oil lamp and search a bit better – maybe there was something he'd missed?

On the way out, from the spot where the mole had asked which exit he wanted to go to, Senka turned left, so he wouldn't wind up in the Old Rags Basement. Walk back past that door, with those eyeless corpses behind it? No thank you, that's a treat we can do without.

Senka felt amazed at his own daring – after a horror like that, how come he didn't go haring out of the Yerokha, and even went hunting for treasure? It meant one of two things: either he was a pretty hard case after all, or else he was as greedy as they come – and his greed was stronger than his fear.

That was what he was thinking when he walked through the side door into the Tatar Tavern. When he got outside the flophouse, he screwed his eyes up at the bright light. Well, well, it was morning already, and the sun was gleaming on the bell tower of St Nikola of Podkopai. He'd spent the whole night creeping around underground.

Senka walked along Podkolokolny Lane, looking at how pure and joyous the sky was, with its lacy white doilies. He should have been looking around, instead of staring at the clouds.

He walked straight into someone – as solid as cast bronze. Bruised himself, he did, but whoever it was didn't even budge.

Oh Lord – it was the Chinaman.

After all these goings-on, Senka had forgotten all about him, but the Chinee was dogged – he'd stayed put in that street all night long. And all for seventy kopecks! If those lousy beads were worth even a three-note, he'd probably have had a fit.

Slanty-eyes smiled: 'Good moruning, Senka-kun.' And he stretched out his stubby hand to grab Senka's collar.

Sod that!

Senka smashed him across the arm with the iron stick out of the vault. That made the nifty heathen pull back sharpish.

Oho, off we go again – the old catch-me-if-you-can routine. Senka spun round and sprinted off down the lane.

Only this time he didn't get very far. As he went running past a fancy gent (what was a dandy like that doing in Khitrovka?), Senka's pocket caught on the knob of his cane. It was weird – the stroller's cane wasn't jerked right out of his hand, like it should have been. Instead, it was Senka who stopped dead in his tracks.

The dandy pulled the cane lightly towards him, and Senka went with it. He looked respectable all right, with a silk stovepipe hat and starched collars. And he had a smooth face too – handsome he was, only not so young any more, his hair was grey at the temples.

'Unhook me quick, mister!' Senka yelled, because the China-man was getting quite close. He wasn't running, just strolling towards them in no great hurry.

Suddenly the handsome man laughed, twitched his black moustache and said, with a bit of a stammer: 'Of c-course, Semyon Spidorov, I'll let you go, but . . . but not until you return my jade b-beads.'

Senka gaped at him. How come he knew his name?

'Eh?' he said. 'What d'you—? What beads are those?'

'The ones that you pilfered from my valet Masa eight d-days ago. You're a smart young man. You've c-cost us a lot of time, making us chase after you.'

That was when Senka recognised him: it was the same gent he'd seen from the back on Asheulov Lane. His temples were grey, too, and he stammered.

'No offence intended,' the gent went on, taking hold of Senka's sleeve in a grip like a vice with his finger and thumb, 'but Masa is t-tired of running after you, he's not sixteen years old any more. We'll have to take p-precautions and put you in irons t-temporarily. That rod of yours, if you please.'

The dandy took Senka's iron stick, gripped both ends tight, wrinkled up his smooth forehead, and then didn't he just twist that rod round Senka's wrists! Real easy, too, like it was some kind of wire!

That took incredible strength! Senka was so shaken he couldn't even do his poor orphan routine.

But the strongman raised his fine eyebrows, as if he was amazed by his own strength, and said: 'Curious. May I enquire where you g-got this thingummy from?'

Senka gave him the appropriate answer: 'Where from, where from? From a stroke of luck. If you want to know more, you can go get . . .'

It was like his hands really were in shackles, there was no way he could pull them from the iron loops, no matter how he wriggled.

'Well, indeed, you're quite right,' the man with the moustache agreed calmly. 'My question is indiscreet. You have every right not to answer it. So where are my beads?'

Then the Chinaman joined them. Senka screwed up his eyes and winced – old Yellow-face would hit him now, like he did Mikheika and the lads.

The words just burst out on their own: 'Tashka's got them! I gave them to her.'

'Who this Taska?' asked the Chinee that the dandy had called Masa.

'My moll.'

The handsome gent sighed: 'I understand. It's unpleasant

and improper to t-take a present back from a l-lady, but please understand me, Semyon Spidorov. I've had those b-beads for fifteen years. One grows accustomed to things, you know. And furthermore, they are associated with a certain rather special m-memory. Let us go to see Mademoiselle Tashka.'

Now, Senka took offence at that. How did he know Senka's moll was a mamselle? Well, of course, Tashka *was* a mamselle, but he hadn't said anything of the sort about her. She could have been a respectable girl. Senka was all set to spring to the defence of Tashka's honour, shout some coarse insult, but he took a closer look at those calm blue eyes and thought better of it.

'All right,' he muttered. 'Let's go.'

They set off back along Podkolokolny, Masa holding one end of the twisted rod. The other tormentor walked on his own, tapping his cane on the cobbles.

Senka felt ashamed, being led along like a little dog on a lead. If any of the lads saw him, he'd be disgraced. So he tried to walk as close as he could to the Chinaman, like they were friends, or they were doing a job together. The Chinee understood Senka's suffering: he took off his jacket and threw it over Senka's shackled hands. He was human too, even if he wasn't Russian.

A crowd of people was jostling around the way into the Yerokha. And over their heads, Senka could see a cap with a badge. A constable! Standing there looking all stern and haughty, not letting anyone in. Senka knew right off what was going on – they'd found the Siniukhins! But in the crowd they were saying all sorts.

Someone, who looked like a ragman (they collected old rags from rubbish tips), was explaining loudly: 'It's this order as was just issued by the orforities. Close down the Yerokha and spray it with infection, 'cause it's spreading bacilluses right across Moscow.'

'What's it spreading?' a woman with a broken nose asked in a frightened voice.

'Bacilluses. Well, to put it simply, that's a mouse or a rat. And you gets cholera from them, 'cause some of them as live in the Yerokha eats these bacilluses when they're hungry, and they swell right up from the rat meat. Well, the orforities have found out about it.'

'Don't tell lies, sir, you're only confusing the good people,' a man emaciated from drink rebuked the ragman. Wearing a tattered frock coat, he was, must have been, one of the pen-pushers, like the late deceased Siniukhin, God rest his soul. 'There's been a murder in there. They're waiting for the superintendent and the investigator.'

'Hah, they wouldn't make all this fuss over a trifle like that,' the ragman said suspiciously. 'Only today two men were stabbed to death across there in the Labour, as if anyone cares.'

The pen-pusher lowered his voice. 'My neighbour told me what happened was horrible. Supposedly they did away with countless numbers of little children.'

The people around him gasped and crossed themselves, and the gent who owned the beads pricked up his ears and stopped.

'Children have b-been killed?' he asked.

The pen-pusher turned round, saw the important-looking gent and whipped off his cap. 'Yes indeed, sir. I did not witness it myself, but Ivan Serafimovich from the Old Rags Basement heard the constable who ran to the station saying to himself: "Didn't even spare the children, the vicious brutes". And something else, about eyes being put out. My neighbour is an extremely honest man, he would never lie. He used to work in the excise office, a victim of fate, like myself. Obliged to waste his life away in such an appalling place because—'

'The eyes were p-put out?' Senka's captor interrupted and handed the pen-pusher a coin. 'Here, take this. All right, Masa, let's go in and t-take a look at what's happened here.'

And he walked up to the door of the flophouse, the Chinaman pulling Senka along behind. But the Old Rags Basement was the last place on God's earth Senka wanted to go.

'Why, what's there to see in there?' he whined, digging his heels in. 'People talk all sorts of rubbish.'

But the gent had already gone up to the constable and given him a nod – the constable didn't dare stop an imposing individual like that, he just saluted.

After they had walked down the steps to the cellars, the dandy murmured thoughtfully: 'The Old Rags Basement? I think . . . that's l-left and then right.'

What an amazing gent, where would he know that from? He walked along the dark corridors quickly, confidently too. Senka was astonished. But he still whined as he was dragged behind: 'Mr Chinaman, why don't we wait here, eh? What do you say to that?'

The Chinee stopped, turned round and gave Senka a light flick on the forehead.

'I not Chinese, I Japanese. Awright?'

Then he went back to towing Senka.

Well, well! And Senka thought Japanese and Chinese were all the same yellow-faced slanty-eyes, but apparently they thought they were different, and they even took offence.

'Mr Jappo,' said Senka, correcting his mistake, 'I'm exhausted, I can't go on.'

And he tried to sit down, like he'd collapsed, but Masa waved a fist at him very persuasively, so Senka stopped talking and accepted his fate.

When they reached Siniukhin's apartment, who was at the door but Boxman himself? As straight and tall as the Kremlin's bell tower. And there was a lit paraffin lamp on the ground.

'Boxman?' the gent said in surprise. 'So you're still in Khitrovka. Well, well, well.'

And Boxman was even more astounded. He gaped at the dandy, wide-eyed and blinking.

'Erast Petrovich,' he said. 'Your Honour!' And he stood to attention. 'I was informed you had changed your Russian domicile for a foreign residence!'

'I have, I have. But I come to visit my native city on occasion, in private. How are you, Boxman, still up to your old tricks, or have you settled down? Oh, I never dealt with you, did I? Didn't have the time.'

Boxman smiled, not very broadly, though, just a bit, *civilly*.

'I'm too old to be getting up to any tricks. It's time I was thinking about my old age. And my soul.'

Well, would you believe it! This gent wasn't any old body – even Ivan Fedotich Boxman paid him respect. Senka had never seen the policeman carry himself so straight for anyone, not even the superintendent.

Boxman squinted at Senka and knitted his shaggy eyebrows together.

'What's he doing here? Has he done the dirt on you some way? Just say the word and I'll grind him to dust.'

The one who was called Erast Petrovich said: 'No need, we've already resolved our conflict. Haven't we, Senya?' Senka started nodding, but the interesting gent wasn't looking at him, he was looking at the door. 'What's happened here?'

'This piece of villainy is a criminological atrocity, the like of which I have never laid eyes on before, not even in Khitrovka,' Boxman reported glumly. 'They've knifed a pen-pusher, and his entire family with him, and in the most fiendish fashion, too. But you'd better be leaving, Erast Petrovich. Back then the order went out that if any policeman saw you, he should report it to the top brass straightaway. The super-intendent and the gentleman investigator might find you here . . . They're due any minute.'

Well, now, Senka thought, *this gent must be a businessman, only not an ordinary one, some kind of super-special one, and all Moscow's businessmen are just lousy punks next to him. The devil himself must have tempted me into filching an important souvenir from a bandit-general prince like that! That's an orphan's luck for you!*

And then Boxman said this: 'The superintendent here now-adays is Innokentii Romanovich Solntsev, the gentleman you wanted to put on trial. And he's spiteful, not one to forget a grudge.'

If he could drag a man like the superintendent to court, then what kind of bandit must he be? Senka was bewildered now.

Erast Petrovich wasn't at all put out by the warning. 'It's all right, Boxman. If God doesn't tell, the pig won't know. We'll make it quick, be out in a flash.'

Boxman didn't try to argue, just moved aside: 'If I whistle, get out quick, don't drop me in it.'

Senka wanted to stay outside, but that lousy Jap Masa wouldn't let him, even though Boxman was there to keep an eye on him. He said: 'You too agire. An' you run fast.'

When they went inside, Senka didn't look at the dead bodies (he'd seen enough of them already, thank you very much). He stared at the ceiling instead.

It was brighter in the room than before – there was another paraffin lamp, like the one in the collidor, burning on the table.

Erast Petrovich walked round the room, leaning down sometimes and jingling something. It was as though he was turning the bodies over and touching their faces, but Senka turned away – he could do without that abomination.

The Japanese was doing some rummaging of his own. He dragged Senka after him, bending down over the cadavers and muttering something Senka couldn't understand.

This went on for about five minutes.

The smell of freshly slaughtered meat was making Senka queasy. And there was a whiff of dung too – that must be from the bellies being slashed open.

'What do you think?' Erast Petrovich asked his Jap, and he answered in his own tongue, not in Russian.

'You think it's a maniac? Hmmm.' The gentleman bandit rubbed his chin thoughtfully. 'Reasons?'

And the Jap switched back to Russian.

'Kirring for money out of question. This famiry extremerry poor. That one. Insane cruerty of it – he didn't even spare the ritter boy. That two. An' eyes. You terr me yourserf, master, sign of a maniac murder is rituar. Why gouge out eyes? It crear – an insane rituar. That three. Maniac kirred them, that certain. Like Decorator other time.'

Senka didn't know who Maniac and Decorator were (from the names they sounded like Yids or Germans) – he didn't understand very much at all really – but he could see the Jap was very proud of his speech.

Only he didn't seem to have convinced the gent.

Erast Petrovich squatted down by the bed where Siniukhin was lying and started going through the dead man's pockets. And him such a decent-looking gent! But then, God only knew who he really was. Senka gazed at the icon hanging in the corner. He thought: *The Saviour saw the horrible things Deadeye did to the pen-pusher, and he didn't interfere.* And then he remembered the way the Jack flung his little knife straight into the icons' eyes, and he sighed. At least the fiend didn't put this icon's eyes out.

'What do we have here?' he heard Erast Petrovich's voice ask.

Senka couldn't resist it, he peeped round Masa's shoulder, and saw a little scale in the gent's hand – just like the ones in Senka's pocket!

'Who knows what this is?' Erast Petrovich asked, turning round. 'Masa? Or perhaps you, Spidorov?'

Masa shook his head. Senka shrugged and gaped like a fool to make it clear he'd never laid eyes on such an odd-looking item. He even said out loud: 'How would I know?'

The gent looked at him.

'Well, well,' he said. 'This is a seventeenth-century kopeck, m-minted in the reign of Tsar Alexei. How d-did it come to be in the home of a pauper, a drunken "pen-pusher"?'

When he heard it was a kopeck, Senka felt rotten. Some treasure that was! A handful of kopecks from some mouldy old tsar.

The door from the collidor opened and Boxman stuck his head in: 'Your Honour, they're coming!'

Erast Petrovich put the scale on the bed, where it could easily be seen.

'That's all, we're going.'

'Go that way, so you don't bump into the superintendent,' said Boxman, pointing. 'You'll come out into the Tatar Tavern.'

The gent waited for Masa and Senka to come out – he didn't seem in any great hurry to scarper from the superintendent. But then, why bother running? If they heard steps, they could just dodge into the darkness and disappear.

'I don't think it's a m-maniac,' Erast Petrovich said to his servant. 'And I wouldn't exclude greed as a motive for the c-crime. Tell me, what do you think, were the eyes p-put out when the victims were alive or dead?'

Masa thought for a moment and smacked his lips.

'Woman and chirdren, after they dead, and man whire he stirr arive.'

'I came to the same c-conclusion.'

Senka shuddered. How could they have known Siniukhin was still alive at first? Were they magicians or what?

Erast Petrovich turned towards Boxman. 'Tell me, Boxman, have there been any similar c-crimes in Khitrovka, with the victims' eyes being put out?'

'There have, and very recently indeed. A young merchant who was stupid enough to wander into Khitrovka after dark was done away with. They robbed him, smashed his head in, took his wallet and his gold watch. And for some reason they put his eyes out, the fiends. And before that, about two weeks back, a gentleman reporter from the *Voice* was done to death. He wanted to write about the slums in his newspaper. He didn't bring any money or his watch with him – he was an experienced man, it wasn't his first time in Khitrovka. But he had a gold ring, with a diamond in it, and it wouldn't come off his finger. So the vicious beasts did for him. Cut the finger off for the ring and put his eyes out too. That's folks round here for you.'

'You see, Masa,' said the handsome gent, raising one finger.

'And you say m-money's out of the question as a motive. This is no maniac, this is a very p-prudent criminal. He has clearly heard the fairy tale about the last thing a p-person sees before he dies being imprinted on his retina. So he's being careful. He c-cuts out all his victims' eyes, even the children's.'

The Japanese hissed and started jabbering away in his own language – cursing the murderer, no doubt. But Senka thought: *You've got a very high opinion of yourself, Your Honour, or whoever you are. You guessed wrong, there's nothing cautious about Deadeye, he's just in a fury 'cause of all that candy cane.*

'A picture on their eyes?' Boxman gasped. 'Whatever next?'

'A fairy tare mean it not true, yes?' asked Masa. '*Tamoebanasi?*'

Erast Petrovich said he was right: 'Of course, it's n-nonsense. There was such a hypothesis, but it was never c-confirmed. The interesting thing here is . . .'

'They're coming!' Boxman interrupted, straining to see. 'Hear that? Sidorenko – he's standing at the door – just barked: "Good health to you, Your Worship" – I told him not to spare his lungs. They'll be here in a minute, two at most. What's this murder to you, Erast Petrovich? Or are you going to investigate?'

'No, I can't.' The gent shrugged and spread his hands. 'I'm here in Moscow on entirely different business. Tell Solntsev and the investigator what I said. Say you worked it out yourself.'

'I shouldn't think so,' said Boxman, pulling a wry face. 'Let Innokentii Romanich bend his own wits to the job. There's enough people already trying to ride into heaven on someone else's back. Never you mind, Your Honour, I'll find out who it is that's up to mischief in Khitrovka, and take his life with my own bare hands, as sure as God's holy.'

Erast Petrovich just shook his head: 'Oh, Boxman, Boxman. I see you're still the same as ever.'

Well, thank God, they finally left that cursed basement. They came into the light of day through the Tatar Tavern, then set off to find Tashka.

Her and her mum lodged on Khokhlovsky Lane. A one-window room with its own entrance – for the trade of a mamselle. Lots of tarts lived like that, but only Tashka's place had fresh flowers on the windowsill every day – to suit the mood of the lady of the house. Senka knew by now that if there were buttercups on the left and forget-me-nots on the right, then Tashka was doing fine, she was singing her songs and setting out her flowers. But if, say, it was stocks and willowherb, then Tashka had had a scrap with her mum, or got landed with a really awful client, and she was feeling sad.

Today happened to be one of those days – there was a sprig of juniper hanging down over the curtain too (in the language of flowers, that meant 'guests not welcome').

Welcome or not, what could he do? He'd been dragged there. They knocked and went in.

Tashka was sitting on the bed, looking darker than a thundercloud. She was chewing sunflower seeds and spitting the husks into her hand – no 'hello' or 'how's things' or anything of the sort.

'What do you want?' she said. 'And what gulls are these you've brought? What for? I've got enough trouble with this trollop.'

She nodded to the corner, where her mum was sprawled out on the floor. It looked like she'd got as tight as a newt again then coughed up blood, and that was why Tashka was in such a rage.

Senka started to explain, but then the Jappo's jacket slipped off and fell on the floor. When Tashka saw Senka's shackled hands, she fairly bounded off the bed, straight at Masa. Sank her nails into his plump cheeks and started yelling:

'Let him go, you fat-faced bastard! I'll scratch your slanty eyes out!' – and then a whole heap of other curses, Tashka had quite a mouth on her. Even Senka winced, and the spruce gent stood there just blinking.

While the Jap used his free hand to fight off the mamselle's assault on his handsome yellow features, Erast Petrovich stepped aside. He answered Tashka's swearing in a respectful voice:

'Well, yes indeed, far from the m-motherland, one becomes unaccustomed to the v-vigour of the Russian tongue.'

Senka had to come to the Jap's defence. 'Stop it, will you, Tashka? Calm down. Leave the man alone! Remember those beads I gave you, the green ones? Are they safe? Give them to these gents, the beads belong to them. Or I'll be for it.' And then suddenly he took fright. 'You haven't sold them, have you?'

'Who do you think I am, some floozie from Zamoskvorechie? As if I'd sell a present that was given to me! Maybe no one's ever given me a present before. The clients don't count. I've got your beads put away somewhere safe.'

Senka knew that 'safe place' of hers – in the cupboard under the bed, where Tashka kept her treasures: the book about flowers, a cut-glass scent bottle, a tortoiseshell comb.

'Give them back, will you? I'll give you another present, anything you like.'

Tashka let go of the Japanese and her face lit up. 'Honest? What I want, Senka, is a little dog, a white poodle. I saw them at the market. Have you ever seen a poodle? They can dance the waltz on their back paws, Senka, they can skip over a rope and give you their paw.'

'I'll give you one, honest to God I will. Just hand the beads back!'

'Don't bother, no need,' Tashka told him. 'It was just talk. A poodle like that costs thirty roubles, even as a puppy. I checked the price.'

She sighed. But it wasn't that sad a sigh.

Then she climbed under the bed, sticking her skinny backside up in the air – and she was wearing only a short little shirt. Senka felt ashamed in front of the others. She was a real harum-scarum. He walked over and pulled her shirt down.

Tashka scrabbled about down there for a while (she obviously didn't want to get her treasures out in front of strangers), then clambered back out and flung the beads at Masa: 'There, you miser, I hope you choke on them.'

The Jap caught the string of beads and handed them to his master with a bow. The gent flicked through the little stones, stroked one, then put them in his pocket.

'Right then, all's well that ends well. You, m-mademoiselle, have done nothing to offend me.' He reached into his pocket, took out a wallet, and extracted three banknotes. 'Here is thirty roubles for you. B-buy yourself a poodle.'

Tashka asked in a matter-of-fact voice: 'So what way is it you're planning to horse me, then, for three red ones? If,' she continued, 'you want it this way or that, I'm agreeable, but if you want it that way or this, I'm a decent girl and I don't let anyone do dirty things like that to me.'

The smooth-faced gent shrank back and flung his hands up in the air: 'Oh no,' he said. 'I don't want anything like that from you. It's a p-present.'

He didn't know Tashka! She put her hands on her hips. 'You clear out of here with your paper money. I takes presents from a client or a mate. If you don't want to horse around, you ain't a client, and I've already got a mate – Senka.'

'Well, mademoiselle,' Erast Petrovich said to her with a bow. 'Anyone should be honoured to have a m-mate like you.'

Then Tashka suddenly shouted out: 'Scarper, Senka.'

She flung herself at Masa and sank her teeth into his left hand, the one holding the end of the bar. The Japanese was taken by surprise and opened his fingers, so Senka made a dash for the door.

The gent shouted after him: 'Wait, I'll f-free your hands!'

Pull the other one. We'll get ourselves free without help from the likes of you. You still haven't made us pay for thieving. How do we know if you're going to give us a bashing? And anyway you can't be far enough away from some freak that even Boxman's afraid of – that's what ran through Senka's mind.

But Tashka, that Tashka! What a girl she was – pure gold!

How Senka Got Rich

Senka might have scarpered, but he still had to get rid of this iron lump. He walked along, pressing his hands to his chest, with the ends of the bar turned up and down, so they wouldn't be so obvious.

He had to clear out of Khitrovka – not just because it was dangerous with that Erast Petrovich about, but so no one he knew would see him looking silly like this. They'd laugh him down for sure.

He could go into the smithy, where they forged horseshoes, and tell them some lie or other about how the iron bar had been twisted on him out of mischief, or as a bet. They were big hefty lads in the smithy. Maybe they didn't have a grip to match the handsome gent's, but they'd unbend it one way or another, they had tools for doing just that. But not for a kind word and a nod, of course – he'd have to give them twenty kopecks.

And then it hit him: where was he going to get twenty kopecks from? He'd given his last fifteen-kopeck piece to the mole yesterday. Or maybe he should diddle the blacksmith? Promise him money then do a runner. Even more running, Senka thought with a sigh. If the blacksmiths caught him, they'd batter him with those big fists of theirs, worse than any Japanese.

So there he was, walking down Maroseika Street, wondering what to do, when he saw a shop sign: 'SAMSHITOV. Jeweller and goldsmith. Fine metalworking'. That was just what he needed! Maybe the jeweller would give him something at least for the silver coin, or even those old kopecks. And if he didn't, Senka could pawn Sprat's watch.

He pushed open the door with the glass window and went in.

There was no one behind the counter, but there was a red parrot bird, sitting on a perch in its cage, and screeching in a horrible voice: 'Wel-come! Wel-come!'

Just to be safe, Senka doffed his cap and said: 'Good health to you.'

It may have been a beast, but it clearly had some understanding.

'Ashot-djan, the door's not locked again,' a woman called from the back of the shop in an odd, lilting voice. 'Anyone at all could come in off the street!'

There was a rustle of steps and a short man popped his head out from behind the curtain. He had a deep-set face and a crooked nose and a round piece of glass set in a bronze frame on his forehead. He sounded frightened as he asked: 'Are you alone?'

When he saw that Senka was, he ran to bolt the door, then turned again to his visitor. 'What can I do for you?'

Someone like him could never unknot an iron bar, thought Senka disappointedly. So what was that about metalworking on the sign? Maybe he had an apprentice.

'I'd like to sell something,' Senka said, and reached into his pocket, but that was no mean feat with his hands shackled together.

The parrot began to mock him: 'Sell something! Sell something!'

The man with the big nose said: 'Shut up, shut up, Levonchik.' Then he looked Senka up and down and said, 'I'm sorry, young man, but I don't buy stolen goods. There are specialists for that.'

'You don't need to tell me that. Here, what will you give me?'

And he plonked the coin down on the counter.

The jeweller stared at Senka's wrists, but he didn't say a word.

Then he looked at the silver coin without any real interest.

'Hmm, a yefimok.'

'Come again?' said Senka.

'A yefimok, a silver thaler. Quite a common coin. They go for double weight. That is, the weight of the silver, multiplied by two. Your yefimok's in good condition.' He took the coin and put it on the balance. 'In ideal condition, you could say. A perfect thaler, six and a half zolotniks in weight. One zolotnik of silver is ... twenty-four kopecks now. That makes ... hmm ... three roubles twelve kopecks. Minus my commission, twenty per cent. In total, two roubles and fifty kopecks. No one's likely to give you more than that.'

Two roubles fifty – well, that was *something*. Senka writhed around again, reached into his pocket for the scales, and tipped them on to the counter.

'And what about this?'

He had exactly twenty of those scales, he'd counted them during the night. They were pretty battered kopecks, but if you added them to two roubles fifty, that would make two seventy.

The jeweller was more impressed by the kopecks than he was by the yefimok. He moved the lens off his forehead onto his eye and examined them one by one.

'Silver kopecks? Oho, "YM" – Yauza Mint. And in enviable condition. Well, I can take these for three roubles apiece.'

'How much?' Senka gasped.

'You have to understand, young man,' said the jeweller, looking at Senka through the lens with a huge black eye. 'Pre-rebellion kopecks, of course, are not thalers, and they go for a different rate. But they dug up another hoard from that time only recently, over in Zamoskvorechie, three thousand silver kopecks, including two hundred from the Yauza Mint, so their price has fallen greatly. How would you like three fifty? I can't go higher than that.'

'How much will that make altogether?' Senka asked, still unable to believe his luck.

'Altogether?' Samshitov clicked the beads on his abacus and pointed: 'There. Including the yefimok, seventy-two roubles and fifty kopecks.'

Senka could barely croak out his answer: 'Fine, all right.'

And the parrot went off again: 'All right! All right! All right!'

The jeweller raked the coins off the counter and jangled the lock of his cash box. There was the sound of banknotes rustling – pure music to Senka's ears. Now this was really something, big money!

The woman's voice sang out again from the back of the shop. 'Ashotik-djan, are you going to take your tea?'

'Just a moment, dear heart,' said the jeweller, turning towards the voice. 'I'll just let this client out.'

The lady of the house appeared from behind the curtain, carrying a tray, with a glass of tea in a silver holder and a little dish of sweets – very neat it looked too. The woman was stout, a lot bigger than her little titch of a husband. She had a moustache under her nose and hands like sugar loaves.

Mystery solved! With a woman like that, you didn't need an apprentice.

'There's this as well . . .' Senka said, clearing his throat as he showed them his hands and the metal bar. 'I'd like to get untangled . . . The lads played a joke . . .'

The woman took one look at his shackled hands then went back behind the curtain without saying a word.

But the jeweller took the bar in his skinny hands, and Senka was amazed when he straightened it out in a trice. Not all the way, but at least enough for him to pull his wrists out. Good old Ashotik!

While Senka was stuffing the banknotes and ten-kopeck pieces in his pockets, his hands nice and free, Samshitov was eyeing up the rod. He dropped something on it from a little bottle and scraped the surface. Then he pulled down his lens, put one end of the rod to his eye, and began to mop his bald patch with a handkerchief.

'Where did you get this?' he asked, and his voice was trembling.

As if Senka was going to tell him that! But he didn't come out with, 'Where from, where from? A stroke of luck. If you want to know more, you can get ****ed,' because Ashot was a good man, he'd helped him out.

So Senka said politely: 'From the right place.' And then he turned to go. He had to think what to do with his sudden riches.

But then didn't the jeweller go and blurt out: 'How much do you want for it?'

Pull the other one – for scrap iron?

But Samshitov's voice was really shaking now.

'It's incredible,' he said, rubbing the rod with a wet rag. 'I've read about the thaler rod, of course, but I didn't think any others had survived . . . And the hallmark of the Yauza Mint!'

Senka watched as the black rod turned white and shiny under the rag.

'Huh?'

The jeweller looked as if he was figuring something out. 'How would you like double the weight? Like the thaler, right?'

'What?'

'Triple, then,' Samshitov corrected himself quickly. He put the rod on the balance. 'There's almost five pounds of silver here. Let's say five on the dot.' He clicked the beads on the abacus. 'That's a hundred and fifteen roubles and twenty kopecks. And I'll give you triple weight, three hundred and forty-six roubles. Even three hundred and fifty. No, four hundred. An entire four hundred! Four hundred, eh? What do you say?'

Senka said: 'What?'

'I don't keep that much money in the shop, I have to go to the bank.' He ran out from behind the counter and gazed into Senka's eyes. 'You have to understand. A commodity like this requires a lot of work. Before you can find the right buyer. Numismatists are a special breed.'

'What?'

'Numismatists are collectors of units of currency – coins and notes,' the jeweller explained, but that didn't leave Senka any the wiser.

In his time, Senka had seen plenty of these numismatists, who loved nothing more than collecting money – his Uncle Zot for starters.

'And how many of them are there, who want these rods?' Senka asked, still suspecting a trick.

'In Moscow, maybe twenty. In Petersburg, twice as many. If you send them abroad, there are lots of people wanting to buy them there too.' The big-nosed jeweller flinched. 'You said "rods"? You mean you've got more of them? And you're willing to sell?'

'At four hundred a time?' Senka asked with a gulp. He remembered how many of those sticks there were underground in the vault.

'Yes, yes. How many do you have?'

Senka said warily: 'I could get hold of about five.'

'Five thaler rods! When can you bring them to me?'

Now this was where he had to show a bit of dignity, not do himself down. Let on what a difficult business it was. Not something just anyone could manage. So he paused for a while then said grandly: 'In about two hours, not before.'

'Ninochka,' the jeweller yelled to his wife. 'Close the shop! I'm going to the bank!'

The exotic bird was delighted with all the shouting and started to squawk: 'To the bank! To the bank! To the bank!'

Senka walked out of the shop to the sound of its screeching.

He had to lean his hand against the wall – he was really staggering.

How about that? Four hundred roubles for a rod! It was just like a dream.

Before he went back underground, Senka called round to Khokhlovsky Lane. To see whether those two had done anything to offend Tashka, and in general – just to say thank you.

Thank God, they hadn't touched her.

Tashka was sitting in the same place on the bed, combing her hair – she was going out working soon. She'd already tarted up her face: black eyebrows and eyelashes, red cheeks, glass earrings.

'That slanty-eyed one sends his regards,' Tashka said as she wound the hair at her temple onto a stick to make it curly. 'And the dreamboat said he would look out for you.'

Senka didn't like the sound of that at all. What did that mean – 'look out' for him? Was he threatening him or what? Never mind, he'd never get his hands on Senka now, he'd never find him. Senka's life was going to be different from now on.

'I tell you what,' he told Tashka. 'You drop all this. You don't need to keep walking the streets. I'll take you away from Khitrovka, we'll live together. You should just see how much money I've got now.'

At first Tashka was delighted, she even started whirling round the room. Then she stopped. 'Can Mum come too?'

'All right.' Senka sighed and looked at the drunken woman – she still hadn't slept it off. 'Your mum can come too.'

'No, she can't leave this place. Let her die in peace. When she dies, you can take me away.'

He tried to talk her round but she just wouldn't listen. Senka gave her all the crunch he'd got from the jeweller. Why be greedy? Soon he'd have all the money anyone could ever want.

And now he had to go back into the Yerokha, where the passage to the treasure was.

They were just carrying the dead bodies out of the doors of the flophouse when he arrived. They flung them into a cart – two large sackcloth bundles, one a bit smaller and one that was tiny.

People stood there, gawping, and some crossed themselves.

Three men came out: an official in specs, Superintendent

Solntsev and a man with a beard carrying a photographic box on a tripod.

The superintendent and the official shook hands, the photographer just nodded.

'Innokentii Romanovich, be sure to keep me up to date with new developments at all times,' the man in specs ordered as he got into a four-wheel carriage. 'Without your agents in Khitrovka, we won't get anywhere.'

'Certainly,' the superintendent said with a nod, stroking his curled moustache.

The parting in his hair gleamed so bright it was almost blinding. He was a fine figure of a man, no denying that, even if he was a lousy snake – everyone in Khitrovka knew that.

'And make a special effort not to get the reporters so ... worked up. No colourful details. There'll be more than enough rumours anyway ...' The official waved his hand forlornly.

'But of course. Don't concern yourself, Khristian Karlovich.' Solntsev wiped his forehead with a pure white handkerchief, then put his cap back on.

The carriage drove off.

'Boxman!' the superintendent yelled. 'Yeroshenko! Where have you got to?'

Another two men appeared out of the dark pit: Boxman and the owner of the flophouse, the famous Afanasii Lukich Yeroshenko. A big man, and his head was worth its weight in gold. A native Khitrovkan, he started as a waiter in a tavern, then rose to tavern keeper. He dealt in swag, naturally, but nowadays he was a respected citizen, he had crosses and medals, went to the governor general's place at Easter to exclaim 'Christ is arisen!' and give him the triple kiss. He had three flophouses like this, a wine business and shops. In short, he was a millionaire.

'The newspapermen will come running soon,' Solntsev told them with a laugh. 'Tell them everything, let them go anywhere they like, show them the scene of the crime. And don't even think of washing away the blood. But don't answer any questions about the progress of the investigation – send them to me for that.'

As Senka watched the superintendent he was amazed. What a brazen rogue, what a louse! He'd promised that man in specs – and now look what he was doing. And he wasn't ashamed to do it in front of people, either. Although to him they probably weren't people at all.

The superintendent was not respected in Khitrovka. He didn't keep his word, he knew no shame and he was incredibly greedy. The others before him had been real numismatists too, but he'd outdone them all. If you're taking a cut from the dives where the mamselles work, then take it, it's your right. But he was the first superintendent who wasn't too squeamish to use the whores for himself. Of course, he chose the pricier ones, the ten-rouble tarts, but there was never any question of the girl getting paid for her trouble, or even getting a present. And he treated his narks to them too. There was nothing worse for a whore than ending up at the Third Myasnitskaya Station when they 'broke their fast'. They picked them up for nothing, stuck them in the 'hen coop', and anyone who felt like it could horse around with them. The grandfathers went to Boxman and asked whether he would let them have the superintendent knifed, or maybe have a big stone dropped on him. Not so as to kill him, of course, but enough to make him see sense. Boxman wouldn't have it. Be patient, he said, His Worship's only just shown up, and he won't hang around. He's aiming high, making his name.

And what else could they do?

Solntsev said to Yeroshenko: 'I'm fining you, Afanasii Lukich. Be so good as to hand over a thousand for the disorder in your establishment. We have an agreement.'

Yeroshenko didn't say anything, just bowed gravely. 'And I'm fining you too, Boxman. I don't interfere in your business, but you answer to me for Khitrovka. If you don't find me the murderer in three days, you pay two hundred roubles.'

Boxman didn't say a word, either, just twitched his grey moustache.

The superintendent's carriage rolled up. His Worship got in and wagged his finger at the crowd, as if to say: 'Look at you, hoodlums!' and rode off. He was just putting on airs, he could have walked – the station was no distance away at all.

'Don't let it bother you, Ivan Fedotich,' said Yeroshenko. 'Your fine's on me, I'll cover you.'

'I'll give you "cover me",' Boxman snarled. 'You won't get me off your back for a lousy two hundred. After the things I've let a crook like you get away with!'

That was Boxman for you. Yeroshenko could hang crosses all over himself, and kiss the governor general to death, but to Boxman he would always be Afonka the Thief.

Senka's visit to the basement was a lot easier than the first time. He borrowed an oil lamp in the Labour, left his cap as a pledge, and got to the chamber very quickly. Less than ten minutes by his watch.

The first thing he did was count the silver rods. But it would take for ever to shift them all. He counted a hundred by one wall, and he hadn't even got halfway. He was dripping with sweat.

And he found the leather sole off a boot, well gnawed by the rats. He pulled some of the stones and bricks from the blocked-off doorway, too, he wanted to see what was behind it. But then he got bored and gave up.

He wore himself out so much that he took only four rods, not five. That was enough for Samshitov, and they were heavy, they weighed about five pounds each.

When Senka got back to the jeweller's shop and was already reaching his hand out to the door, someone whistled behind him – it was a special Khitrovka whistle – and then an owl hooted: Whoo-oo whoo-oo!

He turned round, and there were the lads hanging about on

the corner of Petroverigsky Lane. That was really rotten luck.

But what could he do? He went over.

Prokha said: 'We were told as you'd been picked up.'

Squinteye asked: 'What are you carrying that scrap about for?'

But Mikheika blinked guiltily and said: 'Don't be angry 'cause I grassed on you to that Chinaman. I was dead frightened when he started laying everyone out. You know what Chinamen are like.'

'If you don't like a fright, then stay home at night,' Senka growled, but without any real malice. 'I'd hang one on your ugly mug, you creep, but I ain't got time. Business.'

Prokha said to him, real spiteful: 'What kind of business have you got, Speedy? You were a businessman once, but not no more.'

Senka realised everyone already knew he'd done a runner on the Prince. 'I'll tell you, I've got a job for the Armenian here, putting bars on his windows. See, iron bars.'

'In a jewellery shop?' Prokha drawled, and screwed his eyes up. 'Well, well. You're even slyer than I thought. Who are you with now, then? That Chinaman? And you've decided to do the Armenian over? Now that's slick!'

'I'm on my own.'

Prokha didn't believe him. He took Senka off to one side, put a hand on his shoulder and whispered: 'Don't say, if you don't want to. But you should know: the Prince is looking for you. He's threatening to knife you.'

He gave Senka a pinch and ran off, then whistled and scoffed: 'Be seeing you, *bandit boy*.'

And he darted off down the street with the lads.

Senka realised what Prokha was scoffing at when he saw that Sprat's silver watch was missing from the belt of his pants. So that was why the lousy scum had been all over him like that!

But he wasn't too upset about it. It was just a watch – worth twenty-five roubles at the outside – but the idea of the Prince spreading his threats around, now that really got him down. He'd have to keep his eyes peeled.

Senka walked into the shop and the parrot greeted him, but he was feeling really low. His mind wasn't on the money, it was on the Prince's knife.

He dumped the bars on the counter and the parrot squawked. 'I brought four. That's all there are.'

But when he walked out on to Maroseika Street five minutes later, he'd forgotten all about the Prince.

And there it was, under his shirt, close to his heart, a huge amount of money – four *petrushas*, five-hundred-rouble notes. Senka had never set eyes on anything like that.

He fingered the crisp notes through his shirt, trying to imagine what it was like to live in luxury.

How Senka Lived in Luxury

Story One. *The first step is the hardest*

It turned out to be hard work.

On Lubyanka Square, where the cabbies water their horses at the fountain, Senka suddenly felt like having a drink too – some kvass, or spiced tea, or orangeade. And his belly started rumbling as well. How long could he carry on, walking around empty-bellied? He hadn't had a bite to eat since yesterday morning. He wasn't some kind of monk now, was he?

That was when Senka's problems started.

An ordinary person has all sorts of money: roubles and ten-kopeck coins and fifty-kopeck coins. But Senka the rich man had nothing but five-hundred-rouble notes. What good was that in a tavern or for hiring a cab? Who could give you that much change? Especially if you were dressed up Khitrovka-style: with you shirt hanging outside your trousers, concertina boots and a bandit's cap perched on the back of your head.

Ah, he should have taken at least one *petrusha* from the jeweller in small notes, he could die of hunger like this, like the king in that story, the one they told at college: whatever the king touched turned to gold, so even with all those riches, there was no way the poor beggar could eat or drink a thing.

Senka went back on to Maroseika Street. He tried the shop – it was locked. There was just the parrot, Levonchik, sitting behind the glass squealing something – you couldn't make out what it was from outside.

But it was plain to see – Ashot Ashotovich had stopped trading and gone running after those … what-were-they-called? … numismatist collectioners, to get down to business.

Maybe he should drop in on Tashka? Take back some of the money he gave her?

Well, for starters, she was probably already out walking the street. And anyway, he'd be ashamed. He gave her the beads and took them back again. He gave her money, and now he wanted to take that back too. No, he had to wriggle out of this fix himself.

Maybe he could nick something at the market, before it closed?

Just that morning, Senka would have lifted some grub no problem, he wouldn't have thought twice. But it's easy to steal when you've got nothing to lose and your heart's wild and brave. If you're afraid, you're bound to get caught. And how could he not be afraid, with all that crunch rustling away under his shirt?

He was so desperately hungry, he could have howled. Why did he have to suffer this kind of torment? Two thousand in his pocket, and he couldn't even buy a kopeck bun!

Senka got so annoyed with the low cunning of life that he stamped his foot, tossed his cap down on the ground, and let the tears come pouring out – not in two streams (like in the stories) but in four!

He stood there by a street lamp, bawling like a cretin.

Suddenly a child's voice said: 'Glasha, Glasha, look – a big boy, and he's crying!'

The little kid was walking out of the market in a sailor suit. He had a red-faced woman with him – his nanny or someone like that, carrying a basket. She'd obviously just been to market to do her shopping, and the master's little boy had tagged along.

The woman said: 'If he's crying, he must have troubles. He wants to eat.'

And she dropped a coin into his cap on the ground – fifteen kopecks, plonk.

Senka looked at that coin and started wailing even louder. He felt really hard done by now.

Suddenly there was a clang – another coin, five kopecks this time. An old woman in a shawl had thrown it. She made the sign of the cross over Senka and walked on.

He picked up the alms, and was about to dash off and buy some pies or some buns, but then he changed his mind. So he'd stuff his belly with a couple of buns, and then what? If he could collect three or four roubles, he could buy himself a jacket, and then maybe he could change a *petrusha*.

He squatted down on his haunches and started rubbing his eyes with his fists, not real hard, just enough to give them a pitiful look. And what do you think? The Christian people took pity on the weeping beggar. Senka had sat there for less than an hour before he had collected a whole heap of coppers. A rouble and a quarter, to be precise.

He sat there, blubbing and reasoning philosophically: *When I didn't have half a kopeck to my name, I still didn't go begging on the street, and now look at me. That's what you get for being rich. And it says that in the gospels too, the people who have riches are the greatest paupers of all.*

Suddenly Senka was whacked hard across the tailbone. It hurt. He turned round and there was a beggar with a crutch, who yelled: 'Oh, the ravening beasts! Oh, the jackals! Stealing someone else's bread! My place, since time out of mind! Can't even go away to get some tea! Give it back, whatever you've taken, you little thief, or I'll call our lot!'

And he bashed Senka with the crutch, again and again.

Senka grabbed the cap, almost spilled his booty, then ran off, out of harm's way. He didn't want to mess with beggars – they could easily beat you to death. They had their own council and laws.

He walked across Resurrection Square, trying to think of the smartest way to spend a rouble and a quarter.

And then he was shown the answer.

A messenger boy came darting out of the Grand Moscow Hotel, in a short little jacket with the gold letters 'GMH', and a cap with a gold cockade on it. The lad was clutching a three-rouble bill – one of the guests must have asked him to buy something.

Senka overtook the messenger and struck a deal to hire the tunic and cap for half an hour. As a deposit, he tipped out all the change he'd scrounged at the market. And he promised to pay twice as much again when he got back.

Then off he ran to the Russo-Asian Bank.

He stuck a five-hundred note through the little window and said the words as if he was in a rush: 'Change this for four hundreds, and give me the other hundred in small notes. That's what the guest asked for.'

The cashier shook his head respectfully. 'Well, they certainly have trust in you over at the Grand Moscow.'

'That's because we've earned it,' Senka replied with dignity.

The bank clerk checked the number of the note against a piece of paper – and handed back exactly what he'd been asked for.

Well, after that, when Senka had dressed up in clean clothes and got a fashionable haircut at the 'Parisian' salon, the rich life began to treat him better.

Story Two. *About life in society, at home and at court*

His means were quite adequate to allow him to move into the Grand Moscow Hotel, and Senka got as far as the doors, but then he looked at the electric lamps, the carpets, the lions' faces over the windows, and he lost his nerve. Well, naturally, Senka was dolled up like a real gent now, and there were lots of other expensive duds, still unworn, folded in his brand-new suitcase, but hotel commissionaires and flunkeys were a fly lot, they'd spot a Khitrovka mongrel under his cheviot and silk straight off.

Just look at that general with gold epaulettes they had behind the counter. What would Senka say to him? 'The most excellent room that you've got, please'? And the general would say: 'Where do you think you're going, sticking your swinish snout in the bread bin?' And what was the proper way to approach him? Should he say hello or what? Should he take his cap off? Maybe he should just tip it, the way gents did to each other in the street? And then, weren't you supposed to tip them all in a hotel? How could you hand a tip to someone as grand as the general? And how much? What if he just flung Senka out and took no notice of the swish Parisian haircut?

Senka loitered in front of the door for a long time, but he couldn't build up the courage.

Only this set him thinking. Wealth wasn't a simple thing – that much was clear. It needed special study.

Of course, Senka found a place to live – this was Moscow after all, not Siberia. He took a cab at Theatre Square and asked after a handy place for a visitor from out of town to stay, somewhere decent and proper. And the cabby delivered him like the wind to Madam Borisenko's on Trubnaya Street.

The room was wonderful, Senka had never lived in anything like it before. A great big room with white curtains, a bedstead with bright shiny knobs, and a feather mattress on the bed. In the morning he was promised a samovar with doughnuts and in the evening, dinner if required. Servants did all the cleaning, and in the collidor there was a washbasin and a privy – not quite like Death's privy, of course, but it was clean, you could sit and read a newspaper in it. A right royal mansion, in other words. True, it cost a fair bit, thirty-five roubles a month. By Khitrovka standards that was crazy money – you could stay there for five kopecks a night. But if you had almost two thousand roubles in your pocket, it didn't seem so bad.

Senka settled in, admired his new things, laid them out, hung them up, sat down by the window and looked out on the square.

He had to do some thinking about his new life in this world.

It's a well-known fact that every man turns his nose up at his own lot, and envies other people's. Take Senka. He'd dreamt of riches all his life, though he knew in his heart he'd never have any. But the Lord above sees all things, He hears every prayer. Whether He'll grant them all is a different matter altogether. The Almighty has His own reasons, beyond the ken of mortal men. One of the lame cripples who wander the earth once said: The most grievous test the Lord can set is to grant you all your wishes. There you go, dreamer, choke on that. Weren't you coveting too much? And what are you going to covet now?

And that was how it happened with Senka. God was asking him: 'Did you really want earthly treasures? Well, here's some treasure for you – now what?'

Life without money is rotten – no two ways about it – but even with riches, it's not all as sweet as honey.

So Senka had stuffed his paunch – he'd gobbled down eight pastries in the confectioner's shop, and got belly cramps for his trouble. He'd dressed himself up and got beautiful lodgings, but what came next? What will you wish for now, Semyon Trofimovich?

But Senka's state of philosophical melancholy (brought on by those pastries) didn't last very long, because his dreams took shape of their own accord. He had two: one for earth and one for heaven.

The earthly dream was about turning riches into even greater riches. They named you Speedy, now show some nous, use your noggin.

Any fool could see that if you dragged all the silver sticks in that vault out into the open, no one would buy them except by weight. Where would you find enough numismatists to take them all, one stick each?

All right, let's figure out how much that is, by weight. How many rods are there ... God only knows. Five hundred at least. Five pounds of silver in each one, right? That makes ... two and a half thousand pounds, right? Ashot Ashotovich said that a zolotnik of silver is twenty-four kopecks these days. One pound is ninety-six zolotniks ... Multiply two and a half thousand by ninety-six zolotniks by twenty-four kopecks – that makes ...

He groaned and started totting up figures on a piece of paper, like they'd taught him to do at commercial college. But they hadn't had very long to teach him, and he'd forgotten a few things, he was rusty – so the sum didn't work out.

He tried a different way, simpler. Samshitov said there was 155 roubles' worth of pure silver in a bar. For five hundred bars that made ... fifty thousand, right? Or was it five hundred thousand?

Hang on a minute, Senka thought. *Ashot Ashotovich gave me four hundred for a rod, and I don't suppose he was doing himself down. He might let those numismatists of his have them for a thousand each.*

If the black sticks were worth that much, he'd be better off trading them himself, without Samshitov. Of course, it wasn't an easy business. There were lots of things he'd have to figure out to get started. And the first thing of all was the real price. After that he could service all the Moscow buyers. Then the ones in Peter. And then, maybe, he could find a way to the foreign ones. He'd have to hang on to the rods and flog them one at a time, to the suckers willing to pay more than their weight in silver. Then later, when those fools had had their fill, he could sell the rest of the sticks for melting down.

Thinking like a merchant brought Senka out in a sweat. You needed real brains for a deal like this! For the first time he regretted he hadn't done more studying. He couldn't even work out the future takings properly.

So what did that mean?

Yes, it meant he had to catch up. Squeeze all that ignorance and bad manners out of himself, learn how to make fancy small talk, and it would be no bad thing if he could banter in foreign as well, so he could trade over in Europe.

The very thought of it took his breath away.

And that was only the earthly dream, not the most important

one. The other dream, the heavenly one, set Senka's head spinning good and proper.

Of course, if you thought about it, this was an earthly dream too, maybe even more earthly than the other, only it warmed his heart as well as his head, and the heart was where the soul was. Then again, it made Senka's belly – and other parts of his body – feel hot too.

Before, he was a nobody, just a young pup, no kind of match for Death. But now, if he didn't mess things up, he could be the richest man in Moscow. And then, Senka dreamed, he'd throw all those thousands and thousands at her feet and save her from the Prince and the Ghoul, cure her of the candy-cane sickness and carry her off to somewhere far, far away – to Tver (they said it was a fine town) or somewhere else. Maybe even all the way to Paris.

It didn't matter that she was older. The fluff on his cheeks would sprout into a beard and moustache soon enough, and then he'd really come into his own. And he could touch up his temples with grey, like Erast Petrovich – and why not, it was very impressive.

Only when Senka and Death went to get married, it would have to be well away from any embankment where you could fall in and drown. God takes care of those as take care of themselves.

So there was Senka, already picturing the wedding, and the feast in the Hermitage dining hall, but he knew the money on its own wouldn't be enough. Death had had beaus and lovers with huge fortunes before, that was nothing new for her. And he couldn't win her over with presents. He had to turn himself from a grey sparrow into a white falcon and go soaring way up high before he could fly close to a swan like her.

His thoughts turned to education and cultured manners. He had no chance of being a falcon without them, even if he did have the riches.

There was a bookstall out on the square – Senka could see it from the window. He went out and bought a clever book that was called *Life in Society, at Home and at Court* – how to behave in decent society so they wouldn't boot you out.

When he started reading, he came out in a cold sweat. Holy saints, it was all so complicated! How to bow to who, how to kiss a woman's hand – a lady's, that is – how to give compliments, how to dress when and where, how to walk into a room and how to walk out. If he spent his whole life studying, he still wouldn't remember it all!

'One should never pay a visit earlier than two o'clock or later than five or six,' Senka read, moving his lips and ruffling up his French coiffure. 'Before two o'clock, one risks finding the master and mistress of the house engaged in domestic activities or arranging their toilette; at a later hour, one may appear to be angling for an invitation to dinner.'

Or there was this: 'On arriving to pay a visit and not finding the master and mistress of the house at home, a well-bred individual leaves a card, creased at the upper left side; if the visit is on the occasion of a death or other sad event, the card is creased at the lower right, with the fold slightly torn.'

Blimey!

But the most frightening thing of all was reading about clothes. If you were poor, it was easy: just one shirt and one pair of trousers – nothing to rack your brains over. But oh, the hassle if you were rich! When to wear a jacket, when to wear a frock coat, when to wear tails: when you should take your gloves off, when you shouldn't; what should be check, what should be striped, and what should be flowery. And it seemed, for cultured people, not every colour matched every other one!

But the hardest part of all, though, was the hats – Senka even had to make notes.

The rules went like this. In an office, shop or hotel, you took your hat off only if the owners and countermen were bareheaded too (ah, if only he'd known that back at the Grand Moscow!). When leaving after a visit, you put your hat on outside the door, not in the doorway. In an omnibus or carriage, you didn't take your hat off at all, even in the presence of ladies. When you paid a visit, you held your hat in your hand, and if you were in tails, your top hat had to be the kind with a spring to keep it straight, not the simple kind. When you sat down, you could put your hat on a vacant chair or on the floor but never, God forbid, on a table.

Senka felt sorry for the poor hat, it would get dirty on the floor. He looked at the handsome boater on his table (twelve and a half roubles, that cost). Put it on the floor? Not a chance.

When he was tired of studying society manners, he took another look at his new clothes. A frock coat of fine camlet (nineteen roubles ninety), two piqué waistcoats, one white and one grey (ten roubles the pair), pantaloons with a black and grey stripe (fifteen roubles), trousers with foot straps (nine roubles ninety), button-down half-boots (twelve roubles), and another pair, patent leather (he shelled out twenty-five for them, but they were a real sight for sore eyes). And there was a little mirror with a silver handle, and pomade in a gilded jar – to grease his quiff, so it wouldn't dangle. He spent longest of all admiring the mother-of-pearl penknife. Eight blades, an awl, even a toothpick and a nail file too!

When he'd had his fun, he read a bit more of the book.

Senka went down to dinner, dressed according to the requirements of etiquette, in his frock coat, because 'a simple jacket is only permissible at table in the family circle'.

In the dining room he bowed respectfully, said '*Bonsoir*', and put his hat on the floor – so be it, but he put a napkin he'd taken from the kitchen underneath.

There were about ten people dining at the widow Borisenko's. They gaped at the well-bred young man, some of them said good evening, others simply nodded. Not one was wearing a frock coat, and the fat, curly-headed young man sitting beside Senka was dining in his shirt and braces. He turned out to be a student at the Institute of Land Surveyors, George by name. He lived up in the attic, where the rooms were twelve roubles apiece.

Their landlady introduced Senka as Mr Spidorov, a Moscow merchant-trader, although when they agreed terms for the room, he'd just called himself a trading man. Of course 'merchant-trader' sounded much better.

This George started pestering him straight away, asking what kind of commerce he was engaged in at such a young age, and about his old mum and dad. When they served the sweet (it was called 'dessert'), the student asked in a whisper whether he could borrow three roubles.

Naturally, Senka didn't give him three roubles just like that, and he answered his questions vaguely, but he had an idea for how George could be useful.

Senka couldn't learn everything from just one book. A tutor, that was what he needed.

He took George aside and started lying, saying he was a merchant's son who had worked in his father's business, he'd never had time to study. Now his old dad had died and left all his riches to his heir, but what had he, Semyon Spidorov, ever seen of life, apart from a shop counter? If he could fine someone good-hearted to teach him a few things – proper manners, French and other bits and pieces – then he would pay good money for the privilege.

The student listened carefully and took the hint, and they fixed terms for classes straight off. As soon as George heard Senka was going to pay a rouble an hour, he announced that he wouldn't go to the institute and was ready to put himself entirely at Semyon Trofimovich's disposal all day long.

What they agreed was this: one hour a day studying spelling and fine handwriting; an hour for French, an hour for arithmetic; lunch and dinner were for studying good manners; and the evening class was proper behaviour in society. Seeing as it was a bulk-supply contract, Senka arranged a discount for himself: four roubles a day all told. They were both satisfied.

They lost no time, starting straight after dinner with a trip to the ballet. Senka's tails were hired for two roubles from the musician in the next room.

At the theatre Senka sat up straight without fidgeting, though he soon got tired of watching men in tight underpants jumping about all over the stage. When the girls came running out in transparent skirts, things got a bit more lively, but the music had a really sour edge to it. It would have been deadly boring if George hadn't taken the magnifying glasses from the cloakroom ('binoculars', they were called). Senka got a good look at everything. First the thighs of the dancing girls, then who was sitting in the boxes round the hall, and then he let his fancy wander – a wart on the bald patch of the leader of the musicians, who was waving a stick at the orchestra, so they would keep better order. When everyone *applauded*, Senka stuck the binoculars under his arm and clapped his hands, too, louder than anyone else.

Spending seven roubles to sit in a prickly collar for three hours couldn't be anybody's idea of fun. He asked George if rich people went to get sweaty at the theatre every night. George reassured him: he said you could go just once a week. Well, that wasn't too bad, and Senka cheered up a bit. It was like standing through Mass on a Sunday if you were God-fearing.

From the ballet, they went to the bordello (that was the cultured name for a bawdy house), to learn proper manners with ladies.

Senka was really embarrassed by the lamps with silk shades and the soft couches with bouncy springs. Mamselle Loretta, who was sat on his knee, was plump and springy herself, and she smelled of sweet powder. She called Senka 'sweety' and 'kitten', then she led him into a room and started getting up to all sorts of tricks that Senka had never heard of, even from Prokha.

But he felt ashamed because the lamp was lit, and anyway, there was no way this fat pussycat Loretta had anything on Death.

Phooey!

After that, they spent a long time learning how to drink champagne: you put a strawberry in it, let it settle in and get well soaked, then fished it out with your lips. Then you downed the bubbly booze in one and started all over again.

Well, of course, in the morning his head was killing him. It was even worse than after vodka. But only until George called in.

George looked at his pupil's agony, clicked his tongue and sent one of the servants out for champagne and pâté at once. They spread the pâté on white bread rolls and drank the wine straight from the bottle.

Senka felt a bit better.

'Now we'll do a bit of French, and for lunch we'll go to a French restaurant to reinforce our knowledge,' George told him, and licked his thick lips.

Well, this isn't too shabby, Senka thought, feeling more relaxed. *Not nearly as hard as it looks. The life of luxury is all right by me.*

Story three. *About his little brother Vanka*

Senka enjoyed thinking about his two great dreams, imagining how everything would work out – with love and countless riches. But even with his present riches, which weren't *so* very great, he could already make one dream – which had seemed impossible before – come true. He could appear in all his glory before his brother Vanka.

Of course, he couldn't turn up out of the blue just like that: Hello, I'm your big brother, dressed to the nines, but I'm a slum boy through and through, can't speak a single cultured word. What if Vanka despised his ignorance?

But he could get by without all that much learning in front of a little kid.

Right from the off, Senka had asked George to correct any

words he got wrong when they were talking. And to make sure the student made the effort, he was relieved of five kopecks for every word corrected.

Naturally, he was only too glad to try his best. Almost every other word got a: 'No, Semyon Trofimovich, in cultured society they don't say *collidor*, it should be *corridor*' – and he jotted down another cross on his special piece of paper. Afterwards, in the arithmetic lesson, Senka himself multiplied those little crosses by five. On the first of September 1900, he was stung for eighteen roubles and seventy-five kopecks – and he'd tried to be stingy, not say a single word more than he needed to get by. He started off talking like a book: 'But in this case it seems to me that . . .' And then shut his mouth.

Senka groaned at the huge sum, and demanded a reduction – from five kopecks to one.

On the second of September he forked out, that is, he *paid out*, four roubles and thirty-five kopecks.

On the third of September, it was three roubles and twelve kopecks.

By the fourth of September he'd copped on a bit, that is *got the feel of things*, and it was down to one rouble and ten kopecks, and on the fifth he escaped only ninety kopecks poorer.

Senka decided that was good enough for Vanka, it was time to go. He could now *expound his opinions* for five minutes *with perfect ease*. After all, God had given him a perfectly good memory.

According to *society etiquette*, first he ought to send Justice Kuvshinnikov a letter, saying this and that, and I would like to call on Your Grace with a view to visiting my adored little brother Vanya. But he didn't have the patience for that.

First thing in the morning Senka went to the *dentist* to have a gold tooth put in, and he packed George off to Tyoply Stan to warn them that in the afternoon, *if His Grace was agreeable*, Semyon Trofimovich Spidorov, the *well-to-do merchant-trader*, would call in person, for a *family visit*, so to speak. George dressed up in his student uniform, bought his uniform cap out of hock and set off.

Senka was *extremely nervous* (that is, he was in a real lather) in case the judge said: What the hell does my adopted son want with scummy relatives like that?

But it went off all right. George came back delighted with himself and announced that they were expecting him at three. So not for lunch, Senka twigged, but he didn't take offence; on the contrary, he was glad, because he still wasn't too good with table knives and telling the meat forks from the ones for fish and salad.

It said in the book: 'When paying a visit to children, one should give them a present of sweets in a bonbonnier', and Senka didn't play the tightwad, that is he didn't *penny-pinch* – he bought the very finest tin of chocolate from Perlov's on Myasnitskaya Street, in the shape of the little humpbacked horse from the fairy tales.

He hired a shiny lacquered carriage for a five-rouble note, but his nerves were so bad he set out way too early, and at first he walked along the street with the carriage driving behind him.

He tried to step out the way the textbook said you should: 'In the street, the well-bred, refined individual is easily distinguished. His gait is always steady and measured, his stride is confident. He walks straight ahead, without looking round, and only occasionally stops for a moment in front of shops, usually stays on the right-hand side of the road and looks neither up nor down, but several paces straight ahead of himself.'

He walked that way down Myasnitskaya Street, Lyubanka Street and Theatre Lane. And when he got a stiff neck from looking ahead of him all the time, he got into the carriage.

They drove as far as the apple orchards in Konkovo, all unhurried, but just before Tyoply Stan the passenger told the driver to put on some speed so they would drive up to the judge's house at a spanking pace, looking good, with *real chic*.

He walked into the house in fine old fashion, said *bonjour* and bowed.

Judge Kuvshinnikov replied: 'Hello, Semyon Spidorov,' and asked him to take a seat.

Senka sat there modestly and politely. He took off his right glove, but not the left, the way you're supposed to at the start of a visit, and put his hat on the floor, only without any napkin. And when he'd managed all that, he took a proper look at the judge.

Ippolit Ivanovich had got old, you could see that from close up. His horseshoe moustache had turned grey. The long hair hanging down below his ears was all white too. But his gaze was the same as ever: black and piercing.

Senka's old dad used to say that in the whole wide world you could never find anyone cleverer than Judge Kuvshinnikov, and so, when he gazed into Ippolit Ivanovich's stern eyes, Senka decided he would forget the rules of etiquette and behave with genuine courtesy, as he had been taught, not by George, and not by a book, but by a certain individual (we'll get to him later, we've got ahead of ourselves).

This individual had told him that genuine courtesy was founded not on polite words, but on sincere respect: Respect any person as far as that is possible, until that person has shown himself unworthy of your respect.

Senka had thought about this strange assertion for a long time, and eventually explained it to himself like this: It's better to flatter a bad man than offend a good one – wasn't that it?

So he didn't try to make polite conversation with the judge about the pleasantly cool weather; he said in all honesty, with a bow: 'Thank you for raising my brother, an orphan, as your own son and not offending him in any way. And Jesus Christ will show you even greater gratitude for it.'

The judge leaned forward and said there was no need for thanks, Vanya brought himself and his wife nothing but joy and delight in their old age. He was a lively boy, with a tender heart and great abilities.

Well, that was that. Then they said nothing for a while.

Senka racked his brains – how could he bring the conversation round to seeing his little brother? He started sniffing with the strain of it, but immediately remembered that 'the loud sniffing in of nasal fluid in company is absolutely impermissible', and quickly pulled out his handkerchief to blow his nose.

The judge said: 'That friend of yours who called this morning said you were a "well-to-do merchant-trader" . . .'

Senka thrust out his chest, but not for long, because Ippolit Ivanovich went on like this: 'Where did the money come from, for the shiny carriage, the frock coat and the top hat? I correspond with your guardian, Zot Larionovich Puzyrev. All these years I've been sending him a hundred roubles every three months for your keep, I receive reports. Puzyrev wrote that you didn't want to study at the grammar school, that you are wild and ungrateful and consort with all sorts of riff-raff. And in his last letter he informed me that you had become a thief and a bandit.'

Senka was so taken by surprise that he leapt to his feet and shouted – it was stupid of course, he should have kept his mouth shut: 'Me, a thief? When did he ever catch me?'

'When they do catch you, Senya, it will be too late!'

'I didn't want to go to the grammar school? He was getting a hundred roubles for me?'

Senka choked. What a skunk his Uncle Zot was! Smashing those windows was too good for him, he should have set the house on fire!

'So where does your wealth come from?' the judge asked. 'I have to know before I can let you see Vanka. Perhaps your frock coat was cut from blood and sewn with tears.'

'It's not cut from any blood. I found a treasure, an old one,' Senka muttered, realising as he said it that no one would ever believe *that*.

So much for driving up in grand style and presenting his little brother with the sweets! His old dad was right: the judge was a clever man.

But Kuvshinnikov turned out to be even cleverer than that. He didn't smack his lips in disbelief, he didn't shake his head. He asked calmly: 'What kind of treasure? Where from?'

'Where from? From the Khitrovka basements, that's where from,' Senka replied sullenly. 'There were some silver rods there, with a stamp on them. Five of them. They're worth a lot of money.'

'What kind of stamp?'

'How would I know? Two letters: "Y" and "M".'

The judge looked at Senka for a long time, without saying a word. Then he got up. 'Let's go into the library.'

That was a room covered all over from top to bottom with books. If all the books Senka had ever seen in his life were put together, there still probably wouldn't be as many.

Kuvshinnikov climbed up a ladder and took a thick volume down off a shelf. He started leafing through from his perch.

'Aha,' he said.

Then: 'Hmmm. Yes, yes.'

He looked at Senka over the top of his specs and asked. '"YM", you say? And where did you find the treasure? Not in the Serebryanniki district, was it?'

'No, in Khitrovka, honest to God,' said Senka, crossing himself.

Ippolit Ivanovich climbed down the ladder quickly, put the book on a table and went over to a picture that was hanging on the wall. It was a queer-looking picture, like a drawing of the way pork carcasses were butchered that Senka had once seen in a German meat shop.

'Here, take a look. This is a map of Moscow. This is Khitrovka, and this is Serebryanniki, the lane and the embankment. It's just a stone's throw from Khitrovka.'

Senka went over and tried to take it in. Just to be on the safe side, he said: 'Of course.'

But the judge wasn't looking at Senka, he was muttering away to himself: 'Why, yes! In the seventeenth century that's where the Silversmiths' Quarter used to be, the place where the master craftsmen from the Yauza Mint lived. What do your rods look like? Like this?'

He dragged Senka across to the table where the book was. In a picture Senka saw a rod exactly like the ones he'd sold to the jeweller. And a big picture of the end, with the letters 'MM'.

'The "MM" means "Moscow Mint",' Kuvshinnikov explained. It was also called the New Mint or the English Mint. In the olden days Russia didn't have much silver of its own, so they used to buy European coins – joachimsthalers, or yefimoks. Senka nodded again at the familiar word, but this time in earnest. 'They melted the thalers down and made silver rods like that, then they drew them out into wire, cut pieces off it, flattened them and minted kopecks – "scales", they were called. A lot of kopecks have survived, and even more thalers, but there are no silver billets, or rods, left at all. Well, naturally – they all were all used up.'

'What about this one?' asked Senka, pointing to the picture.

'Well done,' the judge said approvingly. 'You use your head. Quite right, Spidorov. Only one rod came down to our times, minted at the Moscow or New Mint.'

Senka thought about that.

'Why would those silversmiths have dumped the billets and not stamped coins out of them?'

Kuvshinnikov shrugged. 'It's a mystery.' His eyes weren't narrow and piercing now, they were wide-open and glowing, as if the judge was really surprised or delighted. 'Although it's not that great a mystery, if you give it a little thought. A lot of stealing went on in the seventeenth century, even more so than now. Look here, it says in the encyclopedia . . .' – and he ran his hand down the page; '"For so-called 'smelting losses' the craftsmen were beaten mercilessly with a knout, and some had their nostrils torn out, but they were not dismissed, because silversmiths were in short supply". Clearly they didn't beat them hard enough if someone made a secret hoard of silver "lost in smelting". Or perhaps it wasn't the craftsmen they should have beaten, but the clerks.'

The judge turned to his book. Suddenly he whistled. Senka was really surprised: a man like that, and him whistling.

'Senya, how did much did you sell your rods for?'

Senka didn't see the point in lying. Kuvshinnikov was a rich man himself, he wouldn't be jealous.

'Four hundred.'

'It says here that fifty years ago, at an auction in London, this bar was acquired by a collector for seven hundred pounds sterling. That's seven thousand roubles, and in today's money probably a lot more.'

Senka's jaw dropped. Why, that Ashot Ashotovich, what a snake!

'You see, Spidorov, if you'd given your treasure to the state treasury . . .'

'What joy would I get out of that?' Senka snarled, still smarting at the jeweller's treachery.

'Well, the silver was stolen from the treasury. It may have been two hundred years ago, but it's the same state, still Russia. For handing over a treasure trove to the authorities, according to the law, the finder is entitled to a third of its value. So for your five bars, you would have received a lot more than just two thousand. And in addition you would have been an honest man, helping your motherland.'

Senka was about to say that could be put right – but he bit his tongue just in time. He would have to think long and hard before he started blabbing. Kuvshinnikov was sharp-witted, he'd worm the whole thing out of him in a trice.

The looks the judge was giving Senka were knowing enough as it was.

'All right,' said Kuvshinnikov. 'Just give a little thought to where you'd take the bars, if you happened to find any more: to a fence or to the treasury. If you decide to follow the law, I'll tell you how to do it. The newspapers will write about your patriotism.'

'About what?'

'About you not just filling your belly, but loving your homeland, that's what.'

Senka wasn't too sure about the homeland part. Where was his homeland, anyway? Sukharevka, was it, or Khitrovka? Why should he love those lousy dives?

Then Kuvshinnnikov surprised him again. He sighed. 'So, Zot lied to me about the grammar school. And about everything else too, no doubt . . . Very well, he'll answer to me for that.'

The judge turned sad and hung his grey head. 'Forgive me, Senya, for buying off my conscience with a hundred roubles. I could have called to check how you were getting on at least once. When your father died, I wanted to take both of you in, but Puzyrev clung on to you like grim death – he's my nephew, he said, my sister's flesh and blood. But it would seem money was the only thing on his mind.'

Senka's thoughts briefly turned away from money to something completely different: how would everything have turned out if he'd been taken in by Judge Kuvshinninkov instead of Uncle Zot?

But what point was there in eating his heart out now?

Senka asked sullenly: 'Won't you let me see Vanka?'

The judge paused for a moment before he answered. 'Well now, you've spoken to me honestly, and you're not an entirely hopeless case. So yes, you can see each other. Why shouldn't you? Vanya's French lesson has just finished. Go to the nursery. The maid will show you the way.'

And Senka needn't have worried about his little brother.

When they told Vanka his big brother had arrived, he ran out to meet him, jumped right up and threw his arms round Senka's neck.

'Aha! I did it, I wrote him a letter! Senya, you look just the way I imagined you!' Then he corrected himself. 'Not imagined, remembered. You haven't changed at all, even the tie's still the same!'

What a brazen liar the little scamp was!

Senka gave him the bonbonnier and some other presents: binoculars and a penknife – the same one, with the nail file on it. Of course, Vanka immediately forgot all about his brother and started fiddling with the blades – but that was all right, kids will be kids.

Senka shook the judge's hand when he said goodbye and promised to come again in a couple of days.

He walked back almost all the way to the Kaluga Gate, deep in thought.

Seven thousand a rod! If he didn't force down the price, he could live like a king for a whole year – on just one rod.

He had to put his wits to work, use that noggin a bit.

As a certain individual, who has already been mentioned, had taught him: 'He who think rittur, cry man' tears.'

Story Four. *About the Japanese man Masa*

Meaning: 'He who thinks little, cries many tears'. This individual could not pronounce the Russian 'l' because there was no such letter in the language where he was from. But apparently they managed somehow, they got by.

So now it is time to tell you about Senka's other teacher, who wasn't hired, but self-appointed.

It happened like this.

The day after the ballet, when Senka was feeling unwell first thing in the morning, and then was cured by champagne and pâté, he had an unexpected visitor.

There was a knock on the door – a quiet, well-mannered knock. He thought it was the landlady.

But when he opened the door he saw the Japanese, from yesterday.

Senka got an awful fright. Now the Jap would start belting him and asking why he had scampered off before being called to account for his stealing.

The Japanese said hello and asked: 'Why you trembur?'

Senka told him straight: 'I'm trembling because I'm afraid for my life. Afraid you might do me in, mister.'

The Japanese was surprised: 'You mean, Senka-kun, that you afrai' of death?'

'Who isn't afraid of it?' Senka answered. The question sounded like a threat, and Senka backed away towards the window. He'd thought maybe he could leap from the window. But it was a bit on the high side, otherwise he'd definitely have jumped.

The Japanese continued to put the wind up Senka – making out he was even more surprised. 'Why be afrai'? You no' afrai' to sreep at nigh', are you?'

After a dark hint like that, Senka stopped feeling afraid of the height. He backed off all the way to the window and opened the curtain, as if he needed some air. Now if anyone tried to kill him, he could jump up on the windowsill in a single bound.

'But when you sleep,' he said, 'you know you're going to wake up in the morning.'

'An' wake up afta death too. If you rive good rife, waking up wirr be good.'

So now he was playing the priest! That was a bit much, a heathen preaching to a baptised Christian about heaven and resurrection!

With the window so close now, Senka felt a bit bolder: 'How did you find me?' he asked. 'Do you know some magic word?'

'I know. It carred "roubur". I gave boy roubur, an' he forrow you.'

'What boy?' asked Senka, startled.

Masa pointed to a spot about two and a half feet off the floor. 'Rittur boy. Snot face. But run fast.'

The Japanese glanced round the room and nodded approvingly. 'Werr done, Senka-kun, for moving here. It crose to Asheurov Rane.'

Senka twigged – he meant Asheulov Lane, where he and Erast Petrovich had their lodgings. It really wasn't far.

'What do you want from me? I gave back the beads, didn't I?' he whined.

'Master tord me to come,' Masa explained sternly, almost solemnly, then sighed. 'An' you, Senka-kun, rike me. When I was rike you, I was rittur bandit too. If I not meet Master, I woul' grow into big bandit. He is my teacher. And I wirr be your teacher.'

'I've already got a teacher,' Senka growled (he'd lost his fear of death).

'What lessons he give you?' Masa asked, livening up. (Well, actually, he said 'ressons', but Senka had already learned to make out his queer way of talking.)

'Well, there's good manners . . .'

The short-ass was delighted at that. That was the most important thing, he said. And he explained about genuine politeness, which was based on sincere respect for every person.

At the very height of the explanation, a fly started buzzing about over Senka's head. The rotten pest kept flying round and round, it just wouldn't leave him alone. The Japanese jumped up in the air, waved his arm and caught the insect in his fist.

His agile speed made Senka squeal out loud and squat right down – he thought Masa was trying to kill him.

Masa looked down at Senka doubled up on the floor and asked what he was doing. 'I was afraid you'd hit me.'

'What for?'

Senka said with a sob in his voice: 'Everyone wants to hurt a poor orphan.'

The Japanese raised one finger like a teacher. You need to know how to defend yourself, he said. Especially if you're an orphan.

'Yeah, but how do I learn?'

The Japanese laughed. Who was it, he asked, who said he didn't need a teacher? Do you want me to teach you how to defend yourself?

Senka recalled the way the Oriental flung his arms and legs about, and he wanted to do that too. 'That wouldn't be bad,' he said. 'But I reckon nifty battering's difficult, ain't it?'

Masa walked over to the window and set the captured fly free. No, he said, battering people's not difficult. Learning the Way, that's what's difficult.

(It was only later Senka realised he'd said the word 'Way' like it was written with a big letter, but at the time he didn't twig.)

'Eh?' he asked. 'Learning what?'

Masa started explaining the Way. He said life was a road from birth to death and you had to walk that road the right way, or else at the end of the journey you wouldn't have got anywhere and afterwards it was too late to complain. If you crawled along the road like a fly, then in the next life you'd be born a fly, like the one that was just buzzing round the room. And if you crept along through the dust, you'd be born a snake.

Senka thought that was just fancy talk. He didn't know then that Masa was serious when he talked about flies and snakes.

'And what's the right way to walk the road?' asked Senka.

It turned out that doing it right was a kind of self-torture. First of all, when you woke up in the morning, you had to say to yourself: 'Today death is waiting for me' – and not feel afraid. And you had to think about it – death, that is – all the time. Because you never knew when your journey would come to an end, and you always had to be ready.

Senka closed his eyes and said the special words, and he wasn't frightened at all, because he saw Death in front of him, looking incredibly beautiful. (Why be afraid, if she was waiting for you?)

But the more he learnt, the worse it got.

You couldn't tell lies, you couldn't doss about doing nothing, you couldn't sleep on a feather bed (no mollycoddling yourself at all!) and you had to torture and torment yourself, toughen yourself up and in general really put yourself through it.

Senka listened and listened, and decided he didn't want to go through all that agony. He'd already seen more than enough poverty and hunger – in fact he'd only just got a whiff of real life.

'Ain't there any simpler way, without *the* Way? Just so you can fight?'

Masa was upset by that question, he shook his head. There is, he said, but then you'll never beat a tiger, only a jackal.

'Never mind, a jackal's good enough for me,' Senka declared. 'I can walk round a tiger, me legs won't fall off.'

Well, that made the Japanese even more sorrowful. 'Damn your lazy soul,' he said. 'But take off your jacket and you can have your first resson.'

And he started teaching Senka the right way to fall if someone smashed you hard in the face.

Senka learned the skill quickly: he fell correctly, tumbled right over backwards and back up on his feet, and all the time he was waiting for Masa to ask him where a Khitrovka ragamuffin got so much money.

He never did.

But before he left, Masa said: 'The master asks if you want to tell him anything, Senka-kun? No? Then sayonara.'

That was how they said 'see you later'.

And he got into the habit of coming to the boarding house, never missed a day.

If Senka went down to breakfast, Masa was already there, sitting by the samovar, all red from drinking tea, and the landlady was serving him more jam. When he was there, strict Madam Borisenko went all soppy and started blushing. How come he affected her like that?

Then afterwards the Japanese gymnastics lesson began. Truth be told, Masa spent more time jabbering away than teaching him anything useful. The wily Oriental was obviously still trying to drag Senka on to that Way of his.

For example, he was teaching Senka to leap down off the roof of the shed. Senka had climbed up all right, but he couldn't jump, he was afraid. It was fifteen feet! He'd break his leg!

Masa stood beside him, preaching. It's the fear that's stopping you, he said. Drive it away, a man doesn't need it. All it does is stop your head and your body doing their job. You know how to jump, don't you? I showed you, I explained. So don't be afraid, your head and your body will just do it if fear doesn't stop them.

Easily said!

'So isn't there anything in the world you're afraid of, Sensei?' That was what Senka had to call him, 'sensei'. It meant 'teacher'. 'I didn't think there was anybody who didn't have any fear.'

The answer was: There are some people, but not many. The master, for instance, he's not afraid of anything. But there is one thing that I am very much afraid of.

Senka felt a bit better when he heard that. 'What? Dead men?'

No, said Masa. I'm afraid the master will put his trust in me and I'll disappoint him, let him down. Because of my stupidity or circumstances beyond my control. I'm terribly afraid of that, he said. All right, stupidity lessens as the years go by. But only the Buddha has power over circumstances.

'Who does?' Senka asked.

Masa pointed one finger towards the sky. 'Buddha.'

'Ah-ha, Jesus Christ.'

The Japanese nodded. That's why, he said, I pray to him every day. Like this.

He closed his narrow eyes, folded his hands and started droning something through his nose. Then he translated it: 'I trust in the Buddha and do everything I can.' That was their prayer in Japan, he said.

'That ain't Japanese. Trust in God and do right yourself.'

They talked divine matters one other time too.

A lot of flies had appeared in Senka's room. They'd obviously come in for crumbs – he'd become a real fiend for guzzling fancy pastries.

Masa didn't like flies. He caught them, like a cat with its paw, but as for squashing or swatting them – not on your life. He always carried them to the window and let them fly away.

Senka asked him: 'Why do you take all that trouble with them, Sensei? Just swat them, and the job's done.'

And the answer was: You shouldn't kill anyone if you don't have to kill them.

'Not even a fly?'

It makes no difference, Masa said. A soul is always a soul, no two ways about it. Now it's a fly, but if it leads a good life as a fly, in the next it could be a man. Someone like you, for instance.

Senka took offence.

'What's that mean, like me? Maybe like *you*.'

What Masa said to that was: If you go giving your teacher lip, you'll definitely be a fly after you die. Come on now, he said, dodge. And he smacked Senka in the face so fast, there was no way you could dodge it. It fair set his ears ringing.

That was how Senka learned Japanese wisdom.

And every day, at the end of the session, his strange teacher would ask the same thing: Didn't he have a message for his master?

Senka batted his eyelids and kept mum. He couldn't figure out what the master was getting at. Was it about the treasure? Or was it something else?

Masa didn't pester him, though. He waited for about half a minute, nodded, said his 'sayonara' and went off home.

The days flew by fast. A lesson of gymnastics, a lesson of French, reinforced by a session in a French restaurant, then a stroll round the shops and another lesson, on elegant manners, with George, and then it was time for dinner and the practical class. 'Practical class' was what George called trips to the operetta, the dance hall, the bordello or some other society gathering place.

In the mornings Senka slept late, and by the time he had got up and washed, Masa was ready and waiting. And off he went again, just like a squirrel in a cage.

A couple of times, instead of his practical class, he dropped into Khitrovka to see Tashka – after dark, and not wearing any frock coat or tails, of course, but in his old clothes. *Apache style*, as George said.

This was how he did it.

He hired a steady, sober cabby on Trubnaya Street – the cabby had to have a number – and drove to Lubyanka Square with him. He got changed right there in the cab, with the leather hood pulled right down low.

Transformed from a merchant trader into an Apache, he left the driver to wait. Not a bad deal – just sit there, sleep if you like, for a rouble an hour. The only condition was, he mustn't move from the box, or the clothes would be nicked off the seat in a flash.

Stubborn Tashka wouldn't take any of the money Senka tried to give her. And she wouldn't give up her whore's trade, because she was proud. Who takes money from men, she said – not for working, but just like that? A moll or a wife. I can't come and be your moll, because you and me, we're mates. And I won't be your wife, on account of the frenchies (not that Senka had asked her to marry him – Tashka thought that up all by herself). I'll earn as much as I need. And if it's not enough, then you can help me, as a mate.

But Senka's tales of the high life had sparked Tashka's ambition or, rather, her vanity. She'd decided she wanted to make a career as well – move up from a street mamselle to a 'grammar school girl', especially since she was the right age for it.

'Grammar school girls' didn't walk the streets, a madame supplied their clients for them. Compared with a street whore's work, it was much easier and the money was far better.

The first thing she had to do was buy a grammar school uniform, with a cape, but Tashka had money set aside for that.

She already knew a madame too. An honest woman, reliable, who took only a third as her cut. And there was no end of clients who set store by grammar school girls. All respectable men, getting on a bit, men with money.

She had only one problem, the same one as Senka had: not enough culture to conduct a classy conversation. After all, the client had to believe he'd been brought a genuine grammar school girl and not a dressed-up mamselle, didn't he?

That was why Tashka had started learning French words and all sorts of elegant expressions. She'd made up her life story, and she started reciting it to Senka. She wasn't sure of all the words yet, so she kept glancing at a piece of paper. Tashka was supposed to be in the fourth class at grammar school, and an inspector had seduced her and plucked the flower of her innocence, taught her all sorts of tricks, and now, behind Mama and Papa's back, she was earning money for sweets and cakes with her female charms.

Senka listened to the story and, as a man with experience of society, suggested a few improvements. He advised her most ardently to take out the swear words.

Tashka was surprised by this advice. As a Khitrovka girl, she couldn't tell the difference between decent expressions and obscene ones. Then he wrote down all the dirty words on a piece of paper for her, so she could remember them. Tashka took her head in her hands and started repeating *****, ***** , *****, *****, *****. Senka's ears had got used to cultured or, to put it even better, *civilised* conversation, and they fairly wilted on his head.

Tashka had bought herself a poodle with the last money Senka had given her. The dog was small and white, very frisky, and he sniffed at absolutely everything. He recognised Senka the second time he saw him and started jumping up at him in delight. He could tell all Tashka's flowers apart and had a special way of yapping for each one. His name was Pomponius, or just plain Pomposhka.

When Senka called round to see Tashka the second time – to tell her about how he'd seen his little brother and show her his new tooth (and there was one other thing, a money matter), the working girl lashed out: 'What have you shown up here for? Didn't you see I've got a red poppy in the window? Have you forgot what that means? I taught you! Danger, that's what! Don't come to Khitrovka, the Prince is looking for you!'

Senka knew that already, but how could he not come? After his society studies, and especially George's practical classes, he had barely a quarter of the two thousand roubles left. He'd blown fifteen hundred in a week – that was an absolute *disaster* for him. He needed to *restore his financial status* urgently.

So he went down underground and restored it.

He wanted to take two rods, but changed his mind and took only one. No point in flashing it about just for the sake of it. Money to spare needs good care. It was time he started following that principle.

The jeweller Ashot Ashotovich greeted Senka like his long-lost brother. He left the parrot to keep an eye on the shop, took his guest in behind the curtain and treated him to cognac and biscuits. Senka gnawed on his biscuits and sipped on his cognac in a most cultured fashion, then he showed the jeweller the rod, but he didn't led him hold it. Instead of four hundred roubles, he asked for a thousand. Now, would this shark pay up or not?

Samshitov gave him a thousand, all right, didn't even say a word.

So what it said in Judge Kuvshinnikov's book, about the real price, was true.

The jeweller kept pouring the cognac. He thought the Khitrovka halfwit would get drunk and let something slip. He asked whether there would be more rods and when that might be.

Senka was cunning with him. 'That's the last rod for a

thousand, there was only one. You put me in touch with the client, Mr Samshitov, perhaps then more will turn up.'

Ashot Ashotovich blinked his ink-black eyes and sniffed a bit. But he knew his days of taking Senka for a ride were over.

'What about my commission?' he asked.

'The regular rate, twenty per cent.'

Ashot Ashotovich started getting agitated. Twenty's not enough, he said. Only I know the real clients, you can't find them without me. You have to give me thirty per cent.

They haggled and settled on twenty-five.

Senka left the jeweller his address, so he could send word when anything came up, and left feeling very pleased with himself.

Samshitov called after him: 'So I can hope, Mr Spidorov?'

And the parrot Levonchik squawked: 'Mr Spidorov! Mr Spidorov!'

He went back to the cab and changed into his decent clothes, but he didn't ride home in the carriage, he walked. He was going to be prudent from now on. An extra half-rouble was no great expense, of course, but he had to stick to the principle.

On the corner of Tsvetnoi Boulevard he looked round – he had a strange feeling he was being watched.

And who was the figure under a street lamp but his old friend Prokha! Had he followed him from Khitrovka, then?

Senka went dashing over to Prokha and grabbed hold of him by the sides. 'Give me back the timepiece, you louse!'

He'd been walking around for almost a week with a new timepiece, but Prokha wasn't to know that. If you stole from your own, you had to answer for it.

'You're dolled up very handsome, Speedy,' Prokha hissed, and pulled himself free with a jerk. 'Looking for a poke in the mug, are you?'

He slipped his hand in his pocket – and Senka knew he had the lead bar in there, or something even worse.

Suddenly there was the sound of a whistle and tramping feet, and a constable came rushing towards them – to protect the decent young man from the urchin.

Prokha shot off up Zvonarny Lane, into the darkness.

That's right, you ragged prole. This ain't Khitrovka, this is a nice *decent neighbourhood*. He shuddered at the idea – 'a poke in the mug'.

How Senka Was
Death's Lover

Of all the lessons taught by Masa, Senka paid the most avid attention to that supreme branch of learning – how to conquer the hearts of women.

The Japanese proved to be a genuine expert in this area, both in the language of courtship, and the actual horsing around. No, it would be better to put it this way: *in theory and in practice.*

For a long time Senka couldn't understand why the slanty-eye Jap made Madam Borisenko go all bashful like that, why she was so fond of him. One time he came down to breakfast early, before the other guests arrived – and well, well! There was the landlady sitting on Masa's knees, lavishing kisses on his thick neck, and he was just screwing his eyes up in pleasure. When she saw Senka, she squealed and blushed and darted out of the room like a young miss – but she must have been at least thirty.

Senka couldn't resist it, so he asked Masa – that very day, during the break after the morning scuffle. Sensei, he said, how come you have such great success with women? Do a poor orphan the kindness of sharing your savvy.

Well, the Japanese read him an entire lecture, it was just like that time George took Senka to his institute. Only Masa was easier to understand than the professor, even if he was from foreign parts.

In summary, the wisdom came out like this.

In order to unlock a woman's heart, you needed three keys, Masa taught. Confidence in yourself, an air of mystery and the right *approach*. The first two were easy, because they only depended on you. The third was harder, because you had to work out what sort of woman you were dealing with. This was called knowledge of the soul or, in scientific terms, psychology.

Women, Masa explained, were not all alike. They could be divided into two species.

'Only two?' Senka asked in amazement. He was listening very attentively, and really regretted that he didn't have a piece of paper handy to take notes.

Only two, the sensei repeated gravely. Those who needed a father, and those who needed a son. The important thing was to determine the correct species, and without practice this was not easy, because women loved to pretend. But once you had determined this, the rest was simple. With a woman of the first species you had to be a father: not ask her about her life, and in general talk as little as possible – show her the strictness of a father. With a woman of the second you had to make sad eyes, sigh and look up at the sky all the time, so she would understand that you would be completely lost without her.

But if you did not want a woman's soul, and her body was enough, the teacher continued, then it was more straightforward.

Senka exclaimed eagerly: 'Yes, yes, that's enough!'

In that case, Masa said with a shrug, you didn't need words at all. Breathe loudly, make eyes like this, don't answer clever questions. Don't show her your soul. Otherwise it's not fair – you don't want the woman's soul, after all. For her you must be a *rittur animur*, not a person.

'Who?' asked Senka, confused at first. 'Ah, a little animal.'

Masa repeated the phrase with relish. Yes, he said, a *rittur animur*. Who will come running, sniff her under the tail and climb up on her straight away. Everybody wants women to be shy and seem virtuous – women get fed up of that. But why be shy of a little animal? It's only an animal, after all.

The sensei spent a long time teaching Senka about this kind of thing, and even though Senka didn't take notes, he remembered every last word.

And the very next day, an appropriate opportunity for a practical lesson came along.

George invited him to go to Sokolniki Park for a *picnic* (that was when you went into the woods and sat on the grass and ate with your hands, without making any fuss). He said he would bring along two girl students. He'd been after one of them for ages and, he said, the other will be just right for you (by that time they'd already drunk to *Bruderschaft* and were on intimate terms). A modern miss, he said, with no prejudices.

'A tramp, is she?' Senka asked.

'Not exactly,' George answered evasively. 'But you'll see for yourself.'

They got into a fancy gig, and off they went. Senka soon realised the student had bamboozled him. George's girl was plump and jolly, and she kept laughing all the time, but he'd lumbered his comrade with some kind of dried fish with glasses and tight-pursed lips. And he'd done it on purpose, too, so this miserable specimen wouldn't interfere with him trying to get off with her girlfriend.

While they rode along, Four-eyes yammered on about things Senka didn't understand. Nietzsche-schmietzsche, Marx-schmarx.

Senka wasn't listening, he was thinking about something else. According to Masa's science of women, if you made the right approach, with psychology, you could get any woman, even a bighead like this one. What was it Masa had taught him? Simple women love gallant manners and clever words, but with the educated ones, on the contrary, you had to be simpler and rougher.

Maybe he should try it – just to check.

So he did.

She said: 'Tell me, Semyon, what do you think about the theory of social evolution?'

159

He didn't say a word, just laughed.

She started getting nervous and batting her eyelids. I suppose, she said, you probably support the violent overthrow of social institutions. And he just cocked his head and pulled a face – that was his only response.

In the park, when George took his gigglebox for a ride in a boat (Senka's girl didn't want to go, said the water made her feel dizzy), the time came for action.

Senka's mysterious behaviour had driven the young lady into a real state – she kept jabbering on and on, just couldn't stop. In the middle of an endless speech about someone called Proudhon and someone called Bakunin, he leaned forward, put his arms round Four-eyes' bony shoulders and kissed her real hard on the lips. Didn't she squeal! She pushed her hands against his chest, and Senka almost let go – he was no rapist, no sirrah. He was bracing himself for a slap round the face – though with those dainty little hands, she probably wouldn't even make him flinch.

She resisted all right, but she didn't push him off. Senka was surprised, and he carried on kissing her, feeling her ribs with his hands and unfastening the buttons on the back of her dress: maybe she'd come to her senses?

The girl student murmured: 'What are you doing, Semyon, what is this . . . Is it true what George says, that you're . . . Ah, what are you doing! . . . That you're a proletarian?'

Senka growled to make himself seem more like an animal and got really cheeky, slipping his hand in under her dress where it was unbuttoned. The young lady's back was bare at the top, where her backbone stuck out, but lower down he could feel silk underwear.

'You're insane,' she said, panting. Her specs had slipped off sideways and her eyes were half closed.

Senka ran his hands over her this way and that for about a minute, just to make absolutely sure that Masa's theory was correct, and then backed off. She was awfully bony, but then he hadn't started this out of mischief – it was a *scientific experiment*, as they said in cultured circles.

While they were driving back from Sokolniki, the scholarly girl didn't open her mouth once – she kept staring hard at Senka, as if she was expecting something, but he wasn't thinking of her at all, he was having a real epiphany.

So that was the power of learning for you! Knowledge could overcome any obstacle!

The next day at first light he was waiting at the door for Masa.

When his teacher arrived, he led him straight to his room, didn't even let him take his tea.

And he begged Masa in the name of Christ the Lord: Teach me, Sensei, how to win the heart of the creature I adore.

Masa was fine about it, he didn't mock Senka's feelings. He told him to explain in detail what kind of creature they were dealing with. Senka told him everything he knew about Death, and at the end he asked in a trembling voice: 'Well, Uncle Masa, is there really no way I can smite a swan like that with Cupid's arrow?'

His teacher folded his hands on his belly and smacked his lips. Why, he asked, is there no way? For the true admirer all things are possible. And then he said something Senka didn't understand: 'Death-san is a woman of the moon.' There are women of the sun and women of the moon, he explained, they're born into the world like that. I prefer women of the sun, he said, but that's a matter of taste. Women of the moon, like your Death-san, he said, have to be approached like this – and he went through the whole thing with Senka, blow by blow, may God grant him the very best of health.

That very evening Senka set out to see Death – and seek his good fortune.

He didn't dress the way he'd had been planning to earlier – in a white tie with a bouquet of chrysanthemums. He kitted himself out in line with Masa's teachings.

He put on the old shirt that Death had once darned for him, and deliberately tore it under one arm. He bought a pair of patched boots at the flea market, and sewed a patch on a pair of trousers that were perfectly sound.

When he took a look at himself in the mirror, it even made him feel all weepy. He was just sorry that he'd put that tooth in the day before – the gap would have made him look even more pitiful. But he reckoned that if he didn't open his mouth too wide, the gold wouldn't glitter too brightly.

Everything was washed and clean, and he'd been to the bathhouse too. Masa had impressed that on him: 'Poor, but crean, they don' rike dirty admirers.'

Senka got out of the cab on the corner of Solyanka Street and walked up along the Yauza Boulevard. He knocked loudly, but his heart was pounding away even louder.

Death opened the door without calling out, just like she did the time before.

Senka thought she was glad to see him, and the vice gripping his heart loosened a bit. Remembering that tooth, he didn't open his mouth – anyway, the sensei had told him not to wag his jaw unless he really needed to. He was supposed to gaze at her with a pure, trusting look and keep blinking – that was all.

They went into the room and sat down on the sofa, side by side (Senka thought this was a good sign).

He'd had a special haircut done on Neglinnaya Street – 'mon ange', it was called: mop-headed and fluffy on top, with a strand hanging down over his forehead, pathetic but appealing.

'I've been thinking about you,' Death said. 'Wondering if you were alive, if you were starving. Don't stay here long. Someone might tell the Prince. That savage is furious with you.'

Senka had an answer ready. He looked at her through his flaxen strand and sighed. 'I've come to say goodbye to you. I'm not going to get out of this alive anyway, they'll find me and kill me. Let them kill me, I can't bear to be involved in their murderous doings. It contradicts my principles.'

Death was really surprised: 'Where did you pick up fancy words like that?'

Ah, he'd said it all wrong. This was no time to be clever and show off his learning, he had to play on her pity.

'I'm famished, Death, from all this wandering around like a vagabond,' Senka said, and he fluttered his eyelashes – could he coax out a tear? 'My conscience won't let me thieve and I'm ashamed to go begging. The nights have turned cold, it's autumn already. Let me warm up a bit and have a bite to eat and I'll go on my way.'

He was even moved to pity himself, he sobbed out loud. It had worked! Death's eyes were wet and gleaming too. She stroked his hair and jumped up to put food on the table.

Even though Senka was full (before he came out, he'd put away a plate of *poulardes* and artichokes), he still guzzled the fine white bread with sausage and gulped the milk down noisily. Death sat there, resting her cheek on her hand. Sighing.

'You're really nice and clean,' she said in a soulful voice. 'And your shirt's fresh. Who washed it?'

'Who'd wash for me? I get by on my own,' said Senka, looking at her with his eyes glowing. 'In the evening I wash my shirt and pants in the river, and they're dry by morning. 'Course, it's a bit chilly with no clothes on, but I have to look out for myself. Only the shirt's getting a bit shabby. I wouldn't mind, but it's a pity about your needlework.' He stroked the flower sewn on his shirt and turned weepy. 'Look, the shirt's torn under my arm.'

Just like she was supposed to, Death said: 'Take it off, I'll sew it up.'

He took it off.

Mamselle Loretta, the one from the practical class, had said: You've got lovely shoulders, sweetheart, pure sugar, and your skin's so soft and tender, I could just eat it. So now Senka straightened up his sugary shoulders and hugged his sides like a poor orphan.

Death's needle flashed in and out, but she kept glancing at Senka's creamy white skin.

'There was only one moment in my whole miserable life, in all my wretched destiny,' Senka said in a quiet, soulful voice. 'When you kissed me, a poor orphan . . .'

'Really?' Death said in astonishment; she even stopped sewing. 'That was such great happiness for you?'

'There's no words to say what it . . .'

She put down the shirt. 'Lord,' she said, 'then let me kiss you again, what's it to me?'

He turned all pink (that happened quite naturally).

'Ah, then I won't be afraid to snuff it . . .'

But he kept his hands to himself for the time being and just fluttered his eyes – timidly, not brazenly.

Death walked up to him and leaned down. Her eyes were tender and moist. She stroked his neck and his shoulder, then pressed her lips against Senka's so tenderly, so kindly.

He felt like he'd been tossed into a hot stove, right into the flame. He forgot all about his sensei's teachings and jerked upwards towards Death, hugged her as tight as he could and tried to keep kissing her, but in his passion, all he could do was breathe in the minty, dizzying scent of her hair – ah! ah! – and he couldn't breathe it out, he wanted to keep it in.

And something happened, honest to God, it did! Not for long, only a few little seconds, but Death's body responded, it was filled with the same heat, and her gentle, motherly kiss was suddenly firm, greedy and demanding, and her hands slipped round Senka's back.

But those impossible seconds ended – she unhooked Senka's arms and sprang back.

'No,' she said, 'no. You little devil, don't tempt me. It's impossible, and that's an end of it.'

She started shaking her head, like she was trying to drive away some kind of phantasmagorical vision (that was what people said when they saw something that wasn't really there).

'Ooh, you snake, only knee high to a grasshopper, and already as cunning as the devil. You'll make the girls cry all right.'

But Senka was still in the stove, he still hadn't realised it was over, and he reached out to hug Death again. She didn't move away, but she didn't respond either – it was just like hugging a statue.

'Ah, so that's who you do it with, you whore!'

Senka looked round and froze in horror.

The Prince was standing in the doorway with his handsome mug all twisted out of shape and his eyes glittering. Of course – the street door wasn't locked, so he'd just walked in, and they hadn't heard anything.

'Who's this you've taken as a lover, you rotten bitch! A whelp! A lousy little tapeworm! Just trying to mock me, are you?'

He took a step towards Senka, grabbed his numb victim by the neck and jerked him up so that he had to stand on tiptoe.

'I'll kill you,' he said. 'I'll wring your neck.'

And Senka could see he was going to wring it, there and then. At least there was one good thing about that, Senka wouldn't suffer. The Prince could have done what he did with that huckster, cut off his ears and stuck them in his mouth, or even worse, gouged his eyes out.

Senka turned his eyes away so as not to see the Prince's face – he was terrified enough without that. He decided it would be better to look at Death in his final moment, before his soul went flying out of his body.

And what he saw then was wonderful, miraculous: Death picking up the jug with the leftover milk and smashing it down on the bandit's head.

The Prince was startled. He let go of Senka and sank to the floor. Holding his head in his hands, with blood and milk running through his fingers.

Death shouted: 'Don't just stand there! Run.'

And she pushed the shirt she hadn't finished darning into his hand.

But Senka didn't run. Someone else, like a second Senka, said from inside him: 'You come with me. He'll kill you.'

'He won't kill me,' she answered, and so calmly that Senka believed her straight away.

The Prince turned his face towards Senka. His eyes were murky and wild. He jumped to his feet with a jerk, then staggered and clutched at the table – he hadn't properly recovered his wits and his legs wouldn't hold him. But he managed to wheeze out: 'I'll find you, if I have to turn Moscow upside down. Even underground, I'll find you. I'll rip your sinews out with my teeth!'

He was so terrifying Senka just screamed out loud. He shot off as fast as his legs would carry him, tumbled off the porch arse over tit, then dashed this way and that, wondering which way to run.

The second Senka, the one buried farther down, proved cleverer and stronger than the first. Go where the Prince told you to go, it said, go underground. He just hoped he wouldn't have to *emigrate* from Moscow. The Prince would never calm down now until he'd done for the poor orphan.

And if that was how it was looking, he'd better put some money away.

He paid another visit to the treasure vault. And he took a fair lot this time, five rods. He'd decided not to haggle with the jeweller and let him have them for a thousand each. Ashot Ashotovich was welcome to his good fortune.

Only Samshitov never got the chance to relish Senka's generosity.

When Senka came out on to Maroseika Street, he saw two constables in front of the jewellery shop and inside – he could see through the display window – there was a whole crowd of blue uniforms.

Oh blimey! Ashot Ashotovich had traded his last rod of government silver. Someone must have squealed on him. Or maybe Judge Kuvshinnikov was even sharper than he seemed. He'd found out which of the numismatists had picked up Yauza rods and enquired who they bought them from – just like that.

But then, that wasn't so terrible, was it? Senka hadn't given the judge his address. And apart from Senka, no one knew where the treasure was.

The coppers might as well try to catch the wind.

Ah, but no! He'd told the Armenian about Madam Borisenko's boarding house. Big nose would give him away, he was bound to!

Senka didn't hang about making himself obvious in the wrong place. He ran to get a cab.

He had to move out of the boarding house before he was nabbed.

The outlines had emerged of a tendency towards a deterioration in the conditions of Senka's existence, or, to put it simply, things were totally loused up: the Prince was on his tail, so were the police, and there was no one to sell the rods to, but Senka was feeling so cock-a-hoop that he couldn't care less.

The hoofs clip-clopped along the road, the horse twitched its tail, the headwind ruffled the final traces of 'mon ange' from his hair and, in spite of everything, life was wonderful. Senka bobbed along on the seat of the cab, feeling perfectly content.

Maybe not for long, only a few moments, but he *had* been Death's lover, and almost for real.

How Senka's Tongue
Was Loosened

That very evening Senka changed his lodgings. He was going to say goodbye to George, but his teacher had gone off for a wander. And so Senka left English-fashion, like a perfect swine. The only one to see him off to the cab was Madam Borisenko, who had transferred part of her fond feelings for Masa to his pupil. She asked, dismayed: 'And will Masaul Mitsuevich not be calling any more?'

'He'll turn up tomorrow morning for certain,' Senka promised. He still hadn't decided whether he was going to let the Japanese know about his change of address. 'Tell him that Semyon Spidorov said thank you for the trouble he took and wishes him the very best of health.'

Senka had to put as much distance as possible between him and the Prince. So he took off to the back of beyond, even farther west than the Presnya District, and moved into a hotel for railway workers. A good place: nobody knew anybody else, men just spent the night there and then carried on along their way.

And at the same time he changed his name, so no one could pick up his trail. At first he was going to call himself something ordinary, but then he decided that if he was going to change his name, it might as well be something grand, in keeping with his new life. He put himself down in the register of guests *Apollon Sekandrovich Schopenhauer, commercial traveller.*

That night he dreamed of all sorts of things. Steamy scenes of passion (about Death), and frightening scenes of horror (the Prince climbing in through the window, a knife in his teeth, and

Senka getting tangled up in the blanket so he couldn't get out of bed).

At dawn Senka was woken by a loud knocking at the door.

He sat up and clutched at his heart, thinking the Prince and Deadeye had tracked him down. He was all set to scarper down the drainpipe – just as he was, wearing next to nothing – but then he heard Masa's voice.

'Senka-kun, open door!'

Phew! You can't imagine how relieved Senka felt at that. He didn't even wonder how the Japanese had found him there so quickly.

He opened the latch, and Masa walked quickly into the room, followed by (well, blow me down!) Erast Petrovich in person. They both looked gloomy and severe.

Masa stood by the wall, and his master took Senka by the shoulders, turned him to face the window (it was still early, morning twilight) and said briskly. 'Now, Apollon Sekandrovich, no more p-playing the fool. I can't afford to waste any more time on your m-mysterious personality. Tell me everything you know: about the m-murder of the Siniukhins and about the murder of the Samshitovs. This has to be stopped!'

'The Sam . . . Samshitovs!' Senka exclaimed, choking over the name. 'B-but I thought . . .'

Now he'd started stammering too – was it infectious?

'Get d-dressed,' Erast Petrovich told him. 'We're leaving.'

And he walked out into the corridor without bothering to explain anything else.

As he pulled on his trousers and shirt, Senka asked his sensei: 'How did you find me?'

'Cab numba,' Masa replied tersely, and Senka realised Madam Borisenko had remembered the cabby's number, and he'd told them where he took his fare.

So much for keeping things secret and covering his trail. 'And where are we going?'

'To the scene of the clime.'

Oh Lord! What good will this do? But Senka didn't dare argue. This pair would use force, drag him out by the scruff of his neck (we know, we've had a bit of that already).

Senka was feeling terribly nervous all the way to Maroseika Street. And the closer they came, the worse it got. So Ashot Ashotovich hadn't been arrested after all? He'd been done in? Erast Petrovich had said 'the Samshitovs' – so that meant they'd killed his ever-loving wife? Who, robbers? And what did he, Senka Spidorov, have to do with it?

There were no police outside the shop, but there was a string with a seal across the door, and a light burning inside. The street was still empty, the shops hadn't opened, or a crowd of people would have gathered for sure.

They went into the house from the yard, through the back entrance. A police official in a blue uniform was waiting for them – quiet, nondescript, wearing specs.

'You took your time,' he rebuked Erast Petrovich. 'I asked you ... I phoned you at midnight, and now it's half past five. I'm taking a risk here.'

'I'm sorry, Sergei Nikiforovich. We had to f-find an important witness.'

Even though Erast Petrovich had called him important, Senka still didn't like the sound of that. What was he supposed to have witnessed?

'Tell us about this killing,' Erast Petrovich said to the official. 'What was it p-possible to establish from an initial examination?'

'Come this way, please,' said Sergei Four-eyes, beckoning to them. They walked through from the hall into the rooms. 'The jeweller had a kind of office here, at the back of the shop. The living space was upstairs. But the criminal didn't go up there, it all happened down here.' He glanced at his notepad. 'The doctor believes that Nina Akopovna Samshitova, forty-nine years of age, was killed first, with a blow to the temple from a heavy object. Her body was lying just here.'

On the ground by the door there was a rough outline of a

human figure, not a very good likeness, and beside it there was a dark patch. Blood, Senka guessed, and shuddered.

'The criminal tied up Ashot Ashotovich Samshitov, fifty-two years of age, and sat him in this chair. As you can see, there's blood everywhere: on the headrest, the arms, the floor. And both veinous and arterial, different oscillatory fluctuations ... I'm sorry, Erast Petrovich, I'm not being very clear, I don't know medical terminology very well,' the official said, embarrassed. 'You were always at me, trying to get me to study a bit, but the new bosses didn't require it, so I never got round—'

'Never mind that,' Erast Petrovich interrupted. 'I understand: Samshitov was t-tortured before he died. Was a knife used?'

'Probably, or else they stabbed him with a pointed object.'

'And the eyes?'

'What about the eyes?'

'Were the b-bodies' eyes put out?'

'Ah, you're thinking of the Khitrovka murders ...' Sergei Niki-forovich shook his head. 'No, the eyes weren't put out, and the overall picture of the crime is rather different, too. So it has been decided to make this a separate case from the Khitrovka Blinder murders.'

'The Khitrovka B-blinder?' said Erast Petrovich, wincing. 'What a stupid name! I thought only newspapermen used it.'

'It was thought up by the superintendent of the Third Myas-nitsky Precinct, Colonel Solntsev. The reporters pounced on it, although, of course, from a grammatical—'

'All right, to hell with the g-grammar,' said Erast Petrovich, walking round the room. 'Shall we go upstairs?'

'No point. It's quite clear that the killer didn't go up there.'

'Killer? Not killers? Has it been established that there was only one c-criminal?'

'Apparently so. The neighbours testified that Samshitov never served more than one customer at a time, he only let one in the shop then locked the door after them immediately. He was very afraid of being robbed, Khitrovka's not far off, after all.'

'Signs of robbery?'

'None. Nothing's been taken, even in the shop. There are a few trinkets lying in the shop window there, but they're not worth very much. I told you, everything happened in this room.'

Erast Petrovich shook his head and walked through into the shop. The official and Masa followed him. And Senka too – so as not to be left alone in a room splattered with blood.

'And what's this?' asked Erast Petrovich, pointing to the bird-cage.

The parrot Levonchik was lying in it with his head thrown back.

Sergei Nikiforovich shrugged. 'Parrots are nervous birds, sensitive to loud sounds. And there must have been plenty of screaming and groaning . . . His heart gave out. Or perhaps he was left unfed too long.'

'The cage d-door's open. Yes and . . . Aha, t-take a look, Masa.' Erast Petrovich picked up the little body and handed it to Masa.

The Japanese clicked his tongue: 'They wrung it' neck. Murda.'

'Yes, it's a pity the coroner didn't examine it,' the policeman chuckled, evidently thinking that the Oriental was joking, but Senka knew that for his sensei a soul was a soul, whether it was a man's or a bird's.

'How low the p-professionalism of the Moscow d-detective police has sunk,' Erast Petrovich intoned sadly. 'Ten years ago such c-carelessness would have been unimaginable.'

'Don't I know it.' Sergei Nikiforovich sighed even more bitterly. 'Things aren't what they were in your day. You know, I get no satisfaction from the work at all. All they want are results, convictions, they're not interested in proving anything. The triumph of justice doesn't even come into it. Our bosses have different concerns. By the way,' he said, lowering his voice, 'I didn't mention it on the telephone . . . Your presence in Moscow is no secret. I happened by chance to see a secret instruction on the desk of the chief of police: your place of residence is to be determined and you're to be put under secret observation. Someone's recognised you and reported you.'

Erast Petrovich was not in the slightest upset by this news; in fact, he seemed rather flattered: 'It's not surprising, m-many people in Moscow know me. And clearly, they haven't f-forgotten me. Thank you, Subbotin. I know the risks you've taken, and I appreciate it. G-goodbye.'

He shook the man in specs by the hand, and Subbotin muttered in embarrassment: 'Oh, it's nothing. But you should be careful anyway ... Who knows what they've got in mind. His Highness is very vindictive.'

Senka didn't understand who 'they' were – or 'His Highness', for that matter.

From the yard behind Samshitov's shop they walked along a side street to Lubyanka Passage, and then turned into the public garden.

At the very first bench Erast Petrovich gestured, inviting Senka to take a seat. They sat down, Senka in the middle, the other two on either side. A prisoner and his guards.

'Well now, M-Mr Schopenhauer,' said Erast Petrovich, turning towards him. 'Shall we talk?'

'What's it to do with me?' Senka grumbled, knowing this wasn't going to be pleasant. 'I don't know nothing.'

'Deduction t-tells me differently.'

'Who does?' Senka said, cheering up. 'I've never laid eyes on this Deduction of yours. She's a liar, a rotten bitch!'

Erast Petrovich twitched the corner of his mouth. 'This lady, Spidorov (I think I'd b-better address you like that now), never lies. You remember the seventeenth-century silver k-kopeck I found in Siniukhin's pocket after he was killed? Of course you remember it – you ignored it so very p-pointedly. Where would a poor pen-pusher come by a numismatic c-curiosity like that? That is one. Let us continue. At the m-murder scene you deliberately kept turning away and even closing your eyes, although,

173

as Masa has observed, you are c-certainly not short of curiosity. And neither did you d-display the astonishment and horror that are natural at such a sight. You must admit this is strange. That is t-two. To proceed. On that day, there was silver in your p-pocket as well as Siniukhin's, and it was jangling rather loudly. To judge from the sound, the c-coins were small, of a size no longer m-minted in our day. And in your hand you were carrying a rod of p-pure silver, which is entirely out of the ordinary. Where would a Khitrovka g-guttersnipe like you get a small fortune in silver? That is three.'

'Calling me names, now, are you? Swearing at a poor orphan?' Senka asked in a surly tone of voice. 'You ought to be ashamed of yourself, mister, a decent gent like you.'

Masa dug an elbow into his side. 'When Masta say "that one, that two, that three", keep quiet. You frighten away deduction.'

Senka looked round – there wasn't a lady in sight. Who was there to frighten away? But to be safe he held his tongue. So far the sensei had only given him a gentle poke with his elbow, but he could easily belt him a lot harder than that.

Erast Petrovich went on as if he had never been interrupted. 'Although I was not intending to investigate this c-crime, because I am involved in a completely d-different case, your behaviour intrigued me so much that I instructed Masa to look after you. However, the latest b-brutal murder, of which I was informed last night by an old c-colleague of mine, has changed my plans. I have to intervene in this business, because the authorities are clearly not capable of f-finding the killer. The investigating officers cannot even see that these c-crimes are links in a single chain. Why do I think so, you are about to ask?' Senka wasn't about to ask anything of the kind, but he didn't try to argue with the stern gent. 'Well, you see, from M-Maroseika Street to Khitrovka, where the Siniukhins were killed, is only a five-minute walk. These atrocities possess two f-fundamentally similar features that are encountered far too rarely for this to b-be regarded as pure coincidence. The killer is clearly p-pursuing some scheme far too grandiose for him to be d-distracted by mere details such as people or cheap m-medallions in the window of a jeweller's shop. That is one. And another note-worthy f-feature is the diabolical caution that drives the criminal to l-leave no witnesses, not a single living creature, not even one as harmless as a three-year-old infant or a b-bird. That is two. Right, and n-now for you, Spidorov: I am absolutely convinced that you know a great d-deal and can be of help to me.'

Senka had been certain he was going to hear more about the murderer, and was jolted by this abrupt conclusion. Squirming under the keen gaze of those blue eyes, he shouted: 'So they topped that jeweller, what's that got to do with me?'

Masa poked him with his elbow again, harder this time. 'Have you forgotten about the snot-nosed kid? The one who earned a rouble following you? He saw you take the silver sticks into that shop.'

Senka realised there was no point denying it, so he changed tack from market-trader barking to snivelling: 'What is it you want? Why don't you ask properly ... You're just trying to frighten me, beating me in the ribs ...'

'Stop that p-poor-mouthing,' said Erast Petrovich. 'Masa describes you in a most flattering f-fashion. He says that you're not hard hearted, that you have an inquisitive m-mind and – a most v-valuable human quality – you strive towards self-improvement. Previously, before this latest c-crime, Masa simply asked you if you had d-decided to share your secret with us. He was certain that s-sooner or later he would earn your trust and you would want to unburden your heart to him. Now we c-can't wait any longer. No more t-tact or delicacy – I demand that you answer two questions. The first is: what is the murderer l-looking for? And the second is: what do you know about this p-person?'

Masa nodded: *come on, don't be a coward, tell us.*

Well, Senka told them everything, just like at confession. About the bandit deck, and about Deadeye, and about Death, and how the Prince wanted to finish him off, out of jealousy, like.

Well, he didn't tell them *everything*, that goes without saying. He was cagey about the treasure hoard: there was supposed to be something of the kind, but whether it was true or not, Senka didn't know. Well, when people went to confession, they didn't tell the whole truth either, did they?

'So, according to what you say, Spidorov, it seems this P-Prince and his jack killed Siniukhin in an attempt to extort the secret of the t-treasure from him?' Erast Petrovich asked after listening to Senka's rather incoherent story. 'And the Prince p-paid a visit to the antiquary in order to find out your address?'

'It stands to reason. Prokha squealed to him, the rat. He saw me near the shop, I told you! That's why nothing was robbed, the Prince couldn't give a damn for cheap baubles. He wants to get to me.'

'But are you sure the Prince is only l-looking for you out of jealousy?' Erast Petrovich wrinkled up his smooth forehead as if there was something he didn't quite understand. 'Maybe he wants you b-because of the treasure?'

Senka got this sudden aching feeling in his gut: he'd guessed, the wily gent had guessed the whole thing! And now he'd start pestering Senka: You tell me where those silver sticks are hidden.

Just to gain time, Senka started babbling: 'He's so jealous, it's something awful! It's that Deadeye he should be chasing! He's always hanging around Death too. He gives her cocaine, and you know what she gives him. But it's not really 'cause she's a floozy. How can you blame her – when they're on the candy cane, they can't control themselves. It's a real weakness with them . . .'

'In the old days, I b-believe there was a mint in the Yauza District, where they minted silver c-coins,' Erast Petrovich declared thoughtfully when Senka paused for breath. 'All right, I'm not interested in the t-treasure right now. Tell me, Spidorov, c-can you introduce me to this intriguing individual who has d-driven the underworld *beau monde* insane. You say they c-call her Death? What a d-decadent name.'

Senka's heart suddenly felt lighter.

'I can introduce you. But what's going to happen to me, eh? You won't give me away to the Prince, will you?'

How Senka Saw a Scene from Boccaccio

Erast Petrovich, righteous man that he was, didn't abandon the poor orphan to the mercy of fate. In fact, he told him to collect his things and took him off to his own apartment, the one on Asheulov Lane, where Senka had the unfortunate idea (or perhaps it wasn't unfortunate at all, but the very opposite – how could you tell?) of nicking that bundle from the 'Chinee'.

It was a queer sort of apartment, not like what normal people had.

In one room there wasn't any furniture at all, just stripy mattresses on the floor and that was all. That was where Masa and his master did their *renzu*, Japanese gymnastics. Just watching it was frightening. The way they flailed away with their arms and legs, it was a miracle they didn't kill each other. Masa tried to get Senka to join in and scrap with them, but he got scared and ran off into the kitchen.

The kitchen was interesting too. Masa was in charge there. There was no stove, and no barrels of pickled cabbage or cucumbers. But in one corner there was this big cupboard called a 'refrigerator', which was always as cold as an ice cellar on the inside, and there was raw fish in it, on plates. The two tenants cut the fish into pieces, sprinkled it with brown vinegar and ate it just like that, with rice. They tried to give Senka some for breakfast too, but he didn't touch the heathen muck and just chewed a bit of rice. And he didn't drink the tea, either, because it wasn't right at all – a funny yellow colour, it was, and not sweet at all.

Senka was given a place to sleep in his sensei's room – there weren't even any beds there, nothing but mats on the floor, like in Kulakov's dosshouse. *Never mind*, Senka thought, *better to sleep on the floor than in the cold damp ground with a pen stuck in your side. We'll stick it out.*

The weirdest place of all was the master's study. Well, that's what it was called, but it was more like a mechanic's workshop really. The books on the shelves were mostly technical, in foreign languages: the desk was heaped high with strange drawings (they were called 'blueprints', with lots of very complicated lines); there were different-shaped bits of metal lying round the walls, with springs, rubber hoops and all sorts of other stuff. That was because Erast Petrovich was an engineer, he'd studied in America. Even his name wasn't Russian: Mr Nameless. Senka really wanted to ask him what he needed all these thingamajigs for, but on that first day of his life on Asheulov Lane, there was no time for that.

They slept until late, after the kind of night they'd had. When they woke up, Mr Nameless and Masa were off, leaping about on the mattresses and yelling, battering away at each other, then they ate some of their raw fish, and Senka took Erast Petrovich off to meet Death.

On the way they started arguing about what she – Death that is – was like, good or bad.

Erast Petrovich said she was bad. 'Judging from what you have t-told me, Spidorov, this woman revels in her ability to m-manipulate men, and not just any men, but the most c-cruel and pitiless of criminals. She is aware of their atrocities and lives a c-comfortable life on stolen money, but she is not g-guilty of anything herself, as it were. I am familiar with this b-breed, it can be found in all countries and in all classes of society. These so-called *femmes fatales* or infernal women are absolutely immoral creatures, they p-play with people's lives, it is the only game that brings them any pleasure. Surely you can see that she was just t-toying with you, like a cat with a mouse?'

And when he said that Erast Petrovich was really angry, not like himself at all, as if he'd really suffered at the hands of these infernal women and they'd torn his life apart.

Only Death wasn't any kind of infernal woman and she wasn't immoral either, she was just unhappy. She didn't revel in anything, she was simply lost, she couldn't find her way. Senka told Erast Petrovich that. And he didn't just say it – he shouted it out loud.

Erast Petrovich sighed and smiled – sadly, not sneering. 'All right, Spidorov,' he said. 'I didn't wish to offend your f-feelings, only I'm afraid there's a painful d-disappointment in store for you. Well then, is she really so very lovely, this Khitrovka C-Carmen?'

Senka knew who Carmen was, he'd gone to the Bolshoi Theatre to see her with George. She was a fat Spanish woman with a big, loud voice who kept stamping her big feet and sticking her hands on her fat hips. Erast Petrovich looked like a clever man but he didn't understand a thing about women. He could do with a few lessons from his servant.

'Your Carmen's a swamp toad compared with Death,' Senka said, and spat to emphasise his point.

At the turn from Pokrovsky Boulevard on to Yauza Boulevard, Senka half stood up in the cab, then ducked back down and pressed himself down into the seat.

'That's her house,' he whispered. 'Only we can't go there now. See those two hanging about over there? That's Cudgel and Beak, they're from the Ghoul's deck. If they see me, there'll be trouble.'

Erast Petrovich leaned forward and tapped the driver on the shoulder. 'Drive round the c-corner and stop on Solyanka Street.' And to Senka he said: 'Apparently there's something interesting g-going on. I'd like to take a look.'

When they'd driven past the Ghoul's men, Senka straightened up again. 'A look's not very likely, but you could have a listen.'

And he led Erast Petrovich to the house through the back alleys.

The barrel that Senka had rolled up to the window was still standing where he left it.

'Can you get through there?' Senka asked, pointing to the half-open window of the water closet.

Mr Nameless jumped straight up on to the barrel from where he was standing, without any run-up, then he jumped again, pulled himself up with his hands and wormed his way through the small square opening, without any real effort. His heels disappeared inside. Senka climbed in too – not as nimbly, but even so he was in the privy soon enough.

'A strange way of g-getting in to see a lady,' Erast Petrovich whispered, helping Senka to climb down. 'What is behind the d-door?'

'The room,' Senka gasped. 'The sitting room, that is. We could open the door a crack, quiet like, only just a little bit.'

'Hmm, I see you have already p-patented this method of observation.'

And that was the end of the conversation.

Erast Petrovich opened the door a little bit, just a hair's breadth, and put his eye to the crack. Senka tried arranging himself this way and that way (he was interested too) and eventually found the right position: he squatted down on his haunches and pressed himself against Mr Nameless's hip, with his forehead against the doorpost. That is, he took a seat in the stalls.

He couldn't believe his eyes – there had to be something wrong with them!

Death and the Ghoul were standing in the middle of the room with their arms round each other, and that greasy-haired slug was stroking her shoulder!

Senka either sobbed or sniffed – he couldn't tell which it was himself – and he got a quick slap round the back of the head from Mr Nameless.

'Ah, my lovely,' the Ghoul purred in a slimy voice. 'Now that's real consolation, that sweetens life up a bit. Of course, I'm not the Prince, I can't give you gemstones, but I'll bring you a silk scarf, from India. Incredibly beautiful, it is!'

'Give it to your moll,' said Death, backing off.

He grinned. 'Jealous? My Manka's not jealous. I'm in here with you, and she's round the corner, keeping watch.'

'Then give it to her, for her trouble. I don't want your presents. That's not what I love you for.'

'What is it, then?' the Ghoul asked, smiling even more broadly (Senka winced – his teeth were all yellow and rotten). 'The Prince is a real wild one, but I'm better, am I?'

She gave a short, unpleasant laugh. 'No one's better than you in my mind.'

The Ghoul stared at her and screwed his eyes up. 'I can't understand you . . . But then, no one has enough nous to understand you women.'

He grabbed her by the shoulders and started kissing her. In his despair Senka hit his head against the wooden door – loudly. Erast Petrovich smacked him round the head again, but it was too late.

The Ghoul swung round sharply and pulled out his revolver. 'Who've you got in there?'

'Well, aren't you the nervous one, and you a businessman too,' said Death, wiping her lips in disgust. 'It's the draught blowing through the house, slamming the doors.'

There was a sudden whistle. And from close by too – inside the hallway, was it?

A hoarse voice (that was Beak, the one with the collapsed nose) said: 'Manka's given the shout – the superintendent's on his way from Podkolokolny. With flowers. Maybe he's coming here?'

'Walking through Khitrovka, on his own?' the Ghoul asked, surprised. 'With no coppers? That takes guts.'

'Boxman's with him.'

The Ghoul disappeared like a shot. Then he shouted – probably from the hallway: 'All right, darling, we'll talk later. Give my regards to the Prince – that stag has big horns!'

The door slammed and it went quiet.

Death poured some brown water out of a carafe (Senka knew it was Jamaica rum) and took a sip, but she didn't drink it, just rinsed out her mouth and spat it back into the glass. Then she took a piece of paper out of her pocket, unfolded it and held it up to her nose. After she'd breathed in the white powder, she relaxed a little bit and started sighing.

But Senka didn't have any cocaine, so he just sat there numb, as if he'd turned into a block of ice. So an honest young lad with sugar-sweet shoulders and a *'mon ange'* didn't suit her, she couldn't do it with him! But she could with this sticky-lipped slimeball?

Senka moved – and the engineer's fingers beat a warning tattoo on the top of his head: Sit still, it's too soon to come out.

Oh Lord, it couldn't be true! Only it was, she was a whore with no morals at all, Erast Petrovich was right . . .

But this was only the first shock for Senka.

A minute went by, or maybe two, and there was a knock at the door.

Death swayed on her feet and pulled her shawl tight across her chest. She shouted: 'It's open!'

There was a jangle of spurs, and a bold officer's voice said: 'Here I am, Mademoiselle Morte. I promised to come for your answer at exactly five, and as a man of honour, I have kept my word. You decide: this is a bunch of violets, and this is an order for your arrest. Choose for yourself.'

Senka didn't understand at first what violets had to do with anything, but then Superintendent Solntsev – it was his voice – went on to say:

'As I already told you, I am in possession of reliable information from my agents which demonstrates beyond all doubt that you are involved in a criminally culpable relationship with the bandit and murderer Dron Vesyolov, also known as the Prince.'

'And why waste government money on paying your agents? Everybody knows about me and the Prince,' Death answered in a casual voice, sounding almost bored.

'It's one thing to know, and another to have properly documented and signed witness statements and, in addition, photographic pictures taken secretly, according to the very latest method. That, Fräulein Tod, contravenes two articles of the Criminal Code. Six years of exile. And a good prosecutor will tack on aiding and abetting banditry and murder. That's hard labour, seven years of it. It's appalling even to think what the guards – and anyone else whose fancy you tickle – will do with a girl from a simple family like you. I don't envy your beauty. You'll come out a total ruin.'

Then Colonel Solntsev himself appeared in the crack of the door – smart and spruce, with that gleaming parting. He really was holding a bunch of Parma violets ('cunning' in the language of flowers) in one hand, and a piece of paper in the other.

'Well, and what is it you want?' Death asked, setting her hands on her hips, which really did make her look like the Spanish woman in the opera. 'Do you want me to betray my lover to you?'

'What the hell do I want with that Prince of yours!' the superintendent exclaimed. 'When the time comes, I'll take him anyway! You know perfectly well what I want from you. I used to beg before, but now I demand. If you won't be mine, then it's penal servitude! On the word of an officer!'

A steely muscle in Erast Petrovich's thigh twitched – Senka felt it with his cheek – and Senka's own hands clenched into tight fists. What a rotten louse that superintendent was!

But Death only laughed. 'My gallant knight, do you woo all the ladies this way?'

'I've never wooed anyone,' said Solntsev, and his voice was trembling with passion. 'They come running after me. But you

. . . you have driven me out of my mind! What's that criminal to you? Tomorrow or the next day, he'll be lying in the gutter, shot full of holes by police bullets. But I'll give you everything: full upkeep, protection from your former friends, the position you deserve. I can't marry you – I won't lie, and you wouldn't believe me anyway. But love and marriage are quite different substances. When the time comes for me to marry, I won't choose my bride for her beauty, and my heart will still belong to you. Oh, I have great plans! The day will come when you'll be the uncrowned queen of Moscow, and perhaps even more! Well?'

Death didn't answer straight away. She tilted her head, and looked at him as though he was some curious object.

'Tell me something else,' she said. 'I just can't make up my mind.'

'Ah, so that's the way!' said the superintendent, flinging the bouquet down on the floor. 'All's fair in love and war. I won't just throw you in prison, I'll close down that damn orphans' poorhouse you support. It runs on stolen money and it only raises more thieves! Don't you forget, my word's as tough as steel!'

'Now that's more like it,' said Death, smiling at something. 'That's convincing. I agree. Tell me your terms and conditions, Innokentii Romanich.'

The colonel seemed rather taken aback by this sudden compliance, and he backed away a couple of steps, which took him out of view again.

But it didn't take him long to recover. There was a creak of boot leather and a hand in a white glove reached down to pick up the bouquet.

'I do not understand you, Señora Morte, but let that be, it is not important. Only bear in mind that I am a proud man and I will not be made a fool of. If you take it into your head to cheat me . . .' His fist clenched round the violets so tightly that all the stems snapped. 'Is that clear?'

'Yes, that's clear. Get to the point.'

'All right, then.' Solntsev reappeared in the crack. He was about to present her with the bouquet, but then he noticed that the flowers were limp and lifeless, and tossed them on to the table. 'Until I take out the Prince, you will live here. I'll come in secret, at night. And you'd better be affectionate! I don't tolerate coldness in love.'

He took off his gloves, threw them on the table too and reached out for her.

'And won't you be afraid to come to me?' Death asked. 'Doesn't it frighten you?'

The superintendent's hands dropped. 'That's all right. I'll bring Boxman with me. The Prince won't dare stick his nose in with him around.'

'I don't mean the Prince,' she said quietly, moving closer. 'Isn't it a fearful thing to toy with Death? Have you never heard what happens to my lovers?'

He laughed. 'Nonsense. Tall tales for ignorant proles.'

She laughed as well, but in a way that made Senka's skin crawl. 'Why, Innokentii Romanich, you're a materialist. That's good, I like materialists. Well then, let's go to the bedroom, since you're so very brave. I'll give you the sweetest hugging I can.'

Oh, didn't Senka just groan at that! To himself, of course, quietly, but that only made the groan all the more painful. What George said about women was right: *Mon cher*, essentially they are all bedspreads. They lay themselves out for whoever pushes the hardest.'

Senka thought the superintendent would go dashing into the bedroom after what she'd just said, but he jangled his watch and sighed. 'I am ablaze with passion, but I cannot quench the flames now, I've been called to the police chief's office to report at half past six. I'll drop in late this evening. And mind now, no tricks!'

The brazen dog patted Death on the cheek and walked to the door, jingling his spurs.

Death took out her handkerchief and lifted it to her face, as if she was going to wipe her cheek, but she didn't. She sat down at the table and sank her face into her crossed arms. If she had started to cry, Senka would have forgiven her everything, but she didn't cry – her shoulders didn't shake, and he couldn't hear any sobbing. She just sat there like that.

Senka raised his head and gave Mr Nameless a rueful look: *what a fool I am.*

But he shook his head thoughtfully and moved his lips, and Senka guessed rather than heard what he said: 'An interesting individual . . .'

Erast Petrovich winked at him, as if to say: *don't let it get you down.* Then he signalled – the time had clearly come to get involved.

But more footsteps came – not crisp steps, like the superintendent's, but heavy, plodding ones, with a bit of a shuffle.

'Well then, begging your pardon,' said a gruff bass voice.

Boxman! Senka grabbed Mr Nameless by the knee: *Stop, you mustn't go out!* 'His Honour forgot his gloves. He sent me, decided not to come himself.'

Death raised her head. No, there weren't any tears on her face, but her eyes were blazing even brighter than they always did.

'I should think not.' She laughed. 'Innokentii Romanich made such a grand exit. Coming back for his gloves would spoil the whole effect. Take them, Ivan Fedotich.'

She picked the gloves up off the table and threw them to him. But Boxman didn't go straight away.

'Oh, girl, girl, just look at what you're doing to yourself! God gave you all that beauty, and you drag it through the mud, you mock God's gift. That peacock came out of here gleaming like a fresh-polished boot. So you didn't refuse him either. But that titch is nothing, he's not even a peacock – he's a wet chicken. And the Prince, your fancy man, is a festering pimple. Squeeze him, and he'll burst. Is that the kind you really want? You've got fog in your head and a darkness in your soul. You need a straightforward, strong man with a huge fortune, something you can cling to while you catch your breath and get your feet on the ground.'

Death raised her eyebrows in surprise: 'What's this, Ivan Fedotich. Have you turned matchmaker in your old age? I'd be interested to know who you want to match me with. Who is this rich man you talk of?'

Just then an angry voice shouted from somewhere – could it have been the hallway?

'Boxman, you idle good-for-nothing, what are you doing in there so long?'

Boxman finished his piece in a hurry: 'I only want what's good for you, you miserable fool. I have in mind a certain man, who would be your strength and protection and salvation. I'll call in later and we'll have a little talk.'

There was tramping of heavy boots, and the door slammed.

Death was alone again, but she didn't sit down at the table this time. She walked to the far corner of the room, where the cracked mirror hung, stood in front of it and examined herself. She shook her head and even seemed to mutter something under her breath, but Senka couldn't make it out.

'Well now, Semyon Spidorov,' Mr Nameless whispered. 'Pardon the literary allusion, but this scene is straight from Boccaccio. Right, I'll join in and try my luck. I bet my entrance will be even more impressive than the departure of Colonel Solntsev. And you climb back out, there's nothing for you here. Through the window, at the double!' And he pointed the way.

Senka didn't argue. He stepped on to the china bowl (a 'lavatory basin', it was called, they had the same kind in the bordello, and there was another kind of bowl too, for women to rinse themselves off, that was called a 'bidet') and he pretended to be reaching up to the little window, only when Erast Petrovich knocked on the door and stepped into the room, Senka tumbled straight back down again. Resumed his observation post, so to speak.

How Senka Was Disillusioned with People

Erast Petrovich stepped unhurriedly into the centre of the room and tipped his hat (today he was wearing a checked cap with the earflaps turned up).

'Do not be alarmed, dear lady. I will not d-do you any harm.'

Death did not turn round, she looked at her uninvited guest through the cracked mirror. She shook her head and ran her hand across the surface, then she looked over her shoulder, with a surprised expression on her face.

He bowed gently. 'No, I am not a v-vision or a hallucination.'

'Then go to hell,' she snapped, and turned back to the mirror. 'What a nerve you have! I only need to say the word, and you'll be torn to pieces, whoever you are.'

Erast Petrovich walked closer. 'I see you were not at all f-frightened. You really are a m-most unusual woman.'

'Ah, so that was why the door creaked,' she said, as if she was talking to herself. 'And I thought it was a draught. Who are you? Where did you spring from? Did you jump up out of the sewer, then?'

He replied sternly to that: 'For you, m-mademoiselle, I am an emissary of fate, and fate "jumps up" out of anywhere it sees f-fit, sometimes from very strange places indeed.'

At that she finally turned round to face him with a look in her eyes that seemed puzzled, not contemptuous – hopeful even, Senka thought.

'An emissary of fate?' she repeated.

'Why, don't I look the p-part?'

She moved towards him and looked into his face.

'I don't know ... perhaps you do.'

Senka groaned – they couldn't have stood in a less fortunate position. Mr Nameless's tall figure concealed Death completely, and even he was visible only from the back.

'Excellent,' he said. 'Then I shall speak p-poetically, as behoves an emissary of fate. My lady, a cloud of evil has c-condensed above the part of Moscow where you and I now stand. From time to t-time it waters the earth with a b-bloody rain. This cloud of iron-grey is not b-borne away by the wind, it seems to be held in place by some k-kind of magnet. And I suspect that m-magnet is you.'

'Me?' Death exclaimed in an agitated voice, and took one step to the side. Senka could see her clearly now. Her face looked bewildered, nothing like the way it usually was.

Erast Petrovich also moved, as if he wanted to keep some distance between them.

'A wonderful t-tablecloth,' he declared. 'I have never seen such a marvellous d-design before. Who embroidered it? You? If you did, you have genuine t-talent.'

'That's not what you were talking about,' she interrupted. 'What makes you think the blood is shed because of me?'

'The fact, Madame Death, that you have g-gathered around your good self the most d-dangerous criminals in the city. The Prince, a murderer and b-bandit, who supports you. A monster by the name of D-Deadeye, who supplies you with c-cocaine. The Ghoul, an extortionist and low scoundrel, whom you also seem to covet f-for some reason. What do you want with this c-cabinet of curiosities, this collection of aberrations?'

She said nothing for a long time. Senka thought she wasn't going to answer at all. But then she did.

'I suppose I need them.'

'Who are you?' Mr Nameless exclaimed angrily. 'A g-greedy wealth-grubber? A vainglorious woman who likes to imagine herself as the q-queen of villains? A hater of men? A madwoman?'

'I am Death,' she declared quietly and solemnly.

He muttered in a barely audible voice: 'Another one? Isn't that t-too many for one city?'

'What do you mean by that?'

He walked up close to her and said sharply, insistently: 'What do you know about the m-murder of the Siniukhins and the Samshitovs? These c-crimes bear the signs of some strange satanic idolatry: either the eyes are p-put out, or every living thing is exterminated, even a p-parrot in its cage. A genuine b-banquet of death.' His shoulders twitched.

'I don't know anything about that. Who are you, a policeman?' She looked into his eyes. 'No, they don't have people like that in the police.'

He shook his head abruptly, in either annoyance or embarrassment.

'I b-beg your pardon, I forgot to introduce myself. Erast Petrovich N-Nameless, engineer.'

'An engineer? Then why are you interested in murders?'

'There are two phenomena that n-never leave me indifferent. The first is when evildoing g-goes unpunished and the second is a mystery. The f-former rouses an anger in my soul that will not allow me to breathe until j-justice has been restored. And the latter d-deprives me of sleep and rest. In this story both phenomena are evident: m-monstrous iniquity and a mystery – you. I have to s-solve this mystery.'

She smiled mockingly. 'And how do you intend to solve me? In the same way as the other lovers of riddles?'

'That has yet to be s-seen,' he replied after a brief pause. 'But you are quite right, there is a t-terrible draught.'

He swung round, walked straight towards Senka and closed the door; he even propped it shut with a chair. Now Senka couldn't see a thing, and he could hardly hear anything that was happening in the room.

But he didn't even want to hear any more anyway. He crawled

out through the window, feeling sad. With a broken heart, you might say.

Senka was overwhelmed by total and complete disillusionment with human beings. Take this Erast Petrovich: he seemed like a serious man, very dignified, but he was the same kind of randy goat as all the rest of them. And the airs and graces he put on! Who could you trust in this world, who could you respect?

It went without saying that Mr Nameless would have her 'solved' now in a jiffy. Solving a floozie like that didn't take any real effort, Senka thought, beating himself up. Oh, women! Cheap, treacherous creatures! The only one who was true was Tashka. She might be a mamselle, but she was honest. Or was that just because she was still young yet? Probably when she grew up, she'd be like all the rest of them.

How Senka Pulled the Choke Out too Far

Senka felt so sad and disillusioned, he just walked where his feet took him, gazing deep inside himself instead of looking around. And by force of habit his stupid feet took him out on to Khitrovka Square, the last place where Senka should be making a public show of himself. If anyone saw him, they'd whistle for the Prince, and then it would be farewell, Semyon Trifonich, that's the last we'll see of you.

When he realised where he was, he was terrified. He raised the collar of his jacket, pulled the boater down over his eyes and walked off rapidly towards Tryokhsvyatsky Lane – from there it was only a stone's throw to places that were safe.

Then suddenly, talk of the devil, there was Tashka walking towards him. Not alone, though, with a client. He looked like a counter-clerk from a shop. Drunk, with a bright-red face. And one armed draped over Tashka's shoulders – he could hardly even walk.

What a fool she was to be so proud! Why did she need to let herself get pawed and mauled like that for just three roubles? And there was no way of telling her it was a shame and a disgrace – she didn't understand. Of course not, she'd lived in Khitrovka all her life. Her mother was a whore, her grandmother too.

Senka was going to go over and say hello. Tashka saw him too, but she didn't nod, and she didn't smile either. She just made big, round eyes at him and jabbed her finger at her hair. There was a flower in it, she must have put it there for an occasion like this. A red poppy – 'danger'.

But who was the danger for, him or her?

He went across anyway and opened his mouth to speak, but Tashka hissed: 'Clear off out of it, you fool. He's after you.'

'Who is?'

Then the counter-clerk stuck his oar in. He stamped his foot and started making threats. 'What you doin'? Who are you? This little mamselle's mine! I'll rip your face off!'

Tashka punched him in the side and whispered: 'Tonight . . . Come tonight, then I'll tell you something really important . . .' and she dragged her admirer on down the street.

Senka didn't like the way she was whispering. It wasn't like Tashka to frighten him for nothing. Something must have happened. He'd have to go and see her.

He was thinking of waiting on the boulevard for night to come, but then he had a better idea.

Since he was already here, in Khitrovka, why not pay a visit to the basement and lay in a bit more silver? He had the other five rods hidden in his suitcase, wrapped up in his long-johns. It couldn't hurt to have a few more. Who could tell which way fate would take him now? What if he suddenly had to leave his native parts in a hurry?

He took another four rods. So that made nine altogether. That was serious capital, no matter which way you looked at it. Ashot Ashotovich, may he rest in peace, wasn't around any longer, but Senka would just have to hope that some other intermediary would turn up sooner rather than later. Thinking that way was a sin, of course, but the dead had their own interests and the living had theirs.

When he clambered out of the passage into the basement with the brick pillars ('columns' was the cultured word), Senka moved the stones back into place, took two of the sticks in each hand and set off through the dark basement towards the exit on Podkolokolny Lane.

He only had two more turns to make when something terrible happened.

Something heavy hit Senka on the back of the neck – and so hard that his nose smashed into the ground before he even had time to squeal. He still hadn't realised how much trouble he was in when he was pinned to the floor, with a hobnailed boot to his back.

Senka floundered this way and that, gulping at the air. The rods went flying out of his left hand, jangling sweetly on the flagstones of the floor.

'A-a-agh!' poor Senka yelped, as steely fingers grabbed him by the hair and wrenched his head so far back his neck-bones cracked.

Out of sheer animal terror – it had nothing to do with courage – Senka swung the rods clutched in his right hand up behind him. He hit something, then he struck at it again with all his might. And then he struck it once more. Something up there gave a grunt, deep and hollow like a bear's. The massive hand clutching Senka's hair let go, and the boot shifted off his back.

Senka rolled over sideways, spinning like a top, got up on all fours, then on to his feet and dashed off, howling, into the darkness. When he ran into a wall, he recoiled and ran in the opposite direction.

He darted down the steps into the dark night street and ran as far as Lubyanka Square. Beside the low wall round the pool he dropped to his knees, and plunged his face into the water, and it wasn't until after he'd cooled off a bit that he noticed he'd dropped the rods.

To hell with them. He was alive, that was what mattered.

'Where did you g-get to, Spidorov?' Mr Nameless asked as he opened the door of the apartment. Then he grabbed Senka by the arm and led him over to a lamp. 'Who d-did this to you? What happened?'

He'd noticed the bump on Senka's forehead and the swollen nose he'd smashed against the stone floor.

'The Prince tried to kill me,' Senka replied morosely. 'Almost broke my neck.'

And he told Erast Petrovich what had happened. Of course, he didn't say exactly where he'd been, or that he was carrying silver rods. He just said he'd looked into Yeroshenko's basement, on some business or other, and that was where the terrible precedent happened.

'Incident,' Erast Petrovich corrected him without thinking, and a long crease appeared across his forehead. 'Did you g-get a good look at the Prince?'

'What do I need a good look for?' Senka asked, mournfully studying his face in a mirror. What a nose – a real baked potato. 'Who else wants to do me in? The Yerokha riff-raff won't attack just anyone, they take a look first to see who it is. But this lug hit me without any warning, and real hard too. It was either the Prince or someone from his deck. Only not Deadeye – he wouldn't have messed about, he'd have stuck his foil or his little knife straight in my eye. But where's Masa-sensei?'

'He has a prior engagement.' Mr Nameless took hold of Senka's chin and turned it this way and that – inspecting his face. 'You need a c-compress. And mercurochrome here. Does that hurt?'

'Yes!' Senka yelled, because Erast Petrovich had taken a firm grip on his nose with his finger and thumb.

'Never m-mind, it will heal soon enough. It's not b-broken.'

Mr Nameless was wearing a long silk dressing gown and had a fine net over his hair – to hold his coiffure in place. Senka had one like that too, it was called a 'garde-façon'.

I wonder how it went with Death, Senka thought, glancing at the engineer's smooth face out of the corner of his eye. Well, it was obvious enough. A fancy trotter like that wouldn't let his chance slip.

'Well then, Herr Schopenhauer, l-listen to me,' Erast Petrovich declared when he had finished smearing smelly gunk on Senka's face. 'From n-now on you stick with Masa and me. Is that c-clear?'

'Why wouldn't it be?'

'Excellent. Then g-go to bed, and straight into the sweet embrace of Morpheus.'

Senka went to bed all right, but it took him some time to cuddle up to Morpheus. Either his teeth started chattering, or he started shivering and just couldn't get warm. It was only natural. Doom had flitted by awfully close and brushed his soul with its icy wing.

He remembered that he hadn't gone to see Tashka. She'd said she wanted to tell him something, to warn him. He ought to go and visit her, but the very thought of going back to Khitrovka gave him the shakes, even worse than before.

If he slept on it, maybe in the morning everything wouldn't seem so terrible. He fell asleep with that thought.

But the next day he still felt really afraid. And the day after, and the day after that too. He was afraid for a long time, a whole week. In the morning or the afternoon, if it wasn't that bad, he'd think: today's the day, I'll go as soon as it gets dark. But by the time evening came he had that anxious feeling again, and his legs refused to carry him to Khitrovka.

It wasn't as if all Senka did on those days was sit around and feel afraid. There were lots of things to be done, and the kind of things that could make you forget everything else in the world.

It all started when Erast Petrovich made a suggestion. 'How would you like to t-take a look at my "Flying C-Carpet"?'

This was just after they'd had a conversation in which Senka begged him in the name of Christ the Lord to stop calling him 'Spidorov', because that offended him.

'It offends you?' Mr Nameless asked in surprise. 'The fact that I address you f-formally? But I think you consider yourself an adult, d-don't you? Between adults, less formal modes of address

197

require s-some kind of reciprocal feeling, and I am not yet ready to address you in a m-more intimate manner.'

'But you talk to Masa over there like a close friend, don't you? It's like I'm not even a human being for you.'

'You see, Spidorov ... I beg your pardon, I m-mean Mr Spidorov,' the engineer said, beginning to get really annoyed with Senka, 'I address Masa informally and he addresses me formally, because in J-Japan that is the only way in which master and s-servant can converse. In Japanese etiquette the n-nuances of speech are regulated very strictly. There are a dozen or so d-different levels of formality or informality for all kinds of relationships, whenever you address s-someone else. To address a servant in an inappropriate m-manner is quite grotesque, it is actually a g-grammatical mistake.

'But here in Russia it's only the intelligensia that talks to simple people politely, so they can show how much they despise them. That's why the people don't like them.'

Senka barely managed to persuade him. And even then, Erast Petrovich still wouldn't call him 'Senka', like a mate. Instead of 'Spidorov', he began calling him 'Senya', as if he was some little gent's son in short pants. Senka had to grin and bear it.

When Senka started batting his peepers at the words 'Flying Carpet' (he was prepared to expect all sorts of marvels from this gent, even magic), Erast Petrovich smiled.

'It's not magical, of c-course. It's the name I've given to my three-wheeler m-motor car, a self-propelled carriage of my own d-design. Come on, you can take a l-look at it.'

Standing in the coach shed out in the yard was a carriage like a cab with sprung wheels, only it narrowed towards the front, and instead of four wheels, it only had three: the front one was low, with rounded sides, and the two at the back were big. Where the front board would be on a cab, there was a wooden board with numbers on it, and a little wheel sticking out on an iron stick, and some little levers and other fiddly bits and pieces. The seat was box calf leather and it could take three people. The engineer pointed all these things out.

'On the right, where the wheel is, that's the d-driver's seat. On the left is the assistant's seat. The driver is like a c-coachman, only instead of horses, he drives the m-motor. Sometimes you need two people – to t-turn the wheel or hold a lever in place, or just to wave a f-flag so that people will get out of the way.'

Senka didn't twig straight off that this lump of metal would go all on its own, without a horse. According to what Erast Petrovich said (which was probably horse shit anyway), the iron box under the seat contained the strength of ten horses, so this three-wheeler could dash along the road faster than any wild cabby.

'Soon n-nobody will want to use horses for p-pulling their carriages,' Mr Nameless told him. 'They'll all want automobiles l-like this, with an internal combustion engine. Then horses will be liberated from their heavy labour, and in g-gratitude for their service to humanity over the millennia, they will be s-set free to graze in the meadows. Well, p-perhaps the most beautiful and spirited will be kept for races and romantic d-drives by moonlight, but all the others will be retired with a p-pension.'

Well now, I don't know about a pension, Senka thought. If horses aren't needed any longer, they'll just be slaughtered for their skins and meat, no one's going to feed them out of the kindness of their hearts. But he didn't try to argue with the engineer, he was curious to hear what would come next.

'You see, Senya, the idea of a three-wheeled motor car for all kinds of terrain was the subject of my diploma last year at the Technical Institute . . .'

'You mean you were still a student just last year?' Senka asked in surprise. Erast Petrovich looked really old. Maybe thirty-five, or even more – his temples were all grey already.

'No, I took the mechanical engineering course as an external student, in Boston. And now the time has come to make my idea a reality, to test it in practice.'

'But what if it won't go?' asked Senka, admiring the gleaming copper lamp on the front of the machine.

'Oh, no, it goes very well, but that's not enough. I intend to set a record with my three-wheeler, by travelling all the way from Moscow to Paris. The start is set for the twenty-third of September, so there's not much time left to prepare, just a little over two weeks. And it's a difficult business, almost impossible in fact. A similar journey was attempted recently by Baron von Liebnitz, but his automobile wasn't hardy enough for the Russian roads, and it fell apart. My "Flying Carpet" will survive them, though, because the three-wheel design is better suited to bad roads than a four-wheeler, and I shall prove it. And then, there's this, look.'

Senka had never seen Erast Petrovich looking so lively. His eyes were usually cool and calm, but now they were sparkling, and his cheeks were flushed. Mr Nameless was quite unrecognisable.

'Instead of the new-fangled pneumatic tyres, which are perfectly convenient for an asphalt street, but entirely inappropriate for our appalling roads, I have designed single-piece solid rubber tyres with steel wire.'

Senka prodded a black tyre. The pimpled, springy surface felt pleasant to the touch.

'The design is based on the "Patent-Motorwagen" from the Benz factory, but the "Flying Carpet" is far more advanced! On his new "Velo" Herr Benz has only a three-horse-power motor and the gear-wheel drive is attached to the rear axle, while I have moved it to the frame – look! – and I have a motor of almost one thousand cubic centimetres! That makes it possible to reach a speed of thirty versts an hour. And on an asphalt surface up to thirty-five! Perhaps even forty! Just imagine!'

Senka was infected by the engineer's excitement. He sniffed at the seat, and it smelled of leather and kerosene. Very tasty!

'And how do you ride on this carpet?'

'Sit here. That's it,' said Erast Petrovich, delighted to explain, and Senka started swaying blissfully on the springy seat. 'You'll start moving in just a moment. It's quite delightful, there's nothing to compare it with. Only be careful, don't rush. Put your right foot on the clutch pedal. Press it as far as it will go. Good. This is the ignition switch. Turn it. Do you hear that? The spark has ignited the fuel liquid. You open the valves with these levers. Well done. Now pull on the handbrake, to free the wheels. Engage the transmission – that's this lever. Now slowly lift your foot off the clutch and at the same time pull the choke, which . . .'

Senka took hold of the little metal stick that had the strange name 'choke' and pulled it towards himself. The self-propelled carriage suddenly darted forward.

'A-a-agh!' Senka yelled in terror and delight.

He got a sudden sinking feeling in his stomach, as if he was racing down an icy slide in a sleigh. The three-wheeler went shooting out through the gates of the shed, the wall of the house came towards it at high speed, and the next moment Senka's chest crashed into the steering wheel. There was a loud clang and a jangle of broken glass, and the flight came to an end.

There were red bricks right in front of Senka's face, with a green caterpillar crawling across them. His ears were ringing and his chest hurt, but no bones seemed to be broken.

Senka heard leisurely footsteps approaching from behind. He saw that the glass was broken on one dial and it had completely come away from another, and he pulled his head down into his chest: Beat me, Erast Petrovich, beat me within an inch of my life – even that's too good for a bonehead like me.

'. . . which regulates the flow of fuel, and so it should be pulled very gently,' said Mr Nameless, continuing with his explanation as if he had not even been interrupted. 'You pulled it too hard, Senya.'

Senka hung his head and got out. When he saw the flattened lamp, which had been so smart and shiny only a few moments ago, he sobbed out loud. What a disaster.

'Never mind,' the engineer reassured him, squatting down on his haunches. 'In automobilism breakages are an everyday event. We'll fix everything this very moment. Be so kind, Senya, as to bring me the box of tools. Will you help me? It's quite easy to remove a dashboard with two people. If you only knew how badly I need an assistant.'

'What about the sensei?' asked Senka, stopping just as he was about to dash over to the shed. 'Doesn't he help you?'

'Masa is a conservative and a staunch opponent of progress,' Erast Petrovich said with a sigh as he pulled on a pair of leather gloves.

Well, that was true enough. The engineer and Masa had been rowing over progress almost every day.

If Erast Petrovich had just read an article in the morning newspaper – say, about the opening of a railway line to the region beyond Lake Baikal – and he said: Look at this splendid news for the population of Siberia. They used to spend an entire month on the journey from Irkutsk to Chita, but now it only takes a day. They've been given a present of an entire month! There you are, use the time for whatever you like! That is the true meaning of progress – reducing the unnecessary waste of time and effort! Then the Japanese would say to him: They haven't been given a month of life, the time's been taken away from them. The people in this Irkutsk of yours never used to leave home except on important business, but now they'll start spreading out across the face of the earth. That would be fine, if they did it thoughtfully, measuring out the earth with their steps, scrambling up the mountains and swimming across the rivers. But they'll sit down on a comfortable seat and sniff a couple of times, and that'll be all there is to their journey. Before, when a man went travelling, he understood that life itself is a journey, but now he'll think that life is a soft seat in a railway carriage. People used to be strong and sinewy, but soon now they'll all be weak and fat. Fat – that's what this progress of yours is.

Then Mr Nameless would get angry. You're distorting things,

he'd say. Fat? So let there be fat, excellent! And by the way, fat is the most valuable substance in the human body, a reserve of energy and strength for times of stress. We just need to avoid accumulating fat in certain areas of the social organism, it should be distributed equally, that's the reason why social progress or 'social evolution' exists.

But Masa didn't give up. Fat, he said, is a bodily substance, and the essence of a man is spiritual – the soul. Progress will lead to the soul being smothered in fat.

No, Erast Petrovich objected. Why despise the body? It is life, and the soul, if it exists at all, belongs to eternity – that is, to death. It's no accident that the Slavonic word for life, 'zhivot', means 'stomach' in Russian. And by the way, you Japanese also happen to locate the soul in the stomach, in the 'hara'.

Or there was this other time when Erast Petrovich and the sensei started arguing about whether progress changed values or not.

Mr Nameless said that they did change – they moved to a higher level, primarily because a man started to value himself, his time and his effort more highly, but Masa didn't agree. He said it was just the opposite: nowadays hardly anything depended on the individual human being and his efforts, and so all values were in decline. When progress does half your work for you, you can live your whole life without your soul ever waking up and without understanding anything about true values.

Senka listened, but he couldn't decide whose side he was on. On the one hand, Erast Petrovich seemed to be right. Just look at all the progress there was in Moscow: electric trams would start running soon, and they'd put up bright street lamps all over the place, and there was the cinematograph too. Values were getting higher and higher every day. Eggs at the market used to cost two kopecks for ten, and now they cost three. The cabbies used to take half a rouble to drive from Sukharevka to Zamosvorechie, but now they wanted at least seventy or eighty kopecks for the pleasure. Or just look at the price of *papyroses*.

Only, it wasn't that simple. Progress did bring some good of its own. Look at the difference between a shoe made by hand and one from a factory. Of course, the first kind worked out dearer, that's why there were hardly any of them left.

But Senka soon realised that Erast Petrovich didn't understand a thing about values.

They were giving the 'Flying Carpet' a test run on Mytnaya Street. They went round a corner at speed – Erast Petrovich was turning the wheel and Senka was honking the horn – and there was a herd of cows. What did a horn mean to those dumb beasts? So they crashed into the one at the back at full pelt.

It didn't even have time to moo, just flipped over with its hooves in the air, and lay there dead.

Senka felt sorry for the front of the car, not the cow. They'd only just put on a new lamp to replace the one that was smashed against the wall. And a lamp was fifty roubles, that was no joke.

While Senka groaned and gathered up the broken glass, the engineer counted out his recompense to the cowherd for his cow. And how much do you think he gave the man? A hundred roubles! Whoever heard of such a thing? For an old brown cow that wouldn't fetch more than thirty on market day!

And that wasn't the half of it. As soon as that shameless rogue of a cowherd had stuck the hundred note in his cap, the cow got up and walked off, none the worse for wear, its udders wobbling to and fro.

Naturally, Senka took the cowherd by the sleeve and told him to cough up the money.

'In the first place, not "cough up", but "please return". And in the second place, there's no need. Consider it a payment for moral injury.'

So whose moral injury was that? The cow's?

This *incident* had important consequences, and the important consequences led to *epoch-making results*.

Senka was responsible for the consequences, and Erast Petrovich was responsible for the results.

That same day Senka sketched a metal bracket on a piece of paper. It was meant to be attached in front of the lamp, so that cows, goats or dogs could be knocked down without any damage to the automobile. And after supper he subjected Mr Nameless and the Japanese to an interrogation about what prices they paid for things and how much money they paid various people. He was flabbergasted by what they said. Erast Petrovich might be an American engineer, but when it came to simple business matters, he was the biggest fool you could imagine. He paid way over the odds for everything, just gave whatever he was asked, never bothered to bargain. He'd taken the apartment in Asheulov Lane for three hundred a month! And the sensei was no better. Apart from his Way and the women he simply didn't have a clue. Some valet he was.

Senka taught the scatterbrained pair a bit of sound sense about the value of things, and the 'experts' listened open mouthed.

The engineer looked at Senka and shook his head respectfully. 'You're a remarkable young man, Senya,' Erast Petrovich said solemnly. 'You have so many talents. Your idea for a shock-absorbing bracket on the automobile is excellent. The accessory should be patented and named in your honour – say "Spidorov's damper". Or the "antishocker", or "bumper", from the English "bump". You are a born inventor. That is one. And your economic skill is quite astounding too. If you will agree to be my treasurer, I shall gladly entrust you with the management of all my expenditure. You are a born financial manager. That is two. And I am also struck by your technical savvy. You ventilate the carburettor so skilfully, you change a wheel so quickly! I tell you what, Semyon Spidorov: I offer you the position of mechanic until I depart for Paris. And that is three. Take your time before you answer, think it over.'

It's a fact well known that when good luck comes, it doesn't come in dribs and drabs. The sky's pitch black, there's not a single star to be seen, and you could just howl at the misery of it. But then, when the stars do come out, they fill the entire vault of heaven.

Who was Speedy Senka only a little while ago? No one, a dung beetle. But now he was everything: Death's lover (yes, that did happen, it wasn't a dream), and a rich man, and an inventor, and a treasurer, and a mechanic. What a career he'd fallen into now – a much plummier position than a lowly sixer in the Prince's deck.

Senka really had his hands full now. He never even thought about how he ought to go and see Tashka, and how afraid he was, except in the evenings, just before he went to sleep. During the day he didn't have the time.

The three-wheeler had to be cleaned and tuned, didn't it?

He had to go round the shops and buy everything, didn't he?

He had to keep an eye on the cleaner, the yard-keeper, the cook (he'd hired an old woman to cook proper human food, they couldn't keep eating nothing but raw stuff) – didn't he?

With Senka managing everything, the sensei turned into a total idler. He'd spend the best part of an hour on his knees with his eyes closed (that was a way the Japanese had of praying). Or else he'd disappear off somewhere with Erast Petrovich. Or else he had an *assignation*. Or else he would suddenly decide to teach Senka Japanese gymnastics.

And then Senka was supposed to drop all his important business and go running round the yard with him, almost naked, go climbing up a drainpipe and wave his arms and legs around.

Maybe this was all nice and useful, very good for his health, or for defending himself against bad people, but, for starters, he didn't have the time, and what was worse, his bones ached so badly afterwards that he couldn't even straighten up.

Back in Khitrovka there was this old grandfather who used to be an orderly in an asylum. When he talked about the people in there, with all their quirks and whimsies, it was absolutely fascinating. Well now, Senka sometimes felt a bit like that orderly. As if he was living with madmen. They looked like normal enough people, with all their wits about them, but sometimes you could just see the place was a loony bin.

Take Mr Nameless himself, for instance, Erast Petrovich. He wasn't Japanese, was he, he looked like a normal person, but he had these foreign habits. When he was in his study, fiddling with the drawings or writing something, that seemed clear enough. But one time Senka glanced over his shoulder, out of curiosity, just to see what he was drawing, and he gasped out loud: the engineer wasn't writing with a pen, he was holding a wooden brush, the kind you use for spreading glue, and he wasn't drawing letters, but some strange-looking kind of squiggles that didn't mean a thing to Senka.

Or else he might start striding across the room, clicking his green beads, and he could carry on striding about like that for ever.

And then he might sit down facing the wall and stare at a single spot. Once Senka tried to see what was there on the wall. He couldn't see anything, nothing at all, not even a bedbug or some other little mite, and when he tried to ask what it was that Erast Petrovich found so interesting, Masa, who happened to be close by, grabbed him by the scruff of his neck, dragged him out of the study and said: 'When master contemprate, reave him arone.' But then, what was he contemplating, if there was nothing there?

Apart from all the work involved in preparing the 'Flying Carpet' for its long-distance run, Mr Nameless had other mysterious business to deal with, something Senka wasn't let in on. Erast Petrovich disappeared almost every evening at nine o'clock and didn't come back until late, or sometimes he went missing until the next morning. When this happened, Senka was tormented with dark visions. Once he even took the engineer's undershirt out of the laundry pile and sniffed to see whether it smelled of Death (that heady, minty smell that you could never confuse with anything else). It didn't seem to.

Sometimes the master went out in the afternoon as well, but Senka didn't know the reason for his absence.

Once, when Erast Petrovich took longer than usual straightening his collar and combing his hair in the mirror before he went out, Senka suffered an overwhelming fit of jealousy. He just couldn't stop himself, he slipped out of the house as if he was going shopping, then out in the street he fell in behind the engineer and followed him, to see if he was going to meet a certain immoral individual.

He was indeed going to meet someone but, thank God, not the person on Senka's mind.

Mr Nameless went into the Rivoli café, sat down at a table and started reading the newspapers – Senka could see everything through the glass windows. After a while, Senka realised he wasn't the only person interested in Erast Petrovich. There was a young lady standing not far away, in front of a fashionable shop window, and she was looking in the same direction as Senka. First he heard a quiet tinkling sound, but he couldn't understand where it was coming from. Then he noticed that the girl had little bells sewn to her cuffs, and a necklace in the form of a snake; in fact it looked like it was alive. Clear enough, she was one of those decadents, lots of them had appeared in Moscow just recently.

At first Senka thought the young lady was waiting for someone, and he enjoyed taking a look at the lovely brunette, the way you do. But then she gave her head a shake, walked across the street and marched into the café.

Erast Petrovich put down his newspaper, stood up to greet her and offered her a seat. They exchanged a couple of words, and the engineer started reading out loud from the newspaper.

Just what kind of halfwit was he?

Senka didn't watch any more after that, because he felt calm now. Why get himself all worked up if Mr Nameless was so blind? He'd seen Death, he'd spoken to her, gazed into her shimmering eyes, and here he was chasing after some little street cat.

No, this particular individual was beyond Senka's comprehension.

Take the move, for instance.

It was two days before Senka observed the rendezvous at the Rivoli café. All at once – completely out of the blue – Mr Nameless decided to move out of Asheulov Lane. Mr Nameless said they had to. They moved across to Sukharevka, into an officer's apartment in the Spassky Barracks. No one explained to Senka why they had to go, what it was all for. They'd only just started settling in properly: he'd put up all those shelves in the study, hired floor-polishers to wax up the parquet so that it shone, half a carcass of veal had been ordered from the butcher – and suddenly this. And the rooms were paid for two months in advance – that was six hundred roubles down the drain!

They packed in a great hurry, threw everything higgledy-piggledy into two cabs and left.

The new apartment was pretty good too, with a separate entrance, only it was a little while before they could find a place for the three-wheeler. Senka spent two days cajoling the janitor Mikheich, drank four samovars of tea with him, gave him six roubles and then another three and a half before he got the key to the stable (there weren't any horses there anyway, because the regiment had gone off to conquer China).

While Senka was trying to persuade the janitor, Masa-sensei persuaded the janitor's wife – and more speedily too. So all in all, they settled in quite well, they couldn't complain: they had a roof over their heads, the 'Flying Carpet' was in a warm, dry place, they had Mikheich's respect, and pies and stewed fruit from his wife almost every single day.

On the last day of this peaceful life, before everything was sent spinning head over heels again, Senka received visitors at his new residence: his little brother Vanka and Judge

Kuvshinnikov. As soon as they moved out of Asheulov Lane, Senka had sent a letter by the municipal post, saying that he was now living at such and such an address and would regard it as an honour to see his dear brother Ivan Trifonovich, please accept, etc., etc. The judge had replied by letter too: Thank you, we shall definitely come soon.

And he kept his word and came to visit.

At first he looked around suspiciously, wondering whether the place was some kind of thieves' den. When Masa appeared in the hallway wearing nothing but his white underpants for *renzu*, the judge frowned and put his hand on Vanka's shoulder. The youngster gaped wide eyed at the Oriental too, and when Masa slapped himself on the stomach and bowed, he gave a squeal of fright.

Things were looking bad. The judge had already turned towards the door, in order to leave (just to be on the safe side, he hadn't let the cabby go), but then, fortunately, Erast Petrovich came out of his study, and one look at this respectable man in a velvet house jacket, holding a book in his hand, was enough to allay Kuvshinnikov's fears. It was quite clear that a gentleman like that would never live in a den of thieves.

They introduced themselves to each other in the most respectable manner possible. Erast Petrovich called Senka his assistant and invited the judge into his study to smoke Cuban cigars. Senka never found out what they talked about in there, because he took Vanka to the stable to show him the automobile, and then drove his little brother round the yard. He moved all the levers and operated the crafty choke all on his own, and he turned the wheel himself too, while Vanka just hooted the horn and roared with delight.

They drove around like that for a long time and used up half a bucket of kerosene, but that was all right, no one would mind. Then the judge came out, to take Vanka home. He shook hands when he said goodbye to Senka and even gave him a cheery wink.

The judge and his brother drove away.

And in the evening, before he got into bed, Senka looked in the mirror to see whether he had any more hairs in his beard, and he discovered four new ones, three on the right cheek and one on the left. That made thirty-seven altogether, not counting the ones in his moustache.

He thought about going to see Tashka in his usual way and listened closely to see whether his heart would skip a beat.

It didn't.

He told himself to remember the Prince, and how he'd legged it out of that basement.

So he'd legged it to get away from the Prince – was he going to spend the rest of his life trembling with fear?

For more than a week he'd been afraid even to think of showing his face back in Khitrovka, but now, suddenly, he felt the time was right, he could go.

How Senka Cried

He made his way to Khokhlovsky Lane through the yards and back alleys – from Pokrovka Street, by way of Kolpachny Lane. It was a good night for it, with no moon, a fine drizzle and a light mist in the air. You could see damn all just five steps in front of your face. And to make himself less obvious, Senka had put on a black shirt under his short black jacket, and even smeared soot on his face. When he darted out of a gateway on to an alley right at the spot where two Khitrovkans were warming themselves up with wine beside a little bonfire, they gasped and crossed themselves at the sight of the black man. They didn't shout or scream, though – they were too far gone already. Or maybe they just thought they were seeing things.

Senka swung his noggin (his head, that is) left and right as he *reconnoitred*. He didn't spot anything suspicious. There was a dim glow in the windows of the buildings, someone singing, and he could hear loud swearing in the Hard Labour. Just another night in Khitrovka, then. He even felt ashamed for being so lily livered or – in cultured terms – so faint of heart.

He threw caution to the wind and turned straight into the courtyard where Tashka's door was. He had a bundle of presents for her under his arm: a brand new grammar school uniform for her new career, a tennis ball for the puppy Pomposhka and a bottle of 'Double Strength' for her mother (she could drink herself to death, die happy and set her daughter free).

There were flowers in the only window and there was no light on. That was a good sign. If Tashka had a client, the paraffin lamp with the red shade would have been lit on the locker by the bed, and that would have turned the curtain red too. That meant keep your nose out, girl at work. But it was dark, so she must have finished working and gone to bed.

Senka tapped on the window with his finger and called to her: 'Tashka, it's me, Speedy.'

Not a sound.

He called again, but not at the top of his voice – he was still afraid in case anyone else heard him.

They must be out cold. Not even the poodle made a sound, he hadn't scented a visitor. They'd probably had a hard day of it.

Senka scratched his head. What could he do? He didn't want to switch the transmission into reverse at this stage . . .

Suddenly he noticed the door was slightly ajar.

He was so delighted, he didn't even wonder why Tashka's latch wasn't closed in the middle of the night, as if she lived somewhere else, not in Khitrovka.

He darted inside, locked the door and called to her:

'Tash, wake up! It's me!'

Still not a sound.

Had they gone out then? But where could they go at this time? Then it struck him, like a lightning bolt.

They'd moved out! Something had happened to Tashka, and they'd left the apertiment. (Senka knew now that the right word was 'apartment', only that was for proper lodgings, with proper curtains and furniture, but Tashka's place was an apertiment all right, no doubt about that.)

Only she couldn't have just moved out without leaving any message for her mate.

Senka felt for the lamp in the darkness, then reached into his pocket, got his matches and lit it.

Tashka hadn't gone anywhere.

She was lying there, tied to the bed. Half her face was covered with a patch of sticking plaster. Her eyes were absolutely still, glaring angrily up at the ceiling, and her shirt was all torn and covered in brown blotches.

He shuddered and started untying her quickly, but Tashka was stiff and cold. Like a veal carcass in a butcher's cellar.

He sat down on the floor, pressed his forehead against Tashka's stiff side and burst into tears. It wasn't grief or even the fright, he just started crying because that was what his heart told him to do. His mind was blank. He sobbed, wiping his snot on his sleeve, whimpering now and then.

He cried until he couldn't cry any more – it went on for a long time. But that wasn't the worst of it – it was when all his tears were all cried out that Senka started feeling really bad.

He lifted his head and saw Tashka's hand there, really close, tied to the frame of the bed. The fingers on the hand were sticking out in all directions, like the twigs on an old broom, not like they did on living people, and that was more than Senka could bear. He started backing away from those twisted fingers, but his heel hit something soft and he turned round.

Tashka's mum was lying by the wall on her thin mattress. Her eyes were closed, but her mouth was open, and there was dried blood on her chin.

He had the odd thought that he'd never seen her anywhere else but on that tattered mattress. Of course, she'd always been drunk before, and now she was dead. She lived on rags, and she'd died on rags.

But it wasn't really Senka who thought that, someone else seemed to think it for him. This someone had appeared before, and *he* didn't want to cry. He whispered: 'It will be a sin against God if the beast who did this to Tashka is left alive. Just wait, you bloody snake, Erast Petrovich will see you get justice for this.'

That was what the second Senka said after the first Senka had finished crying. And he was right.

As he was leaving, Senka noticed a small ball of white wool right beside the door. When he leaned down, he saw it was the dead puppy Pomponius, and then it turned out that the first Senka hadn't cried all his tears out yet, not by a long way. He still had enough to last all the way back to the Spassky Barracks.

'The same s-scene as with the Siniukhins and the Samshitovs,' Mr Nameless said sombrely as he covered Tashka's face with a white handkerchief. 'Masa, your opinion c-concerning the sequence of events?'

The sensei pointed to the door.

'He smash in door with a singur brow. Walk in. When dog jump at him, he kirr it with his foot, rike this.' Masa stamped, as if he was driving his heel into the floor. 'Then he jump over here.' The Japanese took two long strides across to Tashka's motionless mum. 'She was sreeping. He hi' her on tempur. Kirred her outrigh'. Then he grab the girr, tie her to bed and torture her.'

'He did what?' Senka asked, wincing in pain.

'He t-tortured her,' said Erast Petrovich. 'The same way he t-tortured Siniukhin and Samshitov. Look at her fingers. The m-murderer broke them one at a time. And notice the hair!'

'What about her hair?' Senka asked dull-wittedly.

The engineer moved the handkerchief aside. Erast Petrovich's voice sounded cold and indifferent, as if had been chilled by frost.

'There is b-blood here, on the side of the head. And here. And here. And there are t-tufts of hair on the floor. Some with scraps of skin. He t-tore her hair out.'

'What for? What had she done to him?'

It wasn't right, it was shameful for them to be talking so stiff, as if she was a stranger, but looking at Mr Nameless, Senka could see he was working; only his brain was engaged now, feelings were for later. And anyway, Senka didn't have any more strength for crying, all his feelings had drained out of him with his tears.

'She could have picked up a client who was a lunatic,' he said, replacing the handkerchief so he wouldn't turn all weepy again.

'That happens sometimes in Khitrovka. A mamselle brings back someone who looks normal, but he's a real monster.'

The engineer nodded, as if he was approving Senka's efforts at deduction.

'The sadistic client theory c-could have been taken as the primary one, if not for the s-similarities between this crime and the two that preceded it. The extermination of every l-living thing. That is one. The use of torture. That is t-two. The same district. That is three. And in addition . . .' He pulled the shirt up off Tashka's bare legs and took a magnifying glass out of his pocket. Senka turned away quickly and started coughing to get rid of the lump in his throat. 'Mmm, yes. No s-signs of rape or sexual violence. The killer's interest in his v-victim was not sensual in nature. Let us t-take a look at the lips . . .'

Masa walked over, but Senka didn't look.

There was a quiet rasping sound – that must have been Erast Petrovich tearing the plaster off Tashka's mouth.

'Yes, just as I thought. The plaster was pulled off and stuck back on several times. The torturer kept asking about something over and over again, but the girl didn't answer.'

Senka didn't think it was very likely that Tashka didn't answer a fiend like this. She would have answered him all right, loud and shrill, with her choicest words. But here on Khokhlovsky Lane, no matter how loud you yelled and what filthy words you used, no one would come, no one would rescue you.

'Now this is interesting. Masa, l-look at her teeth.'

'Goo' for her,' the sensei said, with an approving click of his tongue. 'She bi' his finger.'

'Ah, what a shame we d-don't have a laboratory.' The engineer sighed. 'We could take a particle of the criminal's b-blood for analysis. The Moscow police have p-probably never heard of the Landsteiner method . . . But even so, we have to d-draw the investigator's attention to this l-little detail somehow . . .'

Masa and Mr Nameless leaned down over Tashka, and Senka started striding round the room, just to give himself something to do. There were three white daffodils in the window. Did that mean 'I love you' in the language of flowers? Or maybe it was 'you can all go to hell, you bastards'? No one would translate it for him now . . .

'Ah,' said Senka, reproaching himself out loud. 'I should have come earlier, before dark. I was being too careful, so I got here too late.'

Erast Petrovich glanced round briefly. 'Before dark? The murder was committed at least two days ago, most probably three. So you were a lot later than you think, Senya.'

That was true enough. The daffodils in the window were all wilted.

But this was Khitrovka, so no one had noticed anything. If anyone died, they just lay there till the neighbours caught the smell of rotting flesh.

'If it's not a loony, what did he want from Tashka?' Senka asked, looking at the dead flowers. 'What could he get from her?'

'No "what", b-but "who",' the engineer replied, as if he was surprised at the question. 'You, Senya. This stubborn gentleman wants you very b-badly. And you know why.'

'That's a disaster!' Senka exclaimed, throwing his hands up in the air. 'I told Tashka about you and Mr Masa. And I told her you live on Asheulov Lane too. If this killer's so stubborn, he'll find out where we moved to, for sure. He'll find the cabbies who moved the things and intelligate them! We've got to clear out!'

'Not "intelligate", b-but "interrogate",' the engineer said strictly, pulling on a pair of thin rubber gloves. 'And we're n-not going to run anywhere. For two reasons. We are not afraid of this f-friend of yours, let him come – it will m-make things easier for us. That is one. And then, your low opinion of Mademoiselle T-Tashka is an insult to her. She did not give you away, she d-did not tell her killer a thing. That is t-two.'

'How do you know she didn't give me away?'

'Do not f-forget that I had the honour of being acquainted

with this exceptional individual. She was a true c-comrade to you, a "good mate". And apart from that, if she had t-told him, the plaster would have been removed from her m-mouth. It was not, which means that she remained s-silent to the very end.'

And that must have been when the time for deduction came to an end, because Mr Nameless's intent, matter-of-fact expression disappeared, and his face was suddenly immensely sad.

'I feel s-sorry for the girl,' Erast Petrovich said, and put his hand on Senka's shoulder.

The shoulder instantly started trembling, all on its own, and there was nothing he could do to stop it.

Masa picked the puppy up off the floor and set it down carefully on the windowsill, near the daffodils.

'I feer sorry for brave puppy too. In next rife he wirr be born samurai.'

But the unsentimental engineer told him to put Pomponius back on the floor 'in order not to confuse the already rather muddled picture of the crime for the investigator'.

How Senka Used Deduction

Senka and Masa sat in the study, keeping shtum as they watched Erast Petrovich striding round the room and rattling his beads. Senka already knew he mustn't say anything, just wait patiently for whatever came next.

Once the engineer had stopped in the middle of the room, he put the green beads away in his pocket and clapped his hands twice in rapid succession, as though he was suddenly feeling incredibly happy about something.

Even so, the sensei put a finger to his lips: *Sit still and stay quiet, it's not over yet.*

But soon after that Mr Nameless stopped treading the carpet down, sat in an armchair and spoke thoughtfully, as if he was talking to himself: 'So. Three cruel m-murders have been committed: the first and the third were in Khitrovka, the s-second was five minutes' walk from Khitrovka, but still in the area under the j-jurisdiction of the Third Myasnitsky police station. In all, the c-criminal has taken the lives of eight people – two m-men, three women and three children – and, for some reason, a p-parrot and a dog too. In each case one of the victims was t-tortured cruelly before he or she d-died, in an attempt to extort certain information required by the k-killer. There are no clues and n-no witnesses. Such, in brief, are the terms of the p-problem facing us. We know the required result – find the m-monster and deliver him into the arms of justice.'

'An' if not arive, then deriver him to justice dead,' Masa added quickly.

'If the criminal should offer resistance when an arrest is attempted, then, *after having exhausted all the legally permitted measures of self-defence*' – at this point the engineer raised one finger in the air and gave his valet a significant glance – 'it might not prove possible to circumvent the outcome that you mention.'

'I'd like to find the rat and smash his rotten bonce in,' said Senka, putting in his two kopecks' worth.

'Not "b-bonce", but "head". But whatever you call it, first we have to track him down.' Erast ran his eyes over the other members of the meeting there assembled. 'Are there any questions before we move on to d-deduction and practical measures?'

Senka didn't know what to ask, but the Japanese scratched his stiff brush of hair and drawled thoughtfully: 'Sa-a. Masta, why "kirrer", not "kirrers"?'

Erast Petrovich nodded to acknowledge the relevance of the question.

'You gave a very c-convincing rendering of the criminal's actions at Khokhlovsky L-Lane. Why would he n-need an accomplice?'

'That no argumen',' Masa snapped.

'I agree. I ought t-to have asked: Why would the killer need an accomplice, if so f-far he has managed p-perfectly well on his own? In the b-basement Senya was attacked by one person. That is one.' Mr Nameless took out his beads and clacked one of them against another. 'The k-killings at the jewellery shop were also committed by a single individual, as the p-police have established. That is two.' He clacked another bead. 'And finally, at Yeroshenko's d-dosshouse the killer also managed p-perfectly well without anybody else's help. As you recall, Senya told us Siniukhin spoke of one m-murderer, "he". Isn't that right, Semyon?'

'Yes,' said Senka, remembering. 'And Siniukhin called him a "beast" as well.'

He felt a bit ashamed for not telling Erast Petrovich the whole truth back then – he'd kept quiet about the treasure.

It was as if the engineer was listening to Senka's conscience reproaching him.

'So now, if you have no m-more questions, let us move on to the most important s-subject – drawing up a plan of measures to f-find the criminal. And the k-key word here is – treasure.'

Senka shuddered and started blinking rapidly, but the sensei wasn't at all surprised, he even nodded his head.

'Yes, yes, tresia.'

'The criminal's b-behaviour and all the atrocities he has c-committed cease to appear meaningless if we st-string them on that thread.' Mr Nameless looked intently at his beads. 'The logical sequence that emerges here is as f-follows. The pen-pusher from the Yerokha b-basements found some treasure. [Clack number one.] The future m-murderer found out about it. [Clack number two.] He tried to d-drag the secret out of Siniukhin, but he f-failed. [Clack number three.] But before he d-died, the pen-pusher revealed the secret of the t-treasure to our Senya. [Clack number four – this time Senka squirmed, and if the burning feeling in his cheeks was anything to go by, he must have blushed too, but Erast Petrovich didn't look at him, he carried on as if Senka knew all this anyway.] To c-continue. In some unknown manner, the k-killer figured out that Senya knew where the treasure was. [Clack number five.] That is, we d-don't know *how* the criminal f-found this out, but we do know from where. The t-trail that our treasure hunter followed to Senya started f-from the jeweller's shop. [Clack number six.] I believe Samshitov told the k-killer about you and where you could be found – which is c-confirmed by a certain visit paid to Madam Borisenko's b-boarding house. [Clack number seven.]'

Senka started blinking again: *What visit was that, then?* The engineer and the Japanese exchanged glances, and Erast Petrovich said: 'Yes, Senya, yes. The only thing that s-saved you was that you left that evening without l-leaving an address, and a few hours later we b-brought you here. The next day Madam

B-Borisenko informed Masa that someone had been in your room d-during the night. He forced the door, didn't t-touch anything and left. We didn't tell you about it, b-because you were thoroughly f-frightened already.'

Senka propped his chin on his fist, as if he was feeling thoughtful, but it was really to stop his teeth chattering. Holy Mother of God, he'd be lying tied to a bed now, like Tashka, if he'd stayed there that night and decided he ought to sleep on things.

'When you disappeared, the k-killer lost the trail for a few d-days. But then you showed up in Khitrovka, and the c-criminal knew about it straight away, perhaps by chance, perhaps in s-some other way, I don't know which. Somehow he f-found out that you had gone into Yeroshenko's d-dosshouse, and he ambushed you n-near the exit. Your carelessness almost c-cost you your l-life. [Clack number eight.]'

'Never mind, I'm not that easy to catch,' Senka said, trying to blow his own trumpet. 'He tried to take my life but I'm slippery, I wriggled out of his grip, and I gave him a good whack with my stick. He won't forget that in a hurry.'

'If he had wanted to k-kill you, he would have done. Straight away,' said the engineer, pouring cold water on Senka's bravado. 'He's very g-good at it, with a knife or with his b-bare hands. No, Senya, he needs you alive. He would have f-forced you to reveal the whereabouts of the treasure, and then k-killed you.'

When he heard that, Senka propped his chin up again, this time with both fists.

'When the k-killer lost your trail after the murder of the jeweller, he decided to try a d-different approach. Many p-people in Khitrovka knew about your f-friendship with Mademoiselle Tashka. Your admirer knew about it t-too. [Clack number nine.] At first he clearly attempted to extract information f-from her without resorting to extreme m-measures. That was what she whispered about when she walked p-past you – she was trying to warn you of the d-danger. The criminal obviously paid her another visit after the unsuccessful attack in the b-basement. It was no accident that Tashka put three white d-daffodils in the window. If I recall correctly, in the language of f-flowers, that is an alarm signal – "run, run, run".'

Yes, that was right, Senka remembered. Tashka had told him about white daffodils, and how when a signal was repeated, that made the message twice or three times as strong, like an exclamation mark.

'Eventually,' the engineer said, looking at his beads, but not clacking them any more, 'the f-fiend decided to take a more serious l-line with the girl.'

'And still she didn't give me away …' Senka couldn't help himself, he sobbed. 'Damn that rotten treasure. It would have been better if Tashka told him I'd promised to come and see her. Maybe then he wouldn't have touched her. And I'd have given him everything, the lousy rat could go choke on the silver! It's the Prince, isn't it? Or Deadeye?' he asked, brushing his tears away with his sleeve. 'You've probably deduced it all, haven't you?'

'No,' said Mr Nameless, disappointing Senka's hopes. 'I have insufficient d-data. The deceased pen-pusher was too f-fond of his drink, and apparently he couldn't k-keep his mouth shut. If they knew about the t-treasure in the Prince's gang, others could have heard about it too.'

And then there was silence, as Senka struggled with all his might to control his body's reactions: teeth that wanted to chatter, knees that wanted to knock and tears that wanted to flow. For no clear reason, Erast Petrovich started messing up a piece of paper in that stupid way he had. He dipped his brush in the inkwell and scrawled a fancy squiggle. Masa watched the brush carefully. He shook his head and said:

'Not goo'.'

'I can s-see that,' the engineer murmured, and scribbled it again. 'How about that?'

'Betta.'

Honest to God, they were just like little kids! All this important business to deal with, and look what they were doing!

'What are you mucking about like that for?' Senka asked, unable to stop himself. 'Aren't we going to do anything?'

'Not "m-mucking about", but "wasting time". That is one.' Erast Petrovich leaned his head to one side, admiring his scribbles. 'I am not wasting t-time, I am focusing my thoughts with the help of c-calligraphy. That is two. The f-flawlessly written hieroglyph for "justice" has allowed me to m-make the transition from d-deduction to projection. That is three.'

Senka thought for a moment and said: 'Eh?'

Mr Nameless sighed. 'If there is s-something that you didn't understand or d-didn't hear, you should say: "I beg your pardon?" In this case, p-projection signifies the extension of analytical c-conclusions into the practical phase. So, thanks to Mademoiselle Tashka's f-firm resolve, the killer has been left with n-nothing. He does not know where to find you or how to l-look for you. This is good in some ways and b-bad in others.'

'What's bad about it?'

'The c-criminal (I suggest that for the time b-being we call him the Treasure Hunter) cannot d-do anything, so he will not show his hand and g-give himself away.' Erast Petrovich gave Senka a calculating look. 'Of c-course, we could try catching him with live b-bait, that is, deliberately offer you to him, but this gentleman is t-too brutal by half. It could be a risky f-fishing expedition.'

Senka didn't try to argue with that. He'd seen people fishing with live bait – a blay or some other little fish: the pike snapped up the bait first and sank its teeth into its backbone, before it got hauled out to answer for its crimes.

'Isn't there any way we can catch him without live bait?' he asked cautiously.

'There is way,' said the sensei. 'Not rive bait, but dead person. Is that it, Masta? Have I guess' righ'?'

Erast Petrovich frowned. 'Yes. But how many t-times do I have to tell you not to pun. You still haven't m-mastered the Russian language well enough for that.'

Senka wrinkled up his forehead. It seemed like he was the only fool among wise men here.

'What dead person?'

'Masa is thinking of the l-lady who goes by the name of Death,' the engineer explained. 'In s-some way that we d-do not yet understand, all the atrocities that have taken place in Khitrovka over the l-last month are c-connected with that individual. And so are all the m-major characters involved: the Prince, and Deadeye, and other luminaries of the undergound b-business world, and the excessively spry s-superintendent, and even the Treasure Hunter's m-main target.'

That means me, Senka guessed.

'You want to use Death to catch him? You think she's in league with this lowlife?' he asked doubtfully.

'No, I d-don't think that. And what is m-more, she has agreed to help me.'

Well, that was news for him! So when Senka climbed back out through the window, completely disillusioned with people, the two of them had come to some sort of deal, had they? Or rather, he'd talked her round, Senka thought bitterly, and he just couldn't help himself, he asked all casual, like: 'So you gave it to her, did you? Didn't take much persuading, I suppose?'

His voice trembled, the Judas.

The engineer gave Senka a light flick on the forehead. 'Such questions are n-not asked, Senya, and they are certainly not answered. That is one. Women are not to be spoken about in that t-tone. That is two. But s-since all of us, including her, will be working together in a common c-cause, in order to avoid any ambiguity, I shall answer: I d-did not "give it to" that lady and I did not even t-try. That is three.'

Should Senka believe him or not? Maybe he should ask him to swear in the name of God.

He gave Mr Nameless a keen look and decided a man like that

wouldn't lie. His heart suddenly felt lighter. 'But how can Death help us?' he asked, switching to a brisk, practical tone. 'If she knew anything about this Treasure Hunter, she'd have told us. She don't approve of savagery like that.'

Masa grunted suggestively, as if to say: Get ready, now I'm going to tell you the most important part. Senka turned towards the Japanese, but he said something Senka couldn't make out at all: 'Taifu-no meh.'

But the engineer understood. 'Exactly. A v-very precise metaphor. The eye of the t-typhoon. Do you know what that is, S-Senya?' He waited for Senka to shake his head and started to explain. 'A typhoon is a t-terrible kind of hurricane that races across s-sea and land, spreading destruction and t-terror. But at the very centre of this st-storm there is a spot of serene t-tranquillity. Within the eye of the typhoon, all is p-peace, but without this static centre, there would be n-no raging whirlwind. Death is not a criminal, she d-does not kill anyone – she just sits by the window and embroiders f-fantastical designs on cloth. But the m-most ruthless villains in this city of more than a million p-people swarm round her, like b-bees round their queen.'

'Also goo' imaj,' Masa said approvingly. 'But mine betta.'

'Well, m-more romantic, certainly. During the last few days I have p-paid several visits to the house on the Yauza B-Boulevard and had an opportunity to g-get to know this lady better.'

Ah, have you now? Senka was scowling again. 'Well, Erast Petrovich, you sly dog, you find time to get everywhere, don't you? What does "get to know her better" mean?'

'The last t-time we met,' Mr Nameless went on, obviously not noticing how badly Senka was suffering, 'she said she c-could tell she was being f-followed, but she d-didn't understand who was following her. When I went out on to the b-boulevard, out of the corner of my eye I also spotted a shadow lurking round the c-corner of a house. This is encouraging. Mademoiselle Death is n-now our only chance. By killing Tashka, Mr Treasure

Hunter snapped the thread l-leading to you with his own hands. And now, like the old couple in *The Golden Fish*, he is left with a broken tub . . .'

'Eh? Sorry, I mean, I beg your pardon? What tub's that?' asked Senka, who had been listening with bated breath.

All of a sudden Erast Petrovich turned angry: 'I told you to b-buy a volume of Pushkin's works and read the f-fairy tales at least!'

'I did buy one,' Senka said resentfully. 'There were lots of different Pushkins. I picked this one.'

And to prove what he was saying, he took out of his pocket the small book that he'd bought two days earlier at a flea market. It was an interesting book, it even had pictures.

'"*The Forbidden Pushkin*. Verses and p-poems previously circulated in manuscript",' said the engineer, reading out the title. He frowned and started leafing through the pages.

'And I read the fairy tales too,' said Senka, even more offended by this lack of trust. 'About the archangel and the Virgin Mary, and about Tsar Nikita and his forty daughters. Don't you believe me? I can tell you the stories if you like.'

'No n-need,' Erast Petrovich said brusquely, slamming the book shut. 'What a scoundrel.'

'Pushkin?' Senka asked in surprise.

'No, not Pushkin, the p-publisher. One should never publish what an author d-did not intend for publication. Who knows where it will end? Mark m-my words: soon our gentlemen of the publishing t-trade will start publishing intimate c-correspondence!' The engineer flung the book on to the table angrily. 'And b-by the way, correspondence is the very subject that I wanted to t-talk to you about, Senya. Since Death is being f-followed, I can't show myself at her p-place any more. And it is not really f-feasible to keep the house under c-constant observation – any stranger would be sp-spotted straight away. So we shall have to c-communicate from a distance.'

'How do you mean, from a distance?'

'Well, by epistolary m-means.'

'You mean we're going to set up an ambush, with pistols?' Senka asked. He liked the idea. 'Can I have a pistol too?'

Erast Petrovich stared at him absent-mindedly. 'What have p-pistols got to do with it? We are going to write l-letters to each other. I can't visit Death any more. Masa can't go – he's too c-conspicuous. And it wouldn't be a g-good idea for Senka Spidorov to show up there, would it?'

'I'd say not.'

'So the only thing we can d-do is write letters. This is what we agreed. She will go to St N-Nikolai's church every day, for Mass. You will sit on the p-porch, disguised as a b-beggar. Mademoiselle Death will give you her letters when she g-gives you alms. I am almost c-certain that the Treasure Hunter will show his hand. He has p-probably heard about the way you c-cuckolded the Prince.'

'Who, me?' Senka gasped in horror.

'Why, yes. The whole of Khitrovka is t-talking about it. It even g-got into the police agents' reports, an acquaintance of mine in the d-detective force showed me it: "The wanted b-bandit Dron Veselov (known as 'the Prince') is threatening to find and k-kill his lady friend's lover, the juvenile Speedy, whose whereabouts and real n-name are unknown." So, as far as they are all concerned, Senya – you are Death's lover.'

How Senka Read Other People's Letters

There was a big mirror in Erast Petrovich's study. Well, not when they got there, but the engineer had a pier-glass set on top of the desk, and then he laid out all sorts of little bottles and jars and boxes in front of it, so it looked just like a hairdressing salon. In fact there were wigs there too, in every possible degree of hairiness and colour. When Senka asked what Mr Nameless needed all this for, he answered mysteriously that the fancy-dress ball season was about to begin.

At first Senka thought he was joking. But Senka was the first to make use of the facilities.

The day after the deduction and projection, Erast Petrovich sat Senka down in front of the mirror and started mocking the poor orphan something terrible. First he rubbed some nasty kind of muck into his hair, and that ruined the coiffure Senka had paid three roubles for. His hair was a nice golden colour, but that rotten grease turned it into a sticky, mousy-grey tangle.

Masa was watching this cruel abuse. He clicked his tongue in approval and said: 'He need rice.'

'You don't need to t-tell me that,' the engineer replied, concentrating on what he was doing. He took a pinch of something out of a little box and rubbed some little grains or pellets into the back of Senka's neck.

'What's that?'

'Dried lice. Fauna that every b-beggar has to have. Don't worry, we'll wash your hair with p-paraffin afterwards.'

Senka's jaw dropped open and the dastardly Mr Nameless

immediately took advantage of this to paint his golden crown a rotten colour, then stuck some thingamajig wrapped in gauze into Senka's open mouth and arranged it between his gum and his cheek. It twisted Senka's entire mug – his face, that is – over to one side. Meanwhile Erast Petrovich was already rubbing his victim's forehead, nose and neck with oil that turned his skin a muddy colour, with wide-open pores.

'The ears,' the sensei suggested.

'Won't that b-be too much?' the engineer asked doubtfully, but he rubbed his little stick inside Senka's ears anyway.

'That tickles!'

'Yes, I think it really is b-better with suppurating ears,' Erast Petrovich said thoughtfully. 'Now, let us m-move on to the wardrobe.'

He took some tattered rags out of the cupboard, far tattier than anything Senka had ever worn in his life, even during the very worst times with Uncle Zot.

Senka looked at himself in the triple mirror and twirled this way and that. No doubt about it, he certainly made a fine beggar. And the important thing was, no one would ever recognise him. One thing was still niggling him, though.

'The beggars have all the places divvied up between themselves,' he started explaining to Erast Petrovich. 'You have to deal with their head man. If I just turn up on the porch out of nowhere, they'll send me packing, and they'll give me a good thrashing too.'

'If they try to d-drive you away, chew on this,' said the engineer, handing him a smooth little ball. 'It's ordinary children's s-soap, strawberry flavoured. A simple trick, but effective, I b-borrowed it from a certain remarkable t-trickster. Only when the foam starts p-pouring out of your mouth, don't f-forget to roll your eyes up.'

But Senka still had his worries. He walked to the church of St Nicholas the Wonder-Worker on Podkopaevsky Lane, sat down on the very edge of the porch and rolled his eyes right up under his forehead straight off, just to be on the safe side. The hysterical old grandma and noseless old grandad who were begging near by started grumbling and grousing. Clear out, they said, we don't know you, the takings is poor enough already, wait till Boxman comes, he'll soon show you what's what – and all sorts of other stuff like that.

But when Boxman did come and the beggars snitched on the new boy to him, Senka started forcing foam out through his lips and shaking his shoulders and whining in a thin little voice. Boxman looked at him, then looked again and said: 'Can't you bastards see he's a genuine epileptical? Leave him alone, let him eat, and I won't take any remunerations from you for him.' That was Boxman for you – always fair. That was why he'd lasted twenty years in Khitrovka.

So the beggars stopped pestering Senka. He relaxed a bit, rolled his eyes back down from under his forehead and started flashing them this way and that. People really didn't give very much, mostly kopecks and half-kopecks. Once Mikheika the Night-Owl walked past and out of sheer boredom (and to check how good his disguise was as well), Senka grabbed him by the flap of his coat and started whining: *Give a poor cripple a coin or two*. Night-Owl didn't give him anything, and he called him foul names, but he didn't recognise him. After that Senka stopped worrying altogether.

When the bells rang for Mass and the women started walking into the church, Death appeared round the corner of Pod-kolokolny Street. She was dressed plainly, in a white shawl and a grey dress, but even so she lit up the lane like the sun peeping out from behind a cloud.

She glanced at all the beggars, but her eyes didn't linger on Senka. Then she walked in the door.

Oh-oh, he thought. Has Erast Petrovich overdone it? How would Death know who to give the note to?

So when the worshippers started coming out after the service,

Senka deliberately started whining through his nose and stammering – so that Death would realise who he was hinting at: 'Good k-kind people! Don't be angry with a c-crippled orphan for b-begging! Help m-me if you can! I'm not from these p-parts, I don't kn-know anyone round here. Give me a c-crust of bread and a c-coin or two!'

She looked a bit more closely at Senka and started tittering. So she'd guessed all right. She put a coin in every beggar's hand, and gave Senka a five-kopeck piece too, and a folded piece of paper to go with it.

Then she went off, covering her mouth with the edge of her shawl, because she found Senka's disguise so amusing.

As soon as he'd hobbled his way out of Khitrovka, Senka squatted down by an advertisement column, unfolded the sheet of paper and started reading it. Death's handwriting was regular and easy to read, even though the letters were really tiny:

'Hello, Erast Petrovich. I've done everything you told me to. I hung the petal round my neck and he noticed it straight away. [What petal's that, then, thought Senka, scratching his head. And who's 'he'? Never mind. Maybe that'll get cleared up later.] He pulled a face and said you're barmy. Hanging that rubbish round your neck and not wearing the presents I give you. He tried to find out if it was a present from someone. As we agreed I said it was from Speedy Senka. He started shouting. That snot–nosed little pup he said. When I get my hands on him I'll tear him apart. [So it was the Prince she meant! The crumpled piece of paper trembled in Senka's hands. What was she up to? Why was she setting him up like that? Did she want to make sure the Prince did him in? He didn't know anything about any petal! He'd never even seen it, let alone given it to her! After that he skimmed the lines more quickly.] It's hard being with him. He's drunk and gloomy all the time and keeps making threats. He's very jealous of me. It's a good thing he

232

only knows about Speedy. [Oh, yeah, what could be better, thought Senka, cringing pitifully.] *If he found out about the others blood would be spilled. I've tried asking him in all sorts of ways. He denies everything. He says I don't know anything about who's doing these shameless things, I only wish I did. When I find out I'll tell you if you're so interested. But I can't work out if he's telling the truth because he's not the same man he was before. He's more like a wild beast than a man. He's always snarling and baring his teeth. And I wanted to say something about our last conversation too. Don't reproach me for being immoral, Erast Petrovich. Some things are written into people when they are born and they are not free to change them. What is written from above can only be used for evil or for good. Do not talk to me like that again and do not write about this because there is no point.*

Death'

What was it she didn't want him to talk or write about, then? It had to be her indecent goings-on with the superintendent and those other scoundrels.

Senka folded the note back into a little square, the way it was before, and took it to Erast Petrovich. He was dying to ask the clever Mr Nameless a couple of questions about why he'd decided to make the Prince even more furious with a poor orphan. What need was there for that? And what was this 'petal' that Senka was supposed to have given Death?

Only if he asked, he'd let slip that he'd stuck his nose in the letter.

But that came out anyway.

The engineer glanced at the piece of paper and shook his head reproachfully straight off:

'That's not g-good, Senya. Why did you read it? The l-letter's not to you, is it?'

Senka tried to deny it. 'I didn't read nothing,' he said. 'What do I care what's in it?'

'Oh c-come now,' said Erast Petrovich, running his finger along the folds. 'Unfolded and folded b-back again. And what's this stuck to it? Could it be a l-louse? I doubt that b-belongs to Mademoiselle Death.'

How could you hide anything from someone like that?

The next day Senka was given a letter from Mr Nameless, but it wasn't just a sheet of paper – it was in an envelope.

'Since you're so c-curious,' the engineer declared, 'I am sealing my m-missive. Don't t-try to lick it open. This is a patent American g-glue; once stuck, it stays stuck.'

He smeared the stuff on the envelope with a brush, then pressed the letter under a paperweight.

Senka was simply amazed: it was true what they said – even the wise were fools sometimes. The minute he was outside the door, he tore the little envelope open and threw it away. They sold five-kopeck envelopes like that, for love letters, at every kiosk. What was to stop him buying a new one and sealing it without any fancy glue? It didn't say on the envelope who the letter was for in any case . . .

To read or not to read – the question never even crossed Senka's mind. Of course he was going to read it! After all, it was his fate that was being decided!

The note was written on thin paper, and Erast Petrovich's handwriting was beautiful, with fine fancy flourishes.

'Hello, Dear D.

Please permit me to call you that — I cannot stand your nickname, and you will not tell me what you are really called. Forgive me, but I cannot believe that you have forgotten it. However, just as you please. Let me get to the point.

Things are clear with the first individual. Now do the same with the second one, only lead him on to the subject indirectly. As far as I am able to judge, this individual is somewhat cleverer than the Prince. It is enough for him simply to see

234

the object. And then, if he asks, tell him about SS, as we agreed. [Who's this SS, then? Senka rubbed his soot-smeared forehead, and a couple of dried lice fell out of his hair. Hey, Speedy Senka, that's who it was! What were they plotting to do with him?] *Forgive me for returning to a subject that you find disagreeable, but I cannot bear the thought of your subjecting yourself to defilement and torment — yes, indeed, I am certain that it is torment for you — in the name of ideas that I cannot comprehend and which are certainly false. Why do you punish yourself so harshly, why do you immerse your body in the mire? It has done nothing to offend you. The human body is a temple, and a temple should be kept pure. Some may counter: A temple, is it? It's just a house like any other: bricks and mortar. The important thing is not to besmirch the soul, but the body is not important, God does not live in the flesh, but in the soul. Ah, but the divine mystery will never be accomplished in a temple that is defiled and desecrated. And when you say that everything is written into people at their birth, you are mistaken. Life is not a book in which one can only move along the lines that someone else has written. Life is a plain traversed by countless roads, and one is always free to choose whether to turn to the right or to the left. And then there will be a new plain and a new choice. Everyone walks across this plain, choosing his or her own route and direction — some travel towards the sunset, towards darkness, others travel towards dawn and the source of light. And it is never too late, even in the very final moment of life, to turn in a direction completely opposite to the one in which you have been moving for so many years. Turns of this kind are not so very rare: a man may have walked all his life towards the darkness of night, but at the last he suddenly turns his face towards the dawn, and his face and the entire plain are illuminated by a different light, the glow of morning. And of course, the reverse happens too. My*

235

*explanation is confused and unclear, but somehow I suspect
you will understand me.*

E.N.'

Well, that wasn't a very interesting letter. A grand idea that
was, to go smearing someone with all sorts of rotten muck and
sending him halfway across the city, all for the sake of a bit of
philosophical jabbering.

He spent five kopecks on a new envelope and hurried on to
St Nicholas.

Death's shawl wasn't white today, it was maroon, and it set her
face aglow with flickering glimmers of heat. As she walked by
into the church, she scorched Senka with a glance that made
him squirm on his knees. He remembered (God forgive him –
this was not the time or the place) the way she had kissed him
and hugged him.

When she came back out, her eyes still had that same mis-
chievous glint in them. As she leaned down to give him alms
and take the letter, she whispered: 'Hello there, little lover. I'll
reply tomorrow.'

He walked back to Spasskaya Street, reeling.

Little lover indeed!

But there wasn't any reply from Death the next day. She was
nowhere to be seen. Senka spent the whole day on his knees
until it was almost dark. He collected two roubles from his
begging, but what a waste of time! Even Boxman, when he came
round on his beat for the tenth, maybe fifteenth, time, told him:
'You're getting a bit greedy with the begging today, lad. Don't
you go overdoing it.'

Senka left after that.

On the fourth day, which was Sunday, Erast Petrovich sent him
out again. The engineer didn't seem surprised there was no

reply to the last letter, he just seemed saddened.

As he sent Senka off to Podkopaevsky Lane, he said: 'If she doesn't come today, we'll have to abandon the correspondence and think of something else.'

But she did come.

She didn't even glance at Senka, though. As she gave him the money, she looked away, and her eyes were furious. Senka saw a silver scale on a chain round her neck – exactly like the ones from the treasure trove. He hadn't seen Death wear anything like that before.

This time, instead of a piece of paper, Senka was left holding a silk handkerchief.

He walked across to a quiet spot and unfolded it. The note was inside. Senka started reading, taking great care to make sure nothing fell out of his hair and the folds in the paper didn't get twisted.

'Hello, Erast Petrovich. I haven't found out anything from him, in fact I haven't even tried asking him. He spotted my new trinket soon enough with those blank peepers of his, but he didn't ask any questions. He muttered a poem to himself, that's a habit he has. I remembered it word for word. We traded in damask steel silver and gold and now it is time to travel our road. I don't what it means. Perhaps you will understand. [That's Pushkin, Alexander Sergeevich, and what's so hard to understand, Senka thought condescendingly. He'd read The Tale of Tsar Saltan only the day before. And he knew who she was talking about too, it was Deadeye. He just loved spouting poetry.] And don't you dare write to me again about the body or our correspondence is over. I wanted to break it off anyway. I didn't go yesterday because I was angry with you. But today when he left I had a vision. I was lying in the middle of the plain you wrote about and I couldn't get up. I lay there for a long time, not just a day or two. And the grass and all sorts

*of flowers were growing up through me. I could feel them
inside me — it wasn't a bad feeling, it felt very good as they
pushed through me towards the sun. And then it wasn't me
lying on the plain, I was the plain. Later I tried my best to
embroider my vision on to a handkerchief. Take it as a present.*

Death'

Senka hadn't taken a proper look at the handkerchief at first,
but now he could see there really was something sewn on it: up
at the top was the sun, and down below there was a girl, lying
there naked, with all sorts of flowers and grass growing through
her. Senka didn't like this weird malarkey (or *allegory*, that was
the cultured word for it) at all.

Unlike Senka, Erast Petrovich looked at the handkerchief first,
and then opened up the letter. He looked at it and said: 'Oh,
Senya, S-Senya, what am I to d-do with you? You've been
p-prying again.'

Senka fluttered his eyelids to bring out the tears. 'Why are
you always getting at me? You ought to be ashamed. Here I am
slaving away, not a thought for myself. Serving faithfully . . .'

The engineer just waved his hand, as if to say: Go away, don't
bother me, damn you.

And the letter Erast Petrovich sent back to Death said this.

'Dear D.

*I implore you, do not sniff any more of that beastly stuff.
I have tried narcotics on only one occasion, and that almost
cost me my life. I will tell you the story some time. But it is
not even a matter of the danger lurking within this stupefying
poison. It is only needed by people who do not understand if
they are really living in this world or just pretending. But you
are alive and real. You do not need narcotics. Forgive me for
preaching another sermon. It is not my usual manner at all,
but such is the terrible effect that you have on me.*

If the other two individuals notice the object, do not tell them about SS [Well, thanks be for small mercies, Senka thought], *but about a certain new admirer, a man with greying temples and a stammer. This is best for the job at hand.*

Yours, E.N.'

This time Death didn't arrive angry, like the day before, she was in a jolly mood. As she bent down to take the letter, instead of five kopecks she handed him something big, round and smooth and whispered: 'Here's something sweet for you.'

When he looked, it was a chocolate medal! What did she take him for, a little kid?

On the last day of Senka's begging career, which was the sixth, Death dropped a handkerchief as she walked by. As she bent down to pick it up, she whispered: 'Someone's following me. On the corner.' She walked on into the church, leaving the letter on the ground beside Senka. He crawled over and pinned it down with his knee, then squinted at the corner Death had pointed to.

His heart started fluttering.

Prokha was standing at the turn-off from Podkolokolny Lane, leaning against a drainpipe with one elbow, chewing away. His eyes were riveted to the church door. Thank God, he wasn't eying up the beggars.

Ah-ha, so that's what's going on!

The deductions started flitting through Senka's head so fast, he could hardly keep up. That day when he was taking the silver rods to the jeweller, who was it he met right there on Maroseika Street? Prokha. That was one.

And then, on Trubnaya Square, near the boarding house, who was hanging around? That time the constable came running over? Prokha again. That was two.

Who knew about Senka's friendship with Tashka? Prokha yet again. That was three.

And Prokha was spying on Death! That was four.

239

So that meant he was to blame for everything, the rotten slug! He'd done in the jeweller, and Tashka too! Not with his own hands, of course. He was stooging for someone, probably the Prince.

Now what was he going to do? What was the projection that followed from this deduction?

It was very simple. Prokha was following Death, so he would follow Prokha. See who he went to report to and pass on his *communiqué*.

When Death came out of the church, she deliberately turned away and didn't even give out any alms – she floated by like a swan, but she brushed Senka with the hem of her dress. That was no accident. She was telling him to look sharp and keep his eyes peeled.

He counted to twenty and then hobbled after her, limping with both legs at once. Prokha was walking a little bit ahead, not looking back – he obviously didn't think anyone could be tailing him.

They reached the Yauza Boulevard, moving like a flight of storks: Death up at the front in the middle, then Prokha lagging a little bit behind her on the left, and Senka another fifteen paces back on the right.

Prokha loitered outside the door of the house for a bit and started scratching his head. It looked like he didn't know what to do next, hang about or go away. Senka made himself comfy around the corner and waited.

Then Prokha tossed his bonce back (all right, all right, his head), stuck his hands in his pockets, spun round on his heels and set off back at a smart pace. To report to the Prince, Senka figured. Or maybe not the Prince, but someone else.

When Prokha trudged past, Senka turned his back and held his hands down to the baggy front of his pants, as if he was having a pee. Then he set off after his former friend.

Prokha kicked an apple core with the toe of his boot, whistled a smart trill at a flock of pigeons pecking on horse dung (they flapped their wings and fluttered up in the air) and then turned into a courtyard that was just a shortcut back onto Khitrovka Square.

Senka followed him.

The moment he came out of the passageway into the damp, dark yard, someone grabbed him by the shoulder, jerked him hard and swung him round.

Prokha! The pointy-faced bastard had twigged he was being followed.

'Why are you sticking to me, rags and tatters?' he hissed. 'What do you want?'

He shook Senka so hard by the collar that Senka's head bobbled up and down and the thingamajig that made his mug look so twisted came out of his cheek, so he had to spit the fancy dress trick out.

'You!' Prokha gasped, and his nostrils flared. 'Speedy? You're just the one I need!'

And he grabbed Senka's collar with his second hand too – no way he could get out of that. Prokha had a real strong grip. Senka knew he was no match for him when it came to strength and agility. He was the nimblest lad in all Khitrovka. If Senka tried to scrap, Prokha would batter him. If he tried to run, Prokha would catch him.

'Right, you're coming with me.' Prokha chuckled. 'Now don't make a peep or there'll be blood.'

'Where to?' Senka asked. He hadn't recovered yet from the *debacle* of his carefully planned projection. 'What did you grab me like that for? Let go!'

Prokhka lashed him across the ankle with the toe of his boot. It hurt.

'Come on, come on. A nice man I know wants to have a little chat with you.'

If they'd scrapped the proper Khitrovka way, with fists, or even belts, Prokha would have given him a good drubbing double quick. But Senka hadn't completely wasted his time studying those Japanese fisticuffs now, had he?

When Masa-sensei realised Senka would never make a real fighter – he was too lazy and afraid of pain – he'd told him: Senka-kun, I won't teach you men's fighting, I'll teach you women's fighting. This is a lesson for a woman to follow if some ruffian grabs her by the collar and tries to dishonour her. It all came back to Senka in his hour of need.

'As simpur as boired turnip,' the sensei had said.

The idea was to hit the shameless lout with the edge of your left hand, right on the tip of the nose, and as soon as he jerked his head back, smash the knuckles of your right hand into his Adam's apple. Senka must have flailed at the air like that a thousand times. One-two, left-right, nose-throat, nose-throat, one-two, one-two.

So he did that old one-two now; half a second was all it took.

And as they wrote in the books, the result *exceeded all his expectations*.

The blow to Prokha's nose wasn't very strong, barely glanced it in fact, but his head jerked back and blood spurted out of his nostrils. And when Senka landed the 'two' right on the spot of the exposed throat, Prokha grunted and went down.

He sat down on the ground, holding his throat with one hand and squeezing his nose shut with the other, his mouth fell open and his eyes started rolling around. And there was blood, blood everywhere!

Senka felt frightened – had he hit him hard enough to kill him then?

He squatted down on his haunches:

'Hey, Prokha, what's up, not dying, are you?'

He shook him a bit.

Prokha wheezed: 'Don't hit me ... Don't hit me any more! Aah, aah, aah!' He was struggling to catch his breath, but he couldn't.

Before Prokha could come to his senses, Senka turned the

screws hard: 'Tell me who you're stooging for, you bastard! Or I'll give you a smack round the ears that'll knock your peepers out! Well? It's the Prince, isn't it?'

He swung both of his fists back (that was another one of those simple moves – thumping a villain just below both ears at once).

'No, it's not the Prince . . .' Prokha fingered his bloody nose. 'You broke it . . . You broke the bone . . . Oo-oo-oo!'

'Who, then? You tell me!'

And Senka thumped him with his fist, smack in the middle of the forehead. It wasn't a move the sensei had taught him, it just happened all by itself. Senka bruised all his fingers but it had the right effect.

'No, it's someone else, more frightening than the Prince, he is,' Prokha sobbed, shielding himself with his hands.

'More frightening than the Prince?' Senka asked, and his voice shook. 'Who is he?'

'I don't know. He's got a big black beard down to his belly. And black shiny eyes too. I'm afraid of him.'

'But who is he? Where's he from?' Senka was feeling really frightened now. A beard right down to his belly and black eyes. That *was* terrifying!

Prokha squeezed his nose with his finger and thumb to stop the blood pouring out. He said: 'I don'd dow where he's frop, bud if you wand a look, I'll show you. I'b beetink hib sood. Id the Yerokha basebedt . . .'

The Yerokha basement again. That damn place. Where the Siniukhins got their throats cut and Senka almost lost his own life.

'What's the meeting for?' Senka asked, still undecided what to do. 'Are you going to report back about following Death?'

'That's right.'

'And what does your man with the beard want with her?'

Prokha shrugged and sniffed. His nose had stopped bleeding. 'That's none of my business. Well, am I taking you or not?'

'Yes,' Senka decided. 'And you watch out, or I'll beat you to death with my bare fists. This magician I know taught me how.'

'He must be quite some teacher, you can thrash anyone you want to now,' said Prokha, the little brown nose. 'Don't you worry about me, Speedy, I'll do whatever you say. I'm not tired of living yet.'

They walked to the Tatar Tavern, where the way into the Yerokha was. Senka thumped his prisoner in the side a couple of times to keep him frightened and said: 'Just you try to bolt, and see what happens.' To tell the truth, Senka was afraid himself – what if Prokha swung round and socked him in the breadbasket? But he needn't have worried. His new Japanese tricks had made Prokha kowtow something rotten.

'Nearly there, nearly there,' Prokha said. 'Now you'll see for yourself what kind of man he is. I didn't want to stooge for him, he puts the fear of God up me. If you could only help me get free of this butcher, Speedy, I'd be really grateful.'

In the basement they made one turn, then another. So now they were no distance at all from the hall with the entrance to the treasure chamber. And the corridor where Senka almost lost his life was pretty close too. Senka remembered that powerful hand tugging his hair and threatening to break his neck and he started trembling all over and stopped dead in his tracks. He'd set out in fine form to unravel the whole case, but his bravado was almost all gone now. Sorry, Erast Petrovich and Masa-san, everyone has his limits.

'I'm not going any farther ... You go and meet him ... You can tell me all about it afterwards.'

'Ah, come on,' said Prokha, tugging at his sleeve. 'We're almost there. There's this little cubbyhole, you can hide in there.'

But no way would Senka go any farther. 'You go without me.'

He tried to turn back, but Prokha held him tight and wouldn't let go.

Then he flung his arms round Senka's shoulders and yelled: 'Here he is, it's Speedy! I've caught him! Run quick!'

The bastard had a tight grip. There was no way Senka could thump him or break free.

And then came the clatter of footsteps in the dark – heavy feet, moving fast.

The sensei had taught him: If a bad man grabs you round the shoulders, don't try to be clever, just plant your knee in his privates, and if he's standing so as you can't swing your knee or reach him with it, then lean as far back as you can and smash your forehead into his nose.

He butted as hard as he could. Once, twice. Like a ram butting a wall.

Prokha yelled (his nose was already broken anyway) and covered his ugly mug with his hands. Senka took off like a shot. And he didn't have a second to spare – someone managed to grab his collar from behind. The tattered old cloth gave, the rotten threads snapped, and Senka shot off into the darkness, leaving a piece of coarse shirt behind for Prokha's friend.

He just dashed off without thinking, anything to get away. But when the sound of tramping boots fell behind a bit, it suddenly struck him: where was he running to? The hall with the brick columns was ahead of him now, and after that it was a dead end! Both ways out were cut off – the main one and the Tatar Tavern!

They'd catch him now, trap him in a corner, and that would be the end!

He had only one hope left.

When he reached the hall, Senka made a dash for that special spot. He dragged the two bottom stones out of the entrance to the passage, crept into the gap on his belly, then froze. And he opened his mouth as wide as he could, to keep his breathing quiet.

An echo came drifting under the low vaults as two men ran into the hall – one was heavy and loud, the other was a lot lighter.

'He can't go any farther!' Prokha's panting voice said. 'He's here, the louse. I'll go along the right wall, you go along the left. We'll catch him now for sure.'

Senka propped himself up on his elbows to wriggle farther in, but his first movement made the brick dust under his belly rustle. He had to stop, or he'd give himself away, and the treasure too. He had to lie there quietly and pray to God they wouldn't notice the hole down by the floor. But if they had a lamp with them, then Speedy Senka's number was up.

Only, to judge from that dry scraping sound he kept hearing, Senka's pursuers didn't have any kind of light but matches.

The steps kept getting closer and closer, until they were really close.

Prokha, that was the way he walked.

Suddenly there was a clatter and someone barked out a curse almost right above the spot where Senka was lying.

'It's all right, I hit my foot against a stone. It's fallen out of the wall.'

Any moment now, right now, Prokha was going to bend down and see the hole and the bottoms of two shoes sticking out. Senka got ready to jump up on all fours and dart off along the passage. He couldn't run very far, but it would put the end off for a while.

But the danger passed. Prokha didn't spot his hiding place. The darkness had saved Senka, or maybe the Lord God had taken pity on the poor orphan: Ah, sod it, He'd thought, you can live a bit longer, I've got plenty of time to collect you.

He heard Prokha's voice from the far end of the hall: 'He must have squeezed up against the wall in the corridor, and we ran past him. He's crafty, that Speedy. Never mind, I'll find him anyway, don't you ha . . .'

Prokha gagged and didn't finish what he was saying. And the person he was talking to didn't say anything either. There was a clatter of footsteps moving away. Then it went quiet.

Senka was so frightened he just lay there for a while without moving a muscle. He wondered whether he ought to crawl farther into the passage – he could pay a visit to the treasure chamber and pick up a couple of rods.

But he didn't.

For starters, he didn't have any light. And apart from that, the thought of staying there any longer made him feel nervous. Maybe he ought to just leg it while the going was good? What if they'd gone to get lanterns? They'd spot the passage straight off then. And his own stupidity would be the end of him.

He scrabbled out backwards, moving like a crayfish. Everything seemed quiet.

Then he got to his feet, took off his battered old boots and set off towards the corridor on tiptoe, not making a sound. Every now and then he stopped and strained his ears to pick up any rustling or breathing from behind the columns.

Suddenly something crunched under his foot. Senka squatted down in fright. What was it?

He fumbled about and found a box of matches. Had those two dropped them, or was it someone else? No matter, they'd come in handy.

He took another two steps and spotted some kind of low heap on his right. Either a pile of rags, or someone lying there.

He struck a match and bent down.

And he saw Prokha. Lying on his back with his mug pointing up. But then he took a closer look and gasped. Prokha's mug was staring up, but he was lying on his belly, not his back. A man's neck couldn't twist round back to front like that – not if he was alive, it couldn't!

So they were Prokha's matches – and only then did Senka cross himself like you were supposed to and start backing away. And the damn match burned his fingers too. So that was why Prokha gagged like that. Someone had wrung his neck – literally – and double quick. And that was just too much for Prokha, he'd kicked the bucket.

Senka wasn't really sorry for him, he could go to hell. But

what kind of monster was it that could do things like that to people?

And then Senka had another idea. Without Prokha there was no way to find this killer now. A beard right down to the belly was the kind of thing you couldn't miss, of course, only Prokha was lying through his teeth (wasn't he?), God rest his rotten soul. He was lying, sure as eggs is eggs.

After all his deduction and projection Senka had been left with nothing but a broken tub, like the greedy old woman in the fairy tale (Senka had read it, but he didn't like it, the one about Tsar Nikita was better). He could have just told Erast Petrovich about seeing Prokha, couldn't he? But he'd wanted to shine, and look how bright he was shining now. This time he was the one who'd snapped off the guiding thread.

Senka was so upset, he almost forgot to read Death's letter. But he remembered by the time he got to Spasskaya Street.

'Hello, Erast Petrovich. Yesterday evening the superintendent was here. He asked about the silver coin himself. A new rival is it, he said. I won't stand for it. Who is he? I did as you told me and said it was a rich man with pockets full of silver. Very handsome but not young with greying temples. I said he had a slight stammer too. After that the superintendent forgot all about the gold and just kept asking about you. He asked if your eyes were blue. I said yes. He asked if you were tall. I said yes. He asked if you had a little scar on your temple. I said I thought you did. Then he started shaking he was so furious. He asked where you lived and all sorts of other things. I promised to find out and tell him everything. So now the two of us have tied a tight knot and I don't know how to untie it. It's time we met and talked things over. You can't put everything in a letter. Come tonight and bring Senka with you. He knows all the back alleys in Khitrovka. He'll get you away if anything happens. And I wanted to tell you I don't let

*any of them near me, even though the superintendent made
threats and swore at me yesterday. But now he wants you
more than he wants me. I threatened not to ask you about
anything and he left me alone. And I want to tell you I won't
let any of these bloodsuckers near me again because I can't
bear it any longer. Theres only so much anyone can take.
Come tonight. I'm waiting.*

Death'

Senka was in a real tizzy. Tonight, he was going to see her
again tonight!

How Senka Gloated

The engineer and Masa listened to his story without saying a word. They didn't curse him, they didn't call him a fool, but Senka wasn't shown any sympathy either. He didn't hear anything like 'Oh, you poor lad, how awful for you!' or even 'Ah, that's really terrible', not from the likes of them. Even though he tried real hard to impress them.

But then, he only had himself to blame, didn't he?

'I'm sorry, Erast Petrovich, forgive me, and you too, Mr Masa,' Senka said honestly at the end. 'It was a real stroke of luck, and I bungled the whole thing. We'll never find that villain now.'

He hung his head repentantly, but he peeped out from under his eyebrows to see whether they were really angry or not.

'Your opinion, Masa?' Erast Petrovich asked after listening to the story.

The sensei closed his narrow slits of eyes, kind of buried them in folds of skin, and just sat there for two or three minutes. Mr Nameless didn't say anything either, he waited for an answer.

At last the Japanese spoke: 'Senka-kun did werr. Orr crear now.'

The engineer nodded in satisfaction. 'That is what I think t-too. You have nothing to apologise for, Senya. Thanks to your actions we n-now know who the killer is.'

'How's that?' asked Senka, bouncing up and down on his chair. 'Who is it?'

But Mr Nameless didn't answer the question, he changed tack. 'In fact, as far as d-deduction is concerned, the task was not really very c-complicated from the outset. Any investigator with even the s-slightest experience would solve it easily if he p-possessed your evidence. However, an investigator is only inter-ested in the l-law, while my interest in this case extends beyond that.'

'Yes,' Masa agreed. 'Raw ress than justice.'

'Justice and mercy,' Erast Petrovich corrected him.

The two of them seemed to understand each other very well, but Senka didn't have a clue what they were talking about.

'But who's the killer?' he asked eagerly. 'And what put you on to him?'

'Something you t-told us,' the engineer said absent-mindedly, obviously thinking about something else. 'Try exercising your b-brains, it helps develop the personality . . .' And then he muttered some kind of gibberish. 'Yes, undoubtedly justice and m-mercy are more important. Thank God I am now a private individual and d-do not have to act according to the letter of the law. But time, I have so little t-time . . . and there is his maniacal c-caution, we must not frighten him off . . . One single b-blow to finish it. At a single stroke laying s-seven low, like in the folk tales . . . Eureka!' Erast Petrovich exclaimed and slapped his hand down on the table so loudly that Senka shuddered on his chair. 'We have a plan of operations! It's d-decided: justice and mercy.'

'Operation wirr be corred that?' the sensei asked. 'Justice and mercy? A fine name.'

'No,' Mr Nameless said cheerfully as he got up. 'I'll think of a m-more interesting name.'

'What operation's that?' Senka asked plaintively, pulling a sour face. 'You said it was thanks to me you solved the whole thing, but you don't explain anything.'

'When we g-go to the Yauza Boulevard tonight, you'll l-learn all about it there.'

They set off.

Death opened the door as soon as they knocked – had she

been waiting in the hallway? She said nothing, just looked at Mr Nameless hungrily, without even blinking, as if her eyes had been blindfolded just a moment earlier, or she'd been sitting in the dark for a long time, or maybe she'd just recovered her sight after being blind. That was the way she looked at him. She didn't even glance at Senka, never mind saying 'Hello, Senya' or 'How are you?' Then again, she didn't answer Erast Petrovich when he said, 'Good evening, madam,' either. She even frowned slightly, as if those weren't the words she'd been expecting.

They went into the room and sat down. They were supposed to be there to talk business, but something wasn't right, it was like they were talking about the wrong thing. Death didn't say much anyway, she looked at Erast Petrovich all the time, and he mostly looked down at the tablecloth. Sometimes he looked up at Death and then lowered his eyes again quickly. He stammered more than usual, as if he was embarrassed, or maybe he wasn't, you could never tell with him.

Them playing this game of peep for two made Senka feel anxious, he only half listened to what Mr Nameless was saying and all sorts of nonsense kept crowding into his head. To keep it speedy, what the engineer told them, his plan of action, as he called it, was this: they had to round all the suspects up at a certain spot, where the criminal would show his hand and give himself away. Senka stared at Erast Petrovich, as if to say: How come, didn't you say you'd figured out who the killer is? But the engineer flashed his eyes at Senka to tell him to keep quiet. So Senka kept shtum.

And when Erast Petrovich said: 'Unfortunately I c-cannot manage this business without you, m-madam, or you, Senya. I have no other assistants,' Death still didn't look at Senka. That really hurt, he was very upset by that. In fact he was so upset, he wasn't even scared when the engineer starting going on about how dangerous the job they were going to do was.

Death wasn't scared either. She shook her head impatiently.

'Enough. Tell us about the job.'

Senka rose to the occasion too: 'Who cares about that, death comes to everyone sooner or later.'

He tossed his head smartly and tried to catch her eye. And then he realised what he'd said could be taken two ways. About death, or about Death.

'All right.' Erast Petrovich sighed. 'Then let's d-decide who's going to hold which end of the n-net. You, madam, will b-bring the Prince and Deadeye to the spot. Senya will bring the Ghoul. And I will b-bring Superintendent Solntsev.'

'Why bring him?' Senka asked in surprise.

'Because he's under suspicion. All the c-crimes have been committed in his p-precinct. That is one. Solntsev is a cruel, g-greedy and absolutely immoral individual. That is t-two. And m-most importantly . . .' The engineer stared down at the tablecloth again. '. . . he is also involved with you, madam. That is three.'

Death's cheek twitched as if she was in pain.

'You're talking nonsense again,' she said bitterly. 'Why don't you tell me how to lure the Prince and Deadeye out? They're both leery old wolves, they won't just walk into a trap.'

'And what about me?' Senka piped up when he realised he'd have to handle the Ghoul all on his own. 'He won't even listen to me! Do you know what he's like? Him and his gang'll just grab me by the legs and tear me in half! What am I to him? A snot-nosed little kid! He won't come anywhere with me!'

'Yes he will, and he'll c-come running, I'll see to that,' Mr Nameless told Senka, but he was looking at Death as he said it. 'And you two won't have to l-lure anybody out. Just meet them and show them t-to the appointed spot.'

'What spot's that?' Death asked.

And then at last the engineer turned to Senka, and even put a hand on his shoulder.

'Only one p-person knows that place. Well, Ali Baba, will you g-give up the secret of your cave?'

If Erast Petrovich hadn't called him names like that in front of Death, maybe Senka wouldn't have told him. Only what point was there in hanging on to the silver when maybe his life was at stake? And then Death turned her huge eyes towards him and raised her eyebrows just a bit, as if she was surprised by his hesitation . . . That decided it.

'Agh!' he said with a sweep of his hand. 'I'll show you, of course I will. Speedy Senka's no miser!'

But once he'd said it, he suddenly felt sorry: not for all those thousands and thousands of roubles, but for his dream. After all, what were riches, anyway? Not the chance to stuff your belly every day, not a hundred pairs of patent leather shoes, not even your own automobile with a motor as strong as twenty horses. Riches were a dream of heaven on earth, when you got whatever you wished for.

That was horseshit too, of course. No matter how many millions he could offer Death, she still wouldn't look at him the same way she looked at Erast Petrovich . . .

No one was amazed and delighted by Senka's insane generosity, no one clapped their hands. They didn't even say 'thank you'. Death just nodded and turned away, as if it couldn't have been any other way. And Mr Nameless stood up. 'Let's g-go, then,' he said, 'without wasting any more time. Lead on, Senka, show us the way.'

There was no dead body in the underground hall where only a few hours earlier Prokha had tried to hand his old friend over to certain death and lost his own life instead. The basement-dwellers had dragged it away, for sure: they'd taken off the clothes and shoes and flung the naked corpse out in the street, that was the way of Khitrovka.

Senka didn't feel afraid with Erast Petrovich and Death there. He held up the paraffin lamp and showed them how to take out the stones.

'It's a tight squeeze here, but it's all right after that. You just keep going to the end.'

The engineer glanced into the hole, rubbed his fingers on one of the blocks and said: 'Old stonework, a l-lot older than the building of the d-dosshouse. This part of Moscow is like a c-cake with many layers: new f-foundations were laid on top of the old ones, and then n-new ones on top of those. They've been b-building here for almost a thousand years.'

'Are we going in, then?' asked Senka, who couldn't wait to show off his treasure.

'There's no n-need,' answered Mr Nameless. 'We can admire the sight t-tomorrow night. And so,' he said, turning to Death, 'be here, in this hall, at p-precisely a quarter past three in the m-morning. The Prince and Deadeye will come. When they see you, they will be s-surprised and start asking questions. No explanations. Show them the p-passage without saying anything, the stones will already be m-moved aside. Then s-simply lead them through, that's all you have to do. I'll be here soon after that, and that will be the b-beginning of Operation . . . I haven't thought of a n-name for it yet. The main thing is, k-keep calm and don't be afraid.'

Death kept her eyes fixed on the engineer all the time. Fair do's, even in the flickering light of the paraffin lamp he was a handsome devil.

'I'm not afraid,' she said in a slightly hoarse voice. 'And I'll do everything you say. And now let's go.'

'Where t-to?'

She smiled bitterly and teased him: 'No explanations, keep calm and don't be afraid of anything.'

And she walked out of the hall without saying another word. Erast Petrovich gave Senka a confused look and dashed after her. So did Senka, but he grabbed the lamp first. Now what idea had she got into her head?

On the porch of the house, right in front of the door, Death turned round. Her face wasn't mocking now, like it had been in the basement, it seemed to be distorted by suffering, but still unbearably beautiful at the same time.

'Forgive me, Erast Petrovich. I can't hold out any longer.

Perhaps God will take pity on me and work a miracle ... I don't know ... But what you wrote was true. I am Death, but I am alive. It may be wrong, but I can't carry on like this. Give me your hand.'

Mr Nameless didn't say a thing, he seemed overcome by shyness as she took him by the hand and pulled him towards her. He walked up one step, then another.

Senka went up after him. Something was about to happen here!

But Death hissed at him: 'Will you go away, for God's sake! You just can't leave me alone, can you?'

And she slammed the door right in his face – bang! Senka was struck dumb by the cruel injustice of it all. From behind the door he heard a strange sound, a kind of knocking, then a rustling, and something like sobbing, or maybe groaning. No words were spoken – he would have heard, because he had his ear pressed to the keyhole.

But when he realised what was going on in there, the tears started streaming from his eyes.

Senka banged the lamp down on the pavement, squatted on his haunches and put his hands over his ears. He squeezed his eyes tight shut too, so as not to hear or see this lousy rotten world, this bitch of a life in which some got everything and others got damn all. And God didn't exist, because if he could allow someone to be mocked as cruelly as this, the world would be better off without him.

But his woeful blaspheming didn't last very long, no more than a minute, in fact.

The door swung open, and Erast Petrovich came flying out on to the porch as if he'd been pushed from behind.

The engineer's tie knot had been pulled askew, the buttons on his shirt were open, and Mr Nameless's expression was hard to describe, because Senka had never seen anything like it on that self-possessed face before, he'd never even suspected that anything of the kind was possible: the eyelashes were fluttering in bewilderment, there was a strand of black hair hanging down over the eyes, and the mouth was gaping wide in total amazement.

Erast Petrovich swung round and exclaimed: 'B-But ... What's wrong!'

The door slammed, even louder than the last time, when it slammed in Senka's face. He heard the sound of muffled weeping behind it.

'Open up!' the engineer shouted, and almost tried to push the door open, but then he pulled his hands away as if it was red-hot iron. 'I don't wish to f-force my attentions on you, b-but ... I don't understand! Listen ...' and then he added in a low voice: 'Oh God, I c-can't even address her by name! Tell me what it is that I d-did wrong!'

The bolt clanged shut implacably.

Senka watched and he could barely believe his eyes. There was a God, after all! This was it, a genuine Miracle of the Prayer that was Heard!

So how do you like that bitter taste, Mr Handsome?

'Erast Petrovich,' Senka asked in a very sympathetic voice, 'why don't we switch the transmission to reverse?'

'Go t-to hell!' roared the engineer, who had misplaced his habitual courtesy.

But Senka wasn't offended at all.

How Senka Was a Little Kike

In the morning he was shaken awake by Masa, who was dirty and smelled of sweat, and his eyes were red, as if he'd been loading bricks all night instead of sleeping.

'What's this, Sensei?' Senka asked in surprise. 'Just back from a date, are you? Were you with Fedora Nikitishna, or have you got someone new?'

It seemed like a perfectly normal question, quite flattering to a man's vanity, but for some reason the Japanese was very angry.

'I was whe' I had to be! Get up, razybones, it' midday orready!'

And he even waved his fist at Senka, the heathen. And him the one so fond of preaching politeness!

After that things went from bad to worse. The sleepy young man was sat on a chair and his face was lathered with soap.

'Hey, hey!' Senka yelled when he saw a razor in his sensei's hand. 'Leave me alone! I'm growing a beard!'

'Masta's ordas,' Masa replied curtly. With his left hand he grabbed the poor orphan by the shoulder so that he couldn't wriggle and then with his right hand he shaved off all fifty-four of his beard hairs, and his moustache into the bargain.

Senka was afraid of getting cut, so he didn't budge. As the Japanese scraped away the final traces of his nascent male adornments, he muttered: 'Ver' just. "Some have orr fun and othas break their backs".' Senka didn't understand what he was talking about, or what he meant about backs, but he didn't bother to ask. In fact, he decided that for this outrageous attack he was never going to talk to the slanty-eyed pagan again. He was going to declare a boycott, like in the English parliament.

But the mockery of Senka's dignity had only just begun. After the shave, he was ushered into Erast Petrovich's study. The engineer wasn't there. Instead, there was an old Yid in a skullcap and long coat sitting in front of the pier glass, admiring the big nose in the middle of his face and combing out his eyebrows, which were bushy enough already.

'Have you shaved him?' the old man asked in Mr Nameless's voice. 'Excellent. I'm almost f-finished. Sit here, Senya.'

Erast Petrovich was unrecognisable in this get-up. Even the skin on his hands and neck was wrinkled and yellow, with dark spots like old men had. Senka was so delighted, he even forgot about his boycott and grabbed hold of the sensei's arm.

'Oh, fantastic! Make me into a gypsy, will you?'

'We don't need any g-gypsies today,' said the engineer, standing behind Senka's back and rubbing some oil into his hair – it made it stick to his head so that he looked lop eared.

'Let's add a f-few freckles,' Erast Petrovich said to the Japanese.

Masa handed his master a little jar. A few smooth strokes of the hand, and Senka's mug was freckly all over.

'The n-number fourteen wig.'

Masa handed over something that looked like a red bundle of fibres for scrubbing yourself in the bathhouse, but on Senka's head it turned into a tangled mop of ginger hair that hung down over his temples in two matted bunches. Then the engineer tickled Senka's eyebrows and eyelashes with a little brush, and they turned ginger too.

'What shall we d-do with the Slavic n-nose?' Mr Nameless asked himself thoughtfully. 'Add a hump? Yes, I think s-so.'

He stuck a lump of sticky wax on the bridge of Senka's nose, gave it a lick of flesh colour and sprinkled it with freckles. The resulting conk was a work of real beauty.

'What's all this for?' Senka asked merrily, admiring himself in the mirror.

'You're going to b-be the Jewish boy Motya,' Erast Petrovich replied, clapping a skullcap like his own on Senka's head. 'Masa will g-give you the appropriate costume.'

'I'm not going to be no kike!' Senka protested indignantly, suddenly realising that the ginger bunches were Jewish side locks. 'I don't *wish* to.'

'Why not?'

'I don't like them! I hate their ugly hook-nosed mugs! Faces, I mean!'

'What kind of f-faces do you like?' the engineer asked him. 'With snub n-noses? If someone's Russian, do you adore him straight away j-just for that?'

'Well, that depends what he's like, of course.'

'That's right,' Erast Petrovich said approvingly, wiping his hands. 'One should be ch-choosy about whom one loves. And even m-more so about whom one hates. In any case, one shouldn't l-love or hate someone for the shape of his n-nose. But that's enough d-discussion. In an hour we have a m-meeting with Mr Ghoul, the most dangerous b-bandit in Moscow.'

That gave Senka the shakes, and he forgot all about Yids.

'But I reckon the Prince is more frightening than the Ghoul,' he said casually, with a slight yawn.

That was what it said to do in the book on society life: 'If the subject of conversation has stung you to the quick, you should not betray your agitation. Pass some neutral remark on the matter in a casual voice, to show the other person that you have not lost your composure. Even a yawn is permissible but, naturally, only a very modest one, and the mouth must be covered with the hand.'

'That depends on how you l-look at it,' the engineer retorted. 'The Prince, of course, spills far more b-blood, but the most dangerous criminal is always the one to whom the f-future belongs. And the future of criminal Moscow undoubtedly d-does not belong to the hold-up men, it belongs to the m-milkers. The arithmetic p-proves it. The Ghoul's b-business undertaking is less dangerous, because it is less irritating to the authorities, it is actually p-profitable for some representatives of authority. And the milkers make m-more profit anyway.'

'What do you mean? The Prince lifts three thousand a time, and the Ghoul only collects a rouble a day from the shops.'

Masa brought the clothes: down-at-heel shoes, patched trousers, a tattered little jacket. Senka wrinkled up his face in disgust and started putting them on.

'A rouble a d-day,' Mr Nameless agreed. 'But f-from *every* shop, and *every* day. And the Ghoul has about t-two hundred of these sheep that he shears. How m-much does that make in a month? Twice as m-much as the loot the Prince takes from an average j-job.'

'But the Prince doesn't lift loot just once a month,' Senka persisted.

'How many t-times, then? Twice? Three times at the m-most? But then the Ghoul doesn't just take a rouble off everyone. For instance, he's d-decided to take no less than twenty th-thousand off the people we're g-going to see now.'

Senka gasped.

'What kind of people are they, if you can take that much money off them?'

'Jews,' Erast Petrovich replied, stuffing something into a sack. 'A long time ago n-now they built a synagogue not far from Khitrovka. When the present g-governor general was appointed to Moscow nine years ago, he f-forbade them to consecrate the synagogue and d-drove most of the Hebrews out of the old c-capital. But the Jewish c-community has recovered its strength again, its n-numbers have increased, and it is trying to open its house of p-prayer. Permission has been obtained f-from the authorities, but now the Jews have run into p-problems with the bandits. The Ghoul is threatening to b-burn down the building that was erected at the c-cost of immense sacrifice. He is demanding a p-pay-off from the community.'

'What a lousy snake!' Senka exclaimed indignantly. 'If you're a good Orthodox Christian and you don't want their Yiddish chapel anywhere near you, then just burn it down, but don't take their pieces of silver, right?'

Erast Petrovich didn't answer the question, he just sighed. Then Senka thought for a moment and asked: 'So why don't these Jews complain to the police, then?'

'The police are d-demanding even more money for protection against the b-bandits,' Mr Nameless explained. 'And so the m-members of the board of t-trustees have decided to reach an agreement with the Ghoul, and for that they have appointed special representatives. You and I, Senya, I mean M-Motya, are those special representatives.'

'What do I have to do?' Senka asked as they were walking down Spaso-Glinishshchevsky Lane. He didn't like this fancy-dress party nearly as much as the first one, when he was a beggar. It wasn't too bad in the cab, but since they'd got out they'd been called 'filthy Yids' twice, and one tattered raga-muffin had flung a dead mouse at them. He would have boxed his ears, to teach him not to go annoying people for no good reason, but he had to put up with it for the sake of the important job they were on.

'What d-do you have to do?' Mr Nameless echoed as he exchanged bows with the synagogue's caretaker. 'Keep quiet and l-leave your mouth hanging wide open. Do you know how to d-drool?'

Senka showed him.

'Oh, well done.'

They went into a house beside the Jewish chapel. Two nervous gents in frock coats and skullcaps, but without side locks, were waiting in a clean room with decent furniture. One was grey, the other had black hair.

Only it didn't look like they'd been waiting for Erast Petrovich and Senka. The grey-haired one waved his hand at them and said something angrily in a language that wasn't Russian, but the meaning was clear enough: Clear off out of it, I've no time for you right now.

'It is I, Erast Petrovich N-Nameless,' the engineer said, and the two men (they had to be those 'trusties') were terribly surprised.

The black-haired one raised a finger: 'I told you he was a Jew. The name's Jewish too, it's a distorted form of "Nahimles".'

The grey-haired one gulped, and his Adam's apple bobbed up and down. He looked at the engineer in alarm and asked: 'Are you sure you can manage this, Mr Nameless? Perhaps it would be better to pay this bandit? To avoid worse. We don't want any trouble.'

'There won't be any t-trouble,' Erast Petrovich assured him, sticking his sack under a table. 'But it's t-two o'clock already. The Ghoul will be here soon.'

At that very moment someone wailed from outside the door: 'Oi, he's coming, he's coming!'

Senka looked out of the window. The Ghoul was strolling casually up the street from the direction of Khitrovka, puffing on a *papyrosa* and glancing around with an evil smile on his face.

'He's come alone, without his d-deck,' Mr Nameless remarked calmly. 'He's confident. And he doesn't want to sh-share with his own men, the haul's too b-big.'

'Please, after you, Mr Rosenfeld,' said the black-haired man, pointing to a curtain that closed off a corner of the room where there were sofas (an 'alcove' it was called). 'No, I insist, after you.'

The trustees hid behind the curtain. The grey-haired one just had time to whisper: 'Ah, Mr Nameless, Mr Nameless, we put our trust in you, please don't lead us to ruin!'

The Ghoul pushed the door open without knocking and walked in, squinting after the bright daylight of the street. He said to Erast Petrovich: 'Right, you mangy kikes, have you got the crunch? You're the one who's going to cough up, are you, Grandad?'

'In the first place, good afternoon, young man,' Mr Nameless

263

intoned in a trembling voice. 'In the second place, you can stop eyeing the room like that – there isn't any money here. In the third place, have a seat at the table and we'll talk to you like a reasonable man.'

The Ghoul lashed out with his boot at the chair offered to him, and it flew off into the corner with a crash.

'Spieling and dealing?' he hissed, narrowing his watery eyes. 'We've done all that. The Ghoul's word is solid as cast iron. Tomorrow you'll be baking your matzos on charred embers. Well, what's left of the synagogue. And to make sure your brothers get the idea, I'll carve you up a bit too, you old goat.'

He pulled a hunting knife out of the top of his boot and edged towards Erast Petrovich.

The engineer stayed put. 'Ai, Mr Extortioner, don't waste my time on all this nonsense. The life left to me is no longer than a piglet's tail, cursed be that unclean creature.' And he spat fastidiously off to one side.

'You've hit the bull's-eye there, Grandad,' said the Ghoul, grabbing the engineer by his false beard and raising the tip of the knife to his face. 'For a start I'll gouge your eyes out. Then I'll straighten up your nose. What do you want a great big hook like that for? And then I'll snuff you and your stinking little brat.'

Mr Nameless looked at this terrible man quite calmly, but Senka's jaw dropped in horror. So much for the fun of the fancy-dress ball!

'Stop frightening Motya, he's *meshuggah* anyway,' said Erast Petrovich. 'And put that metal stick away. It's easy to see you don't know Jews very well, Mr Bandit. They're very cunning people! Haven't you noticed who they sent out to meet you? Do you see here the chairman of the board of trustees, Rosenfeld, or Rabbi Belyakovich, or perhaps Merchant of the First Guild Shendiba? No, you see the old, sick Naum Rubinchik and the *schlemazel* Motya, a pair that no one in the world cares about. Even I don't care about myself, I've had this life of yours right up to here.' He ran the edge of his hand across his throat. 'And if you "snuff" Motya here, that will be only a great relief to his poor parents. They'll say: "Thank you very much, Mr Ghoul". So let's stop all this trying to frighten each other and have a talk, like reasonable people. You know what they say in the Russian village? In the Russian village they say: You have the merchandise, we have the merchant, let's swap. Mr Ghoul, you're a young man, you want money, and the Jews want you to leave them in peace. Am I right?'

'I suppose.' The Ghoul lowered the hand holding the knife. 'Only you let slip as there was no crunch.'

'No money . . .' Old Rubinchik's eyes glinted and he paused for a moment. 'But there is silver, an awful lot of silver. Does an awful lot of silver suit you?'

The Ghoul put the knife back in his boot and cracked his knuckles.

'Cut the horse shit! Talk turkey! What silver?'

'Have you heard word of the underground treasure? I see from the gleam in your little eyes that you have. That treasure was buried by Jews when they came to Russia from Poland during the time of Queen Catherine, may God forgive her her sins for not oppressing our people. They don't make such fine, pure silver any more now. Just listen to the way it jingles.' He took a handful of silver scales out of his pocket – the same kind of old kopecks that Senka had (or maybe they just looked the same – how could you tell?) and clinked them under the milker's nose for a moment or two. 'For more than a hundred years the silver just lay there quietly all on its own. Sometimes the Jews took a little bit, if they really needed it. But now we can't get to it. Some *potz* in Khitrovka found our treasure.'

'Yeah, I heard that yarn,' the Ghoul said with a nod. 'So it's true. Was it you lot who shivved the pen-pusher and his family, then? Good going. And they say Jews wouldn't swat a fly.'

'Ai, I implore you!' Rubinchik said angrily. 'A plague on your tongue for saying such vile things! The last thing we need is for that to be blamed on the Jews. Maybe it was you who killed the poor *potz*, how should I know? Or the Prince? You know who the Prince is? Oh, he's a terrible bandit. No offence meant, but he's even more terrible than you.'

'Watch it now!' the Ghoul said, swinging his hand back to hit him. 'You ain't seen any real terror from me yet!'

'And I don't need to. I believe you anyway,' said the old man, holding the palm of his hand in front of him. 'But that's not the point. The point is that the Prince has found out about the treasure and he's searching for it day and night. Now we're afraid to go near it.'

'Oh, the Prince, the Prince,' the Ghoul muttered, baring his yellow teeth. 'All right, Grandad, keep talking.'

'What else is there to discuss? This is our business proposition. We show you the place, you and your boys carry out the silver, and then we share it honestly: half for us and half for you. And believe me, young man, that will be a lot more than twenty thousand roubles, an awful lot more.'

The Ghoul didn't think for long. 'Good enough. I'll take it all out myself, I don't need any help. You just show me the place.'

'Do you have a watch?' Naum Rubinchik asked, staring sceptically at the gold chain dangling from the Ghoul's pocket. 'Is it a good watch? Does it keep good time? You have to be in Yeroshenko's basement, right at the far end, where the brick bollards are, tonight. At exactly three o'clock. Poor little dumb Motya here will meet you and show you where to go.' Senka winced under the keen, venomous stare that the Ghoul fixed on him and let a string of saliva dribble off his drooping lip. 'And one last thing I wanted to say to you, just so you remember,' the old Jew went on in a soulful voice, cautiously taking the milker by the sleeve. 'When you see the treasure and you take it away to a good safe place, you will ask yourself: "Why should I give half to those stupid Jews? What can they do to me? I'd better keep it all for myself and just laugh at them".'

The Ghoul swung his head this way and that to see whether

there was an icon in the corner of the room. When he couldn't find one he swore his oath dry, without it:

'May the lightning burn me! May I be stuck in jail forever! May I wither up and waste away! If people treat me right, I treat them right. By Christ the Lord!'

The old grandad listened to all that, nodded his head then asked out of the blue: 'Did you know Alexander the Blessed?'

'Who?' the Ghoul asked, gaping at him.

'Tsar Alexander. The great-grand-uncle of His Highness the Emperor. Did you know Alexander the Blessed? I ask you. I can see from your face that you did not know this great man. But I saw him, almost as close as I see you now. Not that Alexander the Blessed and I were really acquainted, good God, no. And he didn't see me, because he was lying dead in his coffin. They were taking him to St Petersburg from the town of Taganrog.'

'So what are you spouting all this for, Grandad?' the Ghoul asked, wrinkling up his forehead. 'What's your tsar in a coffin mean to me?'

The old man raised a single cautionary yellow finger. 'This, Monsieur Voleur: if you deceive us, they'll carry you off in a coffin too, and Naum Rubinchik will come to look at you. That's all, I'm tired. Off you go now. Motya will show you the way.'

He stepped back, sat down in a chair and lowered his head on to his chest. A second later there was the sound of thin, plaintive snoring.

'A tough old grandad,' the Ghoul said, winking at Senka. 'You make sure you're where you were told to be tonight, Carrot-head. Pull a fast one on me and I'll wrap your tongue round your neck.'

He turned round softly, like a cat, and walked out of the house.

The moment the door slammed shut, the two Jews jumped out from behind the curtain.

They both started jabbering away at once. 'What have you told him? What silver? Why did you make all that up? Where are we going to get so many old coins from now? It's a total catastrophe!'

Erast Petrovich arose immediately from his slumbers, but instead of interrupting the clamouring trustees, he got on with his own business: he took off the skullcap and the grey wig, peeled off his beard, took a little glass bottle out of the sack, soaked a piece of cotton wool and started rubbing it over his skin. The liver spots and flabbiness disappeared as if by magic.

When there was a pause in the clamour, he said briefly: 'No, I didn't m-make it all up. The treasure really d-does exist.'

The trustees stared at him, wondering if he was joking or not. But from Mr Nameless's face it was quite clear that he wasn't.

'But ...' the black-haired one said to him cautiously, as if he was talking to a madman, '... but do you realise that this bandit will trick you? He'll take all the treasure and not give you anything?'

'Of course he'll t-try to trick me,' the engineer said with a nod as he removed his long coat, faded plush trousers and galoshes. 'And then what Naum Rubinchik p-prophesied will come to pass. They'll carry the Ghoul off in his c-coffin. Only not to St Petersburg. To a common g-grave in the Bozhedomka cemetery.'

'Why have you taken your clothes off?' the grey-haired man asked in alarm. 'You're not going to walk down the street like that, are you?'

'Apologies for my state of undress, g-gentlemen, but I have very little time. This young man and I have to m-make our next visit.' Erast Petrovich turned towards Senka. 'Senya, don't just st-stand there like a monument to Pushkin l-lost in thought, get undressed. Good d-day to you, gentlemen.'

The trustees exchanged glances, and the one who was older said: 'Well then, we will trust you. Now we have no other choice.'

They both bowed and left, and the engineer turned to the sack and took out a long Caucasian kaftan with rows of little slots for bullets, a pair of soft leather shoes, a tall astrakhan hat and a belt with a knife. In a jiffy Mr Nameless was transformed into a visitor from the Caucasus. Senka watched wide eyed as he covered his neat and tidy moustache with a different one as black as tar and glued on a beard that was in the same bandit colour.

'You look just like Imam Shamil!' Senka exclaimed in delight. 'I saw him in a picture in a book!'

'Not Shamil, but K-Kazbek. And I'm not an imam, I'm a warrior c-come down from the mountains to conquer the c-city of the infidels,' Erast Petrovich answered as he changed his grey eyebrows for black ones. 'Are you undressed yet? No, no, c-completely.'

'Who are we going to visit now?' asked Senka, hugging himself – it felt pretty chilly standing around in the buff.

'His Excellency, your f-former patron. Put this on.'

'What Excell . . .' Senka didn't finish what he was saying, he gagged and froze, holding the silky, flimsy something that the engineer had taken out of his sack. 'The Prince? Are you crazy? Erast Petrovich, he'll do me in! He won't listen to anything! He'll drop me the moment he sees me! He's a wild man!'

'No, n-not that way.' Mr Nameless turned the short silk and lace underpants round. 'First the d-drawers, then the stockings and s-suspenders.'

'Women's underwear?' said Senka, eyeing the clothes. 'What do I want that for?'

The engineer took a dress and a pair of tall lace-up boots out of the sack.

'You mean you want to dress me up like a bint? I'd rather die first!'

Mr Nameless and Masa had had it all worked out from the start, Senka realised. That was why they'd scraped his face with that razor. Well, sod that! Just how long could they go on mocking a poor orphan?

'I won't put it on, no way!' he declared stubbornly.

'It's up t-to you,' Erast Petrovich said with a shrug. 'But if the

Prince recognises you then he'll d-drop you, as you p-put it, no doubt about it.'

Senka gulped. 'But can't you get by without me?'

'I can,' said the engineer. 'Although it will m-make my job more difficult. But the real p-point is that you'll be ashamed afterwards.'

Senka sniffed for a bit, then he pulled on the slippery girl's pants, the fishnet stockings and the red dress. Erast Petrovich put a light-coloured wig with dangling curls on his victim's head, wiped all the Jewish freckles off his face and blackened his eyebrows.

'Come on, p-push those lips out for me.'

And he smeared Senka's mouth with a thick layer of sweet-smelling lipstick. Then he held out a little mirror. 'Take a l-look at yourself now. A real b-beauty.'

Senka didn't look, he turned his face away.

How Senka Was a Mamselle

'Whoah, whoah, you pests,' the driver barked at his blacks, and the beautiful horses stopped dead on the spot. The lead horse curved his elegant neck, squinted at the driver with a wild eye and stamped his metal-shod hoof on the cobblestones, sending sparks flying.

That was how they drove up to the 'Kazan' lodging house, in grand style. The Bosun selling his whistles and the small fry jostling around him turned to look at the classy landau (three roubles an hour!) and stared at the Abrek, or Caucasian warrior, and his female companion.

'Wait here!' the Abrek told the driver, tossing him a glittering gold imperial.

He jumped down without stepping on the footboard, took hold of Senka the mamselle by the sides and set him down lightly on the ground, then made straight for the gates. He didn't even say the magic word '*sufoeno*' that Senka had taught him, just declared portentously:

'I am Kazbek.'

And the Bosun accepted that, he didn't blow his whistle, just narrowed his eyes a bit and nodded to this handsome Southerner, as if to say: Go on in. He gave Senka a fleeting glance, too, but didn't really take any notice of him – and the tight knot in Senka's belly loosened up.

'More g-gracefully,' Erast Petrovich said in his normal voice in the courtyard. 'Don't wave your arms about. Move with your hips, n-not your shoulders. Like that, that's g-good.'

When he knocked, the door opened slightly and a young lad Senka didn't know stuck his nose out. The new sixer, Senka guessed, and – would you believe it? – he felt something like a pin pricking at his heart. Could it be jealousy?

Senka didn't like the look of the lad at all. He had a flat face and yellow eyes, like a cat.

'What you want?' the lad asked.

Mr Nameless said the same thing to him: 'I am Kazbek. Tell the Prince.'

'What Kazbek?' the sixer asked with a sniff, and his nose was immediately grabbed between two fingers of iron.

The Caucasian warrior swore in a guttural voice, smacked the flat-faced lad's head against the doorpost and gave him a push. The lad collapsed on the floor.

Then Kazbek stepped inside, strode over the boy on the floor and set off determinedly along the corridor. Senka hurried after him, gasping. Looking round, he saw the sixer holding his forehead and batting his eyelids in a daze.

Oh Lord, Lord, now what was going to happen?

In the big room Maybe and Surely were playing cards, as usual. Lardy wasn't there, but Deadeye was lying on the bed with his boots up on the metal bars, cleaning his fingernails with a little knife.

The Caucasian made straight for him. 'Are you the Jack? Take me to the Prince, I want to talk. I am Kazbek.'

The twins stopped slapping their cards down on the table. One of them (Senka had never learned to tell which was which) winked at the young lady, the other gaped stupidly at the silver dagger hanging from the visitor's belt.

'Kazbek is above me. Alone up on high,' Deadeye said with a serene smile, and bounced up to his feet. 'Let's go, now that you're here.'

He didn't ask any questions, just led them through. Oh, this didn't look good at all.

★

The Prince was sitting at the table, looking terrible, all puffy – he must have drunk a lot. He wasn't very much like the handsome fellow Senka had seen that first time (only a month ago!). His fine satin shirt was all crumpled and greasy, his curly hair was tangled and his face hadn't been shaved. As well as empty bottles and the usual jar of pickled cucumbers, there was a golden candlestick on the table, with no candles in it.

Senka's enemy looked up at the newcomers with bleary eyes. He asked the Caucasian: 'Who are you? And what do you want?'

'I am Kazbek.'

'Who?'

'He must be the one who arrived from the Caucasus not long since with twenty horsemen,' Deadeye said in a low voice, leaning against the wall and folding his arms. 'I told you about him. They showed up three months ago. Put the bite on the Maryina Roshcha bandits, took over all the girls and the paraffin shops.'

The Caucasian warrior chuckled, or rather, he twitched the corner of his mouth.

'You Russians came to our mountains and you do not leave. And I have come to you and I shall not leave soon either. We shall be neighbours, Prince. Neighbours can get along – or not. They can talk with their knives, we know how to do that. Or they can be *kunaks* – blood brothers, you call it. Choose which you like.'

'It's all the same bollocks to me,' the Prince replied languidly. He downed a glass of vodka, but didn't take a cucumber to follow it. 'Live any way you like, as long as you don't get under my feet, and if you annoy me, we can get the knives out.'

Deadeye warned him in a low voice: 'Prince, you can't deal with them like that. He's come alone, but we can be certain the others are hiding somewhere not so far away. He only has to whistle and there'll be daggers everywhere.'

'Let them bring on the daggers,' the Prince hissed. 'We'll see who comes off best. All right, Deadeye, don't be so gutless' –

and he laughed. 'What are you glowering at, Kazbek? I'm laughing. The Prince is a jolly man. Right then, *kunaks* it is. Let's shake on it.'

He stood up and held out his hand. That made Senka feel a bit better – he'd been preparing his soul to join the holy saints in heaven.

But the Abrek didn't want to shake hands.

'In our mountains just squeezing fingers is not enough. You have to prove yourself. One *kunak* must give the other the thing most precious to him.'

'Yeah?' The Prince swung his arm out from the shoulder. 'Well, ask for anything you like. The Prince's heart is as open as a Khitrovka mamselle. Look at this candlestick here, it's pure gold. I took it off this merchant just the other day. Like me to give it to you?'

Kazbek shook his head in the shaggy astrakhan hat.

'Then what do you want? Tell me.'

'I want Death,' the Caucasian said in a low, passionate voice.

'Whose death?' the Prince asked, startled.

'Your Death. They say that is the most precious thing you have. Give me that. Then we shall be *kunaks* to the grave.'

Senka was the first to catch on. Well, that was it now, for sure. Now there'd be fountains of blood, and some of it Senka's: *dear old mum, welcome your poor son Senya into heaven with the angels.*

Deadeye caught on too. He stayed where he was, but the fingers of his right hand slipped quietly into his left sleeve. And inside that sleeve there were little knives on a leather cuff. He had only to fling a couple, and that would be the end of the visitors.

The Prince was the last to twig. He opened his mouth wide and tore open his collar so they could see the veins on his neck, but the shout couldn't force its way out – his fury strangled it in his throat.

Kazbek went on as if nothing had happened. 'Give me your woman, Prince. I want her. And for you, see, I have brought the best of my mamselles. As slim and supple as a mountain goat. Take her. I give her to you.'

And he pushed Senka out into the middle of the room.

'A-a-agh!' Senka squealed. 'Mum!'

But his whimper was drowned by the Prince's loud roar: 'I'll rip your throat out! With my teeth! You carrion!'

He picked up the big two-pronged fork for getting cucumbers out of the jar and was about to throw himself on the Abrek, but suddenly out of nowhere a small black revolver glinted in the Caucasian's hand.

'You – hands on your shoulders!' Kazbek said to the Jack. He didn't say a word to the Prince, but his eyes were blazing.

Deadeye raised one eyebrow as he contemplated the black hole of the gun barrel. He showed the Caucasian his empty hands and put them up. The Prince swore obscenely and flung the fork down on the floor. He didn't look at the gun, he stared into the eyes of the man who had insulted him and chewed on his lips in a fury – a trickle of red blood ran down his chin.

'I'll kill you anyway!' he shouted hoarsely. 'I'll get you, even in Maryina Roshcha. I'll rip your guts out for this, and make sausages with them!'

Kazbek clicked his tongue. 'You Russians are like women. A man does not shout, he talks quietly.'

'So she's been with you too, with you!' the Prince shouted, not listening to a word. He wiped away an angry tear and grated his teeth. 'The whore, the bitch, I've no more patience for her!'

'I came to you like a man, honestly,' said the Abrek, knitting his black brows, and his blue eyes glinted with a cold flame. 'I could have stolen her, but Kazbek is not a thief. I ask you like a friend: give her to me. If you do not give her, I shall take her like an enemy. Only think first. I do not take her for nothing.'

He pointed to Senka cringing in the middle of the room.

The Prince gave poor innocent Senka a shove that sent him flying against the wall and sliding down on to the floor:

'I don't want your painted whore!'

Senka had hurt his shoulder and he was terrified, but those words that were meant to be insulting were sweet music to his ears. The Prince didn't want him, Jesus be praised!

'I throw the mamselle into the bargain, so you will not be left without a woman.' The Abrek laughed. 'But the most precious thing I have, the thing I will give you, is silver, much silver. You have never had so much . . .'

'I'll ram that silver down your throat, you filthy swine!' the Prince retorted. And he ranted for a long time, shouting incoherent threats and obscenities.

'How much is "much", my dear fellow?' Deadeye asked when the Prince finally choked on his hatred and fell silent.

'It will take more than one wagon to carry it away. I know you have been searching for this silver for a long time, but I have found it. For Death, I will give it to you.'

The Prince was about to start bawling again, but Deadeye raised one finger: *Ssssh, not a word.*

'Do you mean the Yerokha pen-pusher's treasure?' the Jack asked in a grovelling voice. 'So you've found it? Oh, most artful son of the Caucasus.'

'Yes, now the treasure is mine. But if you wish, it will be yours.'

The Prince tossed his head like a bull driving away horseflies. 'I won't give you Death! Not for all your silver and gold, I won't! She'll never be yours, you dog!'

'She is mine already,' the Caucasian said, stroking his beard with his free hand. 'As you wish, Prince. I came here honestly, and you have called me "dog". I know already that in Moscow you can curse in many different ways, but "dog" is answered with the knife. We shall fight. I have more guards than you, and every one is a mountain eagle.'

Kazbek started backing towards the door, holding his revolver at the ready. Senka jumped up and pressed himself against his master.

'Where are you going, you snake?' the Prince roared. 'You'll never get out of here alive! Go on, fire! My wolves will finish you off!'

One of the twins stuck his head in the door. 'What did you shout for, Prince? Were you calling us?'

Without taking his eyes off the Prince and Deadeye for a single moment, the Abrek grabbed Maybe or Surely just below the chin with his left hand, held him like that for a couple of seconds and let go. The young man collapsed in a heap and tumbled over on to his side.

'Wait, dear fellow!' said Deadeye. 'Don't go. Prince, this man came to you in peace, as a friend. What difference does one woman more or less make? What will the lads say?' Then he started talking in poetry again. 'Dear heart, Prince, do not ponder, I know of a certain wonder.'

Ah-ha, thought Senka, *I know that poem too. That's what the Swan Queen told Prince Gvidon: Don't go getting in a lather, I'll fix you up in fine fashion.*

But the Khitrovka Prince apparently hadn't read that fairy tale, he just looked blankly at Deadeye. The Jack winked back – Senka could see that very clearly from the side.

'Treasure, you say?' the Prince muttered. 'All right. For the pen-pusher's treasure, I'll swap. But the silver up front.'

'On your luck?' Kazbek asked. 'As a thief?'

'On my luck as a thief,' the Prince confirmed, and ran his thumb across his throat, the way you were supposed to when you swore an oath. But Senka spotted another bit of cunning: the Prince held his left hand behind his back, and he had the thumb between his fingers – that meant his word as a thief wasn't worth a bent kopeck. He'd have to tell Kazbek – that is, Erast Petrovich – about this villainous trick.

'Good.' The Abrek nodded and put his weapon away. 'Come to the Yeroshenko basement tonight, to the hall that is a dead end. Just the two of you come, no more. At exactly a quarter past three. If you come earlier or later, there is no deal.'

'We'll come alone, but won't your wolves take their knives to us?' asked the Prince, narrowing his eyes.

'Why go to the basement for that?' Kazbek asked with a shrug. 'If we wanted, we could slice you into kebabs anyway. I need faithful *kunaks* in Moscow, friends I can trust . . . You will be met in the basement and taken to the right place. When you see who meets you, you will understand: Kazbek could have given you nothing and just taken it for free.'

The Prince opened his mouth to say something (to judge from his fierce grin, it was something angry), but Deadeye put a hand on his shoulder.

'We'll be there at quarter past three in the morning, dear fellow. On my luck as a thief.'

The Jack swore without any tricks, both of his hands were out in the open.

'So you're not taking the mamselle?' the Caucasian asked from the doorway.

Senka turned cold. *Ai, Erast Petrovich, why are you trying to destroy me? Holy Saint Nicholas and the Virgin Intercessor, save me!*

But the Prince, may God lop a thousand years off his torments in hell, just cleared his throat and spat on the floor.

Senka was saved.

How Senka Was a Peacher

Outside, once they'd got into the landau and driven off, Senka heaved a bitter sigh and said:

'Thank you, Erast Petrovich, for taking such good care of me. That's the way you treat a true friend, is it? What if the Prince had said "give me your mamselle"? Were you really going to hand me over to be tortured to death?'

'Turn the corner and stop!' the ungrateful engineer ordered the driver in his Caucasian voice. He answered the reproach when they got out of the carriage.

'For the P-Prince only one woman exists. He won't even l-look at any other. I needed you to look f-frightened, Senya – to make our little interlude m-more convincing. And you m-managed it very well.'

And then Senka realised that when Erast Petrovich was wearing fancy dress – as an old Yid or a wild mountain warrior – he didn't stammer at all. That was amazing. And Senka remembered that the engineer had done the whole job on his own, without any help from his partner. He felt ashamed then, most of all for being such a coward and calling on the Virgin Mary and St Nicholas for help. But then, what was there to be ashamed of in that? He was a real person, wasn't he, not some kind of stone idol like Mr Nameless. Erast Petrovich didn't need to pray, Masa-sensei had told Senka that.

They walked along Pokrovka Street, past the Church of the Trinity in the Mud and the magnificent Church of the Assumption.

'Don't you ever pray to God, then?' Senka asked. 'Is that because you're not afraid of anything at all?'

'Why do you think I'm n-not afraid?' Erast Petrovich asked in surprise. 'I am afraid. Only p-people completely without imagination have no f-fear. And since I am afraid, I p-pray sometimes.'

'You're lying!'

The engineer sighed. 'It would be b-better to say "I don't believe you", and best of all n-never to say such things unless it is absolutely n-necessary, because . . .' He gestured vaguely with his hand.

'. . . because you could collect a slap across the face,' Senka guessed.

'And for th-that reason too. And the p-prayer I say, Senya, is one I was t-taught by an old priest: "Spare me, Lord, from a slow, p-painful, humiliating death". That is the entire prayer.'

Senka thought about it. The bit about a slow death was clear enough – who wanted to spend ten years just lying paralysed or withering away? The painful part was obvious too.

'But what's a humiliating death? Is that when someone dies and everyone spits on him and kicks him?'

'No. Christ was b-beaten and humiliated too, but there was nothing shameful about his d-death, was there? All my life I've b-been afraid of something else. I'm afraid of d-dying in a way that people will f-find amusing. People don't remember anything else about you after th-that. For example, the French p-president Faure will not be remembered for c-conquering the island of Madagascar and concluding an alliance with Russia, but for the f-fact that His Excellency expired on t-top of his lover. All that is left of the former l-leader of the nation is a d-dirty joke: "The president died in the p-performance of his duties – in every s-sense". Even on his gravestone the p-poor fellow is shown embracing the b-banner of the republic. People walking by g-giggle and titter – that is the f-fate that I fear.'

'That sort of cock-up couldn't happen to you,' Senka reassured the engineer. 'You're in sound health.'

'If not that k-kind, then some other. Fate loves to j-jest with those who are too concerned for their own d-dignity.' Erast Petrovich laughed. 'For instance, you remember the way the t-two of us were sitting in the water closet, and the G-Ghoul heard a noise and p-pulled out his revolver?'

'How could I forget that? It still gives me the shakes.'

'Well then, if the Ghoul had started f-firing through the door, he would have left us b-both draped across the toilet bowl. What a beautiful d-death that would have been.'

Senka imagined himself and Erast Petrovich lying on top of each other across the china potty, with their blood flowing straight into the sewage pipe.

'Not exactly beautiful, I'd say.'

'Indeed. I wouldn't want to d-die like that. A stupid weakness, I realise that, b-but I simply can't help myself.'

Mr Nameless gave a guilty smile and suddenly stopped dead – right on the corner of Kolpachny Lane.

'Now, Senya, this is where our ways p-part. I have to drop into the post office and s-send off a certain important letter. F-from here on you will act without me.'

'How's that?' Senka asked warily. What torment had the sly Erast Petrovich got in store for him now?

'You will g-go to the police station and deliver a l-letter to Superintendent Solntsev.'

'Is that all?' Senka asked suspiciously, screwing up his eyes.

'That's all.'

That was all right, delivering a letter was no big deal.

'I'll take off the tart's rags and wash the paint off my mug,' Senka growled. 'I feel a right nelly.'

'I feel embarrassed in front of people,' the pernickety engineer corrected him. 'There's no t-time to get changed. Stay as you are. It will be s-safer that way.'

Senka felt a black cat scrape its claws across his heart. Safer? What exactly did that mean?

But Mr Nameless only made the vicious beast scrape away even harder.

'You're a b-bright young man,' he said. 'Act according to the s-situation.'

He took two envelopes out of his pocket, gave one to Senka and kept the other.

Senka scratched at his chest to stop that cat scraping so hard, but his hand ran into something soft – it was the cotton wool Erast Petrovich had stuffed under the dress to give it a woman's curves.

'Why don't I run to the post office, and you go to the super-intendent?' Senka suggested without really feeling very hopeful.

'I can't show my f-face at the police station. Hold on t-to the letter. You have to g-give it to Colonel Solntsev in person.'

There was no address on the envelope, and it wasn't even glued shut.

'That is so you will n-not have to waste any time b-buying a new one,' Mr Nameless explained. 'You'll read it anyway.'

There was no way you could hide anything from him, the sly serpent.

Before Senka had even walked on a hundred steps alone, someone ran up from behind and started pawing his cotton-wool tits.

'Oh, soft and springy, we could have some sweet fun,' a fervent voice whispered in his ear.

He turned his head and saw an ugly mug that hadn't been shaved and smelled of stale vodka and onions.

So this was what it was like for a girl to walk round Khitrovka on her own.

At first Senka was just going to frighten the randy villain, tell him he would complain to Brawn, the biggest pimp in Khitrovka, about this cheek, but the unwelcome admirer went on to lick the false mamselle on the neck, and Senka's patience snapped.

Following the rules of Japanese fighting art, first he breathed out all the air in his lungs (to shift the root of his strength from his chest to his belly), then he smashed his heel into his admirer's shin and then, when the admirer gasped and opened his filthy great mitts, Senka swung round rapidly, jabbed his finger into the top of his belly and winded him.

The lascivious wooer squatted down on his haunches and clutched at his belly. His face turned serious and thoughtful. *That's right, you think about how you ought to behave with the girls.*

Senka turned into a quiet passageway and unfolded the letter.

'Dear Innokentii Romanovich,

I have learned from a reliable source that you have learned from a reliable source that I am in Moscow. Although we have never had any great affection for each other, I hope nonetheless that the orgy of atrocious crimes in the area entrusted to your care concerns you, as a servant of the law, no less than it does me, a man who left behind his former service and the cares of Moscow a long time ago. And therefore, I wish to put a business proposition to you.

Tonight I shall bring together at a certain convenient location the leaders of the two most dangerous gangs in Moscow, the Prince and the Ghoul, and you and I shall arrest them. The nature of that place will not allow you to bring a large number of men — you will have to make do with one deputy, so choose your most experienced police officer. I am sure that the three of us will be enough to carry out the arrest of the Prince and the Ghoul.

The person who will deliver this letter to you knows nothing about this business. She is an ordinary street girl, a simple soul who has undertaken to perform this errand for me for a small payment, so do not waste your time questioning her.

I shall call for you at twenty minutes past three in the morning. Being an intelligent and ambitious man, you will no doubt realise that it would not be a good idea to report my proposal to your superiors. The greatest possible reward you would receive is the benevolent disposition of the municipal

authorities. However, I am not a criminal, and I am not
wanted by the police, so you will earn no titles or medals by
informing on me. You will reap far greater dividends if you
agree to take part in the undertaking that I propose. Fandorin.'

Senka knew what 'dividends' were (that was when they paid
you money for nothing), but he didn't understand that last word.
It must mean 'adieu', or 'please accept, etc.', or 'I remain yours
truly' – basically, what people wrote to give a letter a beautiful
ending. 'Fandorin' had a fine ring to it. He'd have to remember
it in future.

He licked the envelope and glued it shut, and a couple of
minutes later he was walking into the courtyard of the Third
Myasnitsky police station. Curse and damn the lousy place.
Invented for tormenting people and trampling on lives that were
miserable enough already.

There were several cab drivers standing at the gates, holding
their caps in their hands. These violators of the laws of the road
had come to ransom the numbers that had been taken off their
cabs. That cost about seven roubles a time, and even then you
really had to grovel.

Inside the yard there was a jostling circle of men wearing
loose shirts with belts. They looked like a team of Ukrainian
carpenters who had come to Moscow to earn money. The
foreman, with a long, droopy moustache, was walking round
the circle, holding out his cap, and the others were reluctantly
dropping silver and copper coins into it. Clear enough – they'd
been working for the builder without the right piece of paper,
and now the coppers were tapping them for half their money. It
happened all the time.

They said that sort of thing never used to happen here under
the old superintendent, but it's the priest who sets the tone of
the parish.

The moment Senka pushed open the oilcloth-covered door
and stepped into the dark, filthy corridor, a bumptious fat-faced

copper with stripes on his arm grabbed him by the hem of his skirt.

'Well, look at you,' he said. Then he winked and pinched Senka on the side so hard that Senka could have torn his hands off. 'Why haven't I seen you around before? Come to get your yellow ticket amended? I do that. Let's go.'

He grabbed Senka by the elbow and started dragging him off. Senka knew he was lying about that ticket – all he wanted was to use a girl for free.

'I've come to see the superintendent,' Senka said in a stern squeak. 'I've got a letter for him, it's important.'

The copper took his hands off. 'Go straight on,' he said, 'and then right. That's where His Honour sits.'

Senka went where he'd been told. Past the hen coop, full of tramps who had been picked up, past the locked cells with the thieves and criminals (the darlings were singing that song about a black raven – lovely it was, a real treat). Then the corridor turned a bit cleaner and brighter and it led Senka to a tall, leather-bound door with a brass plate on it that said: 'Superintendent: Colonel I. R. Solntsev'.

Senka's polite knock was answered by a stern voice on the other side of the door.

'Yes?'

Senka went in. He said hello in a squeaky voice and held out the letter. 'I was asked to deliver this to you in person.'

He tried to clear off straightaway, but the superintendent growled quietly: 'Where do you think you're going?'

The fearsome colonel was sitting at his desk eating an apple, cutting slices off it with a narrow-bladed knife. He wiped the blade on a napkin, then pressed a knob somewhere, and the blade disappeared with a metallic click.

Solntsev didn't open the envelope straight off; instead he examined his visitor carefully, and his eyes lingered for a long time on her false bosom. (Ah, Mr Nameless had overdone it there, stuffed in way too much cotton wool!)

'Who are you? A streetwalker? Your name?'

'S-Sanka,' Senka lisped. 'Alexandra Alexandrova.'

'What's this letter about? Who's it from?'

Solntsev fingered the envelope suspiciously and help it up against the light. What should Senka say?

'A client gave me it . . . Give it to the colonel, he told me, hand it to him in person.'

'Hmm, intrigues of the court of Burgundy,' the superintendent muttered, opening the envelope. 'Stay here, Alexandrova. Wait.'

He ran his eye over the letter quickly, jerked upright, unfastened the hook of his stiff collar, ran his tongue over his lips and started reading again, taking his time now, as if he was trying to make something out between the lines.

He took so long, Senka got bored. Luckily, there were photographs hanging on the walls and newspaper cuttings in frames behind glass.

The most interesting thing there was a picture from a magazine. Solntsev standing there, a bit younger than he was now, with his hands perched smartly on his hips, and a wooden coffin beside him on the floor. The man in it had a moustache and a black hole in his forehead. The caption underneath read: *'Young district inspector puts an end to the criminal career of Loberetsky the Apache'*.

Under that was an article with the enormous headline: '**Gang of counterfeiters arrested. Three cheers for the police!**'

A photograph without any caption: Solntsev shaking hands with the governor general. His Highness Simeon Alexandrovich was skinny and incredibly tall, with his chin stuck up in the air, and the superintendent was bowing, knees bent, with a smarmy great smile pasted right across his mug (that is, his face).

Another article, not so very old, it wasn't yellow yet: *'The youngest precinct superintendent in Moscow'*, from the *Moscow Municipal Police Gazette*. Senka read the beginning: *'The brilliant operation that resulted in the arrest of a band of robbers in Khamovniki,*

who were given away by one of the members of that criminal asso-
ciation, has drawn attention once again to the talent of Colonel Solntsev
and secured him not only a priority promotion, but an appointment to
one of the most difficult and high-profile precincts in the old capital,
Khitrovka . . .'

He couldn't read any more because the superintendent interrupted. 'Well now. A most interesting message.'

He wasn't looking at the letter as he said that, but at Senka,
and looking at him in a nasty sort of way, as if he was going to
take him apart, unscrew all his nuts and bolts and peer at what
was inside.

'Who do you belong to, Alexandrova? Who's your pimp?'

'I don't belong to anyone, I work for myself,' Senka answered
after a moment's hesitation. What if he named some pimp, even
Brawn, and the superintendent took it into his head to check?
Have you got a mamselle by that name, Brawn? That would be
a real disaster.

'You used to work for yourself,' the superintendent said with
an evil smile. 'But not any more you don't. From this day on
you're going to peach for me. I can tell just by looking at you
that you're a quick-witted girl, you've got sharp eyes. And good-
looking too, buxom. Your voice is disgusting, that's true, but
then you won't be singing at the Bolshoi.'

He laughed. So the rotten snake had decided to recruit Senka
as a peacher! That was what they called mamselles who squealed
on their own kind. If the bandits found out, there was only one
pay-off for that – they'd rip the peacher's guts out.

If a streetwalker was found with her belly ripped open, everyone knew what it was for. But just you try and find out who'd
done it! Even so, there were plenty of little mamselles who
peached. And not just for the fun of it, of course not. When the
coppers started turning the screws, there was no way to wriggle
out.

Now, it made no odds to Senka if they recruited him as a
peacher, but any self-respecting mamselle had to kick up a bit.

'I'm an honest girl,' he said proudly. 'Not one of those whores who squeal on their own kind to you coppers. Find yourself a squealer somewhere else.'

'Wha-at?' the superintendent bellowed in such a terrifying voice that Senka froze. 'Who are you calling "coppers", you little slut? Right, Alexandrova, for that, I'm going to fine you. Three days to pay, and do you know what happens after that?'

Senka shook his head in fright – and this time he wasn't pretending.

But Solntsev stopped yelling and switched to gentle persuasion: 'Let me explain. If you don't pay your fine for insulting me in three days, I'll lock you in a cell for the night. Do you know who I've got in there? Criminals who are sick. They've got consumption and syphilis. According to the latest "humane" decree, we have to keep them separate from other prisoners. But they'll spend the night playing with you, my girl, and then we'll see which one takes a shine to you first – the frenchies or consumption.'

The time had come for Senka to set his girlish pride aside. 'How can I pay?' he said in a weepy voice. 'I'm a poor girl.'

The superintendent chuckled: 'Which is it, poor or honest?

Senka rubbed his eyes with his sleeve – like he was wiping his tears away. He sniffed pitifully as if to say: I'm all yours, do whatever you want with me.

'Right, then,' said Solntsev in a brisk, businesslike tone. 'Did you sleep with the man who gave you the letter?'

'Well . . .' Senka said warily, not knowing what was the best answer.

The copper shook his head. 'My, my, our squeamish friend really has gone down in the world. In the old days he would never have got mixed up with a street girl. He must have seen something in you.' The superintendent came out from behind the desk and took hold of Senka's chin with his finger and thumb. 'Lively eyes, with sparks of mischief in them. Hmm . . . Where did it happen? How?'

'At my apertiment,' Senka lied. 'He's a very hot-blooded gent, a real goer.'

'Yes, he's a well-known ladies' man. Listen, Alexandrova, I'll tell you how you can pay your fine. Tell this man that you've fallen madly in love with him, or something else of the sort, but make sure that you stay with him. If he's seen something in you, then he won't throw you out. He's a gentleman.'

'But where can I find him?' Senka wailed.

'I'll tell you that tomorrow. Hand over your yellow ticket. I'll keep it here for the time being. Better safe than sorry.'

Oh no! Senka started batting his eyelids, he didn't know what to say.

'What, you mean you don't have one?' Solntsev gave a wolfish grin. 'Trading without a ticket? Shame on you! And too proud to peach. Hey!' he yelled, turning towards the door. 'Ogryzkov!'

A constable came in, stood to attention and glared wide eyed at his superior.

'Escort this girl home, wherever she says. Confiscate her residence permit and bring it to me. So you won't be able to do a runner, Alexandrova.'

He patted Senka on the cheek. 'Now that I look a bit closer, I reckon there really is something to you. Fandorin knows a good thing when he sees it.' He lowered his hand and felt Senka's backside. 'A bit scraggy in the basement, but I've got nothing against a skinny bum. I'll have to give you a try, Alexandrova. If you manage to avoid the frenchies, that is.'

And he laughed, the filthy old goat.

How could Death have billed and cooed with this reptile? Senka would rather hang himself.

And suddenly he felt sorry for women, the poor creatures. What was it like for them living in a world where all the men were filthy swines?

And what did 'fandorin' mean, anyway?

How Senka Took an Exam

Senka dealt with the goggle-eyed cooper easily enough. He told him he lived in Vshivaya Gorka by the Yauza, and as soon as they were in the lanes leading to the river, he hitched up his skirt and darted off into an alleyway. Of course, the constable started blowing on his whistle and swearing, but there was nothing he could do. The new peacher had vanished into thin air. Now Ogryzkov was in for a fine from the superintendent, as sure as eggs is eggs.

All the way home Senka racked his brains, trying to think what it was he'd seen or heard in the basement that had let Erast Petrovich and Masa guess who the killer was straight off like that.

He worked his brains as hard as he could, fair wore them out with wild gymnastics, but he still couldn't make two and two equal four.

Then he tried applying deduction to something else. What plan had the brainy Mr Nameless come up with? It was terrifying just to think what a tangled knot he'd tied. What if it all went wrong? Who'd be the one to suffer for it? What if it was a certain young man who was fed up with being a plaything in the hands of the Bird of Fortune? That crazy creature could flap its wings and shower a poor, wretched orphan with its most precious gifts – love and riches, and hope – then suddenly turn tail-on and do its dirt on the lucky devil's coiffure, take back all its gifts and try to filch its victim's life into the bargain.

Senka had bad thoughts about the engineer and the slick way

he had with other people's property. Not a word of thanks for Senka's unbelievable generosity and self-sacrifice. No, you'd never hear anything like that from him. He acted liked it all belonged to him. Invited the rats to dine at someone else's table. Come on, dear guests, take as much as you fancy. And as for that someone else having his own idea, about that treasure, and even dreams, well a smarmy gent like Erast Petrovich obviously couldn't give a rotten damn about that.

Because he felt so resentful, Senka was cool with the engineer. He told him all about delivering the letter and the conversation with the superintendent, but he expressed his insulted dignity by looking off to one side and curling up his bottom lip.

However, Erast Petrovich failed to notice this demonstration of feeling. He listened carefully to the story of how Senka was questioned and recruited. He seemed pleased with everything, and even said 'well done'. That was too much for Senka, and he started hinting at the treasure, saying what a lot of smart-arses there were in the world who liked to make free with wealth that wasn't theirs, but belonged to someone else. But that hint wasn't taken either, he failed to stir the engineer's conscience. Mr Nameless just patted Senka on the head and said: 'Don't be g-greedy.' And then he said in a cheerful voice: 'Tonight I conclude all my b-business in Moscow, there is no m-more time left. Tomorrow at midday is the start of the d-drive to Paris. I hope the F-Flying Carpet is in good order?'

Senka felt his heart sink. That was right, tomorrow was the twenty-third! What with all these harum-scarum adventures, he'd completely forgotten about it!

So, whatever happened, it was the end of everything. Three cheers for the cunning Mr Nameless! He'd got what he wanted from his mechanic (and for nothing, if you didn't count the grub) – his automobile was looking real handsome, it was fine tuned and polished till it shone – but that wasn't even the half of it. The worst thing was that he'd twisted a poor orphan round his little finger, robbed him blind, nearly got the orphan's throat cut, and now he was going driving off to Paris like some fairy-tale prince. And it was Senka's destiny to be left sitting all on his lonesome beside his broken tub. If he was even still alive tomorrow, that was . . .

Senka's lips started trembling, and the corners of his mouth crept down even lower than when he was just acting out insulted pride.

But the heartless Erast Petrovich said: 'Wipe that l-lipstick off your mouth, it looks d-disgusting.'

As if Senka had put the lipstick on himself, just for a laugh!

He went off to get changed, stamping his feet angrily.

While Senka was gone he heard the telephone ring in the study, and when he went back a minute later – to tell Erast Petrovich a few home truths, straight out, no more pussyfooting around – the engineer wasn't there.

Masa was off wandering somewhere too. Meanwhile the day was slipping unstoppably towards evening, and the darker it got outside, the gloomier Senka felt. What on earth would happen tonight?

To distract himself from his dark thoughts, Senka went out to the shed to polish the automobile, which was already shining brighter than the domes in the Kremlin. He wasn't feeling angry now, just depressed.

Well, Erast Petrovich, as they say, may God grant you good luck and the record you're dreaming of. Your three-wheeler is all set up in the finest possible fashion, don't you worry on that score. You'll remember your mechanic Semyon Spidorov with a grateful word more than once on the way. Maybe some day you'll be smitten by a pang of conscience. Or at least a pang of regret. Though that's hardly likely – who are we compared to you?

Just then there was a faint squeak from the louvres (they were kind of like cracks) in the engine cooler, and Senka froze. Was he hearing things? No, there it was again! But what could it be?

He shone his torch into the engine. A little mouse had climbed inside!

Hadn't he told Erast Petrovich the gaps should be smaller? It would be better if there were thirty-six of them, not twenty-four!

And now look! What if that little varmint gnawed through the fuel hose? What a shambles that would be!

While he took off the hood, drove the mouse away, disconnected the hose and connected it again (undamaged, thank God), night fell and Senka didn't even notice. He went back into the house just as the clock struck twelve. The dirge echoed through the apartment and Senka suddenly found it hard to breathe. He felt so afraid and so homeless he could have howled like a stray dog.

Luckily Mr Nameless showed up soon after. Looking quite different from the way he was earlier on: not cheerful and contented now, but gloomy, even angry.

'Why aren't you ready? Have you f-forgotten you're supposed to be playing Motya? P-Put on the wig, the skullcap and all the rest. I won't m-make you up much, it's dark in the b-basement. I'll just g-glue on the nose.'

'But it's too early. We don't have to be there till three,' Senka said in a dismal voice.

'Another urgent m-matter has come up and I have to d-deal with it. Let's go on the M-Magic Carpet. It will be a f-final test before the race.'

Well, how about that? Senka had buffed it and polished it, and now all that work was all down the drain. Though one more trial run couldn't do any harm . . .

Senka put on his kike costume without any more fuss. It was better than being a mamselle.

Erast Petrovich put on a beautiful motoring suit: shiny leather, with squeaky yellow spats. What a lovely sight!

The engineer put his little revolver (it was called a 'Herstal', made to special order in the foreign city of Liège) in the pocket behind his back, and Senka's heart skipped a beat. Would they live to see the start? God only knew.

'You t-take the wheel,' Mr Nameless ordered. 'Show me what you c-can do.'

Senka put on a pair of goggles and squeezed his ears into his oversized skullcap so it wouldn't fly off. At least he'd get a ride before it all ended!

'To Samotechny B-Boulevard.'

They drove like the wind and were there in five minutes. Erast Petrovich got out at a small wooden house and rang the bell. Someone opened the door.

Of course, Senka couldn't control his curiosity – he went to take a look at the copper plate hanging on the door. 'F. F. Weltman, Pathological Anatomist, Dr of Medicine'. God only knew what a 'pathological anatomist' was, but 'Dr' meant 'doctor'. Was someone ill, then? Not Masa, surely, Senka thought in alarm. Then he heard steps on the other side of the door and ran back to the machine.

The doctor was a puny little man, dishevelled and untidy, and he blinked all the time. He stared at Senka in fright and replied to his polite 'good health to you' with a shy nod.

'Who's this?' Senka asked in a whisper when the titch climbed in.

'Never m-mind,' Erast Petrovich replied gloomily. 'He's someone from a completely d-different story, who has nothing to do with our j-job today. We're going to Rozhdestvensky Boulevard. At the d-double!'

Well, once the motor starting roaring, there was no more conversation to be had.

The engineer told him to stop at the corner of a dark lane. 'Stay in the c-car and don't leave it.'

That went without saying. Everyone knew the kind of people who were out at that time of night. Before you could even blink, they'd have a nut or bolt unscrewed, for a fishing weight, or just out of plain mischief.

Senka put a spanner on the seat beside him – just let them try anything on.

He asked the doctor: 'Is someone ill? Are you going to treat them?'

The doctor didn't answer, but Mr Nameless said: 'Yes. S-Surgical intervention is required.'

The pair of them walked over to a house with lit-up windows. They knocked and went in, and Senka was left on his tod.

He waited for a long time. Maybe a whole hour. First he sat there, worrying about seeing the Ghoul in Yeroshenko's basement. Then he just felt bored. And towards the end he started fretting that they'd be late. A couple of times he thought he heard some kind of creaking noise in the house. God only knew what they were getting up to.

Erast Petrovich finally came out – alone and without his leather cap. When he came closer, Senka saw that Mr Nameless was not looking as neat and tidy as before: his jacket was torn at the shoulder and there was a scratch on his forehead. He licked his right hand – the knuckles were oozing blood!

'What happened?' Senka asked, alarmed. 'And where's the doc? Is he staying with the patient?'

'Let's g-go,' the engineer barked. 'Show me your skill. Here's an exam f-for you: if you can get us to Khitrovka in t-ten minutes, I'll take you on the run as m-my assistant.'

Senka pulled on the throttle even harder than that first time. The automobile shot forward and tore into the night, swaying on its steel springs.

The engineer's assistant! To Paris! With Erast Petrovich!

Oh Lord, don't let the motor stall or overheat! Don't let a tyre crack on a big cobble! Don't let the transmission come uncoupled! You can do everything, Lord!

At the corner of Myasnitskaya Street the motor sneezed and died. A blockage!

Senka was choking on his tears as he blew off the carburettor, and that took two minutes at least. That stroke of bad luck meant he didn't make it in time.

'Stop,' said the engineer at the intersection of the boulevard and Pokrovka Street. He looked at his Breguet watch. 'Twelve m-minutes and ten seconds.'

Senka hung his head in shame and sobbed, wiping away the snot with his ginger sidelocks. Ah, Fortune, what a low, mean bitch you are.

'An excellent result,' said Erast Petrovich. 'And the c-carburettor was cleaned in record time. Congratulations. I was j-joking about the ten minutes, of course. I hope you will n-not refuse to accompany me to Paris as my assistant? You know yourself that Masa is n-not suited to play that p-particular role. He will ride behind us in a carriage, c-carrying the spare wheels and other parts.'

Unable to believe his luck, Senka babbled: 'And the three of us will go? All the way to Paris?'

Mr Nameless thought for a moment. 'Well, you s-see, Senya,' he said, 'probably one other individual will g-go with us.' Then he paused and added quietly, rather uncertainly, 'Perhaps even t-two . . .'

Well, we know who one of them is, don't we now, Senka thought with a scowl. After all the fun and games Erast Petrovich had lined up for tonight, there'd be no way Death could stay in Moscow. But who could the other one be? Surely the sensei hadn't decided to steal Fedora Nikitishna away from her husband?

Suddenly Senka felt sorry for the poor doorman Mikheich – how would he manage without his boiled fruit and his pies and Fedora's sweet caresses? But he felt even sorrier for himself. It would be worse than the torments of hell to watch the engineer and Death settling into their love on the way to Paris. And it would be the last straw if that meant the record was never set!

Mr Nameless interrupted Senka's musings when his Breguet jangled again.

'Ten m-minutes to three. Time to b-begin the operation. I'm going to g-get the superintendent. I'll leave the auto at the station – it will be s-safer there. And I'll make sure that Solntsev only b-brings one assistant. And off you go, Senka, to Yeroshenko's d-dosshouse, to the rendezvous. Lead the Ghoul through the underground p-passage, and don't forget that you're an idiot. Don't say anything articulate, just b-bleat. There'll be a critical moment when the P-Prince and Deadeye appear. If it looks as though things may t-turn nasty, the boy Motya can recover the g-gift of speech. Just say: "Silver – over there" and p-point. That will keep them busy at l-least until I arrive.' The engineer pondered something for a moment and muttered under his breath. 'It's not g-good that I've been left without my Herstal, and there's no t-time to get hold of another revolver . . .'

'But how can you go in there with those wolves with no pistol?' Senka gasped. 'You put it in your pocket, I saw you! Did you drop it somewhere, or what?'

'That's exactly what I d-did, dropped it . . . Never mind, we'll m-manage without a revolver. The plan of operations d-does not require any shooting.' Erast Petrovich smiled jauntily and flicked Senka's false nose with his finger. 'And n-now, my Jew, it's up to you.'

How Senka Tried to Keep Up

Agh, he was so sick of this damned Yerokha – this rotten musty cellar smell, this pitch-black darkness, those muffled sounds coming from behind the doors of the 'apertiments' – even in the dead of night the people living underground were still squabbling, or fighting, or singing in their ugly voices, or crying. But as he went farther and farther along the damp corridors, into the bowels of the Yerokha, it got quieter and quieter, as if the earth itself had swallowed up all the sounds of human living, or *existence*, to use the scholarly term. And then the memories came flooding back, a hundred times worse than the stench of the basement and the raucous drunken bawling.

This was where the unknown killer had attacked Senka from behind, pulling his hair and almost breaking his neck – Senka's hand reached up of its own accord to make the sign of the cross.

The Siniukhin family had lived behind that door there – he suddenly thought he could see them staring out of the darkness with their crimson holes of eyes. Brrrr . . .

Two more turns, and there was the hall with the columns, curse the godforsaken place. This was where all the trouble started.

This was the spot where Prokha had lain dead on the ground. Now he'd step out of the darkness, with his fingers spread wide, ready to grab. Ah-a-ah, he'd say, Speedy, you scum, I've been waiting for you for ages. It was your fault I met my death.

Senka dashed on quick to get as far away as he could from that bad place, glancing behind him – just to be on the safe side –

and ready to cross himself if he saw a *phantasmagoria*.

He should have looked where he was going instead.

He ran straight into something, only it wasn't a column, because the supports holding up the ceiling were hard, made of bricks, and this thing he'd run into was springy and it grabbed Senka round the throat with its hands. Then it hissed: 'Here at last, are you? Now, where's this Yiddish treasure of yours?'

The Ghoul! He was here already, waiting in the darkness!

Senka bleated in fright.

'Ah, yes, you're dumb, aren't you?' The terrifying man breathed the words right into Senka's face then let go of his throat. 'Come on then, show me the way.'

He really had come alone! He didn't want to share the riches with his comrades. Now that was real greed for you.

Senka bleated and gurgled a bit more, then led the milker to the corner behind the last column. He pulled out the stones, slipped through the hole and waved his hand: Follow me!

He walked as slowly as he could, even though the Ghoul had lit a lamp and he could have got to the treasure in five minutes. But what was the hurry? He'd only have to spend fifteen minutes billing and cooing with this *villainous malefactor*, until Death brought her own monsters, the Prince and Deadeye. And then . . . but it was better not to think about what would happen then.

Despite all Senka's efforts to go slow and put the moment off, the passage finally led them to that exit lined with white stone. Another three steps, and they were at the secret chamber.

'Gu, gu,' said Senka, pointing to a heap of silver billets.

The Ghoul shoved him aside and went rushing forward. He darted this way and that across the cellar, holding the lamp up high. Shadows leapt across the walls and vaulted ceiling. The milker stopped by the door blocked with a heap of broken bricks and stones.

'This way, is it?'

Senka was still skulking by the way in. He even wondered whether he ought to turn back, leg it and see what happened.

But what was the point? He'd probably just run into the Prince.

'Where's the treasure?' the monster asked, stepping right up close to Senka. 'Eh? Treasure? Understand? Where's the silver?'

'Bu, bu,' the boy Motya replied, shaking his head and waving his arms. To gain time, he said a whole speech like he was talking in tongues: 'Ulyulyu, ga-ga khryaps, ardi-burdi gulyumba, surdik-gurdik ogo! Ashma li bunugu? Karmanda! Shikos-vikos shimpopo, duru-buru goplyalya . . .'

The Ghoul listened to this gibberish then grabbed the halfwit by the shoulders and shook him. 'Where's the silver?' he yelled. 'There's nothing here but trash and scrap iron! Have you pulled a fast one? I'll slice off your ringlets and carve you into little pieces!'

Senka's head bobbed back and forth and he didn't like it one little bit. Just imagine – Senka being so impatient for the Prince to arrive! Where had they all got to, had they fallen asleep in that passage?

Maybe he should reveal the secret of the rods to the Ghoul? Erast Petrovich had said: 'If things look like turning nasty, the boy Motya can recover the gift of speech.' How much nastier could things get? Senka's eyes were almost falling out of his head!

Senka opened his mouth to say something meaningful instead of goobledegook, but suddenly the Ghoul stopped shaking him, jerked his hands away and pricked up his ears. He must have heard something.

Soon Senka heard it too: footsteps and voices.

The milker kicked his lamp, which fell over and went out. Suddenly it was very dark.

But not for long.

'. . . don't you say anything?' a muffled voice said from inside the narrow entrance, and then a bright, narrow ray of light came snaking out, fumbling its way across the vaults and along the walls. The Ghoul and Senka froze, but the light didn't pick them out straight away.

Three people came in. The first, wearing a long frock coat, was holding an electric torch in his hand. The second was a woman. It was the third one, the last to set foot in the chamber, who was doing the talking.

'Fine, don't say anything, then,' the Prince said bitterly. 'You swap me for a black-face and you've got nothing to say? You're a shameless bitch, that's what you are, not Death.'

A match scraped as one of the new arrivals lit a kerosene lamp.

The chamber was suddenly bright.

'Oo-la-la!' the Jack exclaimed under his breath. He quickly put the lamp down on the floor, turned off the torch and put it in his pocket. 'Well, fancy seeing you here!'

'Ghoul!' the Prince yelled. 'Is that you?'

The milker didn't say a word. He just whispered in Senka's ear: 'Well, you Yids really are cunning bastards. Get ready to die, you little shit.'

But the Prince seemed to think he was the one who'd been ambushed. He turned to Death: 'Have you sold me out to this scum, you little slag?'

He raised his fist to hit her, and he was wearing a knuckle-duster too. Death didn't flinch or back away, she just smiled, but Senka howled in terror. A fine operation this was! Now they'd do them both in!

'Wait, Prince!' called Deadeye, turning his head this way and that. 'It's not an ambush. He's here alone, the kid doesn't count.'

The Jack set off across the cellar with his springy stride, muttering: 'There's something wrong here, something wrong. And there's no silver . . .'

Suddenly he turned towards the milker. 'Monsieur Ghoul, you are not here on our account, are you? Otherwise, you would not have come alone, right?'

'Stands to reason,' the Ghoul answered warily, letting go of Senka and sticking both hands in his pockets. Oh Lord, now he was going to start shooting through his pants!

'Then why?' Deadeye asked with a glint of his specs. 'Could it perhaps be on account of a certain treasure?'

The Ghoul's eyes shifted rapidly to and fro, from one enemy to the other. 'So?'

'"So?" – I'll take that as a yes. And who tipped you off?' Deadeye stopped talking and signalled to the Prince not to do anything yet. 'Not a Caucasian gentleman by the name of Kazbek, by any chance?'

'No,' said the Ghoul, knitting his sparse eyebrows. 'An old Yid gave me the nod. And he gave me a guide, this little kike here.'

Deadeye snapped his fingers and rubbed his forehead. 'Right, right. So what does this strange coincidence signify? A chasm opened wide, replete with stars . . .'

'What are you playing at?' the Prince yelled, dashing at Death, but he lowered the hand with the knuckleduster. 'What did you bring us here for?'

'Just a moment, stop babbling,' the Jack said, pulling him up short again. 'She won't tell you anything.' He nodded in Senka's direction. 'Why don't we sound out our little betrayer of Christ first?'

The betrayer sunk his head into his chest, wondering whether he ought to shout out about the treasure now or wait a bit longer.

The Ghoul twitched his chin. 'He's a loony, all he does is bleat. And when he starts flapping his tongue, you can't understand a thing.'

'He doesn't look like a total loony,' said Deadeye sauntering towards Senka. 'Come on now, little gentleman of Jerusalem, talk to me, and I'll listen.'

Senka started back from the crazy maniac. That made the Jack laugh.

'Where to in such great haste, young Yiddish maid?'

He was right, there was nowhere to go. After just three steps Senka's back hit the wall.

Deadeye took out his torch, shone it into Senka's face and

laughed. 'The hair appears to be false,' he said, and jerked the wig off Senka's head. The red side locks and the skullcap slid over to one side. 'Prince, look who we have here. Oh, how many wonderful discoveries—'

'You whore!' howled the Prince. 'So you and your snot-nosed little lover-boy set the whole thing up! Right, Speedy, you tape-worm, this time you're really done for!'

Now was just the right time, Senka realised. If things turned any nastier than this, he wouldn't get another chance.

'Don't kill me!' he shouted as loud as he could. 'You'll never find the treasure without me!'

The Jack grabbed the Prince by the shoulders. 'Wait, we're in no rush!'

But the Ghoul went flying at Senka instead. 'So you're in disguise?' he yelled, and thumped Senka on the ear with his fist.

It was a good thing the crooked wig cushioned the blow, or it would have knocked the life clean out of Senka.

But it still sent him flying anyway. So before they could carry on beating him, he pointed to the nearest heap and shouted: 'That's it, there, the silver! Look!'

The milker followed the direction of the finger. He picked up one of the rods and twirled it in his hands. Then Deadeye walked over, picked up another rod and scraped it with his knife. There was a dull white gleam, and the Ghoul gasped: 'Silver! Well, I'll be damned, it's silver!'

He took out his pen and tried another rod, then another, and another. 'Why, there must be a ton of the stuff in here!'

The Prince and Deadeye forgot all about Senka and also started grabbing too, setting the metal rods clattering.

Senka crept slowly along the wall, moving closer and closer to Death. He whispered: 'Let's clear out of here!'

She whispered back: 'We can't.'

'You what? Any moment now they'll come to their senses and finish me off!'

But Death wouldn't listen: 'Erast Petrovich said not to.'

Senka wondered whether maybe he ought to leave her there, seeing as she was so stubborn. Maybe he would have done too (though that's not very likely) only just then, speak of the devil, who should arrive but Mr Nameless!

They must have been creeping through the passage on tiptoe, because no one had heard them coming.

Three people stepped into the chamber, one after another: Erast Petrovich, Superintendent Solntsev and Boxman. The engineer was holding a torch (which, as it happens, he put out straight away – it was light enough already); the superintendent was holding a revolver in each hand, and Boxman just held up his massive great fists.

'Reach for the sky!' the superintendent cried in dashing style. 'Or I'll drop you where you stand!'

Mr Nameless stood on his left, and the constable on his right.

The two bandits and the milker froze. The Ghoul was the first to drop his silver rod. He turned round slowly and raised his hands. The Prince and Deadeye followed.

'That's my boys!' Solntsev exclaimed cheerfully. 'All my sweethearts are here! All my little darlings! And you too, mademoiselle! What are you doing in a place like this! I warned you to be a bit choosier with your acquaintances! Now you have only yourself to blame!' He glanced quickly at Erast Petrovich and Boxman. 'Get your revolvers out, what do you think you're doing? With this treacherous lot, you never know what might happen.'

'I don't have a f-firearm on my person today,' the engineer replied calmly. 'It will not be n-necessary.'

The constable boomed: 'And I don't need one. I'll lay them out with my fists if need be.'

The superintendent was nobody's fool, thought Senka. He'd chosen the right man for his assistant.

'Madam, and you, S-Senya, stand behind me,' Erast Petrovich said in a voice that couldn't be argued with.

But it didn't cross Senka's mind to object – he ran behind the engineer in a trice and stood right beside the way out. Even headstrong Death didn't dare argue and she stood beside him.

'Innokentii Romanovich, p-permit me to address everyone b-briefly,' Mr Nameless said to the superintendent. 'I have to explain the t-true significance of this gathering to all p-present here.'

'The true significance?' Solntsev exclaimed in surprise. 'But that's obvious – the arrest of these villains. The only thing I'd like to know is how you managed to lure them all in here. And who is that picturesque character?'

Those last words were aimed at Senka, who stepped back into the mouth of the passage, just in case.

'That is m-my assistant,' Erast Petrovich explained, 'but my address will not be c-concerned with that.' He cleared his throat and spoke more loudly, so everyone could hear. 'Gentlemen, I have very little t-time. I have gathered you here in order to p-put an end to everything at once. Tomorrow – or, rather, t-today – I am departing from the c-city of Moscow, and I must conclude all my b-business here tonight.'

The superintendent interrupted him anxiously. 'Departing? But on the way here you told me we would wipe out all these lowlifes together, and that would open up tremendous prospects for me . . .'

'There are s-some things that I find more interesting than your c-career,' the engineer snapped. 'Sport, for instance.'

'What damned sport?'

The superintendent was so surprised that he shifted his gaze from the prisoners to Erast Petrovich. Deadeye didn't miss a beat, he slipped his hand into his sleeve, but Boxman bounded forward and raised his huge fist. 'I'll clobber you!'

The Jack instantly held up his empty palms.

'Interrupt m-me once again, and I'll t-take away your Colts!' Mr Nameless shouted angrily at the superintendent. 'In your hands they're not much use in any case!'

Solntsev just nodded: All right, all right, I'll hold my tongue.

Now that he'd shown everyone who was cock of the walk (at least, that was how Senka interpreted the engineer's behaviour), Erast Petrovich addressed the arrested men: 'And so, gentlemen, I d-decided to gather you here for two reasons. The first is that you were all suspects in the c-case of the Khitrovka murders. I already know who the true culprit is, but n-nonetheless I shall explain briefly how each of you attracted my s-suspicion. The Prince knew of the existence of the t-treasure, that is one. He was s-searching for it, that is two. In addition, in recent m-months he has been transformed from an ordinary hold-up artist into a ruthless k-killer, that is three. You, Mr D-Deadeye, also knew about the treasure, that is one. You are m-monstrously cruel, that is two. And finally, you are p-playing a double game behind your patron's b-back: you despise him, steal from his t-table and sleep in his bed. That is three.'

'What?' the Prince roared, turning towards his adjutant. 'What's that he said about my bed?'

The Jack smirked, but it was a look that gave Senka goose pimples all over.

But meanwhile Mr Nameless had already turned to the Ghoul: 'As f-for you, Mr Milker, you have been obsessed b-by the Prince's rapid ascent. As a vulture who preys on the spoils of others' efforts, you are always attempting to g-grab a chunk of your rival's good f-fortune: loot, g-glory, a woman. That is one. You do not stop short at m-murder, but you only resort to this extreme measure after having t-taken all possible precautions. Like the Khitrovka Treasure Hunter, who is d-distinguished by his positively maniacal c-caution. That is two . . .'

'A woman?' the Prince interrupted – he was listening intently to the case for the prosecution. 'What woman? Death, is that who he means? Don't tell me the Ghoul got his dirty paws on you as well?'

Senka looked at Death and saw she was as pale as death (no, better to say 'pale as a sheet', or 'white as snow', or else it will be confusing). But she just laughed.

'Yes, he did, and your friend Deadeye too. You're all as good as each other – spiders!'

The Prince swung round and launched a punch at the side of the Jack's head, but Deadeye seemed to be expecting it – he leapt back nimbly and pulled a knife out of his sleeve. The Ghoul dug one hand into his pocket too.

'Stop that!' the superintendent yelled. 'Or you'll go down where you stand! All three of you!'

They froze, staring daggers at each other. Deadeye didn't put the knife away, the Ghoul didn't take his hand out of his pocket, and the steel knuckleduster glinted on the Prince's clenched fist.

'Put your weapons away immediately,' the engineer told them all. 'That includes you t-too, Innokentii Romanovich. You m-might shoot by accident. And in any case, this is n-not cowboys and Indians, or c-cops and robbers, but a different g-game altogether, in which all of you are all equal.'

'Wha-at?' the superintendent gasped.

'Oh yes. You were also one of my suspects. Would you l-like to know my reasons? Very well, I'll proceed. You are as ruthless and c-cruel as the other guests here. And you will stoop to any base v-villainy, even murder, to further your own ambition. This is q-quite evident from your entire service record, which is very well kn-known to me. It is to your advantage for the n-new ripper from Khitrovka to become the latest s-sensation in Moscow. It is therefore no accident that you are s-so hospitable to the n-newspaper reporters. First create a bogeyman to set the p-public trembling with fear, then heroically defeat your own c-creation – that is your method. That is exactly how you acted a year ago in the c-case of the famous "Khamovniki Gang" – you c-controlled the gang yourself, through your agent.'

'Nonsense! Wild conjecture!' the superintendent cried. 'You have no proof! You weren't even in Moscow at the time!'

'But do not f-forget that I have many old friends in M-Moscow, including many among the police. Not all of them are as b-blind as your superiors. But that has n-nothing to do with the matter

307

at hand. I only wish to say that p-provocation and entrapment with a b-bloody outcome are nothing new to you. You are calculating and c-cold blooded. And therefore I do not b-believe in your wild, uncontrollable passion for the Prince's l-lady love – you only need the lady as a s-source of information.'

'What, this one too?' the Prince groaned in a voice filled with such pain and torment that Senka actually felt sorry for him. 'You're the greatest whore on God's earth! You've lifted your skirts for all of them, even a lousy copper would do!'

But Death just laughed – a low, rustling laugh that was almost soundless.

'Madam,' Erast Petrovich said, glancing at her briefly, 'I d-demand that you withdraw immediately. Senya, t-take her away!'

The smart engineer had chosen the right moment all right – after he'd stirred them all up like that, they couldn't care less about Death now, let alone little Senka.

And little Senka didn't have to be asked twice. He took hold of Death's hand and pulled her towards the mouth of the passage. Mr Nameless's meet was going to end badly, no doubting that. It would be interesting to watch it to the end, of course, only through opera glasses, from a seat in the top circle. But as for being on stage when they started bumping everyone off – thanks for the offer, but maybe some other time.

Death took two small steps, no more, and then she refused to budge and Senka couldn't shift her. And when he took hold of her sides and tried to pull her, she dug her elbow hard into the pit of his stomach, and it really hurt.

Senka grabbed hold of his belly and started gasping for air, but he carried on peeping out from behind her shoulder, trying to keep up with the action. It was interesting, after all. He saw the superintendent back away to the wall and point one revolver at Erast Petrovich and keep the other trained on the bandits.

'So it's a trap?' he exclaimed, just as flustered as Senka. 'You picked the wrong man, Fandorin. I've got twelve bullets in these cylinders. Enough for everyone! Boxman, come over here!'

The constable walked over to his superior and stood behind him, his eyes glinting menacingly under his grey brows.

'This is not just one t-trap, Innokentii Romanovich, but two,' Mr Nameless explained calmly after the superintendent called him that strange word again. 'As I said, I wish to c-conclude all my business in Moscow tonight. I only stated the b-basis for my suspicions so that you would have the f-full picture. The culprit is here, and he will receive the p-punishment he deserves. I invited the rest of you here for a d-different purpose: to f-free a certain lady from dangerous liaisons and even m-more dangerous delusions. She is a quite exceptional lady, g-gentlemen. She has suffered a great deal and d-deserves compassion. And by the way, in c-calling you all spiders, she has suggested an excellent name for this operation. A most p-precise image. You are spiders, and while f-four of you belong to the species of c-common spider, the fifth is a g-genuine tarantula. So, welcome to Operation Spiders in a Jar. The n-narrow confines of this treasure chamber render the title even m-more fitting.'

The engineer paused, as if inviting the others to appreciate his wit.

'The fifth?' asked Solntsev. 'Where do you see a fifth?'

'Right behind you.'

The superintendent swung round in fright and stared at Boxman, who glared down at his superior from his great height.

'Constable Boxman is my g-guest of honour here today,' said Erast Petrovich. 'A spider of t-truly rare dimensions.'

Boxman barked so loudly, he brought the dust sprinkling down from the ceiling.

'Your Honour must have lost his mind! Why, I—'

'No, B-Boxman,' the engineer retorted sharply. It wasn't very loud, but the constable stopped talking. 'You're the one who has l-lost his mind in his old age. But we'll t-talk about the reason for your mental derangement later. First let us d-deal with the essence of the matter. You were the prime suspect from the very b-beginning, in spite of all your c-caution. Let me explain why.

The vicious m-murders in Khitrovka started about two months ago. A d-drunken reveller was killed and robbed, and then a reporter intending to write an article about the s-slums. Nothing unusual for Khitrovka, if n-not for one certain detail: their eyes were g-gouged out. Then the m-murderer gouged out the eyes of everyone in the Siniukhin family, in exactly the s-same way. There are two circumstances of n-note here. Firstly, it is impossible to imagine any of these exceptional c-crimes occurring on your beat without you f-finding out who committed them. You are the true master of Khitrovka! Superintendents come and g-go, the top dogs in the criminal underworld change, b-but Boxman is eternal. He has eyes and ears everywhere, every d-door is open to him, he knows the s-secrets of the police and the Council. More murders took p-place and the entire city started t-talking about them, but the ubiquitous Boxman d-didn't know a thing. From this I concluded that you were c-connected with the mysterious Treasure Hunter, and m-must be his accomplice. My suspicions were corroborated by the fact that in s-subsequent murders the victims' eyes were not put out. I recalled t-telling you that the theory of images being retained on the retina after death had been d-disproved by science ... But I was still n-not certain that you were the killer and not s-simply an accomplice. Until yesterday n-night, that is, when you killed a young m-man, one of your informers. That was when I finally excluded all the other spiders f-from my list of suspects and focused on you ...'

'And how exactly, if I might enquire, did I give myself away?' Boxman asked, looking at the engineer curiously. Senka couldn't see a trace of fear or even alarm in the constable's face.

But then he had to turn his head to look at the superintendent: 'Are you admitting it, Boxman?' Solntsev exclaimed in fright, recoiling from his subordinate. 'But he hasn't proved anything yet!'

'He will,' Boxman said with a good-natured wave, still looking at Mr Nameless. 'There's no wriggling out of it with him. And you keep your mouth shut, Your Honour. This has nothing to do with you.'

Solntsev opened his mouth, but he didn't make a peep. That was what the books called 'to be struck dumb'.

'You want t-to know how you gave yourself away?' Erast Petrovich asked with a smirk. 'Why, it's very s-simple. There is only one way to twist someone's n-neck through a hundred and eighty degrees in a s-single moment, so fast that he doesn't even have time to m-make a sound: take a firm grasp of the c-crown of the head and turn it sharply, b-breaking the vertebrae and tearing the m-muscles. This requires truly phenomenal physical strength – a strength th-that you alone, of all the suspects, possess. Neither the Prince, nor Deadeye, n-nor the superintendent could have done that. There are not many people in the world c-capable of such a feat. And that's all there is t-to it. The Khitrovka m-murders are not a very complex case. If I had not been involved in another investigation at the s-same time, I would have got to you m-much sooner . . .'

'Well, no one's perfect,' Boxman said with a shrug. 'I thought I was being so careful, but I slipped up there. I should have smashed Prokha's head in.'

'Indeed,' Mr Nameless agreed. 'But that would n-not have saved you from participating in Operation Spiders in a J-Jar. The outcome would still have b-been the same in any case.'

As he peeped over Death's shoulder, Senka tried to figure out what that outcome was. What was going to happen when the talking stopped? The bandits had already lowered their hands on the sly, and the superintendent's lips were trembling. If he started blasting away with those revolvers, that would be a fine outcome for everyone.

But the engineer carried on talking to the constable as if he was sitting by the samovar in a tea-house. 'I c-can understand everything,' said Erast Petrovich. 'You didn't want to l-leave any witnesses, you didn't even take p-pity on a three-year-old child.

But why kill the d-dog and the parrot? That is more than mere c-caution, it is insanity.'

'Oh no, Your Honour,' said Boxman, stroking his drooping moustache. 'That bird could talk. When I went in, the Armenian woman said to me: "Good day, Constable." And the parrot piped up: "Good day, Constable!" too. What if it had said that in front of the investigator? And that puppy at the mamselle's place was altogether too fond of sniffing at things. I read in the *Police Gazette* how a dog attacked the man who killed its master, and that put him under suspicion. You can read a lot of useful things in the newspapers. Only you can't read the most important things.' He sighed wistfully. 'Like how you can suddenly feel like a young man again, when you're the wrong side of fifty . . .'

'You mean there's no f-fool like an old fool?' Erast Petrovich asked with an understanding nod. 'No, they don't write m-much about that in the newspapers. You should have read p-poetry, Boxman, or gone to the opera: "Love humbles every age of m-man" and all that. I heard you t-telling Mademoiselle Death about "a st-strong man with immense wealth". Were you think-ing of yourself? In t-twenty years of ruling Khitrovka, you must have s-saved up quite a lot, enough for your old age. For your old age, yes, b-but hardly enough for a Swan Queen. In any c-case, that was what you thought. And your impossible d-dream drove you into a frenzy, you c-craved for that "immense wealth". You started killing f-for money, something you had never d-done before, and when you heard about the underground treasure t-trove, you lost your m-mind completely . . .'

'That's love for you, Your Honour.' Boxman sighed. 'It asks no questions. Turns some into angels and others into devils. And I'd play the part of Satan himself to make her mine . . .'

'You scoundrel!' the superintendent exclaimed furiously. 'You arrogant brute! Talking about love! Carrying on like this, behind my back! You'll be doing hard labour!'

Boxman said sternly: 'Shut up, you little shrimp! Haven't you realised what Erast Petrovich is driving at?'

The superintendent choked. 'Shrimp?' Then he changed tack. 'Driving at? What do you mean by that?'

'Erast Petrovich has fallen for Death too, head over heels,' Boxman explained as if he was talking to a simpleton. 'And he's decided that only one man's going to leave this place alive, and that's him. His Honour's decided right, too, because he's a clever man. I agree with him. There'll be five dead men left in here, and only one will get out, with these incredible riches. And he'll get Death too. Only we still have to see who it's going to be.'

As Senka listened he thought: *He's right, the snake, he's right! That's why Mr Nameless rounded them all up here, to rid the earth of these monsters. And to free a certain person who wasn't supposed to hear all this – just look at the way her chest's heaving now.*

He touched Death on the shoulder: Come on, let's clear off while the going's good.

But then things began moving so fast, it set Senka's head spinning.

At the words 'who it's going to be', Boxman hit the superintendent on the wrists with his fists and the revolvers went clattering to the stone floor.

In a single moment Deadeye pulled a knife out of his sleeve, the Ghoul and the Prince pulled out their revolvers, and the constable bent down and picked up one of the revolvers Solntsev had dropped – and trained the barrel on Erast Petrovich.

How Senka Tried to Keep Up (continued)

Senka squeezed his eyes shut and put his hands over his ears, so he wouldn't be deafened by the thunderous roar that was coming. He waited about five seconds, but no shots came. Then he opened his eyes.

The picture he saw was like something out of a fairy tale about an enchanted kingdom, where everyone has suddenly fallen asleep and frozen on the spot, just as they were.

The Prince was aiming his revolver at Deadeye, who had his hand raised, holding a throwing knife; the superintendent had picked up one of his Colts and was aiming it at the Ghoul, and the Ghoul was aiming his gun at the superintendent. Boxman had Mr Nameless in his sights, and the engineer was the only one unarmed – he was just standing there with his arms calmly folded. No one was moving, so the whole lot of them looked like a photograph – as well as an enchanted kingdom.

'Now how could you set out for such a serious rendezvous without a pistol, Your Honour?' Boxman asked, shaking his head as if he was commiserating with the engineer. 'You're so proud. But in the Scriptures it says the proud shall be put to shame. What are you going to do?'

'Proud, b-but not stupid, as you ought t-to know, Boxman. If I came without a weapon, it m-means there was good reason for it.' Erast Petrovich raised his voice. 'Gentlemen, stop trying to f-frighten each other! Operation Spiders in a Jar is p-proceeding according to plan and now entering its f-final stage. But first, I must explain s-something important. Are you aware that you are m-members of a certain club? A club that ought to be c-called "The Lovers of Death". Were you not astounded that the most b-beautiful, the most miraculous of women d-demonstrated such benevolent condescension to your ... dubious virtues, to p-put it politely?'

At these words the Prince, the Ghoul, Deadeye and even the superintendent turned towards the speaker, and Death shuddered.

Mr Nameless nodded. 'I see that you were. You were q-quite right, Boxman, when you claimed that if you are the only one to g-get out of here alive, Death will b-be yours. That is undoubtedly what will occur. She herself will s-summon you into her embraces, b-because she recognises you as a g-genuine evildoer. After all, gentlemen, in his own way each of you is a genuine m-monster. Do not take that as a t-term of abuse, it is merely a statement of f-fact. After all the misfortunes she s-suffered, the poor young l-lady whom you know so well imagined that her caresses really were f-fatal for men. And therefore she d-drives away all those whom she does n-not think deserving of death and welcomes only the l-lowest dregs, whose vile, stinking breath p-poisons the very air of God's world. Mademoiselle Death conceived the g-goal of using her body to reduce the amount of evil in th-the world. A tragic and s-senseless undertaking. She cannot possibly t-take on all the evil in the world, and it was not worth s-soiling herself for the sake of a few spiders. I shall be glad to render her this s-small service. Or rather, you will render it, b-by devouring each other.'

Just at that moment Death whispered something. Senka pricked up his ears, but he couldn't make out the words. Except for one: 'late'. What did that mean?

So that was why she'd thrown Erast Petrovich out on his ear! She was afraid her love would cost him his life!

And she didn't give me the push because I'm just a kid to her, either, Senka told himself, straightening up his shoulders.

Mr Nameless had come up with a smart plan, no denying

that. Do away with all of the stinking reptiles at the same time. Only how was he going to handle them without a weapon?

The engineer continued as if he had heard Senka's question: 'Gentlemen and spiders, p-please put your pocket cannons away. I c-came here without a firearm because we can't shoot in this b-basement in any case. I had time to make a close study of the v-vaults, they are in very bad repair, held up by n-nothing but a wish and a promise. One shot or, indeed, a l-loud shout will be enough to bring the Holy T-Trinity down on top of us.'

'The Holy Trinity?' Solntsev echoed nervously.

'Not the Father, the S-Son and the Holy Ghost,' Erast Petrovich said with a smile, 'but the Ch-Church of the Holy Trinity in Serebryanniki. At this m-moment we are precisely below its f-foundations, I checked a historical map of Moscow. The b-buildings of the State Mint used to stand here.'

'He's lying through his teeth,' said the Ghoul, shaking his head. 'The Trinity can't collapse, it's made of stone.'

Instead of answering, the engineer clapped his hands loudly. The heap of earth and rubble blocking the doorway shook, and small stones showered down from the top of it.

'A-agh!' gasped Senka, choking on his own cry, and put his hand over his mouth.

But the others didn't hear him – they were all gazing around wildly and gasping in fright. The superintendent even covered his head with his hands.

Death looked round at Senka for the first time since she had dug her elbow into him. She touched his forehead gently with her finger and whispered: 'Don't be afraid, everything will be all right.'

He was going to say: 'There's no one afraid here', but she turned away again before he could.

Erast Petrovich waited for the spiders to stop twitching and said in a loud, commanding voice: 'Before you d-determine which of you will leave here alive, I s-suggest you tip your bullets out on the f-floor. One accidental shot, and there will be n-no victors.'

'A sound idea,' said Boxman, the first to respond.

Deadeye agreed. 'A bullet has no brains, that goes without saying.'

Well, of course! Those two didn't need revolvers, Deadeye probably didn't even have one.

The Prince narrowed his eyes in fury and hissed:

'I'll bite your rotten throats out!' He threw open the cylinder of his revolver and tipped out the bullets.

The Ghoul hesitated for a moment, but a few more stones tumbled down off the top of the heap, and that convinced him.

The superintendent really didn't want to part with his Colt. He glanced desperately at the way out, wondering whether he could leg it, but Erast Petrovich was blocking the way.

'Come now, Your Honour,' said Boxman, aiming his revolver at his superior's forehead. 'Do as you're told!'

The superintendent tried to open the cylinder, but his hands were shaking. So he just flung the revolver away – it clanged against the floor, spun round a few times then stopped.

Boxman was the last to get rid of his bullets. 'That's better,' he grunted, rolling up his sleeves. 'Those popguns are nothing but trouble. Right, then, let's get down to it and see who comes off best. Only keep it quiet! The first one to yell is the first to die!'

The Prince took his knuckleduster from his pocket. Deadeye backed away into the wall and shook his wrist, and a bright blade glinted between his fingers like a silvery fish. The Ghoul bent down, picked a silver rod up off a pile and swung it a couple of times. It whistled through the air. Even the superintendent wasn't going to be left out. He ran into a corner, clicked something, and a narrow strip of steel leapt from his fist – the same knife he'd used to peel his apple at the station.

The engineer simply walked forward, taking springy steps with his legs slightly bent. Good for Erast Petrovich, the brainbox, he'd twisted them round his little finger. Now he'd start thrashing away with those arms and legs, Japanese-style.

Senka touched Death on the shoulder, as if to say: Watch what happens now! But she said: 'Ah, how well it's all turning out, it's like the answer to a prayer. Let go of me, Senka.'

She turned round, kissed him quickly on the side of the head and ran out into the middle of the chamber. 'And here I am, Death! Speak of the devil!'

She bent down and picked up the pistol the superintendent had thrown away, held it in both hands and cocked the hammer. 'Thank you, Erast Pretrovich,' she said to the stupefied engineer. 'This was a very good idea. You can go now, you're not needed here any more. Take Senya with you, and make haste. And you, my sweet little lovers,' she said, turning towards the others, 'will stay here with me.'

The Prince growled and darted towards her, but Death pointed the pistol at the ceiling. 'Stop! I'll fire! Or do you think I'm afraid to?'

Even the bold Prince backed away at that, her shout was so convincing.

'Don't d-do this!' said Mr Nameless, recovering his senses. 'Please, l-leave, you will only spoil everything.'

She tossed her head and her big eyes flashed. 'Oh no! How could I leave, when God has shown me such kindness? I was always afraid that I would end up lying lifeless in my coffin and everyone would come and look. Now no one will see me dead, and there'll be no need to bury me. The kind earth will shelter me.'

Senka saw Boxman edge over to the Ghoul and the Prince and whisper something to them. But Erast Petrovich wasn't looking at them, only at Death.

'There's no reason for you to die!' he shouted. 'Just because you've convinced yourself that—'

'Now!' Boxman gasped, and all three of them – Boxman, the Prince and the Ghoul – flung themselves on the engineer.

The constable crashed into Erast Petrovich with all the weight of his massive carcass, pinned him against the wall, grabbed hold of his wrists and pulled the engineer's arms out as if he was on a cross.

'Get his legs!' Boxman wheezed. 'He's a great kicker!'

The Prince and the Ghoul squatted down on their haunches and grabbed hold of Mr Nameless's legs. He twitched like a fish on a hook, but he couldn't break free.

'Let him go!' Death shrieked, and pointed the revolver, but she didn't fire.

'Hey, you, Four-eyes, take that gun off her!' the constable ordered.

Deadeye moved directly towards Death, reciting in a cajoling voice: 'Return to me, I beg you, cruel one, a youthful lover's sacred pledge.'

She turned towards the Jack. 'Don't come any closer. Or I'll kill you.'

But the slender hands clutching the revolver were shaking.

'Shoot him! Don't b-be afraid!' Erast Petrovich shouted desperately, struggling to break loose.

But Boxman's mighty hands held him in a vice-like grip, and the Ghoul and the Prince still kept hold of their prisoner.

'Stop, you damned blockhead!' the superintendent howled. 'She'll fire! You'll get us all killed!'

The Jack's thin lips stretched out into a smile. 'Blockhead yourself! Mademoiselle won't fire, she's too concerned for the handsome man with the dark hair. That, my dear copper, is called love.'

He suddenly took two long, rapid strides, grabbed the Colt out of Death's hands and flung it as far away as he could, to the entrance of the passage, then said calmly: 'And now you can finish off Mr Know-all.'

'What with, our teeth?' hissed Boxman, crimson from the strain. 'He's a strong devil, we can barely hold him.'

'Well then,' Deadeye sighed, 'it is the duty of the intelligentsia to help the people. Now, servant of law and order, move aside a little, if you please.'

The constable shifted over as far as he could and the Jack raised his knife, preparing to throw. Now the steel lightning would flash and that would be end of the American engineer Erast Petrovich Nameless.

The Colt was lying on the floor only two steps away from the passage, its burnished steel glittering as if it was winking at Senka: Well, Speedy, how about it?

Ah, to hell with it, he could only die once, it had to happen some time!

Senka dashed to the revolver, grabbed it and yelled: 'Stop, Deadeye! I'll take your life!'

Deadeye swung round and his sparse eyebrows inched up in surprise.

'Bah, the seventh coming. That Speedy again. Why have you come back, you stupid little goose?'

'Hey, kid!' shouted the superintendent, pressing himself back against the wall. 'Don't even think about it! You don't know! You can't shoot in here! The whole place will collapse. We'll be buried alive.'

'L-Landslide!' Erast Petrovich suddenly shouted out at the top of his voice.

Instantly there was a low rumble and the heap of earth and stone blocking off the doorway shuddered and collapsed. The superintendent screamed desperately as a solid, stocky figure dressed in black forced its way out through the rubble. It came tumbling out into the middle of the chamber like a rubber ball, and threw itself at the Jack, screeching like a warrior.

Masa!

Now that was a real miracle!

Erast Petrovich immediately took advantage of his enemies' confusion: the Prince went flying off in one direction, the Ghoul in the other. But the engineer still couldn't break the grip of Boxman's huge hands and, after a brief struggle, they collapsed on the floor, with the constable on top, pinning Mr Nameless down and still holding on tight to his wrists. The Ghoul and the Prince didn't help Boxman this time – the two bandits' hate was too strong. They grabbed each other and started rolling across the floor.

Deadeye flung a knife at Masa, but the Japanese squatted down in good time, and he dodged the second and third knives just as easily. But the Jack didn't stop once he had exhausted the arsenal in his sleeve. He threw back the skirt of his long frock coat, and Senka saw a wooden cane attached to the belt of his trousers.

Senka remembered what Deadeye had in that cane – a big, long pen that was called a 'foil'. And he hadn't forgotten how smartly the Jack handled that terrible shiv either.

Deadeye put his left hand behind his back, moved one foot out in front and started edging forward, tracing out glittering circles with his whistling blade. Masa backed away. What else could he do, with only his bare hands!

'I'll fire! I'll fire right now!' Senka shouted, but no one even looked round.

So there he was, standing like a fool with a loaded revolver, and no one giving a rotten damn about him; everybody was too busy with their own business: Boxman was sitting on the engineer and trying to butt him in the face with his forehead; the Prince and the Ghoul were growling and screeching like two crazy dogs; Deadeye was driving Masa into a corner; Death was trying to drag the constable off Erast Petrovich (but what could she do against a great brute like that?); the superintendent was gazing around like a loony and holding his flick-knife out in front of him.

'Don't just stand there, yerbleedinonner!' Boxman wheezed. 'Can't you see I can't hold him? Stick him! We'll settle things between us afterwards!

The villainous superintendent – and him supposed to be a servant of law and order! – went running across to stab the man on the floor. He threw Death aside and raised his hand, but she grabbed hold of his arm.

'Look at me, you lousy bastards,' Senka shouted in a tearful voice, waving the Colt. 'I'm going to fire now and bury the damn lot of you!'

Solntsev shifted the knife to his left hand and stuck the blade in Death without even a sideways glance. She sat down on the floor with a look of sudden surprise on her face. In fact, her elegant eyebrows rose up in a strange expression of joy. She carefully put her hands over her wound, and Senka was horrified to see blood streaming out between her fingers.

'Move over, damn you!' the superintendent gasped, going down on his knees. 'I'll stick him in the neck!'

Senka stopped worrying about the Holy Trinity crushing everyone. Let it, if this was the way things were. He held the revolver out in front of him and pulled the trigger without even taking aim.

He was deafened straight off, didn't even hear the shot properly, his ears were suddenly blocked, and that was all. A tongue of flame leapt out of the barrel, the superintendent's head jerked to one side in dashing style, as if he was pointing out some direction, and his body instantly followed instructions by falling that way.

After that the end came very quickly, in a terrible, hollow silence.

The ceiling was all right, it didn't collapse, it just dropped a scattering of dust and that was all. But Erast Petrovich managed to pull his left hand out from under Boxman, who had glanced round at the thunderous roar. The engineer made use of this hand by squeezing it into a fist and delivering a short, sharp blow to Boxman's chin. The constable snorted and flopped over on his side like a bull at the slaughterhouse.

Senka turned in the other direction to shoot Deadeye as well, before he could jab that foil of his through Masa. But Senka's help wasn't needed. After driving the sensei into a corner, the

Jack sprang forward, the arm with the foil uncoiled like a spring, and by rights he should have pinned the Japanese to the wall, but the blade just clattered against the stone as Masa skipped to the left and flicked his wrist. Something small and shiny flew out of his hand and Deadeye suddenly swayed like a floppy stuffed doll. He reached up feebly for his throat, but his hand never reached it. The Jack's arms dropped limply, his knees buckled and he collapsed flat on his back. His head tipped backwards and Senka saw a steel star with sharp edges that had bitten deep into Deadeye's throat. There was dark blood bubbling out around it, but Deadeye just lay there quietly, twitching his legs.

The Prince and the Ghoul had stopped rolling around and creating a ruckus too. Senka looked at them and saw that the back of the Ghoul's head was all smashed in, it was covered in dark dents and bruises from the knuckleduster. And the smashed head was lying just where the Prince's throat was supposed to be. The eyes of the man who had hated Senka so much were staring rigidly up at the ceiling. Would you believe it – all those times he'd threatened to rip someone's throat out with his teeth, and someone had ripped his out for him. The Ghoul had drunk his fill of the Prince's blood. The two spiders had devoured each other . . .

Senka thought about all this, so he wouldn't have to think about Death. He didn't even want to look in her direction.

When he did finally glance round, she was sitting propped up against the wall. Her eyes were closed and her face was white and stiff. Senka turned away again quickly.

The resounding silence gradually receded. Senka could hear Boxman hiccuping and Masa grunting as he pulled his magic star out of the Jack's throat.

'The ceiling didn't collapse,' Senka told the engineer in a trembling voice.

'Why should it c-collapse?' Erast Petrovich asked hoarsely, climbing out from under the constable's heavy carcass. 'The stonework here will st-stand for another thousand years. Oof, he must weigh three hundred p-pounds at least ... Don't just stand there, S-Senya! Help the l-lady up.'

So Mr Nameless hadn't seen the superintendent stick his knife in her.

'Won't he come round?' Senka asked, and pointed at the hiccuping Boxman – not because he was worried, just playing for time. He could pretend to himself that Death was just sitting there against the wall: she wasn't dead, just sleeping, or maybe she'd fainted.

'No, he won't come round. That blow was "the talon of the dragon", it's fatal.'

Then Erast Petrovich got up, went over to the seated damsel and held out his hand to her.

Senka sobbed and got ready for the engineer to yell.

But Death wasn't dead at all. She suddenly went and opened those big glowing eyes, looked up at Erast Petrovich and smiled.

'What ... what's wrong?' he asked, frightened.

He went down on his haunches, moved her fingers away and then – Senka had guessed right – he yelled.

'Why did you do it, why?' Mr Nameless muttered as he ripped open her dress and slip. 'I had everything worked out! Masa dismantled the heap of rubble in advance and he was hiding in there, just waiting for the signal! Oh, Lord!' he groaned when he saw the black cut below her left breast.

'I know you would have managed without me,' Death whispered. 'You're strong ...'

'Then why, why?' he asked in a choking voice.

'So that you can live. You can't be with me ... Now you're immortal, nothing can touch you. I'm your Death, and I have died ...'

And she closed her eyes.

Erast Petrovich yelled again, even louder than the last time, and Senka started blubbing.

But she wasn't dead yet. No wonder they used to call her

Lively before she was Death, people didn't get their monikers for nothing.

She lived for a long time after that. Maybe even a whole hour. She breathed, she even smiled softly once, but she didn't talk and she didn't open her eyes. And then she stopped breathing.

She's really beautiful, thought Senka. *And in the coffin, if they wash the dust and dirt off her face and pack flowers round her* (orange blossom was what was needed, it meant 'purity', and a sprig of yew, for 'eternal love') *she'll look a real treat. Her father and mother will collect her, because that's their right, and they'll bury her in the damp ground, and put up a big white stone cross over her, and carve what she used to be called on it, and underneath they'll write: 'Here lies Death'.*

How Senka Read the Newspaper

Once they set off, they tore along the high road for fourteen hours without a break, although they hadn't agreed to do that in advance. They covered almost three hundred versts and only topped up the fuel tank with the can twice. And all that way not a single word was spoken between the driver and his assistant. Senka did what he was supposed to do: tooted the horn, waved the flag, hung out through the door on steep turns, watched to make sure the wheels didn't come loose. The assistant was supposed to follow the route on a map too, but Senka didn't manage that very well. The moment he put his head down, his nose started running, salty water started dripping from his eyes and he got a lump in his throat. He couldn't see the map for his tears, it was just a mass of coloured blotches. But when he looked ahead, into the distance, and let the wind blow his hair about, it was all right, his eyes and his cheeks soon dried out then.

He couldn't tell whether Mr Nameless was crying or not, because he could hardly even see the driver's face under his protective goggles. The engineer's lips were clamped firmly shut all the time, but Senka thought the corner of his mouth was trembling.

But straight after Vyazma the solid-cast tyre on the front wheel split. There was nothing for it, they had to push the three-wheeler back to the town – they couldn't ride on two tyres, could they, it wasn't a bicycle.

The spare tyres and all the other parts were travelling in a horse-drawn carriage with Masa and his female companion, and the carriage had already fallen a long way behind the Flying Carpet. They'd be lucky if it trundled its way to Vyazma by tomorrow evening. So, like it or not, they had to stop over for a night and a day. That was all settled without words too. The sportsmen didn't feel like taking supper and they went to their rooms to sleep.

In the morning Senka walked out of the hotel and shooed away the local kids hanging around the auto without answering any of their stupid questions – he wasn't in the mood for that. Then he set off to the railway station to get a Moscow newspaper.

Right, then, had they printed it or not? He opened the *Gazette* straight off at page five, where they wrote about theatre and sport.

They'd printed it all right – they had to, didn't they?

They're off!

Despite the wind and rain, yesterday at noon devotees of automobile sport, that new religion which is still such an exotic novelty in the wide expanses of Russia, gathered at Triumfalnaya Square for the start of a long-distance drive to Paris. We have written about this event previously and intend to provide continuing comment by means of the telegraph. The spectators saw off the driver, Mr Nameless, and his youthful assistant with enthusiastic applause. The two sportsmen, who seemed quite emotional and preoccupied, avoided any contact with members of the press. Our wish for them is not the sailor's traditional 'seven feet under the keel' (the potholes in the wide expanses of Russia are quite deep enough already), but rather, as the automobilists say, 'firm tyres and a steady spark'.

Senka read the brief article about ten times and he even read the part about the 'youthful assistant' out loud.

After he'd already folded the *Gazette* neatly, he suddenly spotted a large headline on the front page.

When Thieves Fall Out

The bloody drama in Khitrovka

We are now able to report certain details of yesterday's events, which have been the subject of so much rumour and speculation.

On the night of 23rd September, a full-scale battle took place in the infamous Khitrovka slums between the forces of the law and local bandits. The police put an end to the criminal 'careers' of the rival leaders of Moscow's two most dangerous gangs, the Prince and the Ghoul, who both preferred death to arrest. Also killed was an escaped convict, a former student by the name of Kuzminsky, who had figured on wanted lists throughout Russia for a long time.

Unfortunately, there were also casualties among the defenders of public order. The superintendent of the Third Myasnitsky Precinct, Colonel Solntsev, and Senior Constable Boxman died heroically while fighting to defend the citizens of Moscow. The former was still young and had shown great promise, the latter had only two years to go until he drew a well-earned pension. Eternal glory to the heroes.

The high police-master's adjutant refused to give the press any further information, adding only that that a certain female individual killed in the shooting was the Prince's lover (or 'moll' in the criminal jargon).

However, our correspondent has succeeded in establishing an interesting circumstance that is directly related to the Khitrovka tragedy.

See p. 3, the article 'A noble deed' in the 'Events' section

Why, the rotten lousy coppers! Senka thought indignantly. *Lying and twisting everything like that!* There wasn't a word about Erast Petrovich or Masa, even though Mr Nameless had left an envelope for the top police chief at the station, with everything described just the way it had been.

Some heroes, he thought. He ought to write a letter to the editor, that's what he ought to do. Let people know the truth. These newspapermen were all damned liars, anyway. They printed any old rubbish without bothering to check it!

Still fuming, Senka opened page three.

So what was this deed, then?

Aha, there it was.

A noble deed

According to information we have received from a confidential source the battle between the police and bandits in Khitrovka (see p. 1, the article 'When thieves fall out') resulted from an ambush arranged by the police of the Third Myasnitsky Precinct in a secret underground hiding place where old treasure of immense value was stored.

The day before yesterday the Justice of the Peace of the Tyoply Stan District of Moscow Province received a letter written on the instructions of the minor S. Spidorov, who had discovered a fabulous treasure of immense value in the subterranean depths of Khitrovka. Instead of simply appropriating these riches, as the majority of Muscovites would no doubt have done, the noble youth chose to entrust his discovery to the care of the municipal authorities. The whereabouts of the treasure became known to bandits, and the police, having learned about this through their network of secret informers, proceeded to plan the bold operation which is the talk of the whole city today.

On behalf of the inhabitants of the old capital, we congratulate Mr Spidorov on the reward that is now due to him. And we may congratulate ourselves on the emergence of a wonderful new generation, to whom we can entrust the fate of the new-born twentieth century with no qualms or doubts.